SERAPH FALLING

Wayward Orphans Book 2

JEREMY FLAGG

Acknowledgments

I have to give thanks to Miranda Dal Zovo and Karen Diem for writing alongside me as I pounded away at the keys. If it wasn't for Trish Heinrich checking in on my mental health, I might have lost my mind half way through this story. And of course, I have to thank my wonderful editor, Margot Mostert for chasing commas and pointing out plot holes.

The Children of Nostradamus Patrons
Jason Janes
Larry Wilson

Chapter One

2039

"I will not die."

Patches pressed his back against the large cement column holding up the first floor of the soon-to-be office building. He thought he could get inside before they saw him, but he forgot the police in London weren't like the humans patrolling the streets of Chicago. He wished he had his gauntlets or even the suit, anything that'd give him a bit of confidence. From now on, he'd never leave the house without them.

Flashlights swept back and forth near where he entered. He couldn't count how many followed him. Two? Three? To his right, nearly fifty feet away, sheets of plastic fluttered in the breeze, and to the left, a long wall that offered no exit. If he ran, even with his abilities, he wasn't sure he'd reach the windows before they shot. Did it matter? Bullets hurt, but they wouldn't kill him. He feared the officers of London had things nastier than guns.

Patches silently cursed Alyssa and her insistence on them being discreet.

He pressed his palms to the column, hopeful that with enough determination, he'd sink into the cement. Somebody at the Tower probably had that ability, but he wasn't so lucky. He was a stocky guy, and hiding wasn't his thing. Instead, he tapped his fingers against the cold stone, gradually working up to banging his fist. It wasn't much, but his powers created a gentle warmth cascading along his skin.

"We've lost visual."

"Switching to thermal."

He appreciated the heads up. Once they swapped over, it wouldn't take them more than a few seconds to see his footprints. For the last thirty days, he had been learning how to fight. He didn't have Alyssa's discipline or Eve's creativity in a brawl. They would mop the floor with the officers if they were here. It'd be done and over before he could raise his guard.

Their feet scraped along the floor. Neither officer considered a silent approach. It was arrogance, certainty that nobody could match their might. If they were like other officers, their bodies would be laced with muscle enhancers, cognitive processors, and anything else the Body Shop had on sale.

His heart continued its marathon, steadily pounding against his ribcage. Unlike his training sessions, Alyssa's flat tone didn't offer him advice as Eve knocked him off his feet. She understood he hadn't trained for years and that, at heart, he'd rather be a pacifist.

Why are you fighting? The words echoed in his head. He lied every time. They accepted his loyalty to Eve and the desire to find Skits. Even without confessing his truth, the trio suspected the truth. Hell, even Blue, Eve's pet robot, probably knew the truth. He fought for this moment, the building tension in his chest that urged him to run. He had spent his entire life scared, unable to fathom the power housed inside his body.

Patches fought to hide his fear.

Admitting the truth didn't make it any less terrifying. He smashed the back of his head on the column, cracking the cement. He repeated the motion twice more. His powers spread the impact across his skin, converting the kinetic energy into a fire that flowed into his limbs. Concentrating, he diverted the burning along his shoulders, down his torso and into his legs.

"Central? Mitch, they've gone silent."

"Central, can you hear us? Do you see the thermal scans?"

"What the hell?"

Patches wasn't scared of them. He was scared *for* them.

"You gentleman came alone?" It was overkill, but he made sure every word oozed with his Scottish accent. Coarse and hardly understandable, he wanted the officers to know a northerner they hated so much lured them into a trap.

"Don't move." Patches held the laugh. If the skinny man with the thick mustache wasn't Mitch, he couldn't imagine a better name.

Patches took his time as he raised his hands, eyeing both men. Standard issue rifles. Non-functional radios. With the tactical gear, he couldn't tell if they had muscular enhancements. If they had modifications, they paid extra to have them hidden. That lack of knowledge changed his approach. He couldn't risk one of them being fast enough to fire their gun, realize their folly, and reveal a more lethal weapon.

The fire burning in his legs allowed him to push off with enough force that the first gunman didn't have time to fire. Patches ducked low, his shoulder catching the man in the gut. The officer drilled the stock of his rifle along Patches' back, attempting to incapacitate him. The blow almost tickled as his skin dispersed the kinetic energy along the exterior of his body. With the second attempt, Patches' abilities transformed the impact into potential energy captured by his muscles.

Before they could tumble to the ground, Patches stopped himself, grabbing the man by the black vest. He spun faster than a man his size should be able. Without effort, the officer flew, slamming into a cement column. His helmet cracked as he collapsed into a heap.

Patches froze, waiting for the man to move. He spotted him taking in a breath. They wouldn't offer him the same luxury, but he couldn't bring himself to kill. He had already lost sleep over the—

POP. POP. POP. Patches grimaced as all three shots tore through his black t-shirt, smashing against his skin with enough force that it stung. It wasn't the bullets themselves that hurt, but the burning sensation in his veins. One bullet and he might be fine, but after three, he lost control of his powers. Now even the tiniest impact continued to stoke his internal fire.

"Central, we have rogue Children. I repeat—"

"Are you daft, Mitch? They can't hear you," Patches yelled.

"Stop right there!"

Mitch didn't seem to understand what was happening. Patches pitied Mitch. The officer braced his gun and leaned toward the sight. It'd only take a few shots and the pain might render Patches unconscious. He didn't know for certain, and he wasn't going to find out.

Alyssa lunged through the air as if she could fly. The woman maintained a grace like a seasoned dancer. She missed the man, soaring over his shoulder. Patches tried to predict her movements, but when it came to grappling, he was never sure what she'd do next. At the last minute, she grabbed his shirt, turning herself in midair. Leaning back, she guided him into a somersault, ending with her kneeling on his back.

The soldier pushed off the ground, knocking her to the side. Even her fall turned into a smooth roll, leaving her on her knees.

"Central, we have Children."

"Yes, we do."

Eve ran down an alley next to a large, empty office building. She didn't dare glance over her shoulder to see if the officers continued chasing them. Construction materials filled the narrow space. Ducking under scaffolding, she couldn't imagine the guards giving up their pursuit. But without the echoes of feet hitting the ground, she assumed they had chased Patches or Alyssa.

Eve pulled down the black fabric that hid her face. "Dammit," she hissed.

Skidding to a stop, she tucked herself behind a stack of bags holding cement. The crushed rock could stop bullets and their thermal vision. At least for the moment, she could catch her breath. Nothing about tonight was going according to plan. She assumed that at any moment a drone would fly overhead and give away her location. It'd be the cherry on top of a botched operation.

They were supposed to go their separate ways and run until they confirmed they weren't being followed. Alyssa had gone over the plan at least a dozen times, and that was just tonight. Eve had a nasty habit of ignoring Alyssa's orders. She had told Eve to lead the team, but relinquishing control proved the harder task.

Closing her eyes, Eve summons her powers. Buried just beneath her skin's surface, they greedily reached out into the night. They were like an unseen force, mapping the land. She couldn't see them, but she detected two officers carrying lights. Every step scuffed against the concrete floor, creating friction that shone almost as bright as the batteries in their lights. The tiniest amount of heat pinged her radar, and it was as if she could make out their bodies. Even their hearts generated energy, and right now, they pumped frantically from the chase.

"Patches," she whispered, "you owe me."

From this distance, their ripples were hard to pinpoint. She rolled over onto her knee, tightening her eyes. For years she complained about having a passive ability. Detecting the electromagnetic fields didn't make her a better fighter, and she believed it was why Alyssa denied her admittance into the Tower's security team. This useless ability had defeated a Child of Nostradamus capable of manipulating gravity. Passive yes, useless no.

She'd be unstoppable—if she could wield her gifts with any accuracy.

Eve clenched her eyes shut. Their shoes, their bodies, the static electricity, all of it created invisible disturbances in the planet's electromagnetic field. But it was the modules just beneath their ears that created enough disturbance she could feel them coming from miles away.

"Not on my watch," she growled. Tiny pebbles under the palms of her hands should hurt, but they provided a single point of focus. The enhancements allowed the officers to communicate with Central command. Eve decided they had spent enough time on the phone.

Imagining a faint version of herself, she reached a phantom hand into their processors. With a flick of the wrist, the signal dissipated. It wouldn't last for long, but it'd buy Patches enough time to take them out and flee.

She hadn't noticed the tiny disturbance before. But as Patches smashed the back of his head on cement, it lit up the abandoned office. Not only did the impact produce fields, his abilities absorbed enough to make him radiate. He did it again and his body flared to life like a tiny sun. Anymore stored energy and he'd need her to help drain it away.

"Get 'em, boy."

As the two men came upon his location, he probably said something lame. Eve couldn't convince him they were not superheroes. The Scot insisted on having pithy one-liners at every opportunity. But as he hurled one man against an invisible object, he had earned it.

POP. POP. POP.

The gunfire was like a searing light, leaving her blind to the electromagnetic fields. Opening her eyes, she got to her feet before tearing at the plastic sheet covering the window. She caught sight of Alyssa grappling with the second officer.

"Don't dare yell at me for not following the plan," she grumbled as she climbed inside the building. The three of them had been in London for a month, and they had learned almost nothing, at least nothing that could help them find and rescue her aunt. But this was the first time they had a run-in with London's coppers.

As Alyssa dropped the man to the ground, his light smashed, and the room was almost entirely dark. Thankfully for Eve, her powers flared to life on their own, giving her an additional sense. The officer's enhancements were turning back on, giving his muscles—

"Central, we have Children."

"Yes, we do," Eve said.

Eve's anger fueled her abilities. The trio would gladly take Skits from her jailers and never look back. Screw Britain and its insistence that vinegar belonged on fish and chips. Just like she had with their radios, she reached into the energy. Unlike the more disciplined Children, she used her physical hands to help guide her. She imagined grabbing the fields and tearing them away.

They broke. She watched as the computer in the man's head was silenced. Even his muscles stopped creating significant ripples. It wasn't pretty, but whatever made the man tick turned off as she fried his internal electrical systems. Throwing a hand toward the other officer, she repeated the gesture. Fried, which probably meant dead, but she'd deal with the consequences later.

"Go our separate ways, huh?"

"It had been my intention," Alyssa responded.

The only thing left to do was to help Patches control his abilities. Eve caught the worry on his face as he studied the officers' prone bodies. Unlike her, he couldn't fathom the idea of ending a life. She didn't like it, but she compartmentalized and tucked it away for processing later. There'd be tears when nobody watched.

"You gave them a one-line, didn't you?"

Patches took her hand, placing it over his heart. It had become comfortable between them, a friendship forged out of necessity. The more time she spent with the man, the more he reminded her of Conthan, one of her two dads. He had taken the epiphany as a compliment. It wasn't meant as one.

"Gentlemen, you came alone?" Yup, even his one-liners were lame.

She rolled her eyes as she focused on the lines generated by his body. Where she had ripped the officer's magnetic fields, she moved carefully, slowing them as she siphoned the kinetic energy away from his body. No two people at the Tower could have more different gifts, and yet we complimented one another.

Preventing him from turning into a rupturing battery had become second nature. She wouldn't admit it to him, but it allowed her to study her gifts. Without their sessions placating his abilities, she wouldn't have been able to disable the officers. It still wasn't as impressive as hurling lightning, but at least she didn't feel like a weakling.

"Two against one. I like those odds. What about, were you gentlemen looking for me?"

"That's even worse," Alyssa said. "Talk later. We need to get back to the safe house."

With no follow-up, it was off to do what they did best—run.

Chapter Two

2039

The crowd had grown, soldiers wanting to watch their commander in action. Oscar knew they were not there to watch him succeed. Like the politicians, they watched to see if the queen's abomination had a chink in his armor. But instead of polite jabs in the training facility, they were drawn to the possibility of blood.

Weakness had no place in the queen's army.

Politicking wasn't always about fancy dinners and exchanging veiled threats with Lords. He oversaw all military forces, both foreign and domestic. He never planned to put on a demonstration, but as he watched a young cadet run through a cardio routine, he became fixated. When she reached out to the other cadets to ask for a sparring partner, the men shunned her. Oscar wouldn't allow their bravado to prevent her from excelling.

There were two hundred bodies in the facility. Many were running laps around the outside, but in the middle, there were multiple sparring areas set up for cadets to test their one-on-one skills. He had removed his jacket, drawing eyes as he crossed the track, approaching the young girl. For the last half hour, he'd practiced maneuvers, correcting bad habits. As they continued, the youngest cadets had stopped to watch. Eventually, the more seasoned constables joined.

Oscar reached down, helping his opponent off the mat. Despite her youth, she had put up a valiant fight. He respected her nerves of steel. There weren't many new to the police academy that would face him without apprehension. Oscar made a mental note to speak with her commander and offer a word of praise.

"Good match…"

"Niamh," she finished.

"Good match, Niamh."

"Sorry for making it easy, sir."

She had a fiery spirit that matched her bright red hair. In a place known for breaking spirits, it did nothing to dim her vigor. He envied the future laid out before the woman. Despite his life of luxury, Oscar hadn't been given choices in determining the outcome of his life.

"Defense. You've got skill. Don't show it all at once. Let your opponent overplay their hand."

If he were ten years younger, he'd ask to take their match to the pub and see if she could beat him at downing pints. But he—

"Is there a line for the next match?" Oscar turned to see two hulking men at the edge of the mats. Unlike their cadet counterparts, these two men had experience patrolling the streets of London.

"Demonstration is over for today," Oscar said. He turned to Niamh, giving her a slight nod, causing her to salute.

"Only interested in besting little girls?"

Oscar spent most of his waking days proving himself. Unlike his predecessors, they did not grant him all the benefits of royalty. He needed to be better, faster, and smarter. When that didn't command respect, he relied on being the most brutal. The constable's challenge required Oscar to make a point to the room of voyeurs.

"One more match, then." He turned to see one man step forward. "Is your friend scared?" Oscar didn't want a single cadet in the facility to question his abilities.

"Names."

"Murphy," the first man said, then pointed to his companion. "Evans."

Both of them were muscular, far more than reasonable for the average man. Beneath their tracksuits, he expected their skin to be pockmarked with enhancements. He could taste the insecurity dripping from them like sweat. They wanted every advantage, unable to keep up with their peers without mechanical support.

"Rank has no place in this match!" Oscar yelled. He wanted it clarified that he didn't use his position to pressure them. Even with the statement, he'd hear whispers about how he used them to assert himself over the cadets. If there wasn't a new rumor about him, he wasn't doing his job.

Murphy didn't wait for a signal. He charged, arms ready to wrap around Oscar and squeeze the life from his lungs. He sidestepped, dropping low and kicking, causing Murphy to fall with a thud. Perhaps the constable should invest in neural enhancements. Stupidity couldn't be solved with muscles.

Evans at least situated himself before he attempted to drive a knee into Oscar's face. Crouched, he pushed the knee wide before slamming the palm of his hand into the man's groin. He rolled backward as the man attempted a desperate swipe. Neither of these men had any amount of discipline. They relied on their appearance to avoid fights. Oscar detested men like this.

Murphy climbed to his feet, fists balled. He hopped about as if he was in a boxing ring. He threw a jab, but Oscar watched his feet, convinced it was a misdirection. As his other fist swung low, attempting to smash into his kidney, Oscar stepped out of the way, using the man's might to his advantage. Oscar pivoted, launching a kick, driving his toes into Murphy's kidney. The irony made Oscar smile through the grunt.

On your knees. Murphy collapsed onto his knees, cradling his side. Oscar capitalized on the angle and drove his fist downward. His knuckles smashed against the man's jaw, dislodging several teeth. The constable held his position as Oscar brought a knee under his chin. What teeth remained shattered under the pressure.

The audience flinched at the ferocity of the attack. The men had wanted to prove him inferior. Murphy would need his jaw wired shut after this. Oscar considered it payment for forgetting that he remained their commanding officer *and* their prince. He deserved nothing less.

Evans, however, wanted revenge for his swollen testicles.

"I'm going to—"

Silence. Oscar's silent command halted the man's threat. Unlike his predecessor, Oscar refused mechanical enhancements. There were no nanites providing him strength or speed. His senses were average at best. But unlike his progenitor, or by a fluke of fate, he was unlike every human in the room.

Anger rolled off the man, and it mixed with confusion as he attempted to force himself to speak. Oscar admitted the foolishness of robbing the constable of speech. There'd be whispers and accusations. It meant that the fight could only end one way.

Stepping within arm's reach, Oscar ducked the first swipe, returning a jab to the man's stomach. Whatever technology fused itself to the man's muscles rendered the blow useless. Evans relied on brute strength, attempting an uppercut that would have shattered Oscar's jaw if he hadn't retreated.

The man grunted, unable to speak. Oscar smirked.

Evans's form lacked discipline, and he should have spent more time sparring with his comrades. Like his partner, the constable reached out, hoping to scare Oscar into a bear hug. Driving two knuckles into the softest flesh beneath his Adam's apple, Oscar collapsed the man's windpipe. Evans wrapped his hands around his throat, eyes wide in disbelief.

Oscar slammed his heel into the man's leg, shattering his kneecap. Without air, he couldn't howl at the pain. Toppling to his good knee, the man clawed at his throat, desperate for oxygen.

"Let this be a lesson," Oscar yelled. "The chain of command demands respect."

He stepped behind Evans. The room remained silent, but their fear about what unfolded in front of them filled the void. He deserved it. He wouldn't dare. Several individuals silently chanted, "Kill him." None dared to speak up to protect the fallen officer.

Do you know what comes next?

Evans repeated a single thought. *Air.*

Oscar didn't hesitate as he grabbed the man by the jaw. The man's spine cracked, three distinct clicks as he spun the man's head about. The desperate cries for air were silenced. Oscar reveled in the thoughts of the onlookers, each impressed with his prowess. None dared refer to him as the queen's abomination as he stood over the corpse. He had earned their respect for another day, from all but one.

Oscar eyed Niamh in the crowd.

I thought... He's a monster.

Nobody spoke as he walked to the edge of the mats, grabbing his jacket. As he walked away from the corpse, the crowd parted, saluting him as he passed. Only Niamh froze in place, the accusation remaining on the tip of her tongue. He had killed a man to prove a point and maintain the status quo, but her impression of him left him feeling less than.

He stopped only a few feet away from his sparring partner. "Salute your superior."

She reluctantly raised her hand.

Let them see a monster, he thought. Without another word, Oscar exited the facility.

Chapter Three

2039

Patches watched as residents of London made their way along the boardwalk without lifting an eye to see the amazing landmarks peppering the banks of the Thames. From this spot, he could see Tower Bridge, the Tower of London, and further down the river, Parliament, and Big Ben. In a single spot, there was enough history to keep him entertained for days. He tried to maintain a casual gander, but anybody watching would see the wide eyes as he digested the monuments.

Chicago had its charm, a beautiful city of skyscrapers. Glass and steel showed the modern marvels man created. But in London, they maintained a sense of history amidst their advancements. The gothic architecture stood next to skyscrapers, and somehow, both belonged in the landscape. It was easy to get lost in the experience, but instead of enjoying the sights and visiting the museums, he spied. He was barely a functional Child, and yet, somehow, he let himself be thrust into the advanced class.

A woman walked along the promenade, a long

brown jacket flapping in the breeze. She'd have looked like any other stylish European, but the glint of metal from her fingertips caught his attention. Mechanical digits had replaced both hands. As her hair blew back, he could see the side of her face was polished metal. Like so many of the residents in the city, she had spent a significant amount of time at the Body Shop. Unlike America, they proudly displayed their augmented bodies.

A jogger ran past, and like the woman, one leg was entirely mechanical while the other had only reached the knee. It appeared to be normal for the residents of London to flaunt their modifications as if they were nothing more than tattoos. The man had a spring in his step, taking strides that bordered on unrealistic. Nano? Hydraulic? Patches couldn't tell anymore. It seemed to be a place where the British Empire far surpassed the Free Republic's technology.

"Do you think you could take them in a fight?"

Eve sat on the grass next to him. While he had become the reluctant spy, Eve acted as if she were born into it. Every status report she provided, she'd lunge into more insight than necessary. He barely managed a full detail of the conversations he had at the pub, and she seemed to recall the nail color of every person she met, as if it would somehow be the difference between life and death.

"Why would I—"

"You're going to tell me, you haven't thought about it? They all have enhancements. Muscle. Reflexes. I'm pretty sure nobody has their original eyes."

"You know not everybody is a target, right?"

"They could be."

And there he had it. Despite his fondness for the spunky and impulsive woman, they looked at the world through different lenses. He wanted to see the goodness in people and their ability to move beyond the constraints forced upon them. But Eve, she performed a threat assessment on each person, wondering when, not if, a fight would erupt. As much as he hated it, he needed her to fill in his blind spots. She had an obnoxious talent for being right.

Patches sighed.

"I know that sound. What's wrong?"

"At some point, do you think we'll ever get it right?" Patches covered his mouth as he spoke, ensuring prying eyes or security cameras didn't read his lips. "Chicago, wrecked. Troy attacked. Now London? Humanity has done a grand job. It's no different here from home."

"You mean, will the fighting ever stop?"

Patches wanted to help Eve save her aunt. He had never met the woman before, but she was somebody important to Eve and Alyssa. Somehow, a dead psychic thought this trip was important to him, too. But he had to admit, part of him wanted to return to the Tower, to bury himself in books. Was he just pretending to be a guy who liked adventure?

"I guess."

"Never." She didn't hesitate with her answer. While he spent most of his waking hours fumbling through the labyrinth in his head, Eve preferred action. They couldn't be any more different, and yet, somehow, he appreciated that Eleanor bound their futures together.

"You fought to get out of," she grumbled the word Chicago, "and that was a fight. You got to the Tower." She covered her face in the least discrete manner possible. "So here you are, in your new home. Something comes knocking and you beat the shit out of it."

He laughed. It wasn't quite accurate, but he appreciated her embellishment.

"Don't laugh, Mister. I don't wanna fight. You got up and did what you needed to do. You found something you wanted, and you made sure that dream didn't die. I don't think it'll ever stop for you because you stand up when you see a problem."

He hadn't wanted the life of a Child, but he hadn't been given a choice.

"Do you see the injustice here?" Eve turned her head to look down the river toward Parliament.

Somewhere inside those walls, people wielded their power to do harm. They waged a war across Europe, but more than that, they prepared to slaughter Caledonia. The tension had grown to where people waited in anticipation of a formal declaration of war. Those who supported the North were removed from the streets and labeled terrorists. Yes, with only a month in London, he could see the injustice rippling into the world.

"Yes." The word came out more of a growl than he expected.

"Then I think Patches Kilgannon sees more of a fight than he's admitting."

Did he? Once they saved Skits from the Knights, he'd be on the first transport out of London. If they couldn't see the madness unfolding around them, he would not try to pull the wool from over their eyes.

"I need ice cream." Eve, the poster child for lack of impulse control. "Want some?"

"It's like you don't know me."

She patted him on the leg before hopping to her feet

and vanishing toward an ice cream truck. He tried to shake the feeling, but doubt hung around his neck like a noose. Did he see the world more clearly than the residents of London? Or was he looking for a cause, a fight?

"Eve is rubbing off on me," he groaned. But as he eyed Parliament again, he wondered how long it would be before the powder keg exploded.

Alyssa leaned against the concrete wall separating her from the Thames. The wind had transitioned from a gentle breeze to a bluster and the waves grew choppy. The rhythmic smack against the barrier provided a momentary distraction, but as always, her thoughts returned to the mission. No amount of architecture kept her occupied for long. It always came back to "Save Skits."

With Tower Bridge to her side and the Tower of London across the river, she continued to stare into the murky brown waters. The silt-filled river somehow seemed fitting as she chastised herself for not accompanying Skits on this errand. Begging and pleading, she couldn't convince her friend, her sister-in-arms, to walk away from this life. Where Alyssa wanted a reprieve from a life of blood and violence, Skits claimed it was her calling.

"And look where it got you," she whispered. After the Nighthawks defeated the Warden, both of them found themselves soldiers without a mission. When Twenty-Seven, a friend and the acting president of the Free Republic, asked them to infiltrate Quebec, they did so without question. But what started as missions to uphold the peace descended into an area almost as cloudy as the river. Alyssa had killed in the name of peace, ironic as it sounded, but she believed they had done right by the world. But after a time, the blood no longer washed away from under her fingernails.

"I'm sorry I wasn't there for you." She mumbled the words, careful to avoid the prying ears of those who might work for the queen and her legions. Her contact lenses might prevent facial recognition, but her words could easily alert the authorities. The British Empire wasn't so different from the former United States of America. On the surface, it appeared to be a utopia, but the facade was upheld by tyrants. At some point, the queen had started taking her cues from the Warden.

They would have made a lovely couple, she thought.

Further down the boardwalk, she watched Eve and Patches. Together they had protected the Tower from an invasion. Without them, there would have been more freshly dug graves. They had come together because Eleanor changed the course of their futures. She tampered once more, determined to pay penance for crimes Alyssa couldn't discover. The two had bonded in battle, and like her and Skits, they developed a friendship.

Eve held out an ice cream cone, offering it to Patches. Alyssa had never seen him say no to chocolate before and, like always, he accepted it. Unlike Eve, he attempted to enjoy their time in London. She envied their ability to maintain some semblance of normalcy. Alyssa couldn't remember the last time she simply existed. No threat assessments, no saving the world, just—

Her cold exterior warmed at the thought of a kiss, *the*

kiss. Of all the memories she wrapped about her like a cloak, keeping the chill of reality at bay, it came down to his lips pressed against hers. She had fallen for Ned, the bad boy. She almost laughed at the thought of seeing her mother's face if she could introduce them. Alyssa imagined both her parents rolling over in their graves at the thought of their daughter falling for such a fiery, vulgar man.

But she had.

She watched as a carrier drone flew overhead. If her sources were correct, even the postal system's delivery system used cameras to observe the population. She imagined this is what America would have looked like had Genesis Division been left to its own devices. The only difference between their countries was the lack of synthetics patrolling the streets. Instead of robotic protectors, the empire relied on their enhanced police officers. Alyssa would have preferred neither, but at least humans could reason, mostly.

Returning to the Thames, she closed her eyes, listening to a nearby couple walk by. They laughed as if they didn't have a care in the world. She wondered if she and Ned would ever be that couple? Or would they instead have a working relationship, consumed by a need to keep the Tower safe? No. Her lip curled as she fought off a snarl. When she returned, she'd teach herself to be more than a soldier. A woman. A partner. A human. If her muscles could learn to play the piano just by watching, she could learn to be something other than a fighter.

But first, she had one last mission to complete.

"It's not so different from home," Eve said as she and Patches approached. She was learning. No specifics, nothing said out loud that could link them to the Free Republic. As always, her portage did not disappoint.

"It's kind of like—" Eve elbowed Patches in the gut.

"Home," he said. "Kind of like home."

Where Evelyn Cowan took quickly to the life of a spy, Alyssa's other charge hadn't. She admired him for coming on this journey. He assumed the mantle of hero because the world needed him. But unlike Eve, he maintained the heart of a pacifist. The librarian would have rather been tucked away in the dark corners of the Tower, arranging his tombs. Perhaps that's why she admired the man, for his ability to protect those who needed protecting. Ironically, he reminded Alyssa of Eve's father, a gentle soul hardened by the tough lessons life insisted on teaching.

"Is your friend meeting us here?"

Eve casually spun about, putting her back to the wall. The young woman effortlessly switched between speaking with her and scouring the crowd for hints of Alyssa's contact. If she hadn't known better, she'd have assumed Eve had trained for insertion into hostile territories. Nobody watching would guess she was hunting a French spy. Patches, though, he bumbled his way through, so over the top, it bordered on comical. Thankfully, he rode the fine line between novice spy and tourist.

"I haven't seen him," Alyssa said. "But then again, we have a tendency to miss one another. It's the curse of our relationship."

"Then how will we..." Patches slowed his speaking to select his words carefully. He served as their brawn, but thinking on his toes was not his best skill. "How will we meet your gentleman friend?"

Alyssa waved at them to follow. "I have my suspicions you'll meet him soon enough." Strolling down the boardwalk, she stopped, pressing against the concrete again.

"But how will—"

Alyssa held up a finger, silencing Patches. She slid a hand between her and the wall, pulling at a loose brick. She hadn't needed to reach out to the man. It would have been impossible to find him. But for the last week, she sat in the same seat outside a small cafe. The red notebook sitting on the table served as the cue. Whatever network the man had in place, they'd relay the information. The next time she returned to the cafe, the barista, not so subtlety, offered her a fork for her coffee. The distrust between her colleagues required layers of deception. It was another reason she longed to see this part of her life behind her. Alyssa wanted to trust again.

In the empty cavity, she pulled a folded sheet of paper free. With the brick back in place, she casually pointed at a boat making its way beneath the Tower Bridge. The other two watched for a moment before they continued walking down the promenade, looking like run-of-the-mill Londoners. She pressed the paper against her chest, unfolding it and stealing a glance.

"Him?" Eve asked.

She noted the time and place on the sheet before shoving it in her pocket. Tonight, they had a date. "While Patches is drinking away his sorrows, you and I are going to the club."

"Better you than me," Patches said. "Give me a quiet pub any day of the week."

"A club?" asked Eve.

Alyssa had to remind herself that while she'd had

time to experience life outside of the Tower, Eve had been raised under its protective borders. When she returned, she'd speak with the council about ensuring their young people explored the world. She wanted to protect them from a world that feared Children, but she didn't want them to exist in a vacuum.

"Eve." The smile spread across Alyssa's lips. "You are in for a treat."

Chapter Four

2026

"I have a name," Ceann mumbled.

"What's he going on about?" Whisper stood with her back to a metal door strong enough to withstand a bomb. Kerberos ignored his statement, his hand pressed against an access pad to the right of the door. Instead, he growled as it blinked red, before shaking his hand and trying again.

Kerberos slammed his hand down on the panel. "It's encrypted. It'll take a moment."

Ceann watched as the orb floated above their heads. *They* were watching, turning the hunt into a spectator sport. The piece of technology had a sheen to it that left it out of place with the rest of the arena. Croydon once had a reputation for crime, even in a heavily policed Britain. It was only fitting the trio completed their final test in the walled-off ward before induction into the Knights.

"I have a name," Ceann whispered to himself. Whisper had misinterpreted his words. He spoke louder. "We have names. What do we need any of this for?"

They were the bottom of the barrel at the academy, a trio of Children with useful but passive gifts. Most passives didn't survive their first year. They had proven their tenacity, despite their inability to level buildings. For Ceann, that had become a mark of pride. His squad didn't agree.

"Healer." She snarled as she spat the word at him. "Kill the target. To kill him, we need weapons. Get it through your thick skull."

"Got it." The door hissed, opening a crack before Kerberos jerked it the rest of the way open.

Ceann didn't join them as they bolted inside. He eyed the orb overhead, curious if the viewers were cheering for their victory or their failure. Did they even care? The Knights watched, assessing their progress, but the humans, they watched to see his kind pitted against one another. The light glimmered through broken windows into the police station, revealing the copious amounts of dust suspended in the air.

He tore off his gloves, throwing them on the floor as his companions tore through the weapon's locker, looking for ammunition. Ceann had passed the marksmanship tests, but the rifle never felt natural in his hand. He had a name, meaning, like the others in the academy, he had been granted a powerful gift. His hands were the only weapon he needed. If it wasn't true, they'd have tossed his nameless corpse in an unmarked grave.

Something crept in the front of the station. Like many of the buildings, they had left the interior exactly as it had been the day they ordered its occupants to vacate. The front door had nearly been torn from the hinges, probably by previous prey seeking weapons like his companions. The desks in the middle of the room were pointed at one another, so their occupants could sit face-to-face.

Ceann's eyes narrowed, blocking out the light. The dust in the room swirled, moving as if—

"Incoming," he bellowed.

The hunter had become the prey. Dust wrapped around a figure as a man launched himself off a desk. The fist connected with Ceann's jaw, hard enough that blood sprayed across his face. The man crashed into Ceann, sending them both tumbling to the ground. For a second, the man's dark features appeared. With skin black as night, his snarling teeth shone. There wasn't time to study his features as he vanished again.

A gunshot fired, then another. Neither struck their target and before they knew it, their target had vanished.

"Invisibility," Ceann said, spinning over and jumping to his feet. "Bending the light, perhaps? Watch the air."

The door to the front of the station flew open, knocked clean off its hinges.

"Dammit, he got away," complained Whisper.

"Should we follow?"

Ceann ignored his companions as they debated strategy. All that stood between them and advancing to positions as Knights was a single Child of Nostradamus. But what of their prey? Had the Knights offered them freedom should they be killed? They could have hidden anywhere in the city block, requiring hours, if not days, to be found. Instead, he came here, striking quickly. Their prey hadn't scurried away with his tail tucked between his legs.

"He's still here," Ceann said as he clenched his fists.

"He wouldn't be that stupid." Ceann shot Whisper a look, clear that he wasn't joking.

Kerberos raised his pistol, firing at the ceiling. The shot struck one of the old sprinkler systems. Seconds later the others popped from their housing and water rained down in the police station. Ceann welcomed the cold sensation of water leaking down the back of his gray suit, cascading until it turned into a stream flowing down the small of his back.

The dust in the air vanished, consumed by its liquid counterpart. It washed the desks and chairs clean, free from a decade's worth of grime. Just beyond a bank of windows on the far wall, Ceann counted three orbs capturing their defeat at slightly different camera angles. Even the viewers watching were convinced the attacker was inside the station.

"Maybe I was…" Ceann turned slowly to address the duo. Between them, a void stood out in the falling water. It was easy to see the width of the man's shoulder's as droplets ran off his clothes. Even invisible, Ceann watched the muscles ripple as he drew back his hand. Whatever weapon the prey wielded, it attempted to pierce his suit. The armor held in place, promising a nasty bruise.

"Out of the way!" yelled Kerberos. He didn't wait to fire. Three shots. The first missed, but the second struck their target in the shoulder, blood mixing with water. The third struck, but as Ceann looked down, a red stain grew along his suit. He had become a casualty of war. When this was over, and they were knighted, he'd kill Kerberos himself.

Whisper's hand jerked off to the side, and the rifle was knocked away. For all their efforts in securing the guns, they had proven little more than a nuisance to their invisible friend. Her radius snapped, protruding far enough to poke through the sleeve. To her credit, Whisper refused to scream as she swiped with her functioning arm, landing a blow that caused the man to blink into sight.

Underneath the ferocity, Ceann detected the fear. An enemy of the crown, they had marked him for execution. Even if he won this battle, there'd be the next team, and another after that. If they offered him freedom and he believed their words, the man was a fool. For Children who stood against the queen, death was inevitable.

The man caught Whisper's next punch, using her as leverage as he kicked the pistol from Kerberos's hand. Wherever he had come from, they had taught him to fight. He would die, but at least he'd die with dignity.

Ceann let the warmth flow through his body, pooling around the torn flesh and muscle. It only took a few seconds before his abilities reconstructed the damage. It'd take more than a poor shot to fall him.

With her arm flapping, Whisper attempted to rush the man. There were a thousand tactics Ceann would have used before attacking the man with a compromised limb. She could have used her abilities to disorient, but anger drove her decisions.

The sharpness he attempted to shove into Ceann shone in his other hand. The knife looked as if it belonged in a chippy. It wouldn't pierce their suits, but it appeared as if he had learned his lesson. She reached for his neck. It had been a trap, an invitation.

Her momentum made it easy for him to slide the knife an inch above her collar, into the soft spot at the base of her jaw. He turned quickly, jerking the blade free, tearing away the side of her neck.

"Heal her," Kerberos shouted. His teammate had picked up a rifle, swinging it like a club. He struck their target's knee, knocking his leg out from under him. Ceann considered his demands and decided that Whisper had sealed her fate. He needed to take out their target before he slipped away.

The man shoved Kerberos into the weapon's room. With a final kick, his teammate staggered, tripping over the containers they had thrown onto the floor in search of ammo. The door slammed shut, locking Kerberos inside, safe, but useless.

"Smart," Ceann said, getting to his feet. He squared off, tightening his fists. It didn't matter how much damage their prey caused, he'd heal. He had survived lethal wounds before. A steak knife wouldn't be capable of causing more harm than his teachers during training.

"What are your crimes?"

The target couldn't be over thirty. There were no markings on his face, giving away his political or religious affiliation. Had Ceann met him on the street, he wouldn't have given him a second thought. But they had taught them that the best operatives are those capable of hiding in plain sight.

"Je ne suis pas un criminel." He spat at the accusation.

French? The Knights had been on the front lines of the French invasion. The war had been swift, quelling the president and his threats of launching a full-scale war against the British Empire. Was this man part of that scheme?

"Your men took me in my sleep." His grip on the

knife loosened as eyes stared off. "They killed Julia." The man's pain was palpable, but Ceann had already asked more questions than he should have. He'd be chastised for not completing the trial efficiently.

The man's pain turned to rage. He led with his right foot, jabbing with the knife. Ceann didn't fear the blade. When death was removed from the equation, it came down to pain. The gunshot, a broken bone, a knife to the eye. They may not kill him, but they hurt enough that he wished for death.

The healer didn't have flashy powers. His tenacity didn't come from the ability to crush rock between his hands or lasers capable of piercing an armored tank. On the next jab, Ceann snatched the knife, squeezing until the blade pushed against bone. The move startled the man, loosening his grip enough to yank the weapon free.

It clanked to the floor and already his powers stitched together the wound. As the light in his body flowed down his arm, closing the gash, it left a darkness in its wake. Whisper and Kerberos had watched his powers heal wounds a thousand times, never revealing the other side of his gift. In the Knights of Winchester, secrets were traded like currency. Ceann had learned to play their game.

Ceann did nothing to stop the target from rushing him. The man drilled a shoulder into his abdomen, lifting him up before bringing him crashing onto a desk. Fake wood caved inward and the metal frame buckled under his weight. The next strike connected with Ceann's cheek before the man climbed on top of him, hands wrapping around his throat.

"For Julia," he growled.

He admired the inspiration behind the man's brutality. Ceann couldn't remember caring for another human enough to avenge their death. He had become a killer as the Knights made him, but it hadn't given him purpose. Instead, they offered him an outlet for the darkness, the same darkness pulsing in his palms.

Ceann touched a finger to the man's chin, barely more than a caress. The man's veins turned black, reading like a roadmap as they spread through his body. His cells decayed, rotting from the inside. He man didn't have a drawn-out death. His heart and brain broke down, and the light in his eyes vanished.

The man collapsed on top of him. "I'm sorry for Julia," he whispered in the dead man's ear.

From the ceiling, the orbs closed in. They spread wide enough to catch the event from different angles. His superiors could assess his abilities in the field, and for the sick bastards treating him as entertainment, they received a show. Ceann pushed the man off him, rising to his feet before extending his middle finger to the viewers. He'd be detained, perhaps tortured, but at least they would know he loathed their existence. It was the least he could do for Julia.

"You have nearly passed your last trial."

Nexus let the displeasure display on his face. The Knights of Winchester didn't take lightly to a member of their ranks, diminishing their status. Ceann no longer flinched as Nexus wielded his gifts. The invisible force pushed inward on the bones in his hand, pulverizing them until they were bits and pieces.

Ceann cried out, unable to detach from the pain. Like

a switch, the pressure vanished. The light in his body went to work, repairing his commander's punishment. Broken bones healed without fanfare, but Nexus knew this. The pulverized skeleton, however, continued hurting as his body worked on repairing itself.

Kerberos stood nearby, his eyes turned downward. All at the academy knew their superior's penchant for torturing the cadets. It trained them to avoid eye contact in hopes he'd move on to the next in line. This is why Ceann continued staring at the man, eyes locked as he fought to swallow a howl. He didn't speak it out loud, but he wanted every one of the Knights scared of their creation.

"And Kerberos…" The man stifled a whimper. Ceann found him more pathetic than normal. Ironic that the cadet considered his healing abilities useless in the field. Yet, at any moment, the man would wet his trousers.

"Yes, sir."

"Hacking into the officer's weapon locker," Nexus said, "to acquire weapons?"

"Yes, sir."

Ceann watched as Nexus laid the trap. Kerberos walked into it, not realizing he was being led to the slaughter.

"Are we not weapon enough?"

The man raised his eyes, confused by the question. When he realized there was no escaping judgment, he turned to Ceann, hoping for solidarity from his team-mate. Even as a healer, Ceann relied on Nostradamus' gifts. Man-made weapons were as shortsighted as the men who made them. They were Knights of Winchester, and that meant they held them to a higher standard.

"Ceann," Nexus said, "complete your last trial."

Kerberos's jaw went slack, realizing the dead man on the ground wasn't the end of their time in the arena. As Ceann's hand finished healing, it left a darkness in his chest, a void where the light had once been. He wondered if that was why Nexus had crushed his hand.

Justification for the man's cruelty didn't matter. Ceann didn't hesitate as he grabbed Kerberos by the back of the neck. The man batted at his hand, knocking it away, but it was already too late.

"No. No. No." Kerberos watched as the blackness filled his veins.

Ceann grabbed the man, kicking his leg, so he toppled to one knee. Holding the sides of his head, he pushed his powers into Kerberos's body. He'd die either way, but speeding up the process was the only mercy he'd grant the man. His companion didn't deserve it, but unlike Nexus, he wasn't sadistic without reason.

Kerberos spasmed as his body decayed from the inside. The smell of rot already wafted from his nostrils. Ceann pushed the corpse to the ground. If he waited long enough, the man's body would begin decomposing, collapsing in on itself as Ceann's powers finished decimating the man's innards.

"Whom do you serve?"

Nexus spoke the words as if he expected Ceann to state his name. It'd be treason, and he'd be awarded a swift death... if they found a way to kill him. Nexus might believe the Knights of Winchester were loyal to him, but there was only one true master.

Ceann toyed with the idea of stating that he served no master. "I serve Her Royal Majesty." As he dropped his gaze, one of Kerberos's eyes liquified. The man might be dead, but unlike Ceann, at least he was free.

Chapter Five

2039

Patches hadn't taken his usual seat before the barman reached for a pint glass. By the time he took a seat at the bar, ensuring he faced the only door into the pub, the glass was filled with the dark liquid. Guinness was the only beer he could tolerate.

He could hear Alyssa's voice in the back of his head. "Know your surroundings." With a quick glance, he spotted a table with four men in business clothes. Two more sat at the bar, one of them large enough to be intimidating. A young woman and two men were near the front of the pub, laughing as they talked. Only a single man in the back gave him alarm. He appeared out of place, stiff, and his clothes didn't say working class.

"Been a few days," said John, one of the two owners of Jacob's Curiosity, or 'Curi' for short. After a month of stopping in, sitting for a few hours and having a couple of pints, the locals treated him as one of their own.

"Work," Patches lied, "place is killing me."

"I'll never go back to an office. Death by fluorescent lights."

Patches seized the brew and took a deep swig. It had been the same several nights a week since they arrived. Alyssa provided them with new passports and demanded he and Eve memorize their identities. He quickly learned there was an art to lying, and it relied on telling as much truth as possible. The most convincing fibs were half-lies.

"It's like a tower. No windows. Glass and steel, no matter where you look. I spend more time there than I do at home."

"Probably because you're here so much," called Paul from the other side of the bar. The brothers had opened the pub to escape their mundane careers. They were good people making sure the riff-raff were escorted out and the drunks put in a taxi.

Patches never imagined leaving Chicago, let alone traveling across the globe to London. It had been thirty-two days, and he had done little more than plot and plan. Eve had taken to the life of a covert operative. *She should*, he thought. *She'd trained for it*. Patches had to remind himself each night why he had come on this dumb-ass adventure. He might get the luxury of having a pint, but they had tasked him with gathering intel.

"Is it just me, or have you noticed the police increasing their patrols?"

According to the American media, the British Empire waged war between their expansion into Europe and a civil war against the North. In Chicago, the synthetics had once replaced the human police force, but here, they had never relinquished control to robots. After the Battle for Chicago, Patches understood why. On the outside, it appeared as if the British Empire had maintained an existence forty years in the past.

"I don't know how they do things in Yorkshire," John said. He paused, shaking his head. "Stay clear of them. You don't want to find yourself on the wrong end of a rifle."

Patches nodded. "In Yorkshire, chances are they'd buy you a pint before chasing a missing sheep."

"Not here." John waved to a young couple who came in from the rain. Hanging their coats near the door, they took a seat on the other side of the bar. John leaned in close to Patches. "Do yourself a favor. Avoid them while there's a war."

"Isn't there always a war?"

John tapped the end of his nose, giving a crooked smile that said Patches spoke the truth. He held up his glass in a salute before taking another drink.

Either Patches had developed an overactive imagination while trapped in their flat, or Alyssa's training had taken root. The couple across the bar was in their mid-twenties. Married? Patches couldn't spot a ring—no, they must be dating. The small gathering near the front had quieted, but they continued talking. Friends, possibly schoolmates who stayed close to where they grew up. Even the group of co-workers made sense. But the single man in the back had barely moved, his beer still full. Had Patches blown his cover?

"Freaky, isn't it?" Frank said as he took inventory of the cooler.

"What is?"

"Every time Richard drops out of reality. He's a finance guy at a big company, I think. He's off somewhere in a virtual meeting. While here, he looks like an upright corpse."

"Enhancements?"

"I'm not sure how much of him is organic. Speaking of…" Paul leaned over the bar. "What do you think?"

Patches studied the man's face. Strong jawline covered in week-old stubble. His lip held a faint pink scar, probably as old as Patches. It took a moment before he realized Paul's eyes were glancing at the ceiling and then down. His iris reminded Patches of healthy grass, a vibrant green with plenty of depth. But around the outside, a slight golden hue gave away the technology.

"It's impossible to tell."

"I've wanted them for a while. The waiting list for tech is longer than my willy. Next round, I want the neural link like John had installed."

Patches assumed that every person in the bar hid synthetic body parts. This was the advantage of a national healthcare system. From muscle to cognitive processes, the people of the empire, and especially London, had taken the Body Shop to a new level. Even with his abilities, there was a chance somebody in the bar could best him in arm wrestling.

"For me, it'll be another round of muscles," Patches lied. His strength might not come from nanobots or replacement parts, but should he need to prove it, he could.

"Mum made sure I had those."

The frequency with which Londoners rushed to the Body Shop required a mental note. It would certainly be a topic for his debrief.

"She must have. You certainly didn't get her good looks," Patches said into his pint.

The insult grabbed John's attention, causing him to laugh. Even Paul cracked up.

The banter would continue for the next hour or two.

Patches hoped he'd be able to find an angle to inquire about the Knights of Winchester. For the number of times they appeared on television, the locals never discussed their sworn protectors. That in of itself offered insight, but it would not help him free Skits. Pushing the empty glass across the bar, he hoped Alyssa and Eve were having more success.

With the third glass empty, Patches found himself no closer to answers than when he started. Patrons came and went, but nobody sat close enough for him to have a reasonable conversation. Try as he might to talk to the brothers, they remained far too boisterous to ask anything he didn't want the entire pub to hear. Another night turned into a bust, and regardless of what they said about a Scot, the beer had already worked its way to his head.

"Heading out?"

"Aye. If I don't get home now, I'm already half-pished."

"You lightweight," Paul said.

"And for a Scot," came a voice behind Patches.

The man thought he was being stealthy, leaving his post at the back of the pub. Patches had watched him approach in the tap's chrome. His body tensed as he prepared for an altercation. "And what's it to you?"

"Do I detect an accent? Glaswegian?"

In the States, they considered his accent a delight. If he were lucky, they'd pinpoint it as being Caledonian. More often than not, they guessed he was Irish. It'd have made his parents sad to know their son was being mistaken for an Irishman. But in England, Alyssa had made it known that their accents carried a different weight. Unlike her, he didn't have the skill to slip in and out of it as necessary.

"My mom was born there. Dad's from Luss."

"Ah," he said. The man buttoned his coat, taking his time to speak. Patches studied his expression, somewhere between obnoxious and arrogant. He already didn't like the gent. "And what about you?"

"Yorkshire," Patches replied. "Writing a novel?"

Paul laughed at the joke, staying close enough to eavesdrop on their conversation. But Patches didn't find it amusing. If it wasn't his landlord spitting slurs at him for being a Child, now it was a Brit drawing imaginary lines across their empire. Bigots followed wherever he went.

"A concerned citizen, that's all."

"What of it?" Patches slid off the chair, getting close enough he could smell the stink of his breath.

"The last thing we need is another refugee from that godforsaken place. You're— *they're* a drain to us all."

Up to this point, the division between Caledonia and England had only been in the form of micro-aggressions. The Brits refused to honor its namesake, still referring to it by its English name. Fine, he could accept that they were slow to change. But this was the first time one of them did more than whisper behind his back when they heard him speak.

Patches patted the man on the chest. "Get yourself home, you eejit."

He took too long drawing back his fist, his shoulder dipping as he attempted to put his weight into it. Patches had eons to step out of the way or throw up a forearm to block the punch. Alyssa had said to keep a low profile. What was more low profile than a scuffle at the pub? Especially when he couldn't even feel the man's knuckles strike him on the bottom side of his jaw.

Patches rubbed his cheek for dramatic effect. "Your mum hits harder."

The man attempted another punch, but Patches hooked a foot behind his leg and pushed. The man toppled, landing on the floor with a thud. There was no point in making threats, no point in a war cry. Standing over the man, he made it clear that if he wanted to continue the fight, his mystery man wouldn't win.

"Paul," he said, "I'm going to need another pint."

"Richard, on with you!" Paul yelled at the man. "Come back when you've learned some manners."

Patches slammed his foot down as if he might lunge for the man. He scurried backward without a word. Panicking, he bolted for the door. He paused, eyeing Patches as if he might spew one last statement before running into the rainy night.

"Good riddance," said Paul. "As if you could choose where your mum was born. Pint's on the house, mate."

Patches ignored the statement, trying not to let the unintentional jab hit home. He had fled Chicago to find people like him, people with abilities. He had done just that, and now, at the request of a dead psychic, he longed for a place he had hardly settled into. At least there, nobody questioned his differences. He missed the smell of the library and unopened boxes filled with books. Here, even the most accepting of people pitied his heritage.

He returned to his seat. He eyed the door again, half expecting the man to be lurking on the other side of the glass. The city acted like they weren't at war with half the world, but Patches could see it. The fight had reached the streets. For the moment, they waged it with words, but it wouldn't be long before it escalated.

"Aye, one more."

Chapter Six

2039

"What is this?" Eve shouted over the thumping music.

The building appeared no different from an office building. Inside there should be meeting rooms, glass cubicles, and whiteboards filled with corporate mumbo jumbo. From the street, the bass sounded as if there might be an earthquake underway. When Alyssa didn't answer, Eve closed her eyes and let her powers creep outward.

"Holy hell," she mumbled at the vibrations. The music generated a magical wash as it disturbed the electromagnetic field. But if she pushed further into the building, it was as if bombs exploded, not bending, but warping the fields like the Tower shields had. "There is so much interference in there."

"Makes sense," Alyssa said, pushing Eve across the street. In every building, cameras watched the Brits, studying their faces and cycling the information through a central computer. Alyssa assured her their contacts protected them from digital detection, but it didn't prevent her skin from crawling. There were no secrets in

London, and they were trespassers. When would their recon mission turn into an evacuation?

"Are we going to a club?"

"Not any club," Alyssa said. The bank of glass doors was tinted, making it impossible to see the excitement inside. Crowds of people were milling about in their flashiest fashion. Alyssa paused at the entrance, letting the scanner read her retina. Eve followed suit, still creeped out that the technology in London used her eye to do everything from unlocking doors to banking. At any moment, she expected it to flash red or scream that it was contacting the police.

"Welcome to the Ministry of Sound," Alyssa said as she opened the door, and music flooded onto the street.

Eve had never been to a club before. She loved the Tower and the family she discovered there, but in the last month, she realized she had lived a sheltered life. No clubs, bars, and even restaurants were alien concepts.

"I didn't take you for a dancer."

Eve noted the moment of sadness cross her mentor's face. Much like the rest of Alyssa's life, there was a story locked away. During their next dinner, she'd be sure to inquire.

"There is much you've yet to learn. The last time I was in a club was with your fathers."

Eve raised an eyebrow. Her fathers? The same men who argued over which documentary to watch before going to bed at nine at night? *Those* fathers?

"Griffin and you were at a club like this?"

"Not quite." Alyssa let the edge of her lip ease into a grin. "There were more strippers."

Alyssa didn't wait for the confused look. Eve had a

list of questions a mile long. What were they doing at a strip club? Before she could retract the thought, she imagined Griffin stuffing money into a stripper's thong. "Ew. No shower will wash that away."

The stairs led downward, toward the music. Normally, her powers remained dormant until she forced them to the surface. But the vibration of the music and the number of people in the club below took on a life of their own. Where most people would feel claustrophobic, she found herself confined by the lines of energy. As the sound waves ricocheted off walls, it was a chaotic disaster, and Eve hated every minute.

"Take a deep breath," Alyssa said. She rested her hand on Eve's chest, giving the younger woman something to focus on. "It's no different from the music. Find something to ground you." The light tapping of fingers over her heart did the trick, and for the moment, she was in control.

"Thanks." Eve silently kicked herself for having another episode. If she had known the expansion of her abilities required relearning to control them, she'd have gladly kept her passive gifts. "What's the goal?" The mission, *that* she could focus on.

"Find a mark close to the palace. We need intelligence on the chess pieces. While you do that, I need to meet an old acquaintance."

A mark. Is that what Alyssa called them in the Wetworks program? Eve hated knowing that Alyssa and her aunt were part of a kill squad that once served the government. Something about that knowledge tainted her opinion of the women. Even with Alyssa's impeccable ethics, it didn't give them the right to act as jury and executioner. Eve pushed aside the foul taste and focused on the mission.

"Got it."

As they entered, Eve headed straight to the bar. The men in London were no different from the Tower. Until they discovered she could snap every bone in their body, they treated her as a damsel meant to be saved. While she pushed through the crowds grinding against one another, she paused to watch. Her fathers danced when the computer played an old song, but she had never seen them like this. In a room packed with people, Eve felt the isolation creeping in, a reminder that even if she looked like them, she was not one of *them*.

"Like what you see?" It required shouting from the woman at her side to be heard. Eve glanced at her. Dark hair buzzed close to the scalp, no tattoos, but plenty of piercings. She held up a drink in a salute before guzzling the contents.

"I've never been in a club like this." Half-truths had become a way of life.

"Let me welcome you. These are my thousand closest friends. That's DJ Venom in the booth, and Ginger is the only bartender worth her weight." Eve appreciated the rundown, but she couldn't shelve her suspicions. What did— "Let me buy you a drink."

Oh, Eve thought. Unlike the men who insisted on buying her a drink, this woman hadn't eyed her breasts, threatened to touch her, or asked her lewd questions. Perhaps she had been going about intelligence gathering wrong this entire time.

"Let's find Ginger," Eve said.

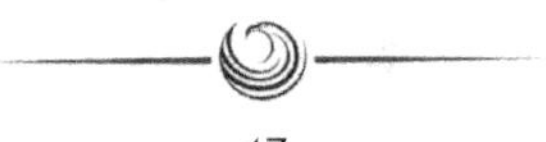

Alyssa glanced over her shoulder as Eve escorted a young woman toward the bar. She held no doubts her mentees could handle themselves in a dangerous situation. But like any good teacher, she hoped they never needed to exercise their more destructive skills. Unfortunately, the Children of Nostradamus weren't awarded the luxury of peace. She admired both Patches and Eve and their determination to face adversity, but she always hoped they wouldn't have to.

Alyssa vanished into the crowd of dancers surrounding the dance floor. Unlike the throngs moving in time to the music, these people settled on swaying hips and bobbing their heads, trying to keep their cocktails from being knocked out of their hands. She never liked the synthetic qualities of music in a club, but she envied the dancers as they lost themselves to the fervor.

While Eve gathered intel, she had a rendezvous with an old acquaintance. France might have fallen to the British Empire, but its people remained determined to fight back. It had taken little coaxing to convince a rebel to help their cause. She only hoped Allah smiled on her tonight and he provided Skits' location. Alyssa pushed back the despair, fearing her friend might not be alive.

"No." The refusal couldn't be heard over the music. "She's alive."

Along the far wall, chest-high tables separated a seating area filled with couches. People gathered around the tables, using them to hold their drinks while they shouted at one another. The lights almost didn't reach the couches, leaving them veiled in darkness. It resembled one of Needles' spy movies. Ironic, considering studios got little else about the occupation correct. Thinking of the man left her heart aching. She wanted nothing more than to complete this mission and return to their courtship.

Antoine. The Frenchman looked out of place in his three-piece suit. Sitting on the furthest couch from the light, he held a martini glass, swirling the contents. He had moved up in status since the last time she fought by his side. The man had traded a ragged beard for a neatly groomed goatee and tactical gear for designer labels. She couldn't help but admire the man's swagger.

Pushing through the crowd, she lifted a drink from one of the round tables, a pint half-filled with amber liquid. Working undercover in a hostile territory didn't mean looking like every other person. The enemy looked for similarities as much as they did differences. No, it was being able to blend in despite your differences. The movies never got this right.

She took a seat next to the man and tightened her hijab, brushing a bit of hair under the fabric. Draping an arm over her shoulder, they appeared nothing more than old friends. The proximity allowed them to talk without shouting.

"You've cleaned up since I saw you last." Speak with vagueness. She did a sweep of the room, but with hundreds of bodies, she couldn't be certain if somebody was monitoring their conversation. Even the cameras hidden within the walls could transcribe their every word, looking for signs of a rebellion. London was no different from any other oppressive government, policing its citizens even more than it did its enemies.

"Et tu, ma petite? You haven't changed at all."

His accent left her cheeks feeling warm. Antoine knew how to disarm with a single phrase. His accent didn't hurt. Alyssa wanted him to read textbooks aloud.

"In town for long?"

"Non." She replied. "I'm visiting, hoping to connect with a dear friend."

"I hoped *I* was the dear friend." He smiled as he took a drink. Unlike her other contacts, Antoine preferred to drag out a meeting with conversation. She always claimed it'd get them killed, but he insisted they partake in civilized discussion before initiating business.

"There's nobody I'd rather share a drink with." Alyssa held out her glass, gently clanking his but never sipping its contents.

Antoine drained his martini. He leaned into Alyssa's neck as if he might kiss beneath her jawline. Were it any other man, she'd break his finger. It came with the territory, and after his first folly, he knew the boundaries. "She is alive. I cannot say for how long."

Alyssa nearly heaved as she sucked in air. In her heart, she knew Allah protected her sister.

She didn't agree with the Wetworks program, not even in the slightest. At first, it had been for the safety of her people, but those in power, no matter how righteous, lost their way. Even Alyssa's friends had abused her talents. She lied to herself that her presence was for the sake of Eve and Patches. But truth be told, guilt motivated her more than she wanted to admit.

She had hidden behind her anger. But when she discovered Skits had sacrificed her freedom to save Registry, she remembered why she loved the woman. They had survived the Outlands, and through trials and tribulations, Alyssa called Skits her sister. It was time to brave the unknown and reunite her family.

"Perhaps I'll visit while I'm here." She hoped his good news didn't end there.

"Alyssa, ma petite chouchou." He turned her head until they were staring one another in the eye. The lights of the club bathed him in neon pinks and blues. He'd have been handsome if he didn't ruin it by insisting he surpassed her body count. Alyssa preferred her men confident in their abilities, much like a certain hacker waiting for her in the States. "You are a woman of many talents, but there is no way your friend can escape."

He rested a hand on her thigh, higher than their friendship allowed. As she attempted to swat it away, he slid something into her palm. He leaned in for another kiss.

"The Knights of Winchester are formidable. My people underestimated them. We paid the price. But it is not them that has us worried. The queen is all that holds this country together. Craignez l'abomination de la Reine."

"Merci, Antoine." She offered a single kiss on his cheek, ready to leave him be. His hand tightened on her wrist, preventing her from standing.

Antoine's eyes went wide as he stared into the crowd. "Alyssa, they're here."

Chapter Seven

2039

All of Caledonia would cry if they discovered Patches was drunk after four pints. Pished, as his father used to say. Paul offered to call him a taxi, but the rules forbid any traceable route back to their flat—even drunk, he heard Alyssa's voice like an angel on his shoulder. Anyway, he needed the fresh air.

The moment he exited the pub, London's notorious drizzle sought every opening in his jacket. Based on the way people spoke, he expected it to be like the whipping rain Chicago was known for. It was more of a constant misting, the type of rain that couldn't decide if it was going to clear or storm. It created a miserable atmosphere. Patches longed for the beaming sun. It always surprised him what made him miss Chicago.

"Next I'll miss the snow," he laughed.

He walked toward his flat a block away. Again, Alyssa's teachings spoke up. Take the most direct route, so the cameras don't spot erratic movement, but make sure he wasn't being followed. The synthetics once patrolled the streets of Chicago, but as he spotted a camera attached to a building, he realized they weren't as oppressive as he believed. London had turned into a police state, and its citizens didn't realize they were—

"Let me go!" yelled a man.

Patches froze as a police officer dragged a man from his flat. Wearing a robe, he attempted to escape the man's hold on his wrist. A second officer stepped out of the flat, rifle strapped to his chest. It wasn't their firepower that worried Patches, it was the speed of the second officer's hand wrapping around their culprit's neck. He lifted his victim off the ground. His robe parted, revealing naked flesh.

"Robert Colquhoun, by order of the queen, you have been deemed a traitor."

"No. No." The suffocating hand of the officer stifled the man's cries.

Patches continued walking. If Alyssa had been sitting on his shoulder, she was silent as he violated at least a dozen of her rules. The first officer opened the back door of his car. Their victim stopped fighting. Patches couldn't tell if he accepted his fate or passed out from the lack of air. The officers weren't sadistic, toying with the man. They did a job with cold efficiency. They might as well be synthetics.

"Stop," the officer yelled. Holding up a hand, he waited for his partner to put the traitor in the back. Once the door slammed shut, they turned their attention to Patches.

"Where are you coming from?"

"Curi's," Patches said. "Had a few pints after work."

The camera mounted on the officer's chest had already scanned his eyes. The computers at Central Command were already dissecting his statement, feeding the information back to the officers. He had no doubt that they were confirming his story, following his path from the pub.

Patches could hear Paul's statement again. "Stay clear of them." Patches realized he had a habit of avoiding good advice. He'd need to think about that more. He never considered himself a rebel, but it was obviously becoming a pattern.

"Patrick," the man said, as if knowing his name would unnerve him. "Be on your way."

Patches glanced at the car. Was the man a traitor, or was this their way of preventing insubordination? Would he receive a trial, or was this drive to rendezvous with exterminators? Every fiber of Patches' being wanted to hit the officers and tear the door from the car. He could do it and be gone in seconds.

"Is there going to be a problem?" asked the second man.

Patches shook his head. "No, officer." Fewer words meant less chance of his accent shining through.

"Rebels and sympathizers have no place here."

Observe. There were whispers of people disappearing, but now Patches had confirmation. As the city settled in for the evening, the officers began a routine of eliminating any opposition to the crown. He wondered if this man was part of an elaborate coup to overthrow the queen or did he express an opinion that didn't follow the majority.

If his feet hit the pavement hard enough, he'd have enough energy stored to overpower them. By the time the second officer punched him, he'd be capable of launching them through the air. If they shot him... Patches shoulder ached at the memory of the last bullet meant to kill him. It sobered him enough to remember that they weren't there to aid a rebellion.

"By her grace," Patches said with a nod.

"By her grace," the officers returned. They moved to their vehicle, watching him as they got in and drove away.

Patches continued walking, eyeing the open door. He'd spend the night beating himself up for not getting involved. All he wanted was a quiet life where being a Child of Nostradamus wouldn't define him. Yet, in the past few months, it had become obvious that destiny demanded more. The old him would have cowered, and now he considered fighting the law. He hardly recognized the man he had become. It both terrified and invigorated him.

He pulled his coat tight, attempting to fend off the intruding drip down his back. As he turned the corner, he found the bigot from Curi's standing to greet him. Unlike before, he had three men at his back, reinforcements for a man incapable of holding his own in a brawl.

"That's one more sympathizer off our streets."

Patches looked back at the flat. "Your doing?"

"We don't want your kind here," said one of his cronies.

"Yer daft," Patches said. If it didn't jeopardize rescuing Skits, he'd have gladly traded blows with the men. He repeated the logic in his head. *Save Skits. Save Skits.* With what he had witnessed tonight, he'd have plenty to debrief Alyssa and Eve. He wasn't sure how any of it would be useful, but it painted a clearer picture of the tyranny at play.

"Do we have a sympathizer?" asked one of his backups.

"A rebel," said the mystery man. "Straight from Scotland."

"Yorkshire, but—"

They spread out, preparing to attack. He could easily barrel through them, but he didn't dare return to the flat for fear of their band following. This was the exact type of attention he wanted to avoid. There could be a thousand cameras watching the event unfold, and Patches doubted the officers would return to intercede before the men lynched him.

"For the Watch."

Fight like a human, he thought. He didn't fear the men. If anything, he worried his abilities might kick in and he'd land a punch snapping a bone. They thought him a Scot, but they didn't suspect he might—

One of Richard's lackeys raised his arm, all metal from the elbow down. A compartment sprung open and a small black disc attached to Patches' jacket. He cried out as a jolt of electricity surged along his abdomen. When he didn't fall, the man fired another. His chest burned as the two tiny objects burned holes in his jacket, electrocuting him. They had proven his invulnerability a fallacy.

"I'll admit, he's tough," said Richard.

Patches swatted at pucks, knocking them from his chest. He slammed his heel against the ground, the energy surging through his body. He was moving before it had time to reach his arms. Lunging at a man, he ignored the raised fists about to connect with his face. He absorbed the impact of the punch powered by hydraulics. The enhancements should have crushed his bone, but they only fueled his abilities. With a thrust of his palm, he struck the man in the sternum, launching him into the street.

There was no point in hiding his abilities. Hiding them wouldn't do any good if they managed a killing blow. He turned to see the fear in their eyes, but even that didn't override the anger. Patches refused to let a group of hate-filled gangsters ruin his night, even if that meant breaking bones.

Richard pulled a small gun from his jacket. Patches laughed, unafraid of a projectile piercing his skin. He stood tall, inviting the blast, prepared to push the energy into his legs. With a flick of his wrist, the nanites from his bracelet would coat his hand, and he'd have the fire-power of the gauntlets to end the scuffle. But the weapon didn't fire with a bang, and there was no blast of kinetic energy rippling along Patches skin. He looked down to see a vial with three needles poking through his shirt. Unlike the discs, the tiny prongs pierced his skin.

"Shit," he hissed, the vial draining into his body.

Tearing it out, he charged, readying to bury his shoulder into the jerk's torso and slam him against the wall. As he bent down, his arms dangled, unable to follow his commands. His foot lagged behind, causing him to trip. Even as he rolled along the pavement, his skin didn't absorb the impact like usual. The side of his head smacked the cement, and he couldn't manage more than a grunt as the wind escaped his lungs.

Richard used the heel of his boot to roll Patches onto his back. "The Long Watch sees all," said the man.

"Clarity brings redemption," responded his collaborators.

Patches watched as the faces gathered, looking down

at him with disdain. He spent years feeling his body betrayed him. He never wanted the abilities of a Child, but they were part of him. With one step toward acceptance, his body betrayed him again. Trapped, he could only look up at the men.

"Redemption awaits you," said the man.

Shit, Patches thought.

"What's an American doing here?"

"What gave it away?"

The girl looked her up and down. "Where to begin?"

Eve looked down, expecting her t-shirt to be glowing with a sign that read, "Out of place." The girl laughed as she pointed to the bartender, an older woman with fiery red hair pulled back in a ponytail. Ginger lived up to her name, and with a wink to Eve's new companion, she felt she was part of an inside joke.

"My parents," she said, leaning close so she didn't need to shout. The woman raised an eyebrow. "They immigrated when I was a kid. Then, well, the world happened." The story was the same for thousands of expats. It left room to maneuver if there were follow-up questions. Alyssa had made sure they knew their false identities to the letter.

"Be careful… my name is Jasper." She held out her hand.

"Evelyn." They shook like old business acquaintances.

"Be careful, Evelyn."

"Funny, Patches keeps saying the same thing."

"Who?"

Eve laughed. "A friend. Kind of like the brother I never asked for."

"He's right though. It's not a good time to be a foreigner in Britain."

"Is it a good time anywhere?" Eve made light of the statement. Jasper appeared like any other local, plain except for the piercing green eyes, tattoos, and piercings. If it weren't for those, she'd easily sink into a crowd and become a phantom memory.

"Be careful of the Watch."

For a month, there had been rumors about the organization. People walked through the streets of London fearful that one of the Watch followed them. But this was the first time somebody offered her a direct warning. Eve was both intrigued and suspicious.

"Who are they, anyway?"

"Assholes," Jasper said, "the whole lot of them. They took a woman in my building. Gone. Like she never existed."

"What happens to them? The people they take, I mean?"

Jasper's glance said everything it needed. They weren't terrorizing foreigners. This organization attempted to purge those unfit to live within their borders. Jasper turned to Ginger, paying for the drinks before handing one to Eve.

"It's a dangerous time to be alive." Eve held up her beer, saluting the fall of civilization.

"You'd think those assholes would do something better with their time. If you're so concerned, go fight in the war. Let a Caledonian kick the shit out of you."

With a single word—Caledonia—her new friend, revealed plenty. She might not have Alyssa's penchant for being a spy, but even she recognized the danger in saying its name aloud. Perhaps meeting desperate men had been a poor strategy.

"To independence," Eve raised her glass again. Jasper returned the gesture. It seemed the woman was a sympathizer, which was dangerous enough on its own. But to refer to the North by its self-given name, it told a long story.

"My best friend is Caledonian. Sometimes I worry about that man."

Jasper raised an eyebrow. "You should. My father is a driver for the palace, and the stories he tells… If the Watch doesn't get to your friend, it's only a matter of time before the crown does."

Interesting, Eve thought.

"Bloody hell," Jasper said. Eve followed her eyes to the men in black descending the stairs. These were the standard officers flooding the streets. The tactical gear and heavy weaponry meant they came looking for a fight. Between her and Alyssa, they could handle six of them, but if they started shooting, innocent clubbers would litter the floor.

"I have to go," Jasper said. Eve realized she wasn't the only one terrified.

"How do I get a hold of you?" Eve needed allies, and Jasper could very well be the first person who knew more than what the government-sanctioned media fed them.

"I'm not somebody you want to know outside the Ministry."

"Be careful, I guess," Eve said.

"Same to you, Evelyn." The woman leaned in, kissing her on the lips. Even in the face of persecution,

Jasper surprised her. She didn't hate it. The woman disappeared into a crowd of oblivious dancers.

"Alyssa," Eve mumbled as she moved in the direction her mentor had headed. She bumped into the tiny woman amidst a throng of people jumping up and down in time with the bass.

"We need to go," Alyssa said.

Eve watched as a bartender pushed their way through a door. She didn't know if there was an exit, but it was better than trying to run between soldiers to flee the club. But as the room caught sight of the soldiers, the patrons made a path, and Eve needed the bystanders to run interference.

The thump and hum of music dominated the room. The shouting, lights, and even the patrons' heartbeats created a chaotic dissonance with the electromagnetic fields. Here, Eve could never isolate them one at a time. It was hard enough within a calm space, but she didn't need to manipulate them like a surgeon holding a knife. Closing her eyes, she reached into the madness and imagined the lines turning back on themselves. The effort made her stagger until Alyssa held her upright. Her abilities pushed back against the lines, hurling them back at their source. It was more than she had attempted before and when she opened her eyes, nothing had changed.

"Dammit." She'd have to practice on something larger than a flashlight when they returned home.

Then the music stopped and the lights burst in a fury of sparks. The darkness spread outward, reclaiming the club. Eve nearly yelped in excitement. She needed to stop referring to her abilities as passive. If manipulating the electromagnetic fields didn't leave her legs weak and her heart racing, it'd be an impressive addition to her arsenal.

"We need to leave," Alyssa whispered in her ear.

Eve closed her eyes, thrusting her abilities outward. Cellular devices. Voices. Body modifications. They all created fields, but none of them were as bright as the weapons held by the soldiers. Powered, they were the type of weapons that didn't simply maim a victim. They eradicated them. This wasn't any contingent of soldiers. It was a death squad, and she couldn't fathom what they'd be after.

Eve turned, taking Alyssa by the hand, and worked her way toward the back of the bar. She couldn't see with her abilities, not like Kevin, but if she kept her focus, she could feel the vibrations and where they met and interacted with solid surfaces. It was enough to get them out of the club before the soldiers switched to their high-tech eyes and pinpointed two patrons, obviously fleeing.

They reached the back of the bar, and Eve had to pause. Her abilities took time to calibrate to the new surroundings. Thankfully, she didn't need to as a man standing in an exit held up his lighter. It was barely enough light to illuminate his face, but it gave her a direction.

"Death squad," Eve whispered.

"I saw," Alyssa confirmed.

"For us?"

"Possibly. Or my contact."

"Are they okay? Should we go back?"

Alyssa tugged at her arm, pulling her toward the light. "He'll find a way out."

Eve might have once believed her mentor, that she

spoke with sincerity. But knowing that she was part of a network doing less than reputable acts in the name of justice, her trust didn't extend as far as it used to. But unless she wanted to charge into a firefight and risk saving Skits, she had to accept her word.

They reached the door. The security lights switched on, blinding Eve. Squinting, she could see the door led into a tunnel. With the electricity turned off, she could sense further, able to tell the tunnels remained empty except for the staff. Somewhere at the end, she had to assume it led to the street, or at least she hoped it did.

"It's safe," she said. Famous last words, she thought, as they yet again ran away from danger. Even with a successful night of gathering intelligence, she didn't like any of this. They were no closer to rescuing Skits, and every day they wasted playing it safe was another day her aunt might not survive. It was finally time for her to push Alyssa into action. It was time to stop hiding in the shadows.

If need be, Eve was prepared to force Alyssa to step down as she took charge of the Sentinels.

Chapter Eight

2039

Patches opened his eyes, but the room remained black. It took a moment before the heat of his breath gave away the hood over his head. They had him seated, and by the echo of the room, it was a large space. How long had he been out? Had they taken him far from the pub or was this a nearby safe house where they disposed of Caledonians?

He pulled at the restraints on his wrists. Had they been plastic or even rope, he'd be more than capable of tearing them off. His captors weren't stupid, instead relying on thin wire capable of severing his hand if he struggled. This wasn't their first time kidnapping somebody. But was this their first time kidnapping a Child? Had they figured it out yet, or did he still have an ace up his sleeve?

"He's awake."

There was movement. At least a dozen people milled about the room. They didn't dare get close to him, all except one pair of boots sauntering up to his chair. Richard snatched off the hood, and Patches finally got a good look at the room. An old Victorian building. There weren't many downtown, so he had to assume they had transported him away from the city center. The room had seen better days, run-down, with shelves broken and walls collapsing under the weight of the second floor.

"Didn't think your night would end like this, Scot?" Richard looked even more punchable now. Patches wanted to ask if he sat at pubs night after night looking for foreigners to harass. How many people had sat in this chair before him? Hopefully, this would be the last time this group *vanished* somebody.

Patches tried not to let out a sigh of relief. This kidnapping had little to do with him being a Child or even their mission to save Skits. This was a good ol' fashioned hate group out to purify their city. That shouldn't bring as much relief as it did. But at least it meant when the time allowed for it, he'd be more than willing to crack their skulls.

"If you wanted a date—"

The man swung his fist, clocking Patches. Unlike before, the blow came with enough force he spat blood. In the pub he had thought himself superior. Now he needed to power up his enhancements to do more than tickle his hostage. Patches let the energy disperse along his skin, storing it away for when he had an opening.

"Don't you dare speak—"

"Or what? You'll hold me hostage and kill me?"

Richard struck him again, knuckles driving into his chin. Patches put on a show, jerking his head to the side and spitting across the room. Right now, he wanted to maintain the element of surprise. They had bested him once before, but that wouldn't happen again. Alyssa always coached using the enemy's weakness against them. For once, he intended to listen to her teachings. Perhaps if he had done it sooner, he wouldn't be sitting here.

"You stain our majesty's land. It won't be long before the prince advances into Scotland and purges those heathens from our land."

Richard turned to one of his compatriots. They all wore dark clothing, not quite a uniform, but enough to show they had given consideration to their outfits. Observe. They didn't appear to have weapons, but the sting from earlier reminded him they invested in her enhancements. Guns remained outlawed by anybody other than soldiers for this very reason. But this ragtag militia had found ways around it.

Radicals, he thought, *good to know things aren't so different from Chicago.*

Richard raised his fist. The skin between his knuckles shifted until metal covered his hand. Patches grit his teeth, preparing for the blow. It'd only take one or two strikes before his body raged with stored energy. At that point, he'd need to break free, or he'd be unable to control his powers. He wasn't sure if the stored energy would prevent the wire on his wrists from slicing into his skin, but he'd have to risk it. He prepared to flick his hand, summoning Registry's gauntlets. They were about to be sorry.

"I'm not from Scotland. I didn't choose my ancestors."

"Your bear their sins."

The man rested a hand on Patches' cheek. The electricity bypassed his skin's ability to redirect kinetic energy. His muscles tensed uncontrollably as millions of needles jabbed into his body. His teeth clenched as his back arched, forcing the wires to slice into his wrists. There was no point in being stoic. A scream ripped from his lungs as he tried to focus the agony into a single breath.

Like a switch, the pain turned off. The device might not be electrocuting him, but his muscles twitched, clinging to the echoes of torment. Sucking in air, he tried to gather his senses, to remember anything other than a moment of agony worse than death. The tech in Richard's hand had been designed to kill. Something wasn't adding up. He needed them to keep talking.

He hissed as he spoke. "The queen has more common sense than to let—"

"Her abomination to take control? That abomination is the rightful heir to the throne."

It was the first time he met somebody who believed the prince should inherit the throne. The conversation went from infuriating to intriguing. It was as calming as a pint at the pub, but maybe these barbarians had the intel he needed.

"She won't allow it," Patches replied.

The men in the room laughed, amused by his statement. They knew more, or at least they believed they did.

"She won't have a say in the matter for long."

"The queen isn't dying soon." The reports of her longevity were almost constant. Heck, there was a daily update on the website of her life expectancy. She might be heading toward her sunset, but she had another decade before her enhancements broke down.

"Who said anything about waiting for her—"

"The Knights of Winchester." He walked into the

trap. Alyssa might be the spy. That made Eve the hot-headed fighter. He worried he brought nothing to their newly formed band of superheroes. But talking, that was a skill he had in spades.

"They won't let anything happen to Her Majesty."

The men laughed as if he had told the world's best dad joke. Richard paced back and forth, flexing his fingers to show off his prosthetic.

Come on, Patches thought, *talk, you asshole.*

"The Knights of Winchester are purists. Who do you think started the Long Watch?"

This. This was the intelligence they had been after, an opening to the Knights. Registry said Skits freed him from the Children of Britain. It meant that there was a good chance they were holding her hostage. First, he'd break free. Then, he'd beat the shit out of these men in the name of Caledonia. Then it'd be taking Richard and putting him in the chair as Patches tortured him for information. It was a sound plan. Eve would be proud of his restraint and determination. A little more informa-tion and then he could free himself.

"Great, you're Children wannabes.

"Feisty," the man said, squatting in front of Patches. "You'll make a fine tribute. By her grace."

"Clarity brings redemption," echoed the others.

"Tribute? For what?"

The man's smirk might as well have screamed, "I know something you don't." He reached for Patches' leg. Try as he might, he couldn't dodge the man's touch. He gritted his teeth, bracing for another round of electro-cution. His muscles tensed as he prepared for the agony to sear through his muscles. The man laughed as he patted Patches on the leg.

"He'll do just fine." Patches' limbs stopped twitching. He'd had enough. It was time to show these men what a Child—*what a Caledonian*—could do.

His muscles were on fire as he pushed energy into his shoulders. Something slid over his face. Not the dark hood from before, but a mask covering his nose and mouth as he exhaled. He thrashed about, the wires cutting into flesh. Jerking his head back and forth, he shot it back, hoping to catch the man in the stomach, but no such luck. If he tried to tear at the bonds holding him in place, he risked losing a limb.

It held fast to his face as he tried to hold his breath. Drained, his lungs begged for air. An odd sensation started in his groin, creeping up his body as he fought the instinct to inhale. Finally, his body won, and he sucked in fast and hard. It tasted of chemicals, and he expected more pain from his tormentors.

Thankfully, the world turned dark.

"We're being followed," Alyssa whispered.

The route to their flat was long and convoluted. There was no reason for somebody to be traveling down this narrow alley unless they were following them. Alyssa kept a running tally of the reasons she had left the Wetworks program. It seemed there was never an end to the reasons she regretted being used by the government to infiltrate hostile territories.

Alyssa looked over her shoulder. Just as she anticipated, the alley remained empty, at least with the naked eye. When she first found herself in the Outlands, she feared her intuition had been tainted by fear, but it had grown into her second power.

The alley was barely wide enough for two people, and filled with rubbish bins. In another hundred feet, it'd widen into the courtyard behind a series of row houses. If *she* were going to spring a trap, that'd be where she lay waiting. The moment they left the alley, they'd be in a kill box.

"They're there," she mumbled. "Can you see them?"

Eve braced a hand on the wall, closing her eyes. She regretted allowing Eve and Patches to come with her. Skits was her responsibility, *her* partner. If she hadn't abandoned the initiative, perhaps they'd be sitting at the Tower telling stories about living in the Outlands. Neither of the kids deserved this life. Add it to the list, a job that put loved ones at risk.

"I see them." Eve opened her eyes, eyebrow raised in confusion. "One person. No weapons."

Alyssa blinked three times in rapid succession. The contact lens came to life, showing a heads-up display. With a couple of rapid glances, she opened a series of videos. Close combat. Grappling. Small arms. Knife. Baton. Tai-Chi. The videos played faster than she could recall the playlist. Her muscles twitched as they learned, absorbing the sensory input faster than her brain.

"Where?" she asked as the display vanished.

"Courtyard."

"Stay behind me," Alyssa said.

"I can—"

"I'm not asking." Alyssa didn't leave room for negotiating. Eve remained her star pupil. None of them learned to fight quicker than her. But no matter how much lecturing Alyssa gave her, she refused to embrace her abilities while training. Now she operated as two people, a capable fighter and a fledgling Child. And if Alyssa was right about the person waiting, Eve would prove more of a liability than a resource.

"I need you to disable the cameras."

"But—"

"Not the time."

Eve nodded. Her expanding skills proved useful time and time again. But it didn't mean she had learned to embrace them. The poor girl continued to feel subpar, as if her gifts didn't measure up to the other Children. She felled two Knights, and still, she lacked confidence. *Eventually*, thought Alyssa. But some things were harder to learn than others.

There was no going back, not with so many soldiers behind them. Alyssa didn't shy away from a fight, but she understood the importance of choosing her opponents. Forward. She zipped up her jacket, happy for the body armor. There were no obvious weapons at hand, but this is where Alyssa took pride in her abilities. She adapted. Swiping one of the metal lids off the rubbish bin, she started in a run.

With a final push, she jumped to the corner of the alley wall, grabbing onto the drain pipe before kicking off. She soared head-first in a controlled flip, taking stock of her surroundings. The garden only had one other exit. Two L-shaped buildings came together, making for a lovely area of green, complete with a non-functioning water fountain in the middle. A stone path circled the water feature, peppered with well-maintained grass and raised planters along the side. There were at least a dozen cameras and close to forty windows overlooking the space. She had faith Eve disrupted the surveillance, but it didn't do anything to stop prying eyes.

The garden appeared empty.

Alyssa hit the ground with a roll, holding the lid as a shield. With a flinch of the eye, the contacts shifted, zooming. They weren't as useful as ocular enhancements, but at least she could remove them at the end of the day. She had fought beside a woman capable of bending light and sound waves, rendering her invisible. Whether mechanical or powers, she— Impressions in the grass.

"Mechanical," she said. With a spin, she used the momentum to chuck the lid. The indentations in the grass shifted, just as Alyssa predicted. She didn't think the makeshift frisbee would fall her opponent. Skidding along the gravel, it did, however, kick up enough dust to make the figure visible. Alyssa skipped, congratulating herself and started into a sprint before the dust settled.

The figure shimmered as if the air had grown dangerously hot. Fire. Heat. Like the former United States, the British Empire purged itself of mentalists. It meant if there were pyro-related abilities, they were rooted in physiology. But if Eve was right, it wasn't a human hiding behind the technology.

The burst of light appeared as a ball of liquid fire hurled in her direction. Alyssa lunged, diving and tucking her shoulder. Somersaulting, she sprang back to her feet, stepping on the edge of the fountain and then pushed off the center spout. Another ball of fire formed, but before the creator could throw it in her direction, she slammed into the person.

The mirage vanished, the cloak falling open, revealing a slender man no taller than her. Both of his hands were bright pink, disguising the scar tissue. But the burned flesh continued up the side of his face, making it impossible to see his features. He lacked a nose and eyelids. Alyssa had met Children with dangerous gifts, victims of their powers. As he raised his hands, she caught a glimpse of the sigil on his shoulder, a sword slicing through a shield.

"Knight," she hissed.

"Child," the man responded.

She almost asked permission to pass, to avoid the inevitable, but he cut that prayer short as his forearms burst into flame. She grabbed the lid, raising it as another burst of flame smashed against her makeshift shield. However, the Knight created fire, it had substance, a burning liquid. Alyssa didn't have access to a video with a quick solution.

Spinning about, she raised her foot, toe posed to strike the man in the head. He raised a forearm, blocking her leg. She hissed as the contact ignited her pants, chewing away at the fabric as it seared her skin. Residue from his skin, combustible sweat? Alyssa might not have a video to stop a fire starter, but adapting served as the cornerstone of her abilities.

"They're coming," Eve shouted.

The man swiped a flaming fist. She knocked it to the side, moving fast enough to sidestep the right hook. They knew how to fight and how to use their abilities. Alyssa commended the Knights on their prowess. Registry had provided plenty of warning. Vanity never followed her into combat, but for once, Alyssa found herself against a formidable opponent. She had something to prove.

She spun about as if she were about to drive a toe

into his skull. She pulled her leg in close, dodging his block. Using her momentum, she brought up her other leg, striking him in the neck. Falling into a handstand, she flipped back and then ran toward the planters. The heat washed along her back as she stepped up, avoiding the burst of fire. It was only a matter of time before he landed a hit. A single ball of liquid fire could incapacitate, and she refused to fall victim to a Knight.

Turning, she watched as the man's arms engulfed in flame. The cloak he wore burned away until it fell from his neck. His eyes narrowed, but not before she caught the wince. Like many Children, his powers came at a cost. Perhaps the battle wouldn't be won with violence?

"It hurts?" She said between breaths.

He looked down at his hands as the fire in his palms intensified. "Pain is for the weak."

"The scars. What have they done?"

Her questions must have struck a nerve. The flames crawled up his bare arms and finally ignited the side of his face. Even with drugs or enhancements, or whatever they did to the poor man, he hurt. But just as Registry warned, the Knights of Winchester maintained a singular focus.

For a split second, the man's fire faltered, flickering as if somebody had flipped the switch to his powers. Alyssa glanced at the alley to see Eve bracing herself against the wall. She wouldn't be able to maintain the cameras and assault the man. But her efforts created a window.

She lunged, diving for the lid. The courtyard lit up as the man screamed, engulfed in flames. She snagged the metal handle, rolling. The splash of fire poured around the edges, hitting the edges of her jacket. Pushing off, she shot upward, but he sidestepped the ending blow, just as she anticipated. She waited until he pulled back his hand, armed with more fire. She hurled the lid, forcing him to turn and deflect the blow.

"You petulant Child."

Hooking her foot on the cloak, she tossed it into the air. The fire spread around the garment, burning holes as she attempted to use it as a flimsy shield. An opponent she couldn't touch, couldn't get close to. From now on, she'd make sure she traveled with her batons. The holes grew, and she tossed them to the side.

"You don't have to do this."

"The Children of Nostradamus are enemies—"

"Registry sent us."

The name made his eyes go wide before the sneer spread across his face. "The traitor. Magus will reward my victory." Did they all talk like brainwashed fools? How much were his own thoughts, and how much was the conditional programming they forced onto young recruits?

She held her ground, waiting for an opening. If Eve could short-circuit his powers, even for a second, she'd drive knuckles into his throat and suffer the burns.

"We only want the woman who saved him."

"She will die."

Will. That's all Alyssa needed to know. His words confirmed Antoine's statement. His body radiated heat, forcing her to squint and turn her face away. She could see Eve running in her direction, a sign that she hadn't been able to turn off his abilities again.

His body flared again, and Alyssa prepared another series of jumps to dodge his liquid fire. His body jerked. One moment he growled, his powers consuming him, and the next he collapsed. Alyssa watched as the man's body hissed, his skin continuing to burn. She wanted to pat him down, to inspect his pockets, but Eve grabbed her arm.

"You?" she asked.

Eve shook her head, pointing toward the other exit. A single red glow came from the space between the buildings. Never did she think she'd thank a synthetic for saving her life. It did, however, raise questions about how Blue continued to defy orders. But for now, she whispered a prayer that Allah had sent her friend's pet robot.

"Skits is alive," Alyssa said.

"We won't be if we don't move."

Alive. Right now, that was the bar for good news. Alyssa thought of all the ways the British Empire resembled the Free Republic. She wanted to believe in the good of people, but yet another nation proved Children were treated as tools. But there wasn't time to dwell on the moral conundrums. Instead, they ran.

Chapter Nine

2039

"The queen's abomination will not sit on the throne."

The words echoed in the back of his head.

Oscar's fingers rolled into a fist. The anger tensed his muscles, but his face remained neutral. They had taught him to hide his emotions, to tuck them away until he found a private place to let them out. Despite his boarding school's teachings, he wanted to drive his knuckles into the flesh of every person who doubted his birthright.

This level of the hospital was off-limits to all but those with top-level clearance. Once a common facility serving the sick of London, they had turned the building into a government-controlled Body Shop. In the upper levels, military, police officers, and members of the ruling class overlaid their organic parts with cybernetic enhancements. Each of them sought to be more than their God made them.

The queen's abomination.

"How dare they?" Oscar drove his knuckles into the wall, cracking the plaster. The outburst did little to satiate his fury. He wanted to do the same to the Lords, who dared to demean the rank of their sovereign.

Not only did they consider their queen's heir a crime against nature, it left Oscar living in the shadow of his— Oscar had never decided on a term for the man who served as the template for his creation. Father? Brother? Twin? While they had created him in the image of a dead prince, they never considered the ethical ramifications.

"Prince Oscar." He turned to see a doctor in a lab coat with a Data pad against his chest. He looked like any other general practitioner, but Doctor Wentworth didn't treat ailing commoners. With degrees in genetic engineering and biotechnology, he only worked with a single patient.

"Dr. Wentworth," Oscar said, pulling his fist from the wall.

"Should we tend to your hand first?"

Oscar shook his head. The pain served as a reminder. "Later, perhaps. Shot first."

One hundred and sixty-one hours. The window between injections had shrunk another thirteen minutes. At this rate, he wouldn't reach his fiftieth birthday, or thirtieth, depending on who did the counting.

He followed the doctor down the hall. "Are you sleeping?"

"When I can."

"Oscar, your body needs to regenerate. The more stress you put on it, the faster the deterioration."

It translated to death. Oscar spent enough nights in the research labs to read between their unique language. Much like the queen, he had a dedicated team of physicians working around the clock to extend his life.

Oscar's mother had long outlived her natural lifespan thanks to the miracles of modern science. He hoped they could do the same for him.

"Nightmares?"

"Not as many. Memory fragments from time to time."

"Diet?"

"The chef follows your guidelines. A little too well, I might add. I'd appreciate ice cream once in a while."

The doctor chuckled. If the queen was his mother by genetics, this man served as his stand-in father. Out of a dedicated staff meant to serve the royal family, only Dr. Wentworth pushed back.

"That's a no. Any fatigue? Muscle spasms?"

"I'm literally a perfect specimen."

"Perfect might be an overstatement."

"Did you just insult me?"

Dr. Wentworth gave a nod. "I believe I did."

Oscar gave a slight laugh. The prince of the most powerful nation in Europe didn't have the luxury of having friends. None of the soldiers who served him would dare a light-hearted jab. With a phone call, Oscar could have the entire hospital shut down and its staff eliminated. But the might he wielded seldom concerned Dr. Wentworth.

Oscar froze as they approached the glass, looking into a large room. Every time he came for injections, he promised himself he'd walk past without hesitating. He, the Prince of the British Empire, Commander of the Queen's Army, had expanded their borders, reclaiming its former glory. But the other side of the window held something that still made his skin crawl.

"They are not you, Oscar."

"I know that," Oscar lied.

His feet turned into lead weights, and taking a single step required concentration. In any other company, he wouldn't dare let them see weakness. He confronted it, staring through the glass to a room full of lab technicians. Past them and their Data pads, through equipment he couldn't explain, stood three large cylinders. Filled with blueish liquid, they held something more terrible than any horror he had witnessed on the battlefield.

"You are unique." Dr. Wentworth placed a hand on his shoulder. "I don't mean that in a medical sense, either. You are your own man with your own experiences. There is no other like you."

The sentiment was lost as a face pushed forward in the middle tube, a face almost identical to his own. As he imagined the man suspended, he had to wonder just how similar they might be. Perhaps they'd be like twins, finishing each other's sentences. It was only made creepier as the adjacent tubes revealed two more faces that greeted him in the mirror every morning.

One of four. Oscar knew the truth, despite what the doctor said. The Queen's Abominations, four identical clones of an assassinated son. Dr. Wentworth could refer to him as one of a kind as often as he wanted. It didn't change the facts.

Ignoring Dr. Wentworth, Oscar let his mind wander. Three copies of the original Oscar, the man the queen birthed, lay dormant. They had grown multiple versions to hedge their bets, but only he had awakened. But unlike the rest of his test-tube clan, he was indeed unique, but not in a way the researchers had been able to document. He let out a long sigh, convinced that his brethren remained asleep in their chambers.

"Commander." The voice in his ear waited for permission to continue.

"Proceed."

"There has been a disturbance at the Ministry of Sound."

"Why does this require—"

"Children. We believe they're Children."

Oscar stiffened. Since introducing the Knights of Winchester, rogue Children had become a thing of the past. Those with abilities were recruited or terminated. It wasn't how he anticipated spending his day, but he'd rather be out there, proving that the empire needed their abomination.

"Do not act until I'm on the scene."

"Duty?" asked Dr. Wentworth.

"Always."

"Then let's make this quick. But one of these days, you're going to stay for an entire appointment. Somebody has to make sure you're taking care of yourself."

"Am I letting myself go?"

The doctor avoided eye contact. "Let's get the injection."

"Arse."

Chapter Ten

2039

"Patches, I hope your night wasn't as productive as ours," Eve called to the back of the house.

She continued checking the window while Alyssa parked Blue in the garage. They would have been home an hour earlier, but it hadn't been until they reached the street with the safe house they discovered their robotic companion had been disabling the cameras as they went. Eve never asked Registry about the new body he created for Blue, but apparently, it came with upgrades.

Eve paused, waiting for Patches to come strolling out of the kitchen. Tossing her boots in the hallway, she turned into the lounge, plopping herself onto the couch. Unlike the Tower, their house had a much homier quality, something she didn't realize she had missed about life before Troy. She pulled one of the throw pillows from the floor and hugged it while she waited. Her finger traced the embroidered puppy, rubbing over where the stitches had pulled loose.

"Patches, it's going to be a late night. We've got

plenty to discuss." In the month since they arrived, tonight felt like their first breakthrough. Her aunt was alive. No idea where, but they could sort that out later. Alyssa had reverted to her spy ways, and something about that didn't sit well with Eve. For now, she kept her opinions to herself and, hopefully, she wouldn't need to discuss her mentor's broad definition of morality. Once Alyssa went to sleep, she'd have the conversation with her bestie-by-default.

They had arrived on a mission to save a single person. Meanwhile, the world around them went mad as tyrants burned it to the ground. She hated to admit it, but she wished she could talk with Dwayne. He'd listen to her speculation and, with a simple sentence, he'd calm her nerves. But for now, she'd have to rely on Mr. Kilgannon.

"Patches?"

She *could* get off the couch and inspect the house or check the cameras on her Data pad. But just like learning to defend herself, she needed to practice. If she had been better, faster, and more accurate, they wouldn't have needed Blue to save them. She silently chastised herself for not being able to disarm the cameras and turn off the Knight's abilities. Anything shy of perfection equated to failure.

Closing her eyes, she relaxed her grip on the pillow and imagined the power in her chest radiating outward. On the table she sensed the circuits in the Data pad, the battery broadcasting a gentle cascade of energy rippling into the universe. The wires in the wall did the same while the lightbulb overhead pushed with more persistence, similar to her own body. In the distance, she sensed Blue. Unlike the household electronics, his power core thrashed, leaving a distinct footprint in the electromagnetic spectrum.

"Where are you?" As her mind wandered through the house, there were no human-sized disturbances until Alyssa approached through the side door. The woman had grabbed her batons from the garage, the power cells were charged and ready to electrocute her next opponent.

A couple of months ago, Eve complained her powers were useless. Passive. They didn't help her fight, making them nothing more than a byproduct of being a Child of Nostradamus. She relied on her strength during training sessions while ignoring her gifts. Had she known their potential, she wouldn't have wasted years shunning them.

For practice, she reached out with her hand. Rubbing two fingers together, the heat produced tiny fields rippling into others. Imagining them pushed forward, she willed them to touch the lightbulb. Opening her eyes, she visualized pulling at the bulb's fields. The bulb dimmed. When she pushed them toward their source, it grew brighter. Before she knew it, the bulb popped, leaving her in a darkened lounge.

"Where's Patrick?"

Eve narrowed her eyes, irked she had blown the bulb. "He's not back from the pub."

"That is unlike him."

"Maybe he's getting lucky."

"Doubtful."

Eve smirked at Alyssa's retort. Unfortunately, she wouldn't understand the humor. Out of them, Patches was the one with a roar-like laughter. He was fast at cracking jokes while training. He didn't seem to improve control over his abilities, but with him around, she was never bored. She focused on the mission, but he reminded her that there was more to life than an objective. The lug had grown on her.

"He returns before us every night."

"Maybe he…" If he was the funny one, she was the impulsive one. He stuck to Alyssa's rules as if they were gospel from on high. From the cereal he ate every morning to the way he checked his pockets before taking off his jacket, everything he did was out of habit.

"Should we go to the pub?" asked Eve.

"It'll be closed by the time we get there," Alyssa said, reaching for the lounge light switch. It clicked twice before she let out a sigh. "Not what I had in mind when I suggested practicing more."

"That's it? We're just going to ignore that one-fourth of the Sentinels are missing?"

"Patience," Alyssa said. "If he doesn't return, then we'll go to the pub and track his steps."

Alyssa walked into the room and picked up the Data pad. The screen lit up her face, accentuating her brown skin. Eve admired how the woman could look demure and non-threatening. Hidden beneath a beautiful exterior, a warrior waited, ready to pounce, which made her insistence on waiting to find Patches even more infuriating.

"Then we should debrief about the club."

Alyssa nodded. "We will. It's been a long evening. We can continue this in the morning. For now, we praise Allah that Skits is alive."

"Mashallah."

"Mashallah," Alyssa echoed.

Eve watched as her mentor's shadow vanished down the hall. It wasn't time to celebrate yet, but Alyssa appeared almost indifferent about Skits. Was it the Knight? Or had her contact at the club said something troubling? Eve had a list of questions, and none of them were getting answered by sitting alone in the dark.

She got up, and in the hallway slid on her shoes. Walking through the dining room, she crossed into the kitchen and slipped out the back door. Without Patches, she relied on the one member of this team that'd listen to her ramblings. She followed the stone path until she reached the garage. Inside, there were boxes scattered about as if real people lived in the house. It looked entirely normal except for the six-foot-tall mech occupying one of the car spaces.

"It's just me, boy." Blue cocked his head to the side. "What? Can't a girl visit her mechanical friend?"

The blueprint for synthetics had been refined until they were efficient killing machines. From the narrow limbs, and the smooth faceplate, to the weapons hidden within his torso, they engineered them to terminate their opponents. Ironically, she was the people he should be killing.

"Something is off with Alyssa." He didn't move. More often than not, he held still, as if she wasn't talking. "We found out Skits is alive. Not that Alyssa seems to care. She skipped the debrief and called it a night." With his head slightly tilted, she imagined a robotic voice gasping in disbelief. "I know, right? I'll get to the bottom of it. I hope."

She pulled a camping chair from one of the wooden tables serving as a workbench. Unfolding it, she took a seat across from Blue. The machine moved, his hydraulics contracting until it appeared he squatted at eye height. "Blue, do you know where Patches is?"

There were moments in which she believed there might be sentience on the other side of the smooth metal plate synthetics used in place of a face. They had originally created him to hunt and murder Children, but a group of rebels reprogrammed him into a freedom fighter. Skits claimed him as her own, and by a stroke of luck, he was the only member of his squad to survive. Her aunt treated him like a puppy, a cute pet that followed her around. Eve wasn't convinced it was the case anymore.

"Did Patches return after he left for the pub?"

Blue shook his head.

"Do you understand me?"

No movement.

"Did Registry change your programming when he uploaded you to this chassis?"

No movement. She swore under her breath. He was even more infuriating than the Tower's computer. At least it acknowledged when it didn't understand a question.

"You saved Alyssa. You defied my orders." They weren't inquiries, but she hoped he'd suddenly have a voice and explain himself. There weren't many people who could understand the complexity of a synthetic's coding. When they returned to the Tower, she'd call Gretchen. Being able to contact the CFO of the largest conglomerate in the world was the perk of her being best friends with Eve's father. "Stay here, Blue. I mean it." She leaned forward, putting her hands on his knees. "I already have to find out where Patches is. I can't handle losing you, too."

Eve was about to stand up when Blue moved his hand. He barely grazed her knuckles with a patting motion. It was perhaps the most human gesture the synthetic had ever made. Did he have the capacity to console? To empathize? While endearing, worrying about Blue's existence posed a slew of moral debates she couldn't discuss tonight.

"Thanks, Blue." She patted him on the side of the head, bringing her forehead to his. "Sleep. Tomorrow we find our friends." It wasn't an empty gesture. The impulsive Eve prepared to make a comeback. She was done observing.

It was time for action.

Alyssa crossed her legs as she got onto the powder-blue duvet folded on the floor. She carefully pulled the pin from her hijab, unfolding the fabric until her hair fell free. The closest door remained open, exposing the only potential hiding spot in the room. She glimpsed herself in the mirror and wondered if Ned would appreciate seeing her without the cotton of her headscarf? She pushed the long brown hair behind her ear, imagining it was him. Their courtship had been ongoing for years, but only recently could she imagine him seeing a more intimate portrait of her. Alyssa didn't hate the idea.

Staring at the tiny device slipped to her by Antoine, she did not know what the spy had given her. Trust didn't come easily, and in her former line of work, it only served as an illusion. She had given him no reason to betray her, but if it served his superiors, they'd easily sell her for the right price.

Pulling out her Data pad, she flipped over the glass. Dating a world-renowned hacker had its benefits. He thought she ignored his rants as he talked about computers and code, but it was in her nature, the very gift Allah bestowed on her through Nostradamus, to learn. She took her hijab pin, bending it back. She examined the corner of the tablet, looking for the etching that allowed it to send and receive signals. With a scratch of her pin, she severed its ability to communicate with the outside world. Even if the device he handed her attempted to disclose her location, it couldn't.

"Ned will want credit when I share this." He'd boast to his friends, but to her, he'd be the first to admit that he was proud. For all his bravado as Needles, a computer genius, as Ned, he was a gentleman. Not hearing his voice for the last month made her sick for home. But every time a security camera turned in her direction, she wondered if it was him ensuring her safety.

Setting Antoine's device on the tablet, she watched the screen come to life. Downloading, she couldn't imagine such a small device capable of storing that much data. When it finished, the screen blinked and went blank.

"Virus?" The screen flashed "Ocular Connection," and before she stopped it, her contacts initiated a download. "You shouldn't be able..."

The room exploded, breaking apart as if the physics of reality no longer applied. Her fingers clutched the duvet, reminding herself that she was in a room in

London. Seconds later, her room transformed into a nearly white void with a screen hanging in the air. In dark letters, a D with a G nestled inside spun on the screen.

"Curiouser and curiouser." She turned her head, and the room shifted as if she were there. Virtual reality was nothing new, but it was the first time the experience was this immersive. It shouldn't surprise her that Genesis Division had created the technology. But why did a French spy have it on a drive?

Reaching out with her hand, she touched the symbol. The room dissolved, replaced by a stone corridor.

"It was you?"

The voice from the Data pad startled her. She reached for the headphones on the floor, sliding them over her ears. She turned about, having to crane her neck to see the owner. But she already knew who she'd find.

"Skits."

Clad in black camouflage, Skits pulled off her visor before pulling the mask off completely. It had been months since Alyssa had seen her friend. She reached out to touch the woman, but her hand passed through the construct. At the top of the list of things she wanted to say, it started with her needing to eat a meal. Skits had a knack for forgetting necessities when on a mission.

"They will kill me. They will kill me." The voice was frantic and desperate, just as Registry had described. The man served as the Knights of Winchester's architect for all things technology, and after years of abuse, he committed his first act of defiance.

Alyssa watched as Registry stepped out from the shadows. If they constructed the construct from the video feeds, it must be somewhere in the queen's palace.

It was grand regarding age, but not nearly as flashy as she expected.

"Not my mission." Skits' voice remained cold, void of humanity. She grabbed Registry by the vest and pinned him to the wall. The man flinched, trained to expect pain. "Why are you helping me?"

"I…" Registry's voice broke. Alyssa thought him a refugee fleeing persecution. She had studied his hollow gaze, but this was the first time she grasped the depth of his fear. "I don't want to die." The words were barely audible.

"You're not—"

"They're coming. He will kill me—us. He will kill us. Please. Please."

Alyssa didn't understand where the mission had gone sideways. But it appeared as if the objective had fallen out of reach. A split-second decision highlighted a break in the persona Skits wore while infiltrating foreign territories. The calm and collected facade washed away, replaced with a fire in her eyes Alyssa hadn't seen since their days in Chicago. The duty-bound woman crumbled, and a smile spread across her lips.

"Sister," Alyssa mumbled. She feared her best friend had fallen not to the Knights, but to her own darkness. But Allah's hand restored something that had once been lost. Alyssa mouthed a silent prayer, thankful for more than her physical safety. From whatever darkness threatened to consume her, a man's plea for his life rekindled her spark.

"Fight," whispered Alyssa. Not for the mission, but for the good in her heart.

"You watched me come in? Go out the same way. Go

to the Iron Horse and ask for Antoine. He'll take you to Blue."

"They will—"

"Kill me. I get it. They can try. Go, before I change my mind."

Before she finished the sentence, Registry pulled free. He took two steps and then paused. "Thank you."

He turned and ran. Alyssa blinked as the image wavered. Alyssa was about to rub her eyes when Skits' arms ignited with her trademark blue fire. The suit burned away, vaporized by the immense heat. There were many Children with impressive gifts, but few compared to her ability to superheat the air until it transformed into plasma.

Skits never shied away from a fight. In her younger days, she started most of them. It made her a scrapper, and borderline fearless. Alyssa wished harm on nobody, but she rallied behind her friend, despite knowing the outcome was less than victorious.

Waving her hand in a circular motion, a blue disc appeared. It protected her as she pushed forward. Guns fired from down the hall, beyond the projection. The bullets hit the wall of liquid fire, consumed until they dissolved into nothingness. With her other hand, she shook it downward until the plasma took the form of a knife.

"Allah protect you."

Skits charged forward, and the camera followed. The first guard she slammed with the shield, burning through his body armor, charring his innards before continuing forward. The next, she knocked his gun away, her hand sliding through his vest and into his ribs.

When Skits turned around, there stood a man, if you could call a head on a metallic body, a *man.*

There was no fineness as he slammed his fist into her shield. When his fist didn't transform into liquid, Skits lunged, attempting to drive her fist into the man's torso. The plasma dispersed and her knuckles punched the man with a loud clank. Alyssa gasped, never seeing an alloy capable of withstanding her friend's abilities.

She might be hot-headed, but as he swiped, she ducked and pushed his arm across his body. Skits had grown into a woman in the Outlands, and brutes like him were a dime a dozen. She adapted almost as quickly as Alyssa could. Skits clapped the man's ears before his elbow drilled into her chest, sending her staggering backward.

As she fell, tucking into a roll, Alyssa held her breath. Skits skid to a stop, crouching low as she studied her opponent. Had Alyssa been there, she'd have used his momentum against him, turning his size into an asset. With careful strikes, she'd test his body and find the weak points. Finally, when she had—

Skits didn't hesitate. She *never* hesitated. Her body flared a brilliant white, causing the video feed to fade until Alyssa could see the bedroom wall. A second later, she was in the hallway. In place of her friend was a fiery elemental coated in blue flames. Skits remained the antithesis of Alyssa's patience. Rolling forward, she caught the man's wrists as he attempted to drive her to the ground. Her hands flared white again, slowly burning through the man's appendages. When his hands tumbled to the ground, she drove her fingers into his chest plate. They sank into metal like a hot knife in butter. Skits crushed whatever made him tick, despite his attempts to bat her away.

A figure walked down the stairs, fading into sight of the camera. The woman was a replica of Skits, down to the finest detail.

"Lux," Alyssa hissed. The shapeshifter had done her best to destroy the Tower from within and nearly succeeded. Alyssa didn't regret throwing her from the roof. She never reveled in the death of an opponent, but she continued cursing the Knight. When her time came, she'd be judged before Him.

Alyssa knew this was where Skits fell. It was like a choreographed dance. Skits attempted to kill Lux, but the assassin moved with ungodly grace. She dodged and sidestepped in a way that Alyssa had only seen watching replays of her own practice sessions. Lux was nearly as good as her, and that was a compliment she rarely offered.

But it wasn't until Skits collapsed on the floor, pinned by an unseen force, that she realized it wasn't Lux who defeated her companion. A man walked down the stairs with his hand held out. Nexus increased the gravitational pull, turning Skits' body into a lead weight until her flames vanished. As he lowered his hand, she cried out, struggling as if the fight wasn't already lost. She lay naked as the last of her plasma evaporated. They had won.

The image faded away until Alyssa remained in her room. Just as she was about to reach for the datapad, she heard Nexus's voice.

"Take her to the pens."

"Yes, sir."

She blinked, gaining her bearings as she released her

death grip on the comforter. Had Registry recorded the events? How did Antoine get the information, and did Genesis Division's newest technology play into the picture? There were more questions than answers, but for now, knowing Skits' location, even if just in name, served as a minor victory.

"We'll rescue you, sister," she whispered.

Now, if only Patches came home.

Chapter Eleven

2028

Ceann finished his beer, chugging the last half of the glass. He pushed the pint across the bar as he nonchalantly studied the faces of nearby men. More than one set of eyes were fixated on him, their judgment and assumptions written by sneers and frowns. His attempt at a night of normalcy had vanished. He cursed himself for believing it'd be different amongst men considered outcasts in London.

He reached for his wallet before the bartender held up his hand. "On the house for the queen's men."

Ceann could hear the fear in the man's voice. This is what he could expect for the rest of his life. The people of Britain, the people he served by safeguarding their queen, feared him. If they knew his crimes, and the brutality that had made him a legend, they wouldn't have maintained their calm. He was not human, and no matter how much he looked like these men, he'd always be a killer in disguise.

He left the King's Arms, and with it, any hope of having a life outside of the Knights.

The fog had rolled in from the Thames, a moist thickness that saturated the streets. Ceann welcomed the spitting rain as it cooled off the city. He could hire a taxi, but the faster he retreated from London, the sooner he'd be in the embrace of the Knights. They might be tyrants, savages playing at peacekeeper, but at least his jailers understood him. But to the throne, they would only know him as the King of Monsters. Perhaps it was time to admit he was more like them than he—

"Please." The plea came from an alley wide enough for two men standing shoulder-to-shoulder. London had a reputation, and those who found themselves in the darkness invited the attention of unsavory individuals.

Ceann slowed until he stood still in the middle of the street. As a Knight of Winchester, his only loyalties were to Her Majesty. What little bits of himself he clung to came second to his position at her side. The mist had already found its way into the crevices of his shirt, leaving him damp. Whatever happened in that alley was between humans, a problem that no longer applied to a Knight of Winchester.

"Please, don't—" The victim's words were cut short, followed by a grunt and groan. Ceann took a step, prepared to ignore the desperate plea, when a shadow broke through the fog.

He recognized the man, the same one who had tried speaking with him in the bar. His face had been beaten, an eye already closing and blood dripping down his chin. Had Ceann been talkative, or allowed the man to buy him a drink, he'd be in the safety of the bar and not running for his life. Despite the best efforts of the Knights, Ceann struggled to maintain his last sliver of empathy.

"It's you." The man stumbled, falling forward. Ceann caught him, supporting his weight as the man tried to warn him of danger.

"What do we have here?"

"Another bender? What are the chances?"

Two men emerged from the alley. Neither of them was large, instead relying on outnumbering their prey. Ceann caught sight of a pipe in one hand and the bulge of a holstered gun. Ruffians, street thugs, degenerates—they were nothing more than men out to get their jollies by preying on those who wanted to mind their own business.

Ceann let the warmth flow down into his arms. The poor man in his hands couldn't see the cut above his eye heal, or the redness of his cheek return to a soft cream color. It might be altruistic to fix the man's ailments, but underneath lie a more sinister motivation. Ceann wanted the light gone. In its place, a void spread through Ceann's chest, a feeling he wore like a second skin.

"Behind me," he whispered to the man.

Feral had taught him to be ruthless, to strike first and leave no prey unscathed. The pipe came from the side, a hard swing that struck his elbow hard enough to break bone. Ceann bit back the pain, the scream trapped in the back of his throat. The other man landed a punch, knuckles digging into his cheek. When the pipe slammed into his stomach, Ceann finally flinched, buckling over as the wind vacated his lungs with a hiss.

"Boyfriend isn't doing so hot."

The heat flowed through his body, a warmth that left his skin tingling. The bone snapped into place and the bloody lip returned to normal. Seconds later, it was as if the bigots had never toyed with their victim. If he could come back from death, nothing these men could do would slow his abilities.

Ceann returned to his feet, spinning his head hard enough to make the vertebrae in his neck crack. The gun flashed before a burst of light filled the street. The bullet drilling through his chest should have hurt, but it was the blood in his lungs that made him angry. Of all the ways he had died, none compared to the sensation of drowning, doubly so when it was his own blood.

The skin repaired itself and Ceann sucked in a deep breath.

"What the fuck?"

The pipe wielder patted his friend on the shoulder. "He's one of *them.*"

Yes, *them.* Ceann grabbed the gunman's outstretched hand. He pulled his attacker close, their lips almost touching. For a moment, he thought about kissing the man, an ironic seal of his fate. But no, he wanted the man to perish with no sense of humanity. This bully didn't deserve attention, none that might make it appear as if this was a crime of passion.

"I'm going to kill you," Ceann whispered.

The gun fired three times before the darkness found its outlet. From down Ceann's arms into the man's skin, the destructive aspect of his powers searched for cells to destroy. Even in the dim city lights of London, the black spread through his veins, causing them to bulge along the surface of his skin. The man's skin turned tight, as if it had stranded him in the desert.

"He's— He— Help!"

Ceann tightened his grip. The bones in the gunman's hands cracked, pulverized until all that remained was taut skin. His companion swung the pipe, striking Ceann hard enough in the head that his jaw shifted, bone popping out of place as the skin tore away from his cheek. The man from the bar hissed, taking several steps back from the impending murder.

Ceann could have had the Body Shop install neural dampeners to all but turn off his pain receptors. Without pain, he'd be near indestructible, but it was one of the few sensations that truly felt real. The Knights could rob him of every emotion, but they'd never be able to take away his pain. Bone ground until it reformed, popping back into place. As his cheek sewed itself together, the skin burned.

He dropped the gunman. His companion turned to run. Ceann grabbed the back of his jacket, and with a jerk, the terrified bully flew up in the air before slamming onto the concrete. Upside down, the man's fear bordered on comical.

He begged for his life. "P-p-please." Struggling to get free, Ceann dropped to his knees, face hovering over the groveling man. Blood from his cheek dripped, splashing against the man's forehead. Ceann hoped he caught sight of teeth before the gash healed. If he was going to sacrifice his humanity, he wanted the world to see him as the monster he believed himself to be. His last sight would be a monster devouring him.

Ceann pressed his hands to the side of the man's head. Without his restraint, the emptiness passed through his fingers into the man's skin. He held the man still as he kicked violently. It'd only last a few seconds as the cells in his body decayed, filling themselves with rot. Had he been feeling cruel, he could flip the switch and breathe life into the man's husk. To this man, he could be both savior and destroyer.

The man's chest collapsed inward as his bones turned brittle. Eventually, his skeleton would crumble, but not before the organs turned to a putrid slurry. Ceann waited for his thrashing to stop, for when the man admitted that there was no running from death. Everybody said they'd stare down the Grim Reaper, but once the brain realized its defeat, the muscles relaxed and invited a quick death.

"Go into death and know I'm the monster who sent you there."

The man's eyes glassed over. Somewhere inside his heart, his blood turned black like oil and ceased functioning. Already Ceann lost track of the deaths caused by his hand. Another body couldn't hasten his descent to Hell. But at least this time, the curse at his call had been used to save a kind man who had found himself in the wrong place at the wrong time.

"You're safe," Ceann said.

Ceann turned on one knee. The bang echoed through the streets, rattling his bones. He couldn't make out the young man's face behind the flash of light. The force of the bullet hurled him backward. Ceann landed on his side. The bullet had torn through his chest, shattering his sternum before ripping through his heart. He couldn't pinpoint the pain as his entire body vibrated.

He reached out to the man he saved, confused, as the gun shook in his hand. "But—"

Blood filled his throat, making his words gurgle. The young man looked on in horror, his hands shaking until the gun fell from his grip. He didn't apologize. The fear written on his face stopped him from doing anything other than protecting himself. Protecting himself from Ceann.

A second later, he couldn't make out the man as he fled. His footsteps grew distant while Ceann bled to death on the streets of London. At any moment, the bullet would be forced to the surface, rejected. Then the healing would begin, and he'd be good as new in a matter of minutes.

He had a few hundred seconds to come to terms with what had happened. The man he saved saw him as he was, a monster, a beast unable to be trusted. Ceann couldn't blame him, he'd have done the same. There was no point in playing the part of a hero for these people. On a late evening, he ventured into London to connect with a part of himself he feared slipping away. Much like his victim with the glassy eyes, he hadn't realized that part of him had long since died.

There was nothing human left in Ceann's heart.

He wouldn't die tonight. But the sliver of humanity he clung to had perished before he entered the King's Arms. He just hadn't admitted it… until now.

Chapter Twelve

2039

Gas. It had only taken gas to immobilize him.

Patches had the notion he was near invulnerable thanks to his abilities. He could withstand the impact of a bullet, but a few shallow breaths of whatever chemical they concocted, and it was lights out. He tried to sort out what they knew about him. The wire they had used to bind him in the chair could have been luck, but it had prevented him from escaping. They were either smart or incredibly dumb, and at this moment, he couldn't tell which.

He opened his eyes to find himself on the floor of a makeshift prison cell. The walls were made of concrete and a metal door had been wielded onto the entrance. A single lightbulb hung from the ceiling. It was the perfect chamber for the opening scene of a horror movie. If he recalled, it hadn't ended well for the prisoner.

Sitting up, he found each of his hands encased in a metal device resembling mittens. He tried wiggling his fingers but found them unable to make the slightest twitch. They were lightweight, extending several inches up his wrists. Not only did they sport impressive enhancements from the Body Shop, but now high-tech handcuffs? Something about this upstart group of domestic terrorists didn't add up.

If he was smart, he'd stomp his feet until he stored enough energy to tear the door off the hinges. He tapped the left mitt on the floor. When nothing happened, he slammed it on the cement. The bolt of pain shot through his body, forcing his muscles to contract.

Gas *and* electricity.

As quickly as it started, the jolts stopped. His muscles continued twitching, and he feared if he looked down, he'd find he had pissed himself. Propping himself against the wall, he worked through the pain, breathing deeply.

"It doesn't make sense." He needed to focus on something other than the memory of pain. "Kidnap a Caledonian. Torture him. Toss him in prison? Why?" If he stored enough energy, could he shatter the cuffs before they toppled him? "Invulnerability." He laughed. Apparently, he had been misusing the word. He thought of the library in Chicago. He missed the quiet of the stacks where he could hide away and be left alone. Ironic that he was enduring forced alone time now. When he got away, this would be his last adventure—*if* he got away.

"Execution."

Patches froze. The voice was barely more than a whisper, enough that he feared he imagined the word. He scooted toward the center of the room and turned to see a narrow grate in the wall. He leaned close, trying to see through the void into the adjacent cell. There was light on the other side, but other than shifting shadows, he couldn't make out the occupant.

"Did you say execution?"

"Aye." With a single word, Patches could hear the ancestry in the man's voice. He wasn't just from Caledonia, he was from the northern lands. His father had a thick accent when he was young, and whenever he grew angry, it was like he had never left his village.

"Caledonian?"

"Ullapool." The man on the other side of the wall grew quiet. Patches listened to the rustle before the man hissed through the grate. "American?"

Patches didn't know if it was worth continuing the lie. Either way, he was a foreigner, trapped for not being British. How much worse could it get? "Yorkshire."

"Bollocks." If Patches didn't know better, he'd swear his father was in the next room. "Tell what lies you will. A Caledonian knows."

Patches smiled at the man's persistence. He wished it were under better circumstances, but he was happy to hear a voice that reminded him of his parents. "Chicago." Alyssa probably shot up in her sleep as he broke protocols. But it couldn't get any worse.

"Patches Kilgannon," Patches added.

"An Irish mutt."

Patches had heard it before. His father's bloodline didn't have roots in Caledonia. Far enough up the tree, he was Irish, but the way his father spoke of Scotland as a boy, there was nothing but Caledonia in his veins.

"Awa' you and chew mah banger."

There came a low whistle from the other room. "And you kiss our mother with that mouth." Patches had long since learned that if you wanted a Caledonian to treat you like family, he needed to dig his heels in and insult them like they were the enemy.

"Calum. Clan MacGregor."

"Why are we here? They jumped me outside the pub and… where is here?"

"We're here because Caledonian refuses to bend a knee to the queen. Her abomination gathers troops at Hadrian. It's only a matter of time before she concedes and lets him wage his war."

"They're going to destroy Caledonia?"

The man coughed with a laugh. "They're going to try."

"Can Caledonia withstand—"

"You really are American. Is it true the robots rose and attacked?"

Patches had assumed that the rest of the world knew what had happened. How could anybody not know that a rogue telepath attempted to slaughter the masses just to prove a point? Did the media really have better things to report? Or was it a case of the country censoring what news got in, or got out, for that matter?

"Nae. Unhinged telepath took over the presidency."

"Oh." It was hard to process for those that survived the onslaught. But saying it out loud, it was damned near laughable. "I guess that's worse."

"What about here, is the North—"

"The Gallowglass," the man jumped in. "The clans have returned—"

"Not for long," came a thunderous voice. Metal screamed as a door opened. Patches ran to the door to see what was happening.

"You two getting cozy? Best friends now?"

Even with his face pressed against the slit in the door,

he could only see the back of their jailer. A single man, and on inspection, no weapons. Calum didn't resist as the man dragged him from his cell. Older than Patches by at least two decades, the Caledonian had seen better days. Like him, he wore street clothes, and he was probably jumped after speaking at a pub, too.

"Asshole. Let him go."

Calum's cuffs slammed together as the man paraded him in front of Patches. It was bad enough that they were torturing Caledonians, but the look on the man's face crushed Patches. There was no fight, as if the Brits had extinguished his fire. Whatever fate awaited him down the hall, he went without a struggle. Patches couldn't stand for it.

He slammed his foot on the ground hard enough that it should have left a crack in the tile. The vibration carried up his leg as a pain radiated from his heel. He repeated it, ignoring the ache in his knee. Nothing. No powers dispersing the kinetic energy, no fire building in his muscles. He'd lived with his abilities for so long that he hardly remembered a time without them.

Patches' cuffs slammed together. He grunted as he tried to separate them. Without his abilities, he couldn't wrestle with the restraints. Patches growled in defiance as he tried to summon his powers again.

"Won't be much fight in yah soon enough."

The electricity didn't just sting, it turned into an all-encompassing pain. It didn't have an origin as it attacked from all sides. Patches fought to hold in the scream, trying to focus on a single point in his throat. He attempted to resist. He failed. The scream echoed around his tiny prison. As he toppled, he spotted Calum's eyes turned downward. Patches' body continued to jerk and convulse.

"They're going to like you, boy."

The man's face hovered near the slit in the door, taking pleasure in the pain. Patches' teeth clenched shut, eliciting a growl as the pain subsided. The electricity might have stopped, but every muscle in his body remembered, and they burned. He worried his heart might stop or that his vision might stay hazy.

The man vanished with Calum, leaving Patches alone. Minutes turned to hours as his muscles relaxed. He crawled to the far corner of the room, furthest from the door. Bracing his back against the stone, he feared that this was worse than he imagined. Strength would not break him free, and with the terrorists holding their finger on his fate, he was no longer worried about saving Eve's aunt. Right now, *he* needed saving.

Patches leaned into his shoulder, attempting to regain his humanity as he wiped the spit from his face. Resting his head against the wall, he spotted markings to his side. In the dim light, he struggled to make out the vertical lines. As his eyes adjusted, his heart sank. The previous occupant, hell, occupants, had been keeping count, but until what? The days until they were stolen from their cells for a worse fate? He bet Alyssa knew the answer. She always did.

Patches let out a sigh. For the first time in his life, he was truly alone.

Chapter Thirteen

2039

Eve could barely keep up with Alyssa as she explained the information Antoine had provided. There was a long list of questions, from who recorded the event to how her contact got his hands on it? Alyssa glossed over the questions, as if Eve's concerns weren't important.

Eve paced to the end of the living room, pausing for a second and then spinning on her heel. She crossed her arms, trying to keep her hands busy. Everything was going wrong, and they had made no progress. Knowing Skits lived did nothing other than ease Alyssa's conscience. At this point, they were worse off than when they started. Right now, she wanted to punch something, to destroy. She admitted it wasn't logical. But if she didn't get the pent-up frustration out, it was going to make her say something she regretted.

"We take it at face value?"

"I trust Antoine." Alyssa raised an eyebrow. "At least with this."

"That's great, really, it is. But *I* don't trust him. How do we know it isn't a trap?"

"We need to accept allies where we find them." Even Alyssa's rhetoric grated on Eve. She paused, pacing long enough to take a deep breath. Alyssa wasn't her enemy. She valued her mentor as if she were a third parent, but right now, Alyssa expected blind trust, a trait she had never acquired.

Alyssa folded her legs, placing her hand on her thighs as if she might meditate. Eve couldn't fathom how the woman maintained a cool demeanor. Eve was ready to crack skulls if that's what it took to find Patches. Alyssa lacked urgency, and this only added to her irritation.

"How do you stay so calm?"

"Does getting agitated help?"

Eve stopped pacing, trying to decide if Alyssa's cold remark was meant as an insult. She needed to focus on something else. Running her hand over the shaved side of her head, she realized she was long overdue for a haircut. She missed Samuel and his almost magical way of putting her to sleep as he cut and colored her neon-pink hair. She'd never admit it, but she enjoyed how he made her feel like a queen.

"Eve, what do *you* suggest we do?"

Eve straightened, feeling as if she were being called out in class. "You want my input?"

"You wanted the Sentinels, you decide."

She had laid the trap. Eve had seen Alyssa carefully lay out scenarios in their workouts that had only one solution. There were many wrong options, and Eve imagined this problem came with a minefield. But for Eve, there was an obvious answer: go hunting for Patches, or confirm if Antoine's intel had any merit. But if Skits had survived this long, did she have more time?

Was Patches somewhere hurt? Could he handle himself as well as Skits? One was a seasoned fighter, and the other was a librarian with more brawn than brains. Could they retrace his steps, or would they be wasting time only to reach a dead end?

Alyssa nodded her head as Eve ran through the many branches of possibility. "Every action has a consequence," Alyssa said.

"No action has twice the consequences," Eve rebutted. Her mentor was full of insightful sayings, but Eve wasn't one of her cadets anymore. This wasn't a theoretical challenge. Lives were at stake.

"Heaven help me," Eve mumbled, "we're going to find Patches."

"Are you—"

She was tired of Alyssa offering her a leadership position and then questioning her decisions. The lights flickered as Eve fought to contain her anger. The kitchen lights flared almost as hot as her temper. She had wanted powers capable of matching her physical abilities in a fight. The request should have been more specific. Now, like her mood, they ran rampant with a life of their own.

"Patches is here because of me. He's my responsibility. We save him. Then we find out if Antoine's information is accurate."

Alyssa nodded, but it did not convince Eve that her mentor supported her decision. When Alyssa offered to join them, she thought it would be a chance to prove herself, to shine on her first actual mission. But now, Eve doubted every decision. Alyssa's presence had her spiraling, and eventually, she'd hit rock bottom. It started with her wanting to be a soldier in the Tower's army, but now the fate of two people rested in her hands.

Right now, she needed to keep her shit together long enough to save her friend.

"Patches. Then, Skits. Pack up. We're out in ten."

Oscar watched the monitor, mesmerized by the woman's movements. Her body twisted and bent into shapes he had only seen from world-class gymnasts. The camera footage scrambled for a second before returning. The Knight's ocular implants only recorded seven seconds of the assault, but it was enough to understand why the techs flagged the footage.

"His readings spiked." The tech pointed at a bar chart. Oscar marveled at the level of data they received from each of the Knights. They couldn't sneeze without it being recorded. "Then it went dead."

"He went dead," Oscar said.

"Yes, sir."

"Replay." Oscar wanted to study the woman. It had been long since trouble brewed on the streets of London. The rioters had been silenced, and those that remained worked in the shadows, chased by his officers. But this? A Child of Nostradamus had entered his borders and eliminated one of the most skilled fighters in their army. He reached into the screen, freezing at a point where he could see her face. Framed by her hijab, her teeth grit hard enough to create a shadow along her jaw. Everything about it exhilarated the man, more than suitable for the public.

"Prince Oscar," a booming voice filled the office.

Unlike the rest of the observation stations, the two technicians here scoured data streams for exactly one thing. Oscar's back stiffened as Magus stood in the doorway, the bright light framing his muscular body. He didn't want to involve his mother's Knights, but they were best suited to handle domestic threats of this nature. Even if he attempted to keep it a secret, Magus had his own network of informants.

"They've finally come," Oscar said.

"Children? In London?"

The man stood closer to seven feet than six, but it was the width of his shoulders that made him intimidating. Unlike many of his subordinates, he chose to clad himself in pristine white. The synthetic body armor he wore hid more weaponry than the man himself. But it wasn't his physical stature that gave Oscar pause. It was how tightly the man was locked away his mind. Violating the thoughts of a Knight might be taxing, but with enough effort, he heard whispers. Not from Magus, which made Oscar question what secrets the Knight stored away.

He bent at the waist, inspecting the monitor. A lock of silver hair fell across his face, making him appear far older than his forty-five years. He stood, slipping his hands behind his back, returning to his regal pose.

"Not keeping track of your Knights, Magus?" Oscar controlled the might of the queen's army, but this one man neutered his efforts. If left to his own devices, Scotland would be under the prince's heel, treated like the pests they had become. With one swift strike, they'd cease to be a problem, but no, Magus, a soldier, stood between him and a well-deserved victory.

"If I wasn't protecting our borders on multiple fronts, perhaps I'd know one of mine had been executed."

Give us the room.

"Give us the room." The whisper sank into their subconscious before they could protest. Trained to remain at their posts, they silently pulled the jacks from their data ports and left. In a few hours, they'd realize their error. With effort, he could wipe the memory from their minds completely, but so far, the result of overextending himself left his puppets delirious.

Magus raised one of his gray eyebrows. It was a subtle victory, but Oscar stowed it away to celebrate later. Their ambitions were the same, but their path to success differed. He didn't doubt Magus' allegiance to the crown, but until it rested on Oscar's head, the man remained a threat. His want to keep the peace and prevent war from falling in their lap left Oscar wondering if the man was a coward or if he thought himself practical.

"If Alyssa Rahim is in London..." Magus stopped talking when the surprise showed on Oscar's face. Whatever advantage Oscar had won vanished with Magus' knowledge of the enemy. "I would think the leader of the military—"

"Cut the bullshit, Magus."

The giant let a smile creep along the edge of his lips, enough to signal that he had won this skirmish. "Alyssa Rahim. Powers: muscle memory." Oscar rolled his eyes. The Knights of Winchester prided themselves on powers, as if it made them godly. "Not impressive enough? How about being a member of the Nighthawks?"

"Oh." With a single word, Oscar replayed a thousand

conversations. As the situation in the States spiraled out of control, the empire locked down its borders, isolating itself from their madness. There had been talks about the potential of reclaiming the country and placing it under British rule. Oscar wondered if he had missed an opportunity for the empire. Not that the crown hadn't taken the opportunity for covert missions on their soil.

"Where there's one…"

"There may be more," Magus confirmed.

Oscar noted the man's concerned tone, a rarity amongst the Knight's elite. He paused, hoping a sense of dread or fear leaked from that finely crafted box he stored his thoughts, but nothing. With a slight nudge, he could feel the air-tight space, a mind hidden from intruders. How had this Knight learned to safeguard against a threat Britain hadn't seen in decades? Oscar speculated about who close to the man might have been a mentalist.

"I will summon the Knights."

Oscar shook his head, turning to the screen. "We need the Knights in the North. It pains me to say this, but the border isn't as secure as I hoped. The French continue to be tiresome. The threat of the European Union… our might is required in France."

Magus didn't need to lord over him. Oscar knew the man thought little of the queen's abomination. He didn't need to read minds to know that the Knight's opinion bordered on treasonous.

"I'll summon the queen's guard. Those not watching Her Majesty—"

"The police. They are at your disposal."

It was faint, but Oscar sensed the surprise in the man. "The queen's guard doesn't have the numbers to patrol the entire city. Let the police serve as the eyes and ears of the Knights." *And as my eyes and ears,* Oscar thought. The Knights might avoid his intrusions, but the police, he could hear their thoughts throughout the city.

"Thank you, sire."

"Do you think they have come for the queen?"

Magus' face remained neutral as he studied the image of Alyssa, her body frozen in motion as she held a singular focus. Oscar found the ferocity in something so beautiful, intoxicating. If under different circumstances, he might beckon her to the palace and enchant her over dinner.

Magus grumbled. "For the sake of the crown... I have a confession."

Oscar glanced at him from the side of his eye. He remained still, arms folded behind his back. If not for his voice, he might as well be a statue taking up space in the small room. Even with the glow of a dozen monitors, he stayed framed within the doorway, making it difficult to read his expression.

"She is not the first."

Oscar turned, nearly stepping against the Knight. While they served the same master, they withheld information, saving it for when it presented a strategic advantage. Magus took every opportunity to undermine him. But to hide a Child of Nostradamus within their borders, that could have him usurped as the leader of the Knights.

"You walk dangerously close to treason, Knight. Should the queen here about—"

"It was she who demanded secrecy."

Now Magus smiled, one he had been holding away for this specific occasion. Oscar didn't want to believe his mother would take a side against him. Unlike the protestors, she always reminded him he was the heir to the throne. While he whispered in her ear, he had never dived into the crevices of the woman's mind. He hadn't believed it necessary. It seemed his respect for his progenitor's mother had been misplaced, an error he wouldn't make again.

"Speak."

"There was a Child. We found her within the palace walls. We captured her."

"An assassination attempt?"

Magus nodded. "We believe so. Nexus apprehended her."

Oscar didn't need to be a telepath to know the Knight continued to withhold information. "What aren't you telling me?"

"She served as a diversion for Registry to flee."

"Dissent amongst your ranks?" Oscar had listened to the Knights of Winchester brag about their recruitment process and how those in their service were loyal without question. If it didn't jeopardize the crown, he'd take pleasure in their organization's shortcomings.

"Nexus and Lux..." Magus' lip twitched. "They are not on border patrol. They went to the States to retrieve—"

Oscar threw his forearm against Magus' neck, shoving him against the doorway. He had heard enough of the man's failings. "You risked war with the Republic? For what? Your vanity?"

"The Children of Troy killed them."

Magus made no move to defend himself. Oscar knew the man could easily throw him against the wall or snap his spine without effort. But he held still, waiting for the next move.

If it wasn't for their superior technology, fighting a war on two fronts would have been impossible. But they maintained France, and soon they'd crush Scotland. But if the president of the Free Republic brought a fight to their door, he wasn't convinced they'd survive. With their actions, the Knights of Winchester had threatened the crown. For that, Oscar would make sure their leadership paid dearly.

"You will tell me *everything*," he growled. "But first, take me to the prisoner."

Chapter Fourteen

2039

"Do you have a plan?" asked Alyssa.

Eve froze on the sidewalk, inspecting the street. Tenement buildings lined the street. It was predominantly a residential area, but small shops had taken over around the intersection. At this hour, people were heading home once they'd finished their after-work pint, or preparing to go out for a much longer night of drinking. But none of them paid her and Alyssa any heed.

She hadn't thought about their next steps as they approached the pub Patches frequented. Ask politely? Then if she didn't get the answer she wanted, beat the shit out of anybody who might have information? It wasn't much of a plan, but she grew tired of playing defense. She wanted to lean into her strengths.

"Ask questions. Get answers."

"And if they don't have any answers to give?"

"Ask again. Harder." Eve stopped and turned to Alyssa, certain she'd have some wisdom to impart. Eve expected Alyssa to argue, to comment on her immature approach, but her mentor held her words in reserve. Her expression, however, spoke volumes. "I know you have something to say."

Alyssa rested a hand on her shoulder. "I know there is a storm raging, but don't lose yourself to the winds."

"Did you just Zen me?"

"Did it work?"

Eve's lip curled. "Fine. I'll save hitting as a last resort."

Alyssa smiled. "Hitting is not my concern. Hit quietly." The smile turned to a smirk. Eve understood. Be angry, but maintain control. Without Patches tempering her impulses, it fell on Alyssa. She didn't want to confess that she needed her mentor, but some lessons required a refresher.

Eve closed her eyes as she covered Alyssa's hand. Her abilities flared to life, stretching across the street and through the bar. The people of London thought the enhancements made them better, as if technology could make up for their shortcomings. It made them faster or stronger, but it didn't make up for their inability to accept themselves. Thankfully, the technology lacing their bones and muscles made them easy to detect. Despite the electromagnetic waves produced by every energy source, enhancements stood out.

"Seven people inside. Two people behind the bar. A bar back in the back room. Couple to the right of the door. Somebody at the bar drinking."

"And the last?"

Eve squinted harder, as if it allowed her to focus. The man in the back of the pub remained statuesque, his body hardly moving. His heart thumped against his chest, surrounded by more advanced technology than accessible by the average consumer. But it was the module nestled behind his ear that interested her. In and out, she could sense it transmitting and receiving information.

"Definite suspect," she admitted.

Eve stepped up to the pub door and swung it open, making a statement as she waltzed inside. She wanted every person in the pub to stare at her. As much as Alyssa wanted them to go undetected and hide amongst the people of London, Eve wanted to play out a suspicion. It might be perfectly normal for somebody to sit in the back of a pub, but not touch their drink? Not move a muscle? She had made up her mind. He'd be the one she questioned.

"What can I get for you lovely ladies?"

"We wanted—"

"A pint each. Something dark with a lot of hops."

Eve wanted to be mad that Alyssa pumped the brakes before the interrogation started, but she was more surprised that she knew about alcohol. Her mentor had more and more secrets. Before the end of the trip, she wondered what else she was going to learn.

"A woman after my own heart," said the bartender.

The man was loud, but with a friendly nature. They took a seat at the bar as he slid glasses in front of them. Eve didn't have time to raise an eyebrow as Alyssa took the glass and drank as if they had rescued her from the desert. A third of the liquid vanished before she came up for air. Eve preferred drinking like a normal person. They were going to have a long talk once they found Patches.

With a quick glance around the pub, she spotted the slender man in the back, hidden in the shadows like a predator. Patches might not have been able to spot the danger, but Eve's skin crawled at the sight of him. It was time to set the trap and let the mice stalk the cat.

"We were supposed to meet a friend of ours here. He's never late."

The bartender leaned on the counter, raising an eyebrow. "He's a fool for standing up such beautiful women."

The blush on her cheeks was genuine. It wasn't often that men flirted with her. At the Tower, most of the guys her age were terrified she'd beat them into the ground. She made a note. When she got back, she'd practice her social skills.

"He's a big fella. Husky. Has facial hair."

"Caledonian accent," Alyssa chimed in.

It would have been dangerous enough to refer to him being Scottish, but to utter the liberated name of Scotland? Eve might have laid the trap, but Alyssa had shone a spotlight on it.

"Shh," he said, leaning closer across the bar. "Careful where you say that. The walls have ears." He glanced back and forth before proceeding. "Patrick? Aye, he's been coming here a lot over the last month. He was here last night for a few glasses. But I didn't see him after he left."

"What time?" asked Eve.

He turned to another man holding a crate of bottles. "Oi, when did Patrick leave?"

"Eleven?"

"Something happen?"

"Nah," Eve said. "I just like to keep tabs on my man." It felt awkward saying it. But somehow, she thought a bartender wouldn't need much convincing of a girlfriend coming to the pub hunting for her boyfriend.

"He's good people. Make sure he stays out of trouble." The bartender gave a glance toward the back of the room. Without saying a word, he had confirmed Eve's suspicion. Whatever business had gone on, he was choosing sides. It gave Eve a bit of hope for the future.

"Finish up and head out?" asked Alyssa.

Eve watched as Alyssa finished her beer. For a woman who didn't partake in alcohol at their weekly dinners, she wasn't a stranger to throwing them back. With another few sips, Eve pushed the glass across the counter and followed Alyssa out of the bar.

"Look at her dress," she gestured toward a woman across the street. Eve was convinced Alyssa had gone mad. "Isn't it lovely?"

"Quite, let's."

Alyssa stopped to read a poster on the side of the pub. She studied it far longer than necessary. When they walked to the end of the block and Alyssa bent down as if she were tying her shoelaces, Eve caught on to the odd behavior. If the man in the pub was going to follow, she didn't want distance between them. Alyssa wanted to choose their battleground.

Waiting for Alyssa, Eve caught their suspect stepping out of the pub. He had taken the bait, just as she suspected. Being a spy wasn't as difficult when the people involved were one-minded. But how did the man cause Patches trouble? And why didn't Patches pile drive him into the ground?

"Do you want to take a shortcut home?" Eve asked.

"Let's. It's rather nice out."

They turned down a walkway that led to a street behind the main row of buildings on the street. Here, there'd be fewer prying eyes should they need more than heated words. But Eve had been too consumed with the man behind her that she didn't spot his accomplices. Four men, leaning against the building as if they had been stationed there to cause trouble.

"What do we have here?" asked a man who spent far too much time at the gym.

"Friends of the traitor?" His stout counterpart asked. Eve detected the signals coming and going from each of them. They had been sending information to the man in the pub. She wanted to kick herself for not being smarter and following the outgoing signal earlier. But at least they found themselves a clue.

"Don't think about running, ladies. You're ours now," said the man from the pub.

Eve's fingers rolled into a fist. "Good."

"We'll go peacefully."

Alyssa stepped in front of Eve for the optics. With three rapid blinks, she attempted to access the video playlist in her contact lens. Nothing. These thugs weren't back-alley ruffians. They had come with a plan, one they repeated until it had become well-rehearsed. She didn't need to ask questions. Without a doubt, they knew about Patches' disappearance.

The closest man, the largest by double, raised his arm until a compartment opened. A black disc flew out, striking Eve. She might not have videos to draw from, but her powers absorbed every bit of information. Perhaps she had grown complacent with rapidly learning her fighting techniques. As she reached into the back of her belt, revealing her batons, she decided it was time to reacquaint herself with the scrapper from a decade ago.

"Cameras," Alyssa said.

A second man launched another of the discs in her direction. Stepping out of the way, she hoped they were more resilient than a bunch of thugs with technology stolen from a self-defense store. The large guy charged Eve, leaving Alyssa with three. Unlike synthetics, she couldn't dispose of them like scrap metal. Restraining herself was the only chance these men had of surviving.

"I don't want to hurt you." She meant it, but men always believed themselves superior.

The one on the left, in a brown leather jacket, walked up to her, his metallic fingers balling into fists. The first transformed, plates moving until it appeared he had industrial-strength knuckles. He stepped forward with his left foot, his right shoulder dipping. He launched the punch at her face, moving faster than she expected, but not fast enough. With one baton, she forced his arm to cross his chest and, with the other, she slammed the tip against the side of his knee with a loud crack.

Even with a punch of electricity, he howled, but didn't drop like she expected. She tried to block the back of his hand, but the force was enough to knock her along the pavement. Rolling to a stop, she gasped for air. She had taken for granted how often she relied on her abilities to soften a blow. But it would not stop her, not when Patches' life was in jeopardy.

"We want to hurt you," he said as he pulled her back by her tunic.

Alyssa grunted as the man nearly snapped her spine. Spinning the baton in her hand, she jabbed it over her shoulder and behind her head. Once. Twice. Three times. On the third, it struck, making a squishy sound. She didn't want to hurt them, but if it came down to her life or theirs, she'd be the one walking away. These men were worse than synthetics. At least the machines didn't have a choice in committing acts of violence. It eased her conscience.

While he covered his face, she rolled away, snapping to her feet. Alyssa cracked the baton against his head hard enough that his skull cracked and he collapsed in a convulsion. She stood, whipping the baton so a streak of blood splashed against the concrete. If anybody from the buildings watched, they'd believe her a cold-hearted killer. Would they sympathize with her for taking out the man? Or would they recognize these gentlemen and consider her a traitor to the crown? Alyssa preferred stopping a power-hungry telepath to navigating international politics.

"One down. Two to go," she threatened.

"We'll go peacefully." Alyssa pushed Eve back, playing the part of the protector. "Don't hurt her." Eve laughed at the charade. Alyssa tried to convince the idiots that she was a helpless woman, but Eve expected that, at any moment, she'd incapacitate them without so much as breaking a sweat.

"Traitor," the big man yelled. The man's prosthetic

housed projectiles. A disc struck her in the shoulder, and tiny needles pricked her skin. It was bad enough that the five men thought to jump two unsuspecting women, but now this brute thought he'd do what? Electrocute her?

"Cute," she whispered.

The pulse from the disc charged up, more dangerous than she suspected. Eve grunted, pushing back against the impending wave about to pump through her body. Even she was impressed with the result. Reaching to her shoulder, she pulled the disc from her shirt, letting it fall to the ground. She dusted off her shoulder, letting the smile spread across her lips.

They had rehearsed the motion. A shorter man with a barrel chest repeated the motion, and launched another puck, thinking they could fall Alyssa.

"Cameras," Alyssa said.

Alyssa leaned out of the way as if the disk was a minor inconvenience. Eve closed her eyes, reaching out. The muscular man had switched his weapon. Something around his hand carried enough of a charge that it might be capable of felling her should he land a punch. Alyssa lacked her usual grace, a sign that something had gone wrong with her contacts. But she had to deal with the lug taking a swing at her.

She caught his wrist, impressed by the strength behind the blow. Holding him still, she decided Alyssa wouldn't be the only one to take out her aggression. "The hunters have become the hunted."

"Cute," he said.

His muscles bulged until the skin tore along his biceps, revealing the hardware underneath. She could taste the static electricity in the air as he leaned forward, his fist closing in on her face. Spinning under his arm, she attempted to wrench the arm from its socket. But the man yanked hard, knocking her off her balance. She had taken on a synthetic battalion, the best of the United Kingdom's Knights, but a punk with a hard-on for personal enhancement knocked her off her game.

The men stopped with their non-lethal weapons, flipping the switch that activated the technology hidden beneath synthetic skin. It was unlike the Body Shop back home. There the technology was always present, augmenting the person. But here, it had slipped by undetected until they powered up. Eve admitted her mistake, but it wouldn't be one she made again.

Alyssa was already moving, and while she mopped the floor with these men, Eve wanted to beat the brute with his metallic arm. The man spun, attempting to drive his elbow into her skull. Throwing up both forearms, she blocked the blow, hissing from the force. She returned a punch to the kidney. His fist vibrated with energy, charged so that connecting knuckles would fry her nervous system.

"Little girl can throw a punch," he said as he turned. He thought he was being scary as he straightened himself, a foot taller than her. "Cute."

"Pulling my punches." Children learned to restrain themselves and to operate with a delicate touch. Eve tightened her fist, blocking his right hook. Leaning in, she hammered her knuckles against his jaw. His head jerked to the side, his lip split and bleeding. It was one thing to trade blows, but nobody, especially not a jackass kidnapping her friend, would get away unharmed. She only needed one of them alive to find Patches. This scum didn't deserve the restraint she normally showed for human life.

With both hands, he attempted to ensnare her in a bear hug. She dropped to one knee, ducking under his reach before driving the heel of her palm into his groin. The wind left his lungs with a grunt. For all that men bragged about their manliness, Mother Nature built them for easy dismissal.

Eve grabbed the man's hand, turning the fist with the shocker inward. She pressed it against his face and let her powers flare, driving the charge from his fist. The bolts of white reminded her of her father's electricity. The scorch marks covered the side of his face as she stepped away. Now that the brute was out of the way, she wanted to speak to the man who orchestrated this attack.

Blocking their entrance, he had stood silently, cheering his henchmen. Eve kicked her toe into the brute, breaking his sternum. *Now* she could move on to the coward watching.

"Hey, asshole. I need to have a word."

The remaining men tried to divide her efforts. The man on her left was the oldest of the bunch, his goatee more salt than pepper. He stepped on the ball of his foot, and Alyssa prepared for him to charge at her. The other man, a redhead with a cleft lip, had found himself a metal pipe, wielding it in his right hand like a baseball bat. Unlike their buddy, they were smarter, waiting for her to make the first move.

Alyssa feigned a step toward the redhead, but stopped, spinning in the other direction. The old man moved with a speed that defied his age. She barely had time to swipe with the batons. He blocked one with his forearm, absorbing the blow. It should have broken the bone, but like his comrade, he hid high-end enhancements. She let the electricity from her baton get her point across.

He screamed as he shouldered into her.

Turning, she glimpsed the man with the pipe swinging. She tucked her shoulder in, somersaulting under the pipe. Landing on her back, she kicked out with her left foot, crushing his knee. Rolling over, she jumped to her feet as the redhead landed a blow against her jaw. The taste of copper filled her mouth, and she prayed she hadn't lost a tooth from the strike.

Before he rebounded, she slammed the baton against his stomach. As he buckled over, she jumped up, driving her elbow into the space where his skull connected to his spine. He landed with a thud and didn't appear to be moving. It wouldn't surprise her if his entire skeleton was laced with a metal alloy.

Alyssa had gone from survival mode to extra levels of irked. Slamming a toe into the man's gut, he skidded along the pavement. They might have the technology, but they lacked the skill to use it effectively. Had she replaced her limbs or enhanced her speed and muscles, she'd be unstoppable. If she couldn't be the fastest or strongest, she'd settle on being the smartest.

The first man's arm hung limp at his side. He was mumbling about the cost of the dead limb. With his good hand, he tore his shirt, exposing the sloppy way his enhancements transitioned to the organic. They were military grade, but whoever installed them ran a chop shop. He roared, a man attempting to be a lion.

She'd had enough of his foolishness. As he clumsily

punched, she tapped his forearm with both batons. The momentum of his fist died, leaving him without a functioning arm. She jumped, snapping the bridge of her foot against his groin, forcing a howl that certainly woke the neighbors. They thought they had stumbled upon sympathizers, and because they were women, they'd be easy prey. She wanted to know how many had fallen victim to this tactic? Had they lured Patches into an alley and captured him?

"I will ask once. Where did you take our friend?" She pressed the batons under his chin.

He struggled to catch his breath. Alyssa shouldn't take pleasure in his pain, but it was a start for the penance he'd need to pay. "You'll hang for treason. Just like your friend."

It wasn't the answer Alyssa wanted.

She dropped the batons and swung her leg, catching his neck in the crook behind her knee. Pushing off, she spun in the air, flipping him onto his back. She hit the pavement with a smack, one of her less graceful moves. It had been worth it to silence the buffoon.

With a long sigh, she checked to make sure none of the men moved. Eve had vanished, pursuing the man who'd led them into the trap. It'd be up to her mentee to get the information while she covered the rear. Brushing fingers over two of their throats, she found they'd never be a threat again. The third man might survive if he received medical attention. She wanted to pity them, but a hardness prevented her from thinking of them as anything more than thugs purifying their country with genocide.

"Allah protect me," she whispered.

She followed the lights in the buildings, checking to

see if any of the residents hid in the shadows watching the fight. Only minutes after it started, she believed them to be free of—

"Dammit," she hissed. A camera on the corner of a tenement building continued moving back and forth. Looking for others, she found similar motions. Eve hadn't scrambled the electronics. Their infiltration of London had ended. At best, the operators wanted to talk to them about the assault. At worst…

"The Knights are coming," she whispered.

Eve hated when they ran. The benefit of fighting synthetics, they came for their prey. He ran further into the alley and then skidded to a halt. Turning, reached into his belt and pulled out a long slender knife. Unlike the big guy she floored, he didn't rush the fight. He assessed her skills before making a move. Finally, a challenge.

"Terro—"

"Yes, terrorist, I get it." She growled. "Where's my friend?"

"Same place—"

Eve ran at him, spinning with her foot snapping out. She hoped with a single metal toe to his side that she'd end his incessant talking. Her toe missed, and she hissed as the knife dragged across her calf. His tech didn't give him strength like his buddy. This one preferred speed, and already she regretted her recklessness.

He spun as he approached, using his long coat as a distraction as he dropped to a knee, expecting to slip the blade across her stomach. Eve leaned back, the tip missing by inches. But he stopped, redirecting his momentum as he stepped closer, attempting another strike. Catching him by the wrist, she spun on her heel, attempting to twist the limb from its socket. But he moved as quickly, matching her speed.

He jerked her close as he dropped the blade from one hand and caught it with the other. She held his arms in place, slamming her forehead against his nose. Rolling backward, he braced a knee against her chest, launching her into the air. She hit the ground in a somersault, jumping to her feet. But he was already on her, trying to position himself to drag the knife across her throat. He snatched the back of her collar, keeping her off-balance.

"Enhancements won't save you," he growled.

"They're not…" She closed her eyes and followed the pulse of electromagnetic energy emanating from his arm. "Enhancements." Eve imagined reaching into the void and slapping away the energy, causing his limbs to tense.

"What the—"

She spun, driving an elbow into his skull. It was amusing to watch as he tried to throw a punch, his shoulders jerking despite his arms not cooperating. She pinned him to the wall, bracing her forearm against his throat. With a smack, she knocked the knife from his hand.

"What are you?"

To stress the reply, she drove her fist into the side of the building, bricks imploding. It hurt, but it did what she needed. His eyes grew wide as she leaned in, a silver gleam glowing around the iris, another enhancement. There was a chance that he broadcasted the entire fight.

There was no point in hiding anymore. The cameras would have caught the entire exchange.

"A Knight?"

She shook her head. Her powers wrapped around him, pinpointing every enhancement in his body. Unlike the big guy, these were more subtle. But to prove her point, she pulled at the electromagnetic fields, shutting them down. Now, he was barely human.

"Children," she hissed.

"Americans," he said as if it were a dirty word.

"Where's our friend?" She pressed hard enough to lift him off his feet. Without his enhancements, he became the victim. She wondered if he thought about the irony of the situation.

"I'll never tell—" she shoved harder, cutting off his words.

"I won't lose sleep killing you." The words should have bothered her, her ability to go from pacifist to killer. She'd unravel the moral implications later, when her friends and family were safe. "Give me a reason."

"The Long Watch will—" She pushed until she cut off his oxygen.

"One last time. Where is our friend?"

"He's already dead."

With a growl, she pushed until the snap reverberated off the walls. His body went limp, and she could sense the electrical pulses in his body diminishing. She had given him an opportunity to win his freedom. Try as she might, she couldn't justify her actions. Dwayne had made it clear that the moment killing became easy, she'd become like them. She'd have to check her definition of easy.

"We need to leave," Alyssa said.

She paused as the man's body slumped to the ground. She didn't utter a word. Eve turned to her mentor. The weight in her eyes told a story laced with sadness. She expected to hear a story of times long gone when they returned to the flat.

"I got a name," Eve said, still trying to tip the scale to justify the death. "The Long Watch."

"The cameras caught everything."

But instead of running, Alyssa bent down and picked up the knife. Without another word, she leaned over the dead man, craning his neck to the side. Sliding the knife along his scalp, even Eve had to fight with her stomach to avoid hurling. The adrenaline of the fight faded quickly and now her mentor sliced into the man as if he were raw meat.

"Even dead men speak," Alyssa said in a flat tone.

Something snapped as she pulled a bloody hand away from his neck. She held up the small processor that had been mounted behind his ear. Inspecting it for a moment, she wiped it down with his jacket. Shoving it into her pocket, she tried wiping the blood from her hands. Should anybody stumble upon them now, they'd have looked like a modern-day Jack the Ripper, butchering their victim at sunset.

"We have clues." Alyssa inspected her hands, considering them clean enough. "We need to get back to the flat and regroup. Ready to clear us a path?"

It wouldn't be enough for them to flee. With the number of cameras in London, they'd be tracked no matter where they went. While she had failed at turning off the cameras before the fight, now she'd need to do it to buy them time before the police arrived. They had been in London for a month without incident. Thanks to a single bigot, they'd now be hunted. If they were lucky, it'd only be the police. But Eve didn't feel lucky right now. Was she prepared to take on the Knights of Winchester again? If it meant saving Patches, she'd damn well try.

Chapter Fifteen

2039

Oscar rarely visited the catacombs. The labyrinth under the Knight's headquarters had become something of a legend. Rumors had it that this is where they sent their less successful recruits. Not all who entered their doors were forged into Knights. Oscar wondered if the whispers were true. Even though they claimed to be nobles, their savagery suggested otherwise.

He watched as Magus stood at the door, hesitating as his hand hovered over the DNA scanner. Did this Knight, the sworn protector of the crown, not trust him? In the time they spent traveling from the palace, he'd never let his defenses slip. Try as he might, Oscar couldn't hear a stray thought or even an emotion from the man. Oscar had questions, but didn't risk showing all his cards, at least not yet.

"Do you hesitate because monstrosities are about to be revealed? Or because of who is about to bear witness?"

The small room outside the elevator appeared benign, another barrier to keep outsiders from discovering their atrocities. Oscar couldn't see the cameras, but he was sure they were watching. Most likely, the room had half a dozen ways to slaughter an intruder. He wondered if they accounted for all the abilities of the Knights-in-training or preferred defenses that could kill them all.

While Magus decided his answer, Oscar had already scanned the minds of the humans on the other side. The Knights might shield themselves away from his intrusions, but their lackeys didn't have the luxury. Through their eyes, he could see corpses strapped to tables as if they discarded cuts of meat. Elsewhere, men forced a young woman into a chair, sliding a needle into the base of her skull as they discussed the weather. The sciences they performed were barbaric, and once he assumed the throne, he'd launch an investigation into their facility. Oscar would have more than enough leverage to bend the Knights to his will.

"Prince?"

Oscar oriented himself to the small room as the door opened. He straightened his back, holding his tongue for a moment as he focused on the feeling of his toes as they wiggled in his boots. *Foolish*, he thought. In the presence of one of the most dangerous men in the British Empire, he had walked away from his body. Whether Magus knew what transpired, it was idiotic to leave himself with no defenses in his presence.

"Proceed," he said.

Immediately inside, Magus turned left. Everything about the architecture suggested they had refurbished it in the last few years. Touching the walls, Oscar suspected they could withstand a bomb.

"Countermeasures for your Knights?"

"Not all with gifts swear allegiance to the crown."

"Until you convince them otherwise?"

Magus stopped walking. "Do you wish to know what measures we take to serve your bloodline? Or is it simply enough that we obey without question?"

It was the first time Magus suggested that not all Knights wished to serve the crown. Oscar understood the weight thrust upon an individual for the greater good. Like his progenitor, he never asked to step into the line of succession. Magus ensured no harm came to him or the queen. Loyalty had never come into question before, but now Oscar wondered if the man felt the same sense of servitude.

"Your loyalty is noted."

Magus whipped about, continuing down the hall-way. The walls gave way to clear glass doors on either side. It was telling to see the number of tiny spaces. The bed, sink, and toilet were more comforts than Knights would supply their prisoners. They, and Magus amongst them, walked a fine line between monster and human.

"This is the assassin."

He stopped. Staring into the cell, he saw a woman nearly his age sitting on the floor. Other than the neon-blue hair, she might almost be forgettable. The scars running up her arm gave away a penchant for danger. This woman had lost as many battles as she had won. He expected her to be furious, using whatever abilities she had to free herself from the cage. But she hardly moved, flicking something against the far wall of the cell.

"Is she contained?"

"Dampeners. Here she's nothing more than human." Magus placed his hands behind his back and turned statuesque. If it wasn't for several strands of shoulder-length hair catching the air from a vent, it'd be difficult to tell he was alive. It was a trick mastered by all of his mother's guards. They were more impressive when they held still.

"Let me guess. The bastard prince wants to ask a few questions?"

"Perhaps. But mostly, I wanted to satiate my curiosity. It seemed you left an impression on my Knights."

"They'd be yours if they hadn't stopped me." Oscar raised an eyebrow. Did she offer him the crown as long as he allowed her to kill the queen? The American assassin held skill in more than physical warfare.

"Should I ask who sent you?"

"They keep asking. But the silver fox here hasn't gotten an answer he likes."

"He's difficult to please," Oscar admitted. "Ms. Ayer, why my mother?"

"Kicks? I woke up one morning and thought, you know who needs a good stabbing in the back? That old broad across the pond."

Oscar withheld his scathing retort. The woman had nothing left to lose. She'd failed at her mission, locked away in the catacombs. She'd never see the light of day again. Behind enemy lines, she had made peace with her short future. Oscar decided it was time to up the stakes.

"They won't free you."

"These Knights aren't so bad. One of them might—"

"The Children of Nostradamus."

Her muscles tensed and she stopped fidgeting with her fingers. He had her attention.

"They didn't tell you? Shame on them." Oscar didn't need to read her mind to know she was currently plucking through her contact list to think who might risk their lives to save her. "There's only an army separating them from you. Then, of course, the Knights."

Oscar studied Magus' face, trying to garner any emotion from the man, but he remained expressionless. "Soon, they'll be here with you. Consider what you'll say to thank them for risking their lives to save yours."

Her fingers balled into a fist. Whoever she settled on, they meant enough to elicit anger. She slammed her fists on the floor before jumping to her feet and slamming a palm against the glass. Oscar held his ground, refusing to back away from her bravado.

"I'll thank them for rescuing me before suggesting we kill the queen's abomination."

Unlike the Knight, her emotions oozed from every pore. Anger. Concern. Worry. Fear. Now that the lives of others were involved, she suddenly had something to lose. Oscar ignored her banging, walking down the hallway toward the elevator. Magus followed, his footsteps almost impossible to hear over her thrashing.

"And what was the point of that, my prince?"

Oscar smiled, finding himself with a leg up on the superhuman. "She believes they're coming to save her."

"We suspected as much."

"They want her, not the queen. Knowledge is power, Magus. We know the game, and with that, we can play to win."

Patches placed his back against the wall, bracing a foot against the surface. Across from him, he waited for the door to open. Since they took his neighbor, there hadn't been another sound from the hallway. There were no cries, no footsteps, no motion he could detect. Instead, he planned to get himself out of the cell.

When feet scuffed against the floor in the hallway, his muscles had tensed in preparation. He had been holding the position for an hour and his legs ached from crouching. He had given up on his abilities. Try as he might, he couldn't summon them and every time he attempted to jerk his hands free from the cuffs, electricity jumped along his skin. If he could just get his hands free, he'd be able to use his gauntlets to fight his way out.

He listened as the hydraulics in the door whined. As it inched its way open, he tensed his muscles, making sure they hadn't fallen asleep. It wasn't much of a plan. Clobber whoever stood there, hoping he could free his hands or shut off whatever inhibited his abilities. Run? Yes, he expected plenty of running.

The door opened.

He pushed off. He focused on his foot placement as he dropped his shoulder. Even without his abilities, he was still stronger than the average man. If he needed, he'd plow them into the wall and if he crushed their ribcage, then so be it. He didn't want to kill anybody, but if it came down to—

Hands grabbed his shirt, and with a quick pivot, they spun him about. He slammed against a brick wall. He barely had time to open his eyes when a young woman held a knife against his throat. She couldn't be older than Eve. On a quick count, she had half a dozen facial piercings and as many in each ear. The silver halo around her iris gave away the enhancements. It explained her speed and strength. He preferred the Free Republic, where only the elite acquired extensive modifications from the Body Shop.

"Try it again and I'll slit your throat."

"You're going to kill me, anyway."

"If the jury says so."

"Jury?" Patches didn't believe that the people holding him in a cell had any intentions of offering a fair trial. They had decided his fate the moment he'd arrived. His only hope was to stay alive long enough for Eve and Alyssa to find him. He needed to bide his time.

"We're not monsters."

"My cellmate would argue."

The blade touched his throat with enough force to remind him his abilities had vanished. Whoever these people were, they had advanced technology.

"Do we have an understanding?"

Patches didn't move or utter a sound.

"I asked you a question." It wasn't the knife held against his throat that concerned him. The girl's face held no anger, no aggression. Whatever went through her mind, killing him didn't appear to concern her. It was one thing to hate him, but she remained the poster child for indifference. That made him more nervous than the bigots who brought him here.

"Yes." He wished it was a lie, but for the moment, it didn't appear he had a choice.

She stepped back, not lowering the knife. Directing him with her chin, he started walking forward. Observe. Alyssa's voice echoed in the back of his head. Take in the situation. Assess.

He walked slowly enough to study the doors on either side of the hallway. Of the six he passed, three of them had their handles lowered in a locked position.

They weren't as advanced as the holding cells at the Tower. The old building had been retrofitted with prison cells. They were welded into place. With enough wailing, he might be able to break them off their hinges. Meanwhile, the floor was littered with broken tiles.

"Hospital?" he mumbled.

Through a door slit, he could see a pair of soft brown eyes watching him march toward his doom. Was she new? Did she know the horrors lurking beyond the double doors?

"We are Gallowglass," she whispered. "Don't beg."

His jailer slammed her hand on the door, forcing the woman on the other side to back away. She shoved him forward. The sign to the side of the double doors ahead confirmed his suspicions. "Doors lock in case of emergency." It explained the sterile smell in the air. He paused at the doors and, with another push from the woman, stumbled through the doors.

He entered hell.

The lobby of the hospital was three stories high, with wraparound balconies lined with doors once used for patients. Hospital equipment still lined the walls, making it appear the desertion had been recent. These assholes had transformed the house of healing into a death pit. Suspended from the balcony, down two stories of rope, hung bodies. They'd covered their heads in burlap sacks, removing their identities. He counted eleven before his brain struggled to process the image.

Patches fell to his knees, losing the fight with his stomach. Without food, the bile rose in his throat. He hurled, spitting up clear liquid. He gasped for air, fighting the convulsions. Was one of the victims Calum? He hadn't heard him return to his cell. Somehow knowing he had talked to one of them when they were alive… He hurled again.

"Get up," she said.

"Sister Jasper," came a booming voice. "Bring us the man."

"Stand," she hissed. Grabbing him by the collar, she pulled him to his feet.

Patches shuffled forward, trying to avert his eyes from the carnage. Unlike him, the three men sitting in cushioned chairs didn't seem to care that eleven lives had been snuffed. They watched him, amused at his discomfort. One of the three men even laughed.

"Brother Vincent," said the woman, "I bring before the jury an alleged traitor."

Observe. Three men, each in street clothes, looking like any other Londoner. The man on the right was the burliest and had a scar reaching from his left eye down his neck. In the middle, Brother Vincent appeared to be a generic corporate middle management. But the man on the left leaned forward, eager for what was about to happen. She had referred to them as a jury, but Patches already knew the verdict.

"You stand before the Long Watch accused of treason. What do you have to say for yourself?"

Did he beg? Was there any point? As Patches stepped in front of the three men, he fought the urge to flee. Along the balcony, he found there to be a dozen more men and women watching from above. He originally thought they were a ragtag group of bigots. But the more he observed, the more he realized they were organized. There was no way they gained the technology that held him prisoner without money backing their efforts. Did the government supply the technology? How deep did their influence run?

"I asked you a question." Brother Vincent's voice demanded answers.

"The guilty have nothing to say," said the scarred man.

"Brother Timothy, we are not cold-blooded killers. The man deserves to defend his name."

Before the Free Republic formed, the United States had hundreds of groups like this. There were thousands of people who persecuted others in the name of right-eousness. There was always some group who believed they were superior to another. Patches thought of the girl in her cage. *Don't beg.* Right now, it was a tall order.

"Who are you?" asked Brother Vincent.

"My family is from Yorkshire."

"Untruth," the man on the left.

"I agree, Brother Daniel."

Patches no longer saw a reason to keep up the charade. Whether they or the Knights killed him, dead was dead. "I'm American. Chicago, to be precise. My parents immigrated from Caledonia."

"Scottish trash," spit Brother Timothy.

"And why are you in the queen's kingdom?"

"I am looking for a friend."

Brother Vincent sat back in his chair, rubbing his chin. "What say you, Brother Timothy?"

"Lies."

"Brother Daniel?"

"Lies."

Patches thought of the library at the Tower. He had hoped to make it home, to be part of something bigger. He wanted nothing more than to run his hands over the unopened spines of books. The smell, the first crack. He longed for a home that had never been. He called the Tower home because he had a room, but he hadn't been there long enough to think of it as anything more than a pit stop. Other than Eve and Alyssa, nobody would be able to identify his body.

Patches straightened his back. He widened his stance, trying to make himself bigger. The girl in the cage asked him not to beg. No matter what the next few minutes held, he refused to give them the satisfaction.

"Oi. I am Caledonian." The words came out in a roar, resonating in his chest as if they had a magical power. The pride caused him to puff up his chest. He knew his lineage, and with his accent, it was hard to hide. In the pit of his stomach, he swore his fire returned. He never imagined a simple statement capable of providing him strength.

"Truth," all three said at the same time.

Brother Vincent stood. "It is time for the jury to convene. Our verdict is law."

Brother Timothy raised his hand in the air before pointing a thumb down. Brother Daniel did the same as Vincent shook his head. He then added his thumb, slowly turning it downward.

"Traitor," Brother Vincent stated. The room echoed as every member of the Long Watch repeated the verdict. "We protect the sanctity of the crown. Because of this, you will be hanged for treason."

Is this where the begging was supposed to begin? Patches found comfort in confessing his lineage, and he refused to back down. He would not take a knee, not to *them*. He had gone from timid librarian to stalking the streets of London to save Skits. If they wanted to believe him to be part of the Caledonian resistance, at least he could go out with a bang.

"Twelve highlanders and a bagpipe make a rebellion." His gram would be proud of him. She claimed he never paid attention to her ramblings, but he had listened every night in the kitchen. With the smell of neeps and tatties in the air, he hung on every word. But it wasn't until now it seemed to apply. His blood boiled, and he would not beg for mercy.

"Tomorrow, the traitor hangs."

Chapter Sixteen

2039

The bloody processor dropped onto the kitchen counter. Specks of red tainted the white laminate. Alyssa stared at the chunk of metal, willing it to answer her questions. She reached into her pocket, pulled out the Data pad and considered making a phone call to headquarters. Needles would most likely pick up and complain about not getting enough sleep. Conthan could open a portal and backup would arrive. She could lean on her friends, but this was something she had to do herself. It hadn't been her idea to come after the queen. If she had stopped Skits, none of them would be in danger.

Eve entered, leaning over the island to inspect the device. In the stark white of the kitchen, her black t-shirt and jeans appeared to absorb the light. Alyssa made a note that when she came traipsing down the stairs, the young woman had set her uniform on the back of the couch. Something was brewing, and if she thought putting on tactical armor was necessary, a serious conversation needed to take place. Eve closed her eyes, her hand hovering over the device before pulling away. A slight shrug confirmed no signals came or went from the tech.

"You don't look well," said Eve, her face giving away her fear. The young woman looked to her for guidance, to be the unmovable force in the face of adversity. But as Alyssa eyed the processor, she felt numb, a feeling that too often reminded her of the regrets in her life. She had to decide between remaining the backbone or being a mentor by showing the cracks in her armor.

"I am tired. I have lived many lives," she confessed. "Some I am proud of. But others… I carry regrets. I want nothing more than to say farewell to the past versions of me, to move on. I find myself exhausted by my past refusing to let go."

"You've done horrible things." Eve didn't hesitate with the statement. Alyssa suspected the woman had questions, or even resentment. But it did not prepare her for how rapidly she loaded the chamber and fired.

"I have."

"You killed in cold blood. Twenty-Seven, a woman who should know better, used you as her personal clean-up crew. What were you thinking?"

"There are unthinkable horrors that transpire. Acts so heinous, I dare not repeat them. Somebody needed to pay. There needed to be a champion who stood up to these tyrants."

Eve pulled out one of the counter stools and plopped herself down. Alyssa wondered if she recognized her habit of playing with her pink strands of hair when she wanted to have tough conversations. Spinning it around her finger, she licked her lips, preparing a monologue. When she flipped her hair back, she let out a long sigh.

"Do you speak for Allah?"

Five words. In all her years of fighting, never had a blow landed as hard. Her gut tensed as she relied on her hands braced on the counter to hold her weight. There were few who knew her as intimately as Eve Cowan. As her student, peer, daughter of her brothers-at-arms, and sister-at-arms, she had insight Alyssa never expected. But with a single question, she stripped away the politics, the feelings and motivations, and struck a blow to her faith that would reverberate for the rest of her life.

"No," she whispered the words.

Eve shook her head. "Twenty-Seven is the damned president of the Free Republic. She did it for whatever reason. To protect the country? To stay in power? I don't really care. I don't know what I'm madder about. Alyssa Ayer, acting like a pawn? Or that you acted as judge, jury, and executioner? Who gave you the right?"

It had been arrogant to believe that by building a new life, she could negate the horrors of the past. The guilt of leaving Skits behind had started a landslide, the descent into the errors of her young self. But to have a woman who respected her, see through her bravado, her ego, and lay it out? It stung.

"I have made errors, terrible mistakes."

Since the day she laid her parents to rest, she had not shed a tear. Mastering her body had been a gift from Nostradamus, but mastering her emotions, that had come from pain. To see Eve's eyes, the disappointment etched into the edges of her eyes, the pressure in her chest mounted, and the carefully placed dam sprung a leak. She let the tear fall, a reminder of the feelings she guarded.

"And you act as if it never happened? I'm not saying

what Skits did was right, but let's be honest, it's who she is. But you? I'm having difficulty reconciling the two women standing before me."

Alyssa had betrayed Eve's trust. The other Nighthawks understood that each of them walked their own path. They had confronted her, but made no judgments. But Eve had been a young girl, taken under her wing, and she hoped to do right by the next generation. Instead, she had lied.

"La hawla wala quwata illa billah."

Eve raised an eyebrow. "What does it mean?"

"When a situation is out of one's control, we seek strength through Allah."

"Bullshit," Eve said. "Allah didn't bless your actions. He didn't move through you."

Alyssa wanted to surrender, to pray for forgiveness, or at least guidance. Without realizing the power of her statement, Eve had called Alyssa's attempts to be pious a scapegoat for inexcusable behavior. Had she embraced her faith as a shield, a justification for her wrong-doings? She didn't sob. There was no sniffling, but the tears ran down her face as if she should be in hysterics. While the dam inside crumbled, she mustered the strength to maintain her facade.

Eve leaned back on the stool. Biting her lip, Alyssa prepared for the next volley, the one that'd shatter her exterior and leave her retrieving the pieces of her fractured self. Had any other person spoken as she did, she'd have brushed it aside. Arrogance and righteousness wrapped about her as a protective coat of arms. Had she been as foolish as the men who attacked them tonight? The confidence she had built over the last decade wavered, and she didn't know how to rebound. Thankfully, Eve took mercy.

"What do we do with the processor? It's not sending any signals."

Alyssa held her words, fearful her voice might crack. When she had a moment, time to rest and reflect, she would admit to her sins before Allah. The guilt hung heavy on her chest, but she needed to correct her wrongs and be the woman Eve respected. It hurt, and she wanted nothing more than to wash away the sadness in Eve's eyes, but for the moment, the dam needed to be patched and she needed to save souls.

"I can turn it on. But you'll need to follow the signal."

Eve nodded, leaning forward, waiting for her to flip the switch.

"If I do this. We are on the run. We compromise the house. They will track us as quickly as we track them. I need you to understand. We will be hunted."

"When aren't we?"

She was so young, and already jaded to the world. Alyssa wanted the next generation to have hope for the future. But it had been a pipe dream, an unachievable reality. They were born into chaos, and at most, she hoped they learned to survive amidst a dangerous world. The truth hurt, but beneath the crushing realization, she sought hope. And more than anything, she wanted to nurture that hope until it shone bright enough to light the ways for others.

Alyssa placed the processor on the Data pad. The computer integrated and, like it had with Antoine's fob, it connected to her contact lenses.

"Genesis has created a link between the computer

and my contact lenses. I can see faint memories of the man."

"Patches?" Eve asked, excitement returning to her voice.

The images flashed quickly and in no order that made sense. She watched the man receive an award from the military, and then in the next moment, she watched him staring at himself in the mirror as a teenager. The audio came in bits and pieces, nothing coherent. There were no controls to slow down the feed, and she—

"I can sense the signal. There are a lot of waves coming and going. But there's one more persistent than the others."

"He knows the prince." Several images flashed, different exchanges with the queen's son. No words followed, but there were enough instances to say they had frequent conversations. But she found one that brought a smile to her face. In the back of a dark vehicle, the thug sat opposite a large man in cuffs with a bag over his head.

"Patches is alive."

"Where?"

Alyssa shook her head. "I do not know. But they took him somewhere." The hope had all but diminished, but at the sight of the young man, it flared. Alyssa breathed a sigh of relief.

"Suit up," Eve said. "I'm getting Blue, and we're going to save our boy."

She might be jaded, but Eve still represented the best of them. Had the mentor become the mentee? Is this why Eleanor set these events into motion? Was the goal not to guide Eve to victory, but to restore her faith and instill a newfound sense of hope? Did the psychic foresee this very event? Whether she believed in the prophecies of a dead woman, the dying flame flickered and returned with vigor.

Alyssa nodded. "Let's save our boy."

It had been hours since the doors to the cell sealed shut. Patches expected them to string him from the balcony and leave his body as another notch for their purification. But it wasn't enough to kill him. They wanted to play with their catch and watch him break. As he paced back and forth in his cell, every time he felt a rush of confidence, a surge that he'd land on his feet and walk away, something swept away another layer of dignity.

He stopped pacing long enough to kick off his shoes and step on his socks. It had become time for extreme measures. With a long sigh, he relaxed his muscles and tried to ignore the warmth running down his leg. After being locked away for the last however long, he couldn't hold it in any longer. Soaked in piss, he could live with. Soggy socks? Even he had limits.

The Long Watch played at being purifiers, and somebody with deep wallets financed their operation. Despite looking for clues, he hadn't been able to find any sign of who they worked for. But the longer they held off killing him, the more time it offered him to come up with a plan.

"Did you see Calum?"

He froze at the sound of the woman in the cell down the hall. He expected to hear a woman banging against the door, followed by threats of death. Patches picked up the sock with his toes, patting down the urine dripping down his leg. When he had gotten it dry enough, he slipped his sneakers on.

"They're all gone."

They left?

"We're prisoners, you idgit. They have cameras, the cuffs, and there are probably mechs outside. Nobody is losing sleep over two Caledonians waiting to die."

"I'm American."

"I figured. Your accent is shite."

"And you're a breath of fresh air. And no, the dead all looked the same. I couldn't tell if he was one of them."

"He is," she said. "They wanted him to give up the resistance."

"Gallowglass?"

"Aye."

"Are you part of it?" It was the first conversation today that didn't end with threats. She might not be a ray of sunshine, but she didn't promise to jam a knife in this throat.

"No, I thought I'd vacation in a prison."

"This is how they're going to break me," he mumbled.

He pressed his face against the door, trying to catch a glimpse of her cell. With his cheek pressed against the metal, he could make out the corner of her prison. He doubted she attempted to make eye contact. That'd be too civil.

"What were you doing in London?"

There was no point in lying. "A friend of a friend came here. She got tossed in a prison. I'm here to bust her out."

"With what army?"

"The army is coming. I came with friends."

She let out a laugh. "They're probably in another detainment center. I'd be surprised if they're not being hunted down by these arseholes."

He decided not to mention that Alyssa and Eve would have no problem tearing the Long Watch apart. It didn't matter if they had five guys or fifty. Between the two of them, they'd be able to hold their own. No amount of tech could compare to the synthetics at the Tower or clobbering two Knights. Some things were best saved for a dramatic reveal.

"I'm not worried about them."

"You should be. These goons aren't the usual bunch of cunts ruining the country."

"Where are they getting the tech?" Perhaps his new friend would be more useful than he thought.

"You ask a lot of questions for somebody looking for a friend."

"I've dealt with groups like this my whole life. I'm not a fan. If I can find her and kick them in the scrote, consider it a double win."

"Mum and Dad were from the highlands?"

"Aye," he admitted. "They moved when they were young."

"Caledonia needs her children." It was the first sincere statement she made. "The clans won't be able to stop the Knights."

"Why not surrender?" He could almost feel the weight of his grandmother's hand on his shoulder. There were many things a Caledonian let roll off their back. But asking them to surrender their freedom? That wouldn't happen. The people were too proud to lay down their arms.

"You know why," she said. It was the first time somebody spoke to him as if they understood his upbringing. He wondered how many mothers from Caledonia raised their boys to be headstrong and cock sure? If they thought piss running down his leg would seize the fight from his bones, they hadn't been reared by a Caledonian granny.

"I do," he said. "Can you remove the cuffs?"

She spoke another insult, but froze. "You want to escape?"

"Sounds like you need help to save your home." No, they wouldn't break him. They hadn't killed him, not yet. There was still fighting to be had.

"And you your friend."

Patches leaned against the door, listening for any whine from the hinges. Stepping back, he threw his weight behind the move. The hinges rattled enough to give him hope. Giving himself a few steps, he charged, slamming his shoulder against the barrier. It inched back.

"I'm not dying here," he growled.

"What are you doing?"

He moved to the far side of the cell. The moment the door opened, he'd have to dodge the cameras or run. He didn't need to get far, just enough outside the hospital to a public space. Even the gun-happy officers would be better suited to deal with the Long Watch.

He braced his toes, leaned forward and charged, his shoulder and back slamming against the door. He flinched and found himself falling, but as the door pounded against the tiled floors, he had won himself a tiny victory. Now he needed to find himself an ally.

Rolling to his feet, he ran to the woman's cell. Without his powers or his hands, he could not tear the door away. For as high-tech as the cuffs were, they sealed the door with a single padlock. He missed his powers—a thought he never believed would come to pass. With them, he could tear the door off the hinges and throw it without effort. Now, a tiny piece of steel vexed him.

"I can't get at the lock."

He attempted to wedge his foot between the door and the wall, but it was impossible. Unless a key miraculously hung nearby, there was no freeing her. He didn't like the idea of leaving the woman behind—

"You need to run. Get help. Do not trust the police. Most are members of the Long Watch. Find your friends and go North. Once you're in Caledonia, go to Grand Central. There's a bar underneath. Tell them Rowan sent you."

"I'll come back," he promised.

"My fate is sealed," she admitted. "Caledonia needs her children."

"Her Children will answer," he said. She might not realize the importance of the statement, or the subtle difference in a word, but he could do more for his ancestors than the average person. Even as she accepted her fate, an impending death at the end of a twenty-foot rope, her eyes maintained a fire. She had been a smart ass and, in a single conversation, grated on his nerves, but he was certain they'd have been friends.

"My name is Patrick Kilgannon."

"We even accept the Irish Caledonians," she said with a laugh. "Now run."

He turned and stepped toward the double doors. Looking over his shoulders, she watched, never letting her confidence falter. He envied her courage. With a slight nod, he turned and ran toward his freedom.

Chapter Seventeen

2039

"I will not let you wage a war we are not guaranteed to win." Repeating Magus' words left a sour taste in Oscar's mouth. The man's hesitation proved he wasn't fit to lead the Knights of Winchester. One of the strongest assets of the crown, and he forced his troops to drag their heels.

Oscar waited for the elevator doors to close before pushing the button to the subbasement. He reeled from the argument with the Knight. They remained on opposite sides of the fence, and even if Oscar had the ear of the queen, he couldn't move without their support. Caledonia would not remain unchecked, leaving the crown a laughingstock in the eyes of the world.

"Arrogant prick."

He had whispered in his mother's ears for years, but it seemed she had been taking counsel with her lapdog more than he suspected. Even as Oscar urged her to take action, she resisted his suggestions. Now he understood why. If it came down to a fight, trading of blows, he'd never win against the awesome power Magus wielded.

He wasn't sure there was enough firepower to fall the man. His invulnerability made him even more annoying. One way or another, Oscar would find the chink in his armor and exploit it.

"Weakness doesn't deserve the ear of the queen."

The door opened and Oscar paused, letting his thoughts wander about the floor. Only a handful of technicians remained at this hour. He let out a sigh of relief when Dr. Wentworth was nowhere to be found. The man treated him as an equal despite being intimately aware of his origins. Even as a replica of the queen's late son, the doctor acknowledged his individuality.

He needed a moment to himself, away from distractions. With a tap of the ear, he shut off his auditory implants and entered the research area of the hospital. The hum of machines created enough white noise to let his thoughts drift. This floor was like a second home, and as a child, he spent more time here than in the palace. He was only two years old when he awoke from inside one of the stasis tubes. The next month was a blur as scientists did tests and tried to find the magical element that had given him consciousness, but not the others.

Oscar knew the secret, luck that defied genetics.

The researchers here worked to cure plagues, slow aging, and find new methods for the synthetic enhancements to improve mankind. For all their tests, they never discovered his secret. Science couldn't explain his abilities. Even the Knights had abilities that could be rationalized by the rules of the universe. But what happened in his brain didn't have an explanation. Oscar had been called a freak his whole life, and part of him liked it. Being a freak awarded him more power than his progenitor. He wasn't a clone. He was an improvement.

Walking along the hall, he reached the glass window, looking into the stasis tubes. He considered it funny that one of those tubes served as the place of his birth. There remained three replicas. Genetically they were identical to him, but he still considered them sleeping siblings. Oscar fantasized about having brothers as he grew. Would they have gotten along or would they have had a rivalry?

He lost himself in the maybes of a past that never came to fruition. But between these thoughts, he caught glimpses of his progenitor, the man who supplied his genetic code. He fought to push them aside, to remind himself that he was his own man, even if the world saw the face of their dead prince. Slamming his palm against the glass, he cursed his father.

It was bad enough to look like the prince, but to also have his memories circulating in his consciousness... Oscar growled. If he didn't focus, he lost himself in their narrative. He assumed the role, the mantle left behind by the man, but he was determined to forge his own path. Even the name Oscar, he envied the Knights of Winchester and their absurd naming practices. What would he name himself, given the opportunity?

"I am not him," he whispered.

No.

Oscar spun about, fists raised. He half expected Dr. Wentworth to be present, studying him. For years he had listened to the thoughts of others, eavesdropping on their most intimate conversations. He could whisper to them, but never had they spoken back. His kind had been wiped from the British Empire and should they discover a Child developed into a mentalist, the hostility assured the Knights would eliminate them. They hadn't found a mentalist over the age of six in a decade.

"Who's there?" he asked.

Throwing his thoughts into the facility, he couldn't find anybody nearby. Despite knowing the difference, he touched his ear, making sure it wasn't a whisper from his communicator.

If he had survived, he might have considered reaching out to the man who nearly destroyed America. He didn't want the madness, but to have somebody capable of showing him the grandeur of his abilities would be amazing. The Prime Minister of Canada had announced being a mentalist when he took office, and so far, he appeared stable. Oscar thought about revealing his secret in hopes of better establishing his individuality.

Oscar moved along the window until he reached the door leading into the stasis room. As it hissed open, he stepped inside. The lights above created a dim glow. Inside the tanks, he could see the bubbles shimmering, oxygenating the fluid so his brothers could breathe. Like him, they were born into a world against their will, forced to play a role they never wanted. If he had been stronger, he'd have shattered their tubes, freeing them from a life of servitude. But more than their freedom, he wanted to connect.

He approached the first tube with the oldest version of himself. Pressing his hand against the glass, he hoped the man's eyes would open. But like every other time he visited, his hopes went unanswered.

"Will you ever wake up?"

The pressure in Oscar's inner ear mounted, as if he

were aboard an airship. Holding his nose, he blew until he heard a pop. He raised an eyebrow, curious at the sudden sensation. Behind his eyes, a tingling grew until he rapidly blinked.

His hand returned to the glass. "Are you in there?"

Yes.

The reply had been faint, barely a whisper from down a long corridor. Was it his imagination? His need for connection? Or had somebody whispered to him in the only way they knew how?

"I hear you, brother."

Chapter Eighteen

2028

In the massive hall, the entire queen's court held their breath as she proceeded from the throne to the edge of her pulpit. She wore a ceremonial gown, far more flowy than she normally did for her public affairs. Nearly her hundred-and-second birthday, she moved toward a squire holding a sword across a pillow.

A gasp broke the silence as she rested her hand on the hilt of the sword. Her wrinkled fingers tightened one by one until she held the weapon. The squire lowered the pillow, bowing down as he backed away. Frail and showing every bit of her age, Ceann thought she'd drop the blade and rely on one of her Knights to carry out the ceremony. His doubts vanished as she held it above her head, turning for the crowd so they might admire her showmanship.

The chamber erupted in cheers. Her military leaders and head of state applauded her strength. Ceann watched those closest to the crown fall victim to the fervor of an age-old tradition. Behind her, seated on either side of the throne, was her most devout. Nexus, captain of her Knights, and Oscar, her abomination of an heir, watched with less enthusiasm. Neither of the men let their emotions get the best of them as the queen turned forward, sword clasped in her right hand.

Ceann turned in his seat, counting the paces to the door. If he turned and ran, it'd only be seconds before he reached the double doors. Within a minute, he'd be in front of the palace. The daydream crumbled as he tried to imagine his next steps. Fleeing would mark him as an enemy of the throne, and there would be no returning to society with the Knights of Winchester on his heels.

He pushed away the fantasy.

Oscar, Prince of the British Empire and the commander of her human military, spoke from his seat. He cleared his throat. "Ceann, squire to the Knights of Winchester, kneel before your monarch."

Ceann straightened his uniform, padded to resemble a modern suit of armor. Never had he seen the Knights wear such foolish outfits before today. Behind him sat the queen's elite guard, ten of the Knights chosen to serve as her personal protectors. They each wore a similar uniform, void of rank, equals in the eyes of the queen.

Nexus nodded, giving his approval. Ceann stepped forward, aware that every eye followed him as he moved from the audience to stand before the queen. She might be a foot shorter than he, but her eyes held a sharpness only possessed by the young. Despite her age, she'd gladly challenge him to a duel and expect to win.

"Kneel," came her son's voice.

He eyed the stool set before the queen. It had been years since he had trained with the Knights, working his way through their ranks. With each step upward, he could almost taste the freedom, the ability to think for himself again. But as he studied the stool, he realized the Knights of Winchester continued to rob him of freedom. Even as he found himself before the queen, he imagined removing one set of shackles for another. Ceann's freedom had been a myth offered as a means of control.

It hadn't even been twenty-four hours since he unleashed his gifts on ruffians in the street of London. They had earned the might of his powers. They forfeited their lives when they attacked an innocent man. His hands had long since stained red with the blood of his victims. The man he attempted to rescue, filled with terror, had shot him, leaving him for dead. Even if Ceann could escape, he'd never fit in amongst the people of Britain. The Knights had ensured that only they could tolerate his inhumane ways.

Oscar had scooted to the edge of his chair. The man had barely reached his twenties. Cloned from the queen's son before his untimely demise, he was the spitting image of his genetic benefactor. For all intents and purposes, he was a perfect replica. But despite the queen naming him as successor, the people waited, ready to rise against him should he assume power. While her biological son had won the heart of the people, it was the same admiration that turned them against his clone. It was one of the few moments the queen feared losing her station. Ceann found the petty squabbles of politicians to be childish.

"Kneel," the man repeated.

Into servitude he went, dropping to his knee. Yet another master pulling at his bonds.

"Sir Ceann, Knight of Winchester." She raised the sword into the air before gently letting it touch his shoulder. She dragged the blade back, the refined edge cutting through his uniform and drawing blood from his shoulder. "It is with your life and blood that you serve the crown." She moved to the other shoulder, repeating the motion.

"Rise, Sir Ceann, Knight of Winchester, and take your place by my side."

Ceann stood, meeting the woman's eyes. She gestured to her side, commanding him to fall in line. She had watched his trials. Lux had clarified that should he upset the queen today, she'd ensure he died. For now, he accepted the shackles, standing at her side like a proper subject.

"Enough with the formalities," she bellowed. "Feast." With a single word, the tension in the room faded. Doors at the far end of the hall opened and men and women flooded the space with silver trays holding the empire's finest wines.

The squire took the queen's sword before she vanished into the crowd. But even as she moved amongst her most loyal, the Knights followed, prepared to strike down any who might do the matriarch harm.

Ceann held his position, watching as the humans went about their dance. They spoke in code, taking inventory of who supported their causes. There would be discussions of law and the direction of the country. None of it interested him. The King of Monsters wanted nothing to do with the plight of humans.

"I watched as you killed that man." Nexus stood behind him, close enough to feel the heat radiate from his uniform. "Did you hope to find comfort in his arms? Or were you hunting for your next target?"

Ceann should have suspected that he was being

watched. "Neither. I wanted to remember why we fight."

"You have many gifts, but lying isn't one of them."

"I have nothing to hide."

"Says the man who fraternizes with commoners."

"No different from a man who takes a commoner for a mistress."

Ceann turned to see the man's twitching lip. He pretended to be above the humans, superior to them, because Nostradamus had chosen him. Despite his arrogance, he served a human master. Like Ceann, he remained shackled by a sense of duty beaten into them. But it was the *human* lover they whispered about behind closed doors. The Knights had watched Ceann on his excursion, but not even Nexus evaded their watchful eye.

"Watch yourself, Knight."

His superior's hand tightened, balled into a fist as he summoned his abilities. Ceann casually looked at a large white box nestled in the corner where the wall met the ceiling. The ceremonial room contained a dozen similar devices, each of them used to nullify the abilities of Nostradamus' chosen. They might maintain their strength, but those with external abilities like Nexus, they were nothing more than average.

"Another time," Ceann promised.

"Sir Ceann, we are honored to have another graduate of the academy serving us." Oscar inserted himself, offering a hand to Ceann. Whispers about the royal made it seem as if he were a sniveling weakling. But the man carried himself as if he belonged, and between two Knights capable of extraordinary feats, that caught Ceann's attention.

"It's my pleasure to serve the crown," Ceann said. He might not care for having masters, but they awarded him the privilege of carrying out monstrous deeds. For now, it was an uneasy relationship.

"A Scot?"

"At one time, yes." His ancestry had bought him more than a few lashes at the academy. With a war brewing between the crown and the newly liberated Caledonia, they treated him as less than.

"They are relentless savages. Twice this week, they've attempted to overrun the blockade with little more than spears."

Nexus laughed. "I still think the Knights should sweep through the country and—"

"Appreciated, truly," Oscar said. "But the queen's army has this under control. Once we finished securing the borders of France, we'll turn our attention to the North."

Ceann was bored of the men's politics. They spoke of conflict as if neither had witnessed a battlefield. While there were records of Nexus defending the queen against a coup for the throne, he had yet to see the man do more than lord over cadets.

"Will you be leading the charge?" Ceann asked.

The question left Oscar speechless. The man raised an eyebrow, studying Ceann's lack of expression. "Spoken like a grunt. I'll be the first to see the flag of Scotland crushed."

He turned to Nexus. "Your second in command—"

"Magus?"

Oscar nodded. "He seems to think our way forward is through a peaceful resolution with the traitors." There was a bit of smug satisfaction in his words. Ceann disliked politics due to the cloak and dagger, the inability to speak and be straightforward. "Is there discord in the Knights of Winchester?"

The commander of the human army steered Nexus into a minefield. Ceann admired a human who had unsettled his superior. If Nexus admitted Magus was a pacifist, it'd mark him as an unfit leader. If he confessed to entertaining the idea, he'd be seen as weak. The court might speak of Oscar as an unfit monarch, but the man knew his audience and how to manipulate them.

"The Knights value diversity amongst our ranks. Magus wants to ensure we are not missing any solution that benefits the queen or her future successors."

Ceann staggered, taking a step away from the men. Shaking his head, he found the rage between the two men palpable, as if he could taste the anger in the air. For a moment, he believed Oscar might lunge, sinking his thumbs into Nexus's eyes. It would serve him right, and perhaps Ceann would let him land a blow before interfering. It now made sense why the inhibitors prevented their abilities.

Neither man moved.

"When we reclaim Glasgow—"

"They will never support an abomination."

The insult made Ceann's eyes go wide. The man's constitution never faltered. For him to bait Oscar, he must be closer to breaking the man than Ceann believed.

"Remember who you serve, Knight."

"I serve the crown."

Ceann dared to take Nexus by the arm. Pulling him away from the conversation, Oscar smiled, convinced he had won the argument. He frequently imagined shackles clasped about his wrists and ankles. But now, it was clear, Nexus wore a similar set of chains. The Knights of Winchester might have a place of prestige next to the throne, but they were nothing more than powerful servants.

"He must never be allowed to wear the crown," Nexus said.

Ceann might consider himself ruthless in a fight, but with the nuances of politics, he remained unarmed. But even he understood Nexus's words.

"Aye, sir," he agreed.

Chapter Nineteen

2039

He slammed against the exit. Unlike the cell door, it held firmly in place, refusing to give an inch. It was the last set of doors exiting the lobby and, like the others, they remained secure. He kicked again, frustrated that his strategy of getting out quickly reached a dead end. Staring at the narrow glass slits in the metal frame, he debated if he could wiggle his hips through.

He relented. "It's a hospital. There must be exits everywhere."

Patches walked into the lobby, careful to keep his eyes from looking up. There were eleven bodies still hanging from the balcony, but now, two more nooses had been dropped over the ledge. He didn't need to be a genius to know they were meant for him and Rowan. If he didn't find a way out... his skin crawled at the thought of the coarse rope tightening around his neck. His powers might save him from a broken neck, but even he needed to breathe.

"Keep moving," he said as he ran across the lobby. He tried the doors leading to another wing, but found they were secured. Without his abilities, a simple locked door turned into an unbreakable barrier. Patches cursed, growling at the humility.

"Windows," he said. He pivoted, running toward the stairs.

As he climbed to the second story, he froze. The bodies hung at face level, and he couldn't avoid looking at the limp corpses suspended from the upper floors. Leaning against the wall, he forced himself to see them, to see the fate of those who didn't meet the British Empire's mold. At first, he thought eleven bodies were bad, already eleven too many. But knowing there were more places like this spread across the country, he wondered how many bodies hung in a similar manner.

The bile churned, and he swallowed to keep from hurling. It was bad enough to kill them. But to leave them as trophies, victories against an entire race of people, he couldn't fathom the hate. The cut along his neck should have been reminder enough, but he'd never sleep again without seeing the ropes or the burlap sacks robbing them of their identities.

Patches fought back the tears. "No crying," he said. The only way he could make this right was to get out and find help. If he could come back and free the woman, it would be an act of defiance, a step toward saying this was unacceptable. It wasn't much, but it motivated him to escape.

From the front of the lobby, chains rattled as somebody removed them from the doors. Had they seen him? Were there really cameras or was that a myth to force obedience? He didn't want to find out.

Run. There was no other thought. He bolted along the balcony, expecting at any moment for the Brothers to pour inside the lobby. His foot caught on a fallen wire rack, sending him reeling toward the balcony. He braced for the fall, the restraints smacking against the wall. The shock pulsed through his body, enough that if he hadn't relieved himself earlier, he'd certainly do it now. His muscles twitched, but he refused to fall to his knees.

The first step seemed to take forever. One foot in front of the other. The zaps stopped, and muscles along his neck twitched as he continued staggering his way forward. The doors below burst open as he reached an exit from the balcony. He was getting closer. If only he could outrun *them*.

"Do. Not. Fall."

"Do we have a plan?"

Eve narrowed her eyes as Alyssa slid into her body suit. "I hit the bad guys until somebody tells me what I want to know. Any questions?"

Eve hopped out of the van and zipped up her jacket, pressing a spot on the collar, the fabric tightened and she could feel the electric hum run through the threads. Registry had gone above and beyond. The body armor had been his parting gift; a thank you for saving his life. She hoped the suit did the same for her.

Alyssa slid out of the van, pulling the hood over her head. Clad entirely in black, she reminded Eve of the ninjas in old movies. The only thing she was missing was a giant red sash and sword.

Much like London, the school before them had long since fallen into disrepair. If it weren't for the faded 'academy' sign on the gate, she'd have assumed it was an English mansion. Inside, more bad people waited. If they had touched Patches, she'd tear off their arms and beat them with their own limbs. With a collapsed roof, boarded-up windows and a rickety metal fence, it looked like the perfect place for a massacre.

"When killing becomes easy…" Alyssa mumbled.

Eve wanted to laugh at the irony. The warning from her father seemed like a distant memory, and to be reminded by a woman who killed without hesitation. "Special rules for special people," Eve said. Someday she might forgive Alyssa, but tonight she'd use it as fuel. The anger had set in and whatever came next, it'd serve as therapy.

"Eve…"

"They know we're here." Eve's heart raced and her skin crawled until she swatted at the phantom bugs on her arm. Somewhere inside the building, the electromagnetic fields warped and distorted. The electric currents being turned reminded her of Registry's body armor. It couldn't be a coincidence.

"How many?"

"Enough," Eve growled. One or one hundred, none of them left without damage. She flexed her arms until an electrical current flowed down her sleeves. As she rolled her fingers into fists, she smiled at the power she commanded.

She would owe Registry a thank you.

"Sister?" A man had opened the front door of the school. He stepped out and walked into the overgrown courtyard. Eve thought it laughable that he assumed a wrought-iron fence offered any semblance of protection.

Eve walked forward until she reached the gate. While the metal appeared rusted, a newer square lock pulsed, electrifying the fence. They weren't complete buffoons. They prepared for outsiders.

"I'm not your sister," Eve called back.

Eve imagined her hand reaching into the lock, pulling at the lines generated by its power source. It was as much an art as a science. Bat away this field, and pull at that one. Without moving a muscle, the lock hissed, popped open, and fell to the concrete.

"Who the fuck do you think you are?"

He stepped outside the doorway, and now she could see the exoskeleton bonded to his body. The humans of London were fast to sell their souls as they climbed their way atop a fearful ladder. Eve thought it cute that they attempted to keep pace with Children.

"I asked you a question," he yelled. To emphasize his question, he pulled a gun off his back, pumping the stock and pointing it in her direction.

"I think you might know where a friend of mine is. I want answers." If he wanted drama, she gladly matched him. She kicked the gate, knocking it off its hinges. Eve wanted to see if he had enough smarts to be fearful.

"You and what—"

"For God's sake." She stepped to the side and turned to the van. She couldn't have whispered the word any softer. "Blue."

The door of the van tore open, thrown to the side in a shower of sparks. As Blue stepped out, the old rubber tires popped and hissed. She took a bow, gesturing to the open gate. Blue ran forward, his toes digging into the ground in a spray of concrete. He jumped forward, his torso spinning as his legs tucked underneath him. The transformation from humanoid to canine took seconds.

"Registry." Eve didn't know if she should curse the architect or add it to the list of thanks.

Blue bound through the fence, faster than she had ever seen him move. The man fired, forcing Blue to bound to the side. Without losing momentum, he leapt toward the man, transforming into the seven-foot-tall robot. The second shot fired, striking Blue in the shoulder, causing him to jerk to the side. But his sheer weight carried him forward.

The man spun to the side, stepping out of Blue's path. Blue came to a stop, holding his pose on one knee with his arm held out toward the man. Eve waited for the goon to take a shot. Blue stood up, turning his arm. Only then did she see the long blade protruding from his forearm. The man's weapon fell as his chest separated from his lower body with a sploosh.

"First blood," Eve said. As she looked back for Alyssa, she found her mentor had vanished. A second later, she sensed a disturbance in the electromagnetic field as Alyssa ran toward the building.

Now she needed to crack some skulls for Patches and for shooting her robot.

Patches regained his footing, shaking off the shock. He shouldered another door, hoping it'd give way to a patient's room. He could see the light of the moon shining under each of the thick wooden doors. His shoulder went numb as he tried his thirteenth, no, fourteenth door. If he didn't make his way out of the hall soon, it'd only take a single bullet in the narrow corridor to end his escape.

Behind him, he heard shouting, one man barking orders. He couldn't make out their words, but they couldn't be far away. He changed his plan. If he couldn't get to a window on the second floor, he'd continue going up. If he could get to the roof, there'd be a fire escape, and then he'd make his way toward the city to find help.

Kicking the last door, just to be sure, he confirmed that each of them had been locked. With a deep breath, he tasted the remnants of cleaning chemicals. Gritting his teeth, he continued running. He had worried if a door opened, he'd find more bodies. He imagined them piled high, their burlap covers hiding their taut faces. At least they'd have been given the dignity of being cut down. The thought that the men left them there, admiring their handiwork, made his stomach churn.

He rounded the corner and headed down another long, white corridor. Skidding to a stop, he found the exit sign with the universal image of a man walking on zigzag lines. The bar in the middle used to open it had been smashed in, leaving it slightly ajar. He barreled forward, careful not to smash the cuffs off the doorjamb.

"Almost free," he muttered.

Up the stairs he went. The voices grew louder, and at this pace, they'd be on him before he escaped. With no other exits available, they'd follow his path with error. When he got back to the Tower—if he got back—he'd make it a ritual to go to the gym. He'd never skip leg day again. He just needed to reach the roof and get outside.

Rounding the corner, he nearly cheered. One more flight and the red exit sign greeted him. The voices downstairs grew louder. No time to dawdle. The burning running down his legs threatened to cripple him, but he'd worry about it later. If he couldn't walk for a week, at least he'd be alive to complain about the pain.

"Almost. There."

He took the steps two at a time. When he reached the top, the air changed. It wasn't the stuffy smell of disinfectant. Fresh air. The first kick shoved the door backward. The second broke it from its hinges. He didn't dare celebrate the victory. He needed to find the fire escape and get away.

In the darkness, it was hard to tell just how far the hospital roof stretched. He ran to the edge, careful to slow before hurling himself off the top. There were enough lights around the facility to see they were just outside of the city. The buildings were further apart and less crowded than in the middle of London. If he screamed now, would any of the residents hear him? Would they care?

There wasn't much time before the Long Watch made it to the roof. He needed to find his escape, and fast.

The woman's fist pulverized a chunk of the wall as Eve ducked out of the way. With enhancements, speed and strength came at a premium. Most could only afford one or the other. The beefy woman had sunk every penny into her muscles. When natural muscles were no longer an option, she replaced her arms with synthetic limbs. Eve almost complimented the adorable back-alley cybernetics.

As she drove her fist under the woman's jaw, her knuckles flared. Electricity arced, jumping from her fist along the woman's shoulders. If the electricity hadn't been impressive enough, the suit augmented her strength. The woman's head snapped back, her spine cracking as blood sprayed across the hallway.

Eve didn't wait for the body to hit the ground. Grabbing the woman's shirt, she spun, using her as a shield as a man jumped out of a classroom door, gun drawn. The spray of bullets pelted the woman's hide, but none penetrated.

She was about to toss the body to the side when a disc slid across the floor. Bomb? Electromagnetic pulse? Eve tried to drop the body on the device, but it simultaneously flashed and whistled at a volume that made her scream. The bang left the room spinning. Disoriented, she couldn't access her powers.

She was unable to see more than blurry shapes because of the sunspots in her vision. The man didn't have a chance to raise his weapon as a white rectangle picked him up by the skull. He screamed when Blue slammed him into the wall. By the third, his body hung limp and Blue tossed him to the side.

The synthetic stood next to her, his body covering her the best he could. She patted him on the chest and found that more of his body was covered in dark red gore than not. She had considered him Skits' pet robot and almost forgot that they designed him to be a ruthless killing machine. There was no point in dwelling on the ethics of what happened within the academy. Right now, she was thankful for a guardian capable of cutting through the cheap-ass enhanced goons.

"Good boy," she said. "Alyssa, any luck?" She knew her hearing was shot and that she yelled louder than necessary. If her mentor responded, she couldn't make out her words. "On our own, Blue."

The wall exploded and she could barely see the blur tackling Blue. The figure, a man, maybe, was almost the same size as the synthetic. Instead of clothing, he wore a silver body suit. No, that *was* his body. Instead of having his limbs replaced, all that remained resembling a human was from the chest up.

Blue's fist shot forward, but the man caught it. When the blade sprung out, it smacked against the man's shoulder, causing sparks but not penetrating. The man laughed louder than the ringing in her ears before spinning with Blue, tossing him toward Eve. She rolled out of the way as Blue transformed midair. The canine's nails screeched along the tile before he ran toward the brute.

Eve nearly spat at the taste as the air sizzled with power. Without moving his feet, the man caught Blue out of the air. Even as he transformed, the man slammed him against the wall. As Eve's hearing returned, she could make out his faint laughter.

She crawled to her feet as he hammered Blue against the floor.

"Asshole," she yelled.

"Little girl feeling brave?"

She wished Patches were here. Eve would have loved to see the bruiser land a punch and Patches do nothing more than laugh. He'd knock the behemoth of a man on his ass. Instead, she'd have to do it in his honor. When she rescued him, she'd have to regale him with the boxing match he missed out on.

"Tell me where my friend is." She turned her body, narrowing her gait. "And I won't kill you."

It had stopped being a threat.

Patches refused to let the tears form.

"God damned assholes."

They had installed a flood light at ground level. In the darkness between the wings of the hospital, they had torn the fire escape from the wall and laid it for all to see. He thought back to the locked doors, the wedged-open stairwell. It had all been a setup. If that didn't convince him, the two bodies surrounded by dark puddles confirmed it.

"Monsters," he whispered. Along the pavement they had taken white paint, drawing smiley faces with arrows. He'd have hurled if the despair didn't paralyze him. They had given him a chance to escape. Hope. But it was all part of a sick and twisted game. Had the woman in the other cell been a plant? He assumed she was just as bad. His faith in the world shattered.

"You can return with us or take your chances."

Patches turned to see Brother Vincent. There were at least a dozen people gathered behind him. They had been waiting for his escape. Did they do this with every Caledonian they captured? Now they watched him with sick amusement as he weighed his options. From four stories, he'd never survive the impact against the cement below. He knew it. They knew it.

His choices were simple, die by his own volition, or die at their hands. He looked over the ledge again, wondering if the two bodies below had the same internal dialogue. They had been brave enough to risk it. Bones protruded from their legs, proof they had taken their lives into their own hands.

Patches stared at their lifeless corpses. He wanted to

believe he could muster the strength to risk it, to defy these assholes at every turn. Slowly, he turned. Dropping to one knee, then both, he admitted to himself that he wasn't brave.

"Can't even take his own life?" Brother Timothy mocked. The words stung almost as much as the electricity they pumped into his body. Convulsing, he fell to the ground.

"Another coward," the man boasted. The crowd cheered loud enough to be heard over his own screaming. Killing him wasn't the victory they had been after. Breaking him had been their goal from the moment they arrived.

The Sister broke away from the crowd, approaching him. The current died. His teeth continued chattering as he twitched. She dipped to one knee, pulling the knife from her boot. She held it near his neck, able to end it at any second. Part of him wished she would do what he couldn't. He needed somebody willing to pull the trigger and end his suffering.

She leaned close, as if she wanted a closer inspection as the blade touched his throat. His eyes refused to focus enough to see the piercings, but he recognized the brutality written across her face. She held his life in her hands, and he nearly begged her to claim the ultimate prize.

"Caledonia needs her children," she whispered. "We are Gallowglass."

With a tight fist, she drove her knuckles into his skull. The dark of night closed in and he fought to remain conscious, but it was a losing battle. He closed his eyes and focused on the cold under his cheek. Had she just...

"Smug, annoying, Scottish accent."

"A traitor to the crown." Brutus only needed prompting before he turned chatty. Eve needed him to release Blue. She could fry the man's cybernetics, but her lack of finesse put the synthetic in danger. "You'll find him hanging from the rafters."

Bait. Eve knew the man attempted to knock her off her game. Even if he lied, the idea of Patches hanging limp filled her with rage. His body swinging, lifeless… the moment the image crossed her mind, she screamed. He came to London out of a sense of loyalty, and she hadn't upheld her end of the bargain. Patches could be dead, and it'd be her fault.

The man slammed Blue into a wall. The robot already attempted to pull itself free. "Blue, stay." It was her turn to be the hero.

Eve extended her middle finger. As the man stomped toward her, she watched him stifle his step, metering his pace as he brought back his right fist. It'd have been easy enough to reach out with her abilities and screw with his electronics or give him a seizure. Easy, but not as gratifying.

At the last second, she stepped to the side, letting his fist pass inches from her face. Slamming her fist into his rib cage sounded like a tiny explosion. Electricity shot from the suit, skidding along the surface of his steely hide. As he spun, she ducked under his elbow. Instinct had her thrusting a palm into his testicles, but she paused at the lack of sex organs.

His knee nearly caught her in the chin before she stopped it. He had traded a fleshy body for brute strength. The blow had her somersaulting backward and landing in a crouch. As he came in, swinging with the back of his hand. She braced herself, catching his wrist. Her feet slid, and she tumbled, but she stopped the man's strike.

The confusion was almost priceless. Eve smiled through grit teeth. "Don't. Fuck. With. Children." His eyes widened. His tiny pea brain assumed she was a Knight. She didn't correct him. Even better if he thought his countrymen betrayed him.

Digging her fingertips into the metal, she jumped up, slamming both her feet against his torso. She'd seen Alyssa perform the move on the synthetics at the Tower. As she pulled at his arm, the metal sheered, tearing from his shoulder before she lost her grip and flew backward.

"Bitch."

He tried to grab her, but she braced a foot against the wall and pushed off. Launching over the man, she reached out, grabbing his head. It wasn't as graceful as Alyssa, but she held onto his skull as she slammed against his back. A man his size normally wouldn't be able to reach her, but his arm rotated until he had access to her face.

Pushing her knee against his spine, she leaned back, pulling at his head. The man's hand wrapped around her face, tightening. It stopped as his skull pulled from his spine, the skin tearing from under his chin. With a final growl, she landed on her ass, half of the man's crushed skull in her hands. It took her a moment before her brain processed the clumps of hair and skin poking through her fingers.

Eve's stomach turned.

She only had a second to see a woman holding a gun

a few feet away. At this range, there wouldn't be any way she missed Eve's face. The woman couldn't be much older than her, and somehow that made it less terrifying. Eve tried to summon her powers, but the gore dripping from her hands made it impossible to focus.

The woman's head jerked to the side, spinning it a hundred and eighty degrees. Before her body fell, Alyssa's black silhouette stepped out of nothing. Pulling the mask off her face, she eyed the brute's upright corpse.

"That's all of them." She held out her hand.

Eve looked from her mentor's outstretched fingers to her own. There was enough of the man's face that she could make out where his eye should be. She spun over, throwing the gunk to the side. Her body betrayed her, and she vomited, splashing her dinner along the academy floors.

"Patches isn't here." Alyssa acted as if nothing was amiss. Eve wanted to curse but continued emptying the contents of her stomach. They had slaughtered people, a *school* full of people, and for what? Nothing?

"But I think I know where he is," Alyssa added.

Good, Eve thought. At least the bits of skin under her nails and the blood oozing down her fingers had been worth something. But for now, she let her body take control and start another volley of heaving.

Chapter Twenty

2039

Alyssa watched in silence as Eve approached the mass grave.

She wanted to apologize for not being able to keep Eve safe, not from harm, but from the ferocity of the world. The girl had come to Troy a teenager. Young enough to rebound from the brutality of her childhood, and she managed to flourish under her father's guidance. For a while, Alyssa thought the girl might lead a normal life.

That was a lie. Normal had been a myth Alyssa allowed herself to believe.

Eve fell to her knees next to the shallow hole. The zealots inside hadn't bothered to cover the bodies, instead leaving them outside for the elements and rodents. Some wore plastic bags over their heads, but most remained frozen in their last moments of terror. Nearly two dozen men and women had been slaughtered and left here without remorse or reverie. At least there were no children.

The shadow of night hid the details of their bodies.

Eye color. Makeup. Wedding bands. Not knowing about them and their lives almost made it bearable. But as the wind shifted, the smell of rot filled her nostrils, decay with a tinge of sweetness. She wished it was the first time, but it triggered memories she would rather have forgotten.

Alyssa left the comfort of Troy to wage a war against the injustice. The first time she agreed to a mission, handed to her by the president of the Free Republic, she didn't hesitate to say yes. Atrocities like this had become commonplace, and she willfully assumed the burden. She witnessed countless horrors hoping others wouldn't. The burden had grown tiresome, and she admitted that alone, she couldn't stop them.

Then she turned to the next generation of Children. She trained kids to be soldiers hoping they'd never need their skills. It was for their well-being, and for a time, Alyssa believed it. One-by-one, she robbed them of their innocence. She built an unescapable prison. No matter the decisions she made, she felt the weight in her heart.

"La hawla wala quwwata illa billah." Even as she muttered the words, she acknowledged the disgrace. When she passed from this life, she expected harsh judgment. Not even her faith could wipe away the stain on her heart.

Eve sobbed quietly, hiding her face.

There were countless people she owed apologies to. The Sentinels, Dwayne, Conthan, and even Ned, they all deserved an explanation for her actions. But none of them touched her heart like the young girl before her. If she could have saved one person from this life, she'd have considered it a victory. But yet again, Alyssa's actions invited disaster in the lives of those she loved.

"I'm sorry," she whispered.

"For what?" Eve spun on her knees, wiping the tears from her face.

Alyssa didn't know where to begin her atonement. "I never wanted this for you. I hoped to spare you this reality."

"You didn't kill them," Eve spat back. Her lip twitched in anger. The tears continued rolling down her face, making her look even younger.

"This is why I joined the Wetworks program. I didn't want anybody in the Tower to witness this side of mankind."

Eve's eyes softened before she glanced at the grave. Alyssa wanted to close the distance between them, to wrap her arms around Eve and promise everything would be okay. But it would be another lie, and she couldn't continue the facade. When Eve stood and turned, she saw in her eyes the very thing she had wanted to prevent. Rage had replaced the girl's innocence.

"I want them dead," she said. "I want each one of them to pay."

Alyssa let her eyes water, refusing to dismiss the pain in her chest. Twice today she had cried. Those words, even in anger, would evoke Dwayne's warning. But as Eve let out a screeching roar, Alyssa understood her pain. There were a thousand things she could say, words that would make her fathers proud, but none reached her heart.

Alyssa wanted to prevent Eve's pain, but this was a road the girl needed to travel. Just as Conthan had walked it before her, dancing along a line of good and evil, Eve needed to make her own decisions. But she wouldn't be alone.

"Each and every one," Alyssa confirmed. Eve's eyes shot up, confused by her words. Even she expected Alyssa to offer a prayer or sagely advice.

"We fight for a reason. I arranged for the Sentinels to exist because I believed they could stand up for those who couldn't. I allowed them to play at being soldiers. But none of them could stomach this." Alyssa moved to Eve's side, staring at the face of a young man, dark shadows wrapping around his neck. They had choked him, and after he died, they dumped his body. His eyes remained open, searching the heavens for Allah.

"We fight for those who can't."

"I'm sorry," Eve whispered. "I... I didn't understand."

"You shouldn't have to, child."

Eve's fingers slipped into Alyssa's hands as they stared at the carnage. The ground rumbled as Blue approached from behind. Alyssa wanted to say a prayer, but after the inner turmoil, she felt as if it would be hollow, ignored by Allah. Even as she slipped further from grace, she held hope that somehow she'd find her way back and reclaim the parts of her soul she sacrificed.

"What?"

Clanking, Blue stopped before the shallow grave. In his hands, he held a pair of shovels, and Alyssa's eyes went wide. Without a command, a synthetic, an invention of man designed to destroy, held compassion? Could the hand of Allah be speaking through a machine?

"Astaghfiru lillah," she muttered. "He speaks."

"Alhamdulillah," Eve said, squeezing Alyssa's hand.

The girl's insistence on understanding her faith was one reason they had grown close. The girl she first met working on a car engine with Dwayne had grown into a powerful young woman. And much like Blue's gesture, perhaps she hadn't seen the grace of Allah clearly until now.

"We honor the dead." Eve took the shovels, handing one to Alyssa. "Then we avenge them."

She slammed the shovel into the ground, lifting the first of many loads of dirt. The man's eyes were glassy, as if he was shocked to see two women standing above him with shovels. Alyssa wondered if he'd view them as devils severing his tie to the physical world, or as angels. As she dropped the dirt onto his chest, nothing about the thoughts in her head were angelic.

And so, they did for those who could not for themselves.

Chapter Twenty-One

2039

"I tried." The Sister's face didn't have the same ferocity as before. Her emotions fled across her face, and for a second, he believed her. He had questions, more than he could remember at this point. "You should have had another twenty-four hours. Something changed."

"What about her?" Patches nodded to the other door.

"I'm doing what I can," she whispered. "They can't discover I'm Gallowglass."

"Why are you telling me this?"

She pulled him from the cell. They were going through the motions. Brother Timothy had shouted for her to retrieve him in preparation for his execution. She slowed the process, and despite that, she continued to march him toward his death.

"Remove the cuffs," Patches begged.

She walked behind him, a hand wrapped around the back of his neck. He could feel the strength in her grip and at any moment, she could snap his neck. He almost preferred that thought over hanging from a noose.

"I can't," she whispered. "They'll kill us both. I have orders."

He wanted to believe she was one of the good guys, but after last night, he had his doubts. It'd be an ultimate victory for him to find comfort in an escape only to discover she had played him. Before being locked up, he'd have said mankind didn't have the ability for that level of depravity. Right now, he wanted to watch humanity burn. They were twisted individuals and deserved no mercy.

It was time to put it all on the line. He only had one card left to play.

"I'm a Child of Nostradamus."

She froze, her hand relaxing against his neck. He clenched his eyes shut, waiting for a strike across the back of the head. Seconds passed without movement or pain. Patches opened an eye, wondering what was happening behind him. When he tried to turn around, her nails bit into his skin.

"Prove it," she whispered.

"The cuffs. They're doing something to my powers. I—"

"American," she whispered. "The Tower?"

Patches nodded. "I came with two others. We're looking for a friend. The Knights most likely have her."

"Then she's dead." Her tone didn't leave any room for negotiation. It came as an absolute. "I'm sorry. We're at war." Her voice quieted, as if she spoke to convince herself. "My country needs me. I can't let them down."

The idea of dying had never crossed Patches' mind. Being invulnerable made him numb to the possibility. Even when he fought Nexus, there had been a cocky idea that he couldn't lose. But as her grip tightened, nails biting into his skin, he confronted reality. He didn't want to die. There would be no stoic facade, nor staring death in the eye. He'd struggle, kicking and screaming if he must. He didn't care for a graceful end.

"Don't fight me," she whispered. She lifted him enough that his feet almost dragged along the floor. He might get away but, laced with enhancements, she'd easily be able to outrun him.

"Sister Jasper." Brother Timothy held open the double doors leading into the lobby. "What's taking you? Do you require help?"

She continued pushing until Patches was within arm's reach. He tried swinging the cuffs, hoping to knock the man in the head. Timothy caught Patches' wrists. The smile grew until he bared his teeth.

"I'll enjoy watching you hang, traitor." Brother Timothy wasn't a liberator, or even a protector of the crown. Patches had seen nationalists before. This man was a sadist who found an outlet by serving the queen. It had less to do about his country and more to do with suffering. Patches imagined after his body swung from the rafters, Brother Timothy would go home and jerk off to the image.

"Fuck you," Patches growled.

"Take him to the third floor." Brother Timothy gave a slight bow, dropping his gaze. The man didn't see Patches as a threat. After yesterday, Patches understood why.

Jasper continued pushing until they reached the elevator. They filled the lobby with at least two dozen men and women. They gathered to watch the show. It was bad enough that they persecuted innocent Caledonians, but to take pleasure in their execution, it tightened

Patches' stomach. There was something wrong with the people of London. It was another thought that justified Caledonia's insistence they gain their freedom.

She pressed the button, never stepping into his line of sight. The doors opened, and she shoved him inside. They had twenty seconds to speak freely.

"I'll remove the cuffs like I always do. They'll fall, then I push." She turned him about so she could impress the urgency of her words. "Will you survive?"

"Why are you doing this?"

At any moment, she could remove his cuffs. He'd stand a chance, and he'd be able to fight his way free of the Long Watch. London would be a safer place, and he could free the woman from her cell. He didn't understand her insistence on playing a role when she could be saving one of her own. He wanted to spit at her, to knock her against the wall. She acted as if she were a savior for her people, but she'd gladly sacrifice one of her own. Patches growled at the hypocrisy.

"Will you survive?" she asked again.

He'd never thought about if his powers could withstand a snap of the neck. Jasper didn't leave him any options. He wasn't sure how quickly his power would return, and even if he survived the initial snap of his spine, would it mean he'd asphyxiate?

The elevator slowed before it lurched into place on the third floor. The ding bordered on deafening as the doors rolled open. Jasper pulled him from the elevator, returning to her role on the Long Watch. There was no care in her movements, shoving him along until he nearly tripped.

"Sister Jasper," said a wide man. His facial hair had turned unwieldy, desperate for a razor. Patches noted the way he held the rope, sliding the knot back and forth with an almost child-like glee.

Panic set in. Patches ducked low, Jasper's nails cutting into his skin as he pulled free. Leaning forward, he charged the man. His shoulder caught the man's torso, but he hardly budged. His elbow drove down on Patches' back at the same time the noose wrapped around his neck. It had been his last chance to flee, to regain his freedom. Without his powers, he couldn't manage a simple strike without being knocked to the floor. For all of Alyssa's training, he relied on the one thing these assholes had stolen from him.

"I like it when they struggle," the man laughed.

Jerked about, Patches sat on the ledge, his back facing the crowd below. If there were any doubts about what was about to happen, the knots suspending previous victims served as a reminder. They were going to murder him for a misguided cause.

"Prepare the cleansing," came a voice below. The cheers made Patches noxious.

The man tightened the noose even as Patches struggled. He gripped the front of his shirt, as if he might hurl him from the ledge.

"The restraints," Jasper said. "I'm not fishing them off another swinging corpse."

"You're no fun, Sister."

She bumped him to the side, pushing her thumb into the top of the restraints. Patches couldn't feel his hands even as the cuffs loosened. She pulled them free, handing them to her compatriot. Her face hardened, jaw tightening until he could see the sharp edges of her chin.

Do you deserve to be saved, Child?

Patches' eyes widened at the whisper grazing his ear.

"We have found you guilty." There was no ceremony as she slammed her palm into his chest. The force knocked him over the ledge. Patches screamed as he fell backward, trying desperately to catch the ledge before he toppled to his death.

Save me, he begged.

He reached for the rope, hoping to slow his descent. Seconds stretched for eternity, but with numb fingers, he couldn't grasp the noose. His lungs ran out of air just as the cord tightened. His body jerked, the noose clenched his throat, and pain shot through his body.

The world turned dark.

"You've arrived in time to witness our victory."

Oscar didn't comment on the man's determination to impress the future ruler of the British Empire. Brother Vincent had gone above and beyond to purge the streets of Scots, sometimes *too* eager. If the Long Watch wasn't kept in line, they'd cause panic. Oscar made a mental note to adjust the man's thinking. With a simple suggestion, he'd dial down his rage.

"You're taking more pleasure than normal." He didn't need telepathy to know the man was elated with his newest acquisition. With a simple thought, he could wade through the man's memories, but he always hated the stain of fanaticism and how it lingered for hours.

"He attempted to flee. We gave him the opportunity to end his suffering. The man could have jumped. Like the others, he is weak. He couldn't end his own life, so we have to do it for him. It's a theme with the Scots."

Oscar had offered Magus the use of the police to help

expand his reach. But even Magus didn't know about the growing militia Oscar put in place. Every day, new fanatics joined, and eventually, it'd reach a point where he could use them to shape public opinion. Nobody would dare to question his ascension to the throne, not even Magus himself. But first, he needed to ensure that the Long Watch upheld their end of the bargain.

"I have brought more toys for the Watch."

"Thank you, sir." Brother Vincent saw the weapons as favor being bestowed upon him for his efforts. Oscar didn't care why the man did his job, as long as he continued to expand his—the prince's—reach. Eventually, they and the police of England would be enough to secure his hold on the country. Even if Magus wanted him gone, he wouldn't be bold enough to risk the optics.

The men and women in the room grew agitated, as if a current ran through their bodies. Each of them believed they were foot soldiers in a war against the North, and today brought the fruits of their hard work. Their glee, with an impending execution, left the taste of blood in Oscar's mouth. He touched his lips, ensuring the taste of old pennies wasn't coming from him.

"Tell me more about this traitor." He could easily invade Vincent's skull and pull the secrets from the crevices of his psyche. The taste of metal prevented him from diving any further into their broken minds.

"We found him in a pub. He asked questions, a lot of them. We have no doubt he's working with the Gallowglass."

Oscar snarled at the mention of the terrorists. They believed themselves to be freedom fighters, working to liberate their precious Scotland. Just as his forces infiltrated the North, they waged a secret war against his rule. Unlike the peasants they sent, his operatives were putting themselves into place to destroy Scotland from the inside.

"Brother Vincent, how often have you believed you found their spies?"

The man dropped his head, the stench of defeat radiating. Oscar rested his hand on the back of Vincent's head, his fingers sliding along the smoothness of his scalp. The man's skull fit in the palm of his hand, and with enough force, he could collapse the Parietal bone. Even if his fingers weren't strong enough, Oscar had become more than comfortable with his other skills.

Vincent groaned as Oscar tore at the thoughts, eliminating his usual graceful intrusions. Just beneath the surface, he caught sight of the Scot standing on the roof. Vincent offered him the chance to take his own life, but he fell to his knees, unable to jump to his death. The satisfaction of reducing his captive to nothing more than a captured animal excited Vincent. Oscar wondered how much of his arousal was genuine and how much from the suggestions he received during their encounters.

"It's time," Vincent whispered.

Oscar watched as a woman across the lobby shoved her captor inside the elevator. In minutes, he'd join the other eleven bodies swinging from the balcony. How long did they leave them dangling like rag dolls? As the bodies rotted, did they cycle them out? He didn't dare search Vincent's mind for answers. There was only so much depravity he could tolerate in a single day.

Instead, Oscar let go of Vincent's head, wiping his hand along his jacket. Stepping from his body, Oscar reached out to the man in the elevator. He wanted to discover his secrets. If Vincent was right, the man could have useful information. For a second, Oscar saw through the man's eyes as he pleaded with the woman escorting him to his demise.

The man pushed Oscar away.

"No," the telepath whispered. He imagined himself flying from the balcony, slipping through the cracks of the elevator and diving head-first into the man's chest. The visual had proven effective in the past, but the man inside somehow kept him at bay. That had only ever happened with the—

"He's a Child."

"What?"

"Your prisoner isn't human."

Oscar watched as the woman pushed him along. He attempted an escape, but one of Vincent's minions fell the Child. Even the weakest of Children held dangerous abilities. Oscar watched as the man strung the noose around his neck. It was only as they removed the cuffs around his wrist that Oscar realized the technology he supplied Vincent's men was the same used by the Knights. Without knowing it, they had captured and neutralized a Child.

"Did you say he's a Child of Nostradamus?"

Are you worth being saved, Child?

Oscar let his thoughts drift across the lobby, imagining he whispered the words in the man's ear. He might not be able to enter his mind like Brother Vincent, but he could still speak with him. Even without entering his mind, the fear poured off his body like cheap cologne.

The woman's palm slammed into the man's chest, sending him toppling from the balcony ledge.

Save me.

The panicked words slammed into Oscar, as loud as

if they were being screamed. He wrapped his fingers around the balcony railing. Squeezing, he thought of the thousand ways a Child of Nostradamus could serve him. How had he evaded the Knights? Was he one of the Gallowglass? There were questions that needed answering, and instead of doing their due diligence, Brother Vincent and his lot were more obsessed with purifying London than protecting it.

The rope tightened and the man's body swung about. The change in direction would have snapped his spine. He dangled just beneath the first floor, swinging back and forth, his body limp. There were no screams, no cries for mercy. One moment, his thoughts screeched in terror. Then nothing.

The room filled with cheers as the onlookers celebrated another victory.

"Dammit," Oscar said.

"Did you say he was a—"

"What's this?"

The dead man's limbs twitched. Seconds later, he flailed, reaching for his neck. He had crossed over, vanishing into the darkness. But somehow, he continued to fight.

Oscar stepped back as the man's eyes opened. He pulled at the rope. Even if he survived the snap of the neck, he fought to breathe. Oscar had to decide. Who served as the stronger asset? Did he risk his plan for an uprising for a single man?

"Brother Vincent," Oscar whispered, "kill yourself."

Without question, Vincent reached into the back of his pants and produced a handgun. He opened his mouth, shoving the barrel as far as it would go. He didn't blink as he pulled the trigger. The back of his skull exploded, forcing Oscar to turn his head as blood splattered across his face.

This faction of the Long Watch couldn't live to expose his newest ally.

"Kill each other," he hissed.

Patches' body convulsed.

The energy rolled along his skin. His entire body burned as his gifts diffused the snapping motion from the rope. If he concentrated, he might push the fire into his shoulders and arms, but he panicked as his lungs begged for oxygen.

A bang startled him back to the present. They attempted to murder him, but by the grace of Nostradamus, he survived. Reaching for his neck, he clawed at the rope, his nails scraping at the fibers.

Something struck the rope, and the tension vanished. The air whipped past him as he finished the last ten feet of his descent. Hitting the floor, he continued pulling at the rope until he loosened the noose. Chucking the rope, he opened his eyes.

Carnage erupted in the hospital lobby.

One of the jury had a knife in his hand. He slammed it into the chest of a nearby woman. With a turn, he held on with two hands, yanking it free from her ribcage. She crumpled with a gurgle of blood. When he turned about, he spun the blade in his hand. His eyes held no fear as he dragged the serrated blade across his throat. He hit the ground.

Patches ran his hand along his neck, the impressions of the twisted fibers leaving an indent in his neck. Had he died? Even the electrocutions hadn't left him feeling this sore. He struggled to keep his stomach from tightening. Bile rose in his throat and he was about to—

A gun fired from the balcony, and it appeared there was a similar fight between the Long Watch. It only lasted a minute before the lobby of the hospital turned quiet. Nowhere did a member of the group of bigots remain standing.

"What the hell?" Patches didn't want to stay to find out what madness had gotten into them.

"There will be more," a voice called from the stairs. "We won't have much time."

The man coming toward him wore a uniform. His importance could be counted by the medals adorning his chest. Patches didn't trust the man, nor the scene that unfolded around him. Were they blanks? Did they put on a show so he'd run again, only to find out this had been another depraved act?

"Who are you?"

The man's buzzed head and wide shoulders said military. He appeared like somebody who had spent a lifetime serving. Patches let the fire in his muscles pool in his fist as he prepared to fight his way from the hospital. He wouldn't hold back, not if it meant being free. If he had to pulverize the man—

"We need to get out of here," said the man.

Patches flinched as another shot fired, the bang echoing in the lobby. "What happened?"

"Their greed got the best of them." It wasn't an answer. But right now, searching for answers meant staying in the hospital. Patches wanted to thrust the fire into his legs until it gave him the speed of an Olympic runner.

"Who are you?"

The man's eyebrow raised as if it was a foolish question. "You're not a Brit?"

"American," Patches said. "You haven't answered my question." He reached across his torso, finger hovering just above his watch. The next words out of the man's mouth decided if he lived.

"Oscar," he said. "Prince Oscar, next in line for the crown."

"The queen's abomination," Patches whispered. He had spent the better part of a month learning the attitudes of the people. There were few who favored the replicant's ascension. Those who remembered the original prince found this version to be an abomination. Even those who tolerated the man's existence didn't want him to sit upon the throne.

"So I've heard," he said. "We need to leave. When they don't report in, the Long Watch will send more. Unless you're in the mood for a fight, we shouldn't be here when they arrive."

There were few humans capable of challenging the Knights of Winchester. The rumors of animosity between the prince and the Knights flooded the pubs as if it were a poorly kept secret. He didn't have time to decide, but anybody who held disdain for the empire's Children, they were an ally. It might provide him with the information he needed to find Skits. Perhaps this man had answers.

Patches turned toward the bank of locked doors. Without the cuffs, he'd tear them off their hinges. Freedom waited for him a hundred feet away. He'd be back at the house within an hour, and he'd be able to go back to normal.

Normal. He touched the rope burns. "It'll never be normal," he said. They had broken him, pushed him to where he and death were on a first-name basis. Even if he returned to Eve and Alyssa, he'd never be able to put into words the creeping sense of dread. He had died.

Into the belly of the beast he went. "Lead the way," he said. There was no returning to the quiet life of a librarian. He didn't know what it meant, but he wouldn't rectify this growing unease surrounded by books. He said farewell to freedom, to a life he never had a chance to live.

Chapter Twenty-Two

2039

"What happened here?" asked Eve.

Alyssa grew tired of having to make sense of madness.

Even with Blue's feet stomping through the hospital lobby, it had an eerie quiet that only came from abandoned buildings... or graveyards. Alyssa froze at the sight of the first bloodied body on the floor. One body led to the next until it blurred into carnage. Blood splattered across the white tile, red enough to suggest a recent massacre. Wicked men dying horribly didn't warrant a second thought.

Her eyes traveled up, and she froze. Much like the mass grave, these sadists took pride in their savagery. Eleven bodies, hanging from the third-floor balcony, waited to be liberated. With each atrocity, her hope for a brighter future slipped away.

"What fresh hell..." The ride from the academy to the hospital had been quiet as they attempted to fight off the imagery of the grave. But with dirt under their nails,

there would be sleepless nights before the horror became
a memory.

"More righteous men," Alyssa said.

Eve drew back her foot and kicked a corpse. The
body slid through its fluids. Alyssa's eye raised as she
spotted a glint of metal on the man's neck. She feared
with the men dead, they had lost their lead. But the very
technology they believed made them superior also made
them liabilities.

"It's another dead end."

"Not yet."

"The dead can't speak."

Alyssa didn't claim to be talented with technology.
She left the computers at the Tower to Ned. But after
watching over his shoulder, she'd learned a thing or two.
Thankfully, Eve's rage had offered another solution.
"But they can. If he has a data port, he has a processor."

"And?"

Alyssa spun the bag hanging on her shoulder until
she retrieved the Data pad. If it hadn't been for
Antoine's trick the other night, she might not have
thought about using the processor like this. It might
have saved them trouble had she considered it for the
man who led them to the academy.

"This is going to take a few. Blue, stand guard
with—"

"I'm going to look for survivors."

They both knew the likelihood of survivors was non-
existent. Eve's determination to fight against the darkness
snaking its way under her skin gave Alyssa hope. She
prayed for a victory, anything to restore a sliver of faith,
hope that not all was lost. If not for her, then for Eve.

While Eve wandered away, Alyssa kneeled next to the man. Her knees squished as they slid about in the blood. No matter how hard she scrubbed in the shower, it'd never wash away the grime of today. But the thought of being coated in the man's blood was the straw threatening to break the camel's back. She knew the dry-time of blood and the way it congealed. The good news was they weren't far behind whatever happened here. They were getting closer.

She pulled a cord from her Data pad and plugged it into the man's neck. If she were lucky, she'd be able to access the last few minutes before somebody shot him. With how things were going, she expected little. It'd be another in a string of unfortunate events.

After a minute of pounding away at the screen, she wanted to scream. It had been years since she felt helpless. As she kneeled on the floor, fighting against despair, she thought of her parents. Killed in a car crash, she found herself in a similar position inside her house as grief threatened to consume her. For most of her life, she remained stoic, a woman with a plan forward. The universe robbed her of the confidence she'd spent a lifetime building.

Blue's feet thudded as he approached. The servos in his knees hummed as he knelt on the other side of the body. He weighed a ton and could decimate a room full of people in seconds. He reached over, plucking the Data pad from her hands in a delicate way she'd have never imagined.

"Blue, what are you doing?"

Skits joked Blue was more than a synthetic, that he was as alive as either of them. Alyssa loved her friend's eccentric manner. She'd talk to him for hours, carrying on a conversation as if the robot responded. Skits walked a fine line between self-entertaining and lunacy, or so she thought.

Blue held the Data pad in one hand while he placed the other against the glass. She grimaced, expecting him to break the computer. The screen flashed several times, objects moving quicker than her eyes could follow.

"Are you..."

Before she finished the statement, the Data pad was linked to her contacts, and she was no longer kneeling on the floor. The dead man was looking about the room, observing his co-conspirators. She couldn't be sure about the timeline or when the shooting would begin. But as he looked up to the third story, she let out an audible gasp.

"Patrick."

It had been days since seeing him, and she had all but given up on finding her ward. But as he walked across the balcony with a woman pushing him from behind, she nearly cheered. She almost yelled for him, hoping he'd hear her voice speaking through the dead man.

"Oh no," she whispered.

As the dead man admired the bodies dangling with nooses around their neck, she realized the fate that awaited Patches. She almost pulled at the contact lenses to inspect the bodies in real time. Had she not seen him hanging? No, she would have spotted him, and Eve would have sworn vengeance.

The man rubbed his hands together, growing excited as the event approached. Alyssa watched as seconds dragged out, wondering why Patches didn't toss his captors to the side before fleeing. Either he chose to stay, or they prevented him from using his abilities. Genesis Division worked tirelessly to create technology that could inhibit their powers, but last she heard, they were months away from success.

"Lillian," she cursed the mega corporation's president. It wasn't the first time the woman kept secrets. It'd be addressed when she returned to the Tower.

Patches attempted to flee, but another man subdued him with ease. It confirmed that they had found a way to nullify his powers. She'd worry about technology capable of inhibiting their abilities—

"No," she cried out.

Patches flipped over the balcony, falling toward the lobby floor. She tried to take a step forward but nearly fell over. As she placed her hand in the tacky fluids, she remembered that what she saw wasn't real. Patches' body jerked, snapped, and then nothing. The asshole had the audacity to give the performance a golf clap.

"They killed him," she whispered.

Suddenly, gunfire erupted. She prepared to jump to her feet when the man staggered. He pulled out a handgun and started firing. Alyssa held her breath, waiting to see if he landed a killing blow on his attacker. But instead of firing at a person, he took aim at the rope. Through his eyes, she watched as he narrowed one eye. The dead marksman missed.

"What?"

Alyssa nearly yelped as Patches' body convulsed. The man took another shot, and it struck the rope. Patches fell, but before she confirmed his survival, the body she occupied jerked violently. He attempted to turn and point the gun at his attacker, but he didn't manage a shot before he died. As his body collapsed, she watched one of the Long Watch fire into his body again.

"Killed by one of your own? Curious," she said.

As her vision returned, she stood, wiping her hands off on the man's jacket. Something about the situation left her filled with questions. But for now, those questions could wait. Patches lived.

"Something's wrong," Eve whispered.

She studied the woman on the ground, the gun in her hand still pointing toward her chest. While they had shot the big guy in the lobby multiple times, this one had a single shot in her chest.

The hospital hadn't been used for its original purpose for years. The gurney had been tossed in a pile along a wall, discarded and unused. Dust had settled along the floor, and none of the assholes had considered cleaning. There had been enough foot traffic to give away dozens, if not hundreds, of footprints. They weren't a ragtag group of concerned citizens. They had transformed into an army.

Eve pulled the gun from her hand, noting that it was turned inward. After a second of pulling at the magazine, she tore it free. It had all but two bullets, and with one in the chamber, Eve raised an eyebrow. An attacker hadn't shot her. For some reason, she had taken her own life. It seemed out of character for people who believed themselves superior.

"What happened here?"

Tossing the weapon on the woman's chest, she turned her attention to the massive doors that had been installed along the hallway. One had been left open, and all but one were empty. Inside the makeshift cell, a woman lay against the back wall, blood covering her face. Eve almost walked away when she saw the splatter on the wall. She hadn't been shot like the others. The prisoner had bludgeoned herself against the cement.

"They killed themselves? Why?"

The hospital held an eerie quality, as if at any moment a loud crash would break through the silence. Every step she took echoed, and her breathing sounded like a deafening roar. She stopped worrying about a random terrorist attacking and feared their lingering ghosts would jump from behind a door.

She left their prison ward and ventured up the spiral staircase in the lobby. Reaching into her boot, she pulled a knife free, preparing to cut down the bodies. From the third story, she could see a growing number of dead bodies below. It was impossible to tell what had unfolded, but it had been chaos. The bigots had gone insane and attacked one another. There was something at play she couldn't identify.

She focused on the true victims. There wasn't a place to bury them inside the hospital, but at least she could offer them the dignity of not swinging for all to gawk at. Eventually, law enforcement would check the space, and hopefully their families would find peace.

Approaching the first rope, she gripped the knife. Whoever would do this deserved a painful death. After the academy, she hoped to find one of them alive. It wouldn't be punching and kicking to stay alive. When she pinned them to the ground, she wanted to wrap her hands around their necks and squeeze. When their eyes rolled back, she'd give them just enough air so they could see her face again. She'd deal with the remorse later. Right now, she wanted to see their light go out.

Stopping with the knife on the rope, she growled. That thinking was the very reason she had grown angry with Alyssa. She couldn't be mad at the woman for turning into an assassin when she was prepared to walk the same path. Internally, she tried to convince herself that it was different. If they labeled her a killer, it'd be for a good cause.

The rope snapped, and the first of eleven bodies hit the ground. When she reached for the fourth rope, she peered over the edge and saw the next one didn't have a body. On the floor, she spotted the noose, torn apart.

"Patches," she whispered. Hope. It dwindled in a sea of darkness, but it reminded her why they had come. She prepared to move on when she heard a scraping noise. Holding her breath, she listened intently, hoping to hear Patches' Scottish accent.

"Patches, are you there?"

As she rounded the corner, she spotted two bodies on the floor. A man had crumpled over, a gunshot to the forehead. A woman with bright neon-pink hair rested on her stomach. Eve was about to step around her when the woman's arm shot out, dragging her along the floor.

Eve's eyes went wide. With lightning speed, she dropped to the ground, flipping her over and straddling her chest. With the knife pressed against her throat, Eve prepared to sever her head from—

"Jasper?"

In a city of millions, it couldn't be a coincidence the only resident she knew was amongst the bodies. Her fingers tightened on the blade.

"What's going on? What are you doing here?" Eve

leaned closer as the woman's eyes fluttered open. She didn't make eye contact, instead groaning as she came to her senses. "Were you following me at the club?"

Eve leaned in close enough to feel the woman's breath on her face. The knife pressed against her skin, drawing a sliver of red. "What the fuck is going on?"

"Eve? What—"

With an ounce more pressure, Jasper inhaled and held her breath. Eve hardly remembered the girl from the club. Instead of the talkative partygoer, a sinister woman capable of hanging people had replaced her because of their country of origin. Had she known, perhaps killing her at the club could have saved one of the deceased.

"They killed each other. They shot—" Jasper's voice turned to panic. "They shot themselves. It's like they were mind controlled."

Eve leaned back on her heels and Jasper tried to scoot away. With a pivot, she pinned Jasper underneath her knee. The woman wouldn't get away, but there was something more worrisome. The Children of Nostradamus told stories of a bogeyman, one who nearly destroyed the world. Those old enough remembered, and at the heart of every story, was a maniac capable of controlling people with nothing more than a thought.

"Telepaths," Eve hissed. "It seemed he did us a favor by stopping the Long Watch."

"No," Jasper said as she tried to sit up. Eve pushed her back to the floor. The woman winced in pain. She held onto Eve's wrist, trying to pull herself upright. "They were tying up loose ends."

"Interesting," Eve said. As much as she wanted to

believe there were heroic telepaths out there. It seemed being able to read the minds of every human made them cocky and more than a little mad. Jasper was more than likely right, at least about this.

"Who are you?" Eve shoved her back. With her hand on the woman's sternum, it'd only take leaning forward to make it so she couldn't inhale. Eve fought the temptation.

"You're going to answer my questions. If I don't like what I hear, I'm going to remove a finger for every dead Scot. But Eve, there's eleven, you say. I guess that's when I kill you."

No matter how much she cooperated, Eve planned to remove at least one finger. Even if she answered every question, the conversation would end with her screaming for mercy. Then there would be decisions about how she died.

"Gallowglass."

"English, please."

"I'm a Glaswegian. The Gallowglass, they're the underground resistance. We were sent to infiltrate the Long Watch." She might have questioned her words, but she shared a thicker version of Patches' accent.

"You killed your own people?"

Jasper's silence spoke volumes. Tears rolled down her face. Either she deserved an award for acting, or her story had credit. Had Jasper done it for a greater good? Is that what she told herself as she lay awake imagining their faces? Eve didn't care which side of this war Jasper favored. She had murdered innocent people.

"We're losing." She bit back a sob, her voice growing quiet. "My people are dying every day."

Eve imagined the knife sinking into the girl's neck.

She could take a life and avenge the men and women strung about the hospital. It wouldn't bring them back, but it was the only thing she could do for them. Spinning the knife in her hand, she brought it to Jasper's chest. With a single thrust…

"Eve."

She held still, refusing to turn and make eye contact with Alyssa. With one word, she gave Eve pause, enough to see she had already pierced the skin above Jasper's sternum. A tiny red dot formed, a dot that moments ago she wanted to see pool into a puddle. She wanted revenge, but Jasper told the truth. She was nothing more than a wayward freedom fighter. The irony of Eve's rage toward the woman was not lost on her.

"You're his friends," Jasper whispered. "You're Children. He… is he alive?"

"He's alive," Alyssa confirmed.

"Alyssa." Eve's lips quivered as she spoke. "We have bigger problems. I think there's a telepath on the loose."

There was silence. When Eve glanced over her shoulder, she caught a moment of horror on Alyssa's face. Buried trauma came bubbling to the surface.

"It's happening again," Alyssa sighed.

No Child alive could hear of a rogue telepath without worrying there was another disaster coming. They weren't all bad, but when one man committed genocide, it made it hard not to lump them together.

"We won't let it happen again."

"Prince Oscar," Jasper said.

"What about him?"

"He supplies the weapons to the Long Watch. He was here. I saw him when Brother Vincent shot himself."

"Do you think... the prince is a telepath?" Eve looked over her shoulder to see Alyssa's face. The woman's steely gaze didn't give away her feelings on the matter. That, on its own, was telling. Inside her mentor, a turbulent storm brewed.

"Where are you going?" Jasper asked.

Eve slid the knife into her boot and stood. Reaching down, she offered a hand to the woman. She didn't have to agree with her. In fact, right now, she hated the woman more than the misguided bigots slaughtering Scots. At least they weren't sacrificing their own. But their mission was about to change, and they'd need allies, even if they weren't good people.

"I will follow your lead," Alyssa said.

"Save Patches. Then we kill the prince."

Words Eve never expected to say.

"What happened back there?"

In the back of the black SUV, Patches sat next to Oscar, surprised by the man's calm demeanor. He escorted him from the hospital into the vehicle, where a driver waited for him. There were no words spoken as they peeled away from the building. Patches kept turning in his seat to check that the hospital had long since faded from view.

In the tight space, Patches couldn't be subtle as he rubbed the spot where the noose had tightened about his neck. For several seconds, the world had turned black. He tried to come to grips with the idea of dying. Had they killed him? Did whatever deity on the other side thrust him back into his body? Never had the librarian grappled with an intimate knowledge of death, and now he wondered if there was a God watching over him.

"Factions within the Long Watch have become turbulent. It seems somebody didn't like how things were being run."

Patches' nose scrunched up as he caught a whiff of himself. While trapped in the cell, he hadn't worried about his smell. Now, sitting next to royalty, he realized just how disgusting they made him. Between the vomit and urine, he had reached a level of offensive no human should experience.

"Wait. Why were you there?"

The prince reached inside his jacket and pulled out a beefy handgun. He adjusted the holster, sliding the weapon back into place. "The people of the British Empire may not like me, but I am sworn to protect them. Whoever pulled the trigger first saved me the trouble."

"Oh."

"Between you and me, I wish I had gotten the satisfaction of at least one of them."

Patches had been their prisoner, taunted and tortured until he welcomed death. He had imagined a thousand different ways to kill them. But as the thoughts crept into his head, he threw down mental barriers. He could hate them, but there was a line in the sand he refused to cross. Hurt them, yes, but he had seen more than enough death in the last few days. They didn't deserve his mercy, but it would have been a final act of defiance.

"Where are we going?"

"Back to the palace. I want the head of the Knights to hear about your experiences. The tech…" Oscar eyed Patches' wrists. "It belongs to the Knights, and I have concerns about how it fell into the Long Watch's hands."

Patches rubbed his wrists. It made sense that the technology belonged to Children. Did they find a use for cuffing their own kind? He wondered if it had been another invention belonging to Registry. Alyssa talked about Children with powers wildly out of control, and it could help bring a sense of normalcy to their lives. But somehow, he doubted the Knights had the same altruistic intentions behind the invention.

"Your Knights are supplying bigots with technology to kill Caledonians?"

The prince flinched at the mention of the North. Patches didn't expect the man to be passive about a war. There was no point in being naïve, but at least he didn't correct him. Could there be a reluctant ally in the man? The son of the queen must know something about Skits. If Eve were here, she'd strong-arm him until he relented and supplied her with a location. He shook off the idea. How would Alyssa handle the situation? That was more his speed.

"Magus has no love for Scotland. It borders on pathological at this point. If he had his way, he'd wage a war that left them in chains."

"And you?"

Prince Oscar leaned back in his seat, pondering the phrase. "I want to see my country unified."

Patches studied the man's face. His jaw tightened at the statement. He might not be lying, but it was obvious that his words were carefully chosen. Patches didn't trust him, not in the least. He owed the queen's abomination for saving him, but this was the same man who declared the French heretics. The people of London didn't respect him and openly defied his future rule. Patches couldn't neglect the opinion of the people.

"Magus has the queen's favor. He whispers in her ear, but once she discovers he's in league with the Long Watch, perhaps she'll listen to reason."

Patches threw caution to the wind. "Isn't she your mother?" Could he unnerve the man and discover his intentions? He half expected the driver to slam the brakes and the prince to shove Patches from the vehicle.

"Our relationship is complicated. She has defended my right to the throne, as our traditions demand. But, like the rest of the empire, there are questions. There has always been resentment at the sight of my progenitor's face."

Progenitor? It was an interesting way to refer to the man they had cloned him from. Patches had never seen a photo of the original Prince Oscar. Were they identical? Were there any aspects of the two men that differed?

"You have questions. Don't beat around the bush."

"Are you really his clone?"

"They say the queen's son died in a tragic accident."

"You don't believe them?"

"I forget the naïveté of those not raised in a palace."

Patches fought the eye-roll. Was the man so removed from the commoners that he forgot what average life was like? How could the man expect to lead if he didn't understand the lives of his people?

"We refer to it as court intrigue. But it's more like a constant sparring match. Allies and foes shift allegiances for their own gain. It's not outright hostile, but it can be the difference between success or failure. When you're the queen's son, a tragic death is never as simple as an *accident.*"

"Who would kill him?"

Oscar snarled. "My mother's kin have never

expressed interest in ruling. No, there's only one man with the gumption and the resources to challenge my ascension."

"The Knights?"

Oscar nodded. "He's a tyrant in the making."

Patches had a thousand questions. Most of them would reveal his lack of knowledge about the British Empire. He bit his tongue, not wanting to anger the man before he asked about Skits. Even if he didn't know her whereabouts, he had the resources to find her.

"Screw it," he started. "I came to London to find—"

An explosion shattered the windows. The world spun as the SUV smashed onto its side. The driver screamed as his body tumbled from the side, to the roof, and then to the other side of the vehicle. Patches couldn't make heads or tails as he slammed about in the car. He clobbered Oscar before wrapping his arms around the man. Patches protected the man's head the best he could, absorbing every impact as he went.

Metal screeched along the pavement as the vehicle slid to a stop.

Patches shook his head. The burning came in like a flood, pouring itself through his skin, waiting for an outlet. It wasn't the worst he felt, but he wasn't far from reaching the threshold where he'd need Registry's gadgets.

"What happened?"

Oscar didn't respond. The man was shaking his head, wiping his eyes, trying to recover from the blast. Patches crawled over him and slammed his palm into the door. It tore from the vehicle, sheering to one side. There was no point in being subtle, not if it meant dying.

Smoke surrounded the SUV, and parts were scattered

across the street. The wind pulled at the gray mist, revealing a man kneeling in the intersection with something on his shoulder. Nearly a block away, four more people emerged between parked cars, each of them holding weapons.

"It's the Long Watch," Oscar said. "They've found us."

Chapter Twenty-Three

2039

"It's the Long Watch," Oscar said. "They've found us."

As Patches grabbed his hand, he attempted to push at the man's mind. Frazzled and disoriented, he hoped to break down the barriers that protected the Child. Still, his defenses held fast. But the worry radiating off him came with a sour taste. He wasn't as confident as he portrayed.

Patches pulled him through the door. "How'd you tear it off?" Play dumb. Let the man come to him. Oscar had sowed the seeds of doubt. Telepathy wasn't his only skill. They had bred Oscar to be the best at political intrigue.

"Surprise," Patches said, "I'm a Child of Nostradamus."

"What?" Play stupid. The false sense of security had done its job perfectly. The worry came with anger, a bitter hatred that nearly choked Oscar. He only needed a suggestion, a direction, and he'd get a demonstration.

"They will not let us go," Oscar said.

He let his thoughts drift outward, touching the

minds of their attackers. With a suggestion, he could repeat the scene from the hospital. They would turn on one another and seconds later, they'd be free. Instead, he reached into their thoughts and pulled at their rage. For reasons they couldn't identify, their hostilities focused on Patches. Oscar prepared for a spectacle as they attempted to kill the man.

The Scot slammed his right foot on the ground. The second time he did it, the pavement cracked under his heel. Something moved along his right fist, the skin vanishing under a sheen of metal. He wore gauntlets similar to those he had seen on the Knights of Winchester. Perhaps he had more in common with his mother's guard than he first assumed.

Oscar considered challenging Magus for years. As the leader of the empire's military force, he thought about sending in their elite teams to eradicate the Knights. But he admitted their superiority on the battle-field. Without numerous casualties, they'd decimate his ranks, and then they'd come looking for blood. Then, even the queen couldn't protect him. War against the Knights would leave the empire in shambles. Now, he had an ally, somebody untainted by their years of condi-tioning. But first, he needed to see if the man stood a chance against the head of the Knights.

Kill him.

Patches moved with speed, impossible for a man his size. He dropped his shoulder and stampeded toward the man with the rocket launcher. Each step launched him ten feet forward. As the man stood, Patches slammed his shoulder into the man's gut, launching him twenty feet into the air, before slamming against the hood of a car. A woman whipped her arm to the side, her arm splitting down the middle. A blade flipped from her forearm, unfolding until it was nearly as long as she was tall.

She swiped, not moving as fast as the burly man. He ducked underneath, and smacked her arm, bending the metal at the elbow until her arm turned useless. Dropping to his knee, he held up the palm of his hand. The light flared and a burst of energy scorched her chest. She didn't scream as the second blast incapacitated her. All that time and money acquiring enhancements and she didn't last more than a few seconds against Patches.

"Impressive," Oscar muttered.

As another man stood behind the Child, his chest opened, and a small gun with three barrels rolled out. Their trips to the Body Shop gave them state-of-the-art weaponry, but it still bordered on comical how they integrated it into their bodies. He fired three shots, jerking Patches' head forward. Oscar held his breath. If bullets killed the man, then he wasn't—

Patches turned slowly, unbothered by the shot. "Impressive, indeed." He'd need to inquire about how his powers functioned to better understand the man's worth.

He spun about, his fist striking the man's neck. His head folded over as his body flipped through the air. Patches fired from his mitt, the shot catching the man in the torso.

When the woman approached, it was laughable by comparison. No enhancements about her. She wielded a crowbar like a club. Patches held still as she pulled back and struck his arm. He remained frozen as she wound up, and this time struck him across the jaw. Neither strike moved the titan. Pulling the weapon from her hand, he threw it. The crowbar vanished into the sky, but that didn't stop her from throwing a punch.

With a smack from the back of his hand, the woman sailed into a nearby building. If she survived, it'd be a miracle.

It was down to the last man. Unlike his companions, he contained more hardware than he did original organic parts. Seven feet tall, the muscles in his chest threatened to tear open his vest. He growled, even his voice sounding digitized. Oscar remained mesmerized by humans willing to cut away their flesh to be the fastest, strongest, or most powerful. But at least now, he'd see Patches in action.

"Traitor," the man yelled.

Unlike before, the force of the man's punch jerked Patches' head to the side. When he kicked the Child in the stomach, it sent him reeling. Oscar bit his bottom lip, reminding himself he couldn't cheer the man for pummeling the Scot. When Patches held up the glove, the man's arms transformed, forearms widening like bracers. He threw up his arms, the blast doing nothing more than irritating the man.

He drew back his fist, preparing to slug Patches again. But this time, the Child caught his hand. The man tried to pull away, but Patches' fingers sank into the metal. He used him for leverage, slamming his fist repeatedly into the human's metallic face. Just when Oscar thought he might deliver the killing blow. The man's chest parted and a blast of energy struck Patches, launching him into the side of a car hard enough to fold the vehicle in half.

The Child of Nostradamus didn't move. Oscar listened carefully for his thoughts, but found his mind silent. The man thumped his chest like a gorilla, turning about as if adoring fans might shower him with flowers. But the few Brits watching the fight scurried away. Oscar prepared to tear at the man's thoughts until he was nothing more than a gurgling mess.

"That all you got?"

Brazen, Oscar thought. When Patches let a smile spread across his face, Oscar rallied. It appeared as if the young man was more powerful than he expected. But there was still one test remaining. He needed to know if Patches could finish his opponent—*at any cost.*

Kill him, now. Oscar found it surprising how little nudging he needed to provide members of the Long Watch. Their nationalism made them terrifying. Brits opened their doors to watch the fight. Oscar thought about hurling innocents at the Child for good measure. But he decided not to jeopardize the lives of his citizen unless required.

Patches held up his gloved fist. A laser struck the man's forearm shield. When it did nothing, the ray intensified. The red LED turned a brilliant white, and seconds later, the man's forearm and shield fell to the ground. Patches flexed his hand, and the gloves vanished, receding into his watch. Oscar made a note of the man's tech, something that seemed foolish considering his abilities.

Patches pushed off the car, launching him twenty feet into the street. His knee nailed the man in the chest. He slid backward, the toes of his shoes kicking up asphalt. Even with a single hand, the man tried to punch Patches again. The metallic limb closed around his throat. When Patches didn't respond, the man let go, confused at how to stop the Child.

"Kill him," Oscar whispered.

Patches didn't seem to tire from the exchange. Did it have something to do with his powers, or was he generally a powerhouse when it came to trading blows? It didn't matter, so as long as he took the next—

Patches grabbed the man's head, and with a fast spin, he killed the man. Instead of letting him fall over and tumble to the ground, Patches kicked him backward. Lying in a heap, Patches stood over the body. The glove covered his hand again, and this time, three bursts of energy left the man's upper body scorched and kicking up plumes of smoke.

Oscar gasped at the abrupt silence. The rage from his compatriots was replaced with something even more seductive. He manufactured their emotions, heightened thanks to his prodding. But the sheer anger radiating from the Scot had grown intense enough that he nearly suffocated. He might not penetrate the Child's mind, but as he loomed over the remains of the last of the Long Watch, Oscar didn't need to read his mind.

Already, his thoughts raced with the possibilities. There were only two people standing between him and the crown. His mother he could control, but the other had proved more wily. But now, he had a weapon that promised to turn the tide.

"Magus won't be able to stop me," he said.

"If she attempts to escape," Eve barked, "kill her."

The weapon on Blue's forearm sprung up, and he held his arm at face level with the woman. The laser would kill her and cut through the back of the truck. Overkill, but it got her point across. Eve didn't quite know what to do with Jasper at this point. From here on, she improvised the plan.

They had found a moving truck old enough to not have GPS. Jasper and Blue sat in the back while Alyssa sat in the driver's seat, waiting for direction. She had been fired up and ready to beat the shit out of anybody who crossed her, but as her adrenaline waned, logic fought for dominance. But every path forward she considered came with strings and impossible odds.

Alyssa had stepped back and offered Eve the ability to lead. But in doing so, she spiraled at the endless options. She considered storming the palace and committing an act of war against the British Empire. Would the Free Republic come to her aid? She had only met President Twenty-Seven once. The others spoke of her as if she was a great warrior, but Eve only saw a politician who never said what she meant. Most likely, the president would hang them out to dry to keep the peace.

She ran her fingers over a button on Eleanor's jacket. The psychic had seen countless possibilities and somehow navigated her way a century into the future. Eleanor had pushed and pulled each of them in the hope of reaching an unknown outcome. Had she seen this moment? Did the psychic know the best possible future? Eve understood why Dwayne and Conthan cursed the woman as much as they admired her. Understanding a psychic could be maddening.

"There isn't a solution," she whispered.

"Victory isn't linear," Alyssa said. The woman rested a hand on Eve's thigh, squeezing it gently. "Leadership is often weighing bad options against other bad options."

"How did you do it?" Eve whispered.

"I think we both know that my decisions continue to reveal unintended consequences."

If Eleanor had seen this path, how did she know it was the best outcome? Had she needed to see another alternative? Ten? One hundred? Infinite? Eve turned in her seat to see Jasper engaged in a staring contest with an eyeless Blue.

"Where are the Gallowglass?"

"What? They're not—"

"They didn't leave you to act on your own. You report to somebody."

"Well, yes. But—"

"Where are they?"

Eve needed more information. Her impulse control begged to take over. She'd break down the doors to the palace, and if they were lucky, they wouldn't die within seconds. Without knowing more, she didn't expect to make it very far, and even if she did, what about the Knights? She'd nearly died taking out Nexus. They had bred their Children to fight. No, even she admitted that dying by stupidity wasn't a smart choice.

"Blue. If she doesn't answer in three seconds, kill her."

"You wouldn't."

"Two."

"Fine," Jasper growled. "They're not going to like this."

"Good. Cause I already don't like it." Eve turned around in her seat, fastening her seatbelt. She waited for a moment. "One."

"Head to Westminster."

"What's your plan?" asked Alyssa.

"We need intelligence and allies."

"Rebels?"

Eve nodded. Despite the weight of the world pressing on her shoulders, she couldn't help but smile. She might have decided, but it was based on a story that she once heard around the dinner table. "If I remember correctly, didn't you find yourself in a bunker once with an arrogant hacker?"

"You have the tenacity of an Ayer and the cunning of Cowan. Here I thought our stories made you… how did you put it? Wanting to jam a fork in your eye?"

Eve had repeated that phrase every time the adults revisited their glory days. They spoke about it as if there had been nothing but triumphs. It was only once guests left, and the lights were shut off, that she heard her fathers recollect the names of those they lost. At the time, it bored her to tears. She'd never hear the end from either father.

"I'll apologize for being crass when we celebrate."

"They'll be proud of you, Eve."

Eve pointed forward. "First, let's give them something to be proud of."

Jasper cleared her throat. "How familiar are you with the Church of Nostradamus?"

Chapter Twenty-Four

2033

Even Ceann listened when *she* summoned.

The Knights stationed with the queen roamed Buckingham, a skilled detail with perfect timing. Their movements bordered on robotic, confirming each of them had implants, allowing them to communicate without words. In the eyes of the queen's human sycophants, they were the most elite of the Knights. But for Ceann, he pitied those who lacked even the ability to think for themselves.

"She is waiting." Barrier stood at seven feet, a hulking woman fitting her name. Her gray suit stood out against the ornate gold filigree of the hallway's wallpaper. He couldn't imagine why the queen insisted on meeting with him in her home instead of Parliament. He couldn't put his finger on it, but something about the summons felt off.

"Any idea why I've been summoned?"

"No."

Ceann didn't bother asking the woman additional questions. Unlike the rest of the Knights, this branch of their order was committed to only the queen, and ready to sacrifice their lives for her safety. He wondered what they thought about the recent cries from the people for her to name a successor. Did Barrier's unit have the ability for independent thought?

They reached a door, and she turned, facing Ceann. She scanned his body slowly, pausing at his belt.

"They relieved me of any—"

"Your belt."

The woman didn't leave room for discussion. Ceann unfastened the belt cinched about his waist. As he unfastened it, he saw the blade that served as a buckle. It had gone undetected through the scanners, but whatever technology replaced her organic eyes, it had seen the sharp edges.

Ceann surrendered the belt.

"I will be waiting." The statement came as a threat and a promise should he make a wrong move, she'd terminate him. Opening the door, she stood to one side, gesturing for him to enter.

Ceann entered to one of the most powerful women in the world reclining on an ornate sofa while holding a delicate white teacup. Behind her, Oscar took his time inspecting books on a shelf. Neither made a move to acknowledge his presence as he stood at attention in the doorway. The queen blew her tea before sipping to test the temperature.

"Ceann, please sit." She gestured to a matching armchair sitting opposite her.

"Yes, ma'am."

She continued drinking her tea as if the problems of the world couldn't penetrate the walls of her home. Ceann suspected that might indeed be possible. Despite the centuries of history within the palace, he had spotted the technology interwoven in its corridors. No, the woman wasn't helpless. In fact, he believed this nothing more than a ruse as she studied him.

"Speak your mind." She returned the cup to its saucer. Her clothes were elegant, but modest for the wealth at her fingertips. Crossed ankles and hands resting softly in her lap revealed years of finishing school. But not even the healthiest human reached her age without the aid of science. Behind those eyes, technology pumped through her veins, leaving Ceann curious as to what other enhancements she might hide.

"You're studying me, ma'am. Tactical assessment."

The lines around her lips deepened as she smiled. "I suppose I am. I've read your reports, Ceann. Your file is filled with accolades. For every promising statement, there is another detailing your inability to follow orders. Quite the paradox?"

They had properly educated him on how to behave in the presence of Her Majesty. He refrained from speaking until she granted permission.

"Knights and your pageantry. Be done with it, child. Speak." Her command defied her age.

"I serve the crown," he said. She wanted him to speak his mind, one of the leading reasons he knew the programmers by name. "I serve as a slave. There are no handcuffs, no bonds the eye can see. But they exist just the same. I serve Her Majesty. You can have my body, but this..." Ceann tapped his temple. "Not even the Knights have broken me."

"Talented *and* arrogant. It seems to be a trait amongst your people." Oscar slammed the book shut, the crack louder than necessary. He slid it on the shelf before standing behind his progenitor's mother. "You're more like them than you'd think."

"Hush, Oscar." She waved at him, shooing him away as one does a child. Ceann found the simple gesture far more familial than he expected between the two. Their public appearances told a narrative much different from the one playing out in front of him.

"Do I detect an accent? Highlands, perhaps?" she asked.

Ceann had little doubt she knew his heritage. They had mapped his lineage back four generations to study the Nostradamus Effect within families. Heritage had become a sore spot as tensions continued to rise between the crown and Caledonia.

He tried to recall the faces of his parents. There were no memories of them, and even when his imagination attempted to fill in their features, their faces remained blank. Even his accent had diminished over time, or so Nexus reminded him at every opportunity.

"Aye."

"Perhaps our ancestors were once neighbors." Six words revealed a fact unknown to the rest of the world. Had the Queen of England confessed to having Caledonian blood in her veins?

"Mother," Oscar chided. "Some truths should remain hidden."

"I am the most powerful woman in the world. Hell, the most powerful person. Let the unwashed masses whisper about our lineage. Commoners have nothing better to do than gossip about their rulers."

Ceann noted her ability to go from casual conversation to reminders about her station. The queen hadn't conquered the European Nations without ruthless ingenuity. He couldn't hide the smile. He nearly laughed as he realized the woman wielded her age as a disguise. Beneath the wrinkles and slow movements, there was a cunning that kept her in power.

"Ceann, it's funny you should mention being a slave. Neither of us chose these roles. As a youth, I wanted nothing more than to escape the prim and proper ways of royalty. A girl born into a patriarchy. I did not choose my husband. Much like you, I defied my elders."

"Your Majesty, the similarities are superficial. Are you aware of the life of Knights? The torture? The dehumanizing—"

"I watched my son murdered to prevent the lines of succession."

Ceann bit his words. The official word had been a German assassin had been sent to murder the entire royal family. While he killed her son and husband, she had gotten away.

"My husband was a terrible man who did horrific things. I would like to think it didn't impact me. But as I slid the knife across his throat, there was satisfaction in watching the light in his eyes diminish."

She reached for her cup, taking another sip as if she hadn't just spoken of treason. She spoke openly, making a claim that could galvanize the people and give credence to the rebels in Caledonia. Either she believed him insignificant, or that he would never utter these words to another soul.

"He was a bastard, but he had given me Oscar. I overlooked his tyranny. But nothing is more dangerous than a woman seeking revenge. If only he could see Oscar now."

"We have an offer for a man known for his ferocity."

They were prepared to buy his silence. It came dangerously close to politics. If he refused and asked to return to his post, either of the people across from him could have him killed. Even if his powers made it impossible, they'd simply bury him in a box in an unmarked grave, left to rot for eternity.

"You're buying my silence?"

Oscar joined his mother, taking a seat by her side. He laughed, a condescending sound that filled the study. Even his mother smiled at the confusion. Ceann couldn't quite figure out the game, but he understood he was being played.

"Not your silence, Knight. We are offering your freedom. If you complete this, we will have you removed and your records scrubbed. You'll be left to your own devices, free from servitude."

"An offer never given to me," the queen added.

Ceann said nothing, wanting his jailers to lay their cards on the table.

"There is a growing menace in the States," Oscar started. "We want him terminated."

"Lux is known—"

"I know of your resident assassin. We need a Knight we can motivate."

"Control," Ceann corrected.

"Ceann, I don't have many years left in this world. I have spent my life ensuring the safety of my people. But there is a threat that has gone unchecked for too long."

"Shouldn't it be left to the Americans?"

"They're infants playing make-believe. Their inability to deal with their own corruption will spill into the rest of the world. And I have no intention of letting my son inherit a broken world."

Ceann let his face go slack at the statement. The woman was anything but a fool. But admitting that Oscar was indeed next in line to wear the crown put Ceann's life in jeopardy. A secret that important to the well-being of Great Britain, they'd kill him should he refuse their offer.

"I do this task, and I walk away a free man."

"Free," the queen assured.

"Who is the target?"

"Jacob Griffin."

"Why?"

Oscar shook his head. "Everything you need to know is on this." He pulled a clear glass screen from his pocket and pushed it across the table. "Nothing more, nothing less."

Freedom. He had never entertained the possibility. He had spent years making a name for himself as one of the most terrifying Knights of Winchester. A legend used to scare children. Was it possible for the King of Monsters to walk away? Could he shuck the horrors he had seen, had caused, and lead a life of normalcy?

"When do I leave?"

"Speak with Registry. He'll make sure you have transportation and enter the States undetected."

Ceann leaned forward, reaching for the phone before the queen rested her hand on his. The woman's eyes had hardened, no longer the casual woman who attempted to lure him into a false sense of security. From the side of his eye, he watched as Oscar's lips moved and the queen spoke.

"Fail your mission, Ceann, King of Monsters, and you'll find yourself at my mercy. I will kill you without hesitation."

She withdrew her hand, allowing him to take the phone and slide it into his pocket. He stood, nodding his head. They couldn't be trusted, not with the information they had given him. But for the first time since he killed Feral, he held hope.

"I expect nothing less."

Chapter Twenty-Five

2039

"A church?"

"It's an Abbey," Jasper corrected.

"In name. It hasn't housed an Abbot in years." Eve turned around in her seat to give Jasper a snarl. Were all Caledonians this arrogant, or was she lashing out because Blue held a gun to her head?

"So you're not just a pretty face."

They parked close enough that Eve had to strain to see the entire massive building. Unlike the surrounding buildings, it stood out with its spires and intricate brick-work. A block over the buildings lacked the attention to detail. Here, it was easy to spot the natives. They walked with a purpose, hardly looking up from their feet.

"Children have an uneasy relationship with a religion that idolizes us as deities," Alyssa said. "How does this relate to the Church of Nostradamus? I thought the monarchy had outlawed it."

"Caledonia has found an ally in the church. Whether we agree with their beliefs is beside the point. We treat them with respect, and in return, their networks have helped us infiltrate key positions throughout the city."

"That's how you got the position at the palace?" Eve said.

She had wondered about the connection, and now it fell into place. These Gallowglass people were moving themselves into spots throughout the government, biding their time until they were called upon. Eve wanted to ask if there was already a plan in place. Disrupting the infrastructure? Terror? Killing?

"Will there be hostiles?" Alyssa asked.

"Blue, wait here. We'll come back when it's safe."

"I'm being escorted by two unknown women. What do you think?"

Alyssa leaned back in the driver's seat. Her eyes blinked quickly and seconds later she turned to Eve. "Ready?"

"Already searching."

Eve opened the door and hopped out of the truck. She didn't wait for Alyssa to bring Jasper. Crossing the street, she ignored the hundreds of people strolling about London. She imagined that once upon a time this area had been busy, filled with tourists wanting to see ancient structures in the middle of the city. With the borders all but closed, only the residents passed by, and none of them seemed overly concerned with a single woman or the abbey occupying their neighborhoods.

Tapping her ear, she turned on the communicator. "Read me?"

"Five by five."

Eve didn't worry about Alyssa. Her mentor had probably stormed a church in her days abroad. For her, this was a typical visit to a foreign power. But for Eve, storming a church would go on the list of things she never expected to do. But after burying bodies and cutting down corpses, she had something to prove. Just the thought of the victims tightened her chest. She needed that anger. Tonight, it served as fuel.

The abbey walls were thick, and unlike the rest of the city, it served as a dead zone. There were a million interactions with the electromagnetic fields, but inside the church, it was almost peaceful—Almost.

Standard electrical ran through the walls, outlets and lights, mostly. The power rolled off her until she walked with closed eyes. As she focused, it was as if the world lit up and an imaginary image of the church formed. Instead of bricks and timber, she watched lines spread their way through the night. Inside, she searched for the densest sources of energy. Nearly a dozen people moved through the abbey. None of them seemed out of sorts, maids and janitorial staff going about their business after hours.

She almost missed it. Scanning the rooms, she found a conduit drawing more electricity than anywhere else in the building. It vanished into the floors, and— Eve's eyes shot open as she stood at the massive doors to the abbey.

"Nothing."

"What's that?"

"There's something under the church. But I can't feel it. It's a void."

"No sledgehammers," Alyssa said.

It was code to rely on stealth. For the Sentinels with abilities that made them brutes on the battlefield, it served as a reminder that subtlety had its place. Eve touched her collar, letting the electricity run through her suit. Once she zipped up Eleanor's jacket, she pulled at the door, breaking the lock before entering. She left the door ajar for Alyssa and Jasper while she did the recon.

Inside, she proceeded into the main hall. Even at night, lights dimly shone across the nave. The walls were massive, spanning stories. If the war ever ended, she'd have to convince her father to teleport here to admire the architecture. Moving toward the back of the church, she followed the vibration of power being pumped beneath the building.

"How do I access the basement?" Silence. "Alyssa?"

She turned back to see Alyssa at the door with Jasper. Her mentor waved her forward. That a church disrupted communication devices shouldn't come as a surprise. If there was a resistance inside, it'd make sense that they'd have precautions against people violating their base of operations.

Eve inched closer to the back of the church, her foot scraping across metal on the floor. She dropped to her knee, touching the grate. She prepared to tear it off when the church went silent—no, not silent, dead.

"What the hell?" The vibrations vanished. There were no more electrical currents flowing through the building despite the lights remaining on. She hadn't experienced a silence like this since her powers first manifested. The white noise of the world had been deafening at first, but as she learned to control it, it remained a constant hum in the background. But now, it was as if the entire planet held its breath.

"Leave, and I won't have to hurt you."

Eve smiled. Challenge accepted.

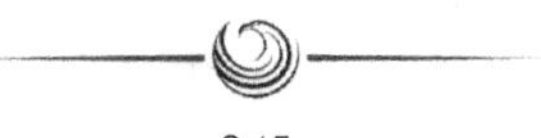

Patches stared in the mirror with ornate trim. He spent an hour in the bathroom washing away the grime and inspecting the rope burns on his neck. When he returned to his room, they had laid a garment bag out on the bed. He had never worn a suit before, especially not one that fit him with such precision. Even the turtleneck struck him as deliberate, high enough to hide the red marks under his jaw.

A knock at the door tightened his muscles. "Calm down."

Before he could answer, a gentleman in a suit with tails entered. His lack of hair reflected the light from the chandelier. "Is there anything I can help you with before dinner?"

"Dinner?"

"Do they not eat where you come from?"

Patches couldn't decide if the man was making a joke at his expense or if the words were sincere. He took the man at face value.

"How do I look?"

"Like a fine gentleman. It fits perfectly."

Patches' eyes went wide, and he dashed over to the bed. Scooping up small silver cufflinks, he approached the butler with a bit of embarrassment. It was bad enough that his entire apartment could fit in the bedroom, or that the mirror probably cost more money than he'd make in a lifetime. But being unable to dress himself? That's when he couldn't disguise the blush.

"I've never had cufflinks before."

The butler escorted him to the mirror and started sliding the cufflinks into place. Once he finished, he flattened a crease and adjusted the shoulders. The butler stepped to the side, revealing his reflection. A fine gentleman might be a stretch, but he was more formal than he had ever appeared in his life.

"Have you worked for…"

"Her Majesty," the butler whispered. "Once you've been introduced, address her as ma'am."

He might need the man to stay close by for the duration of the evening. "Have you worked for *her* for long?"

"My adult life. My father served her father. It's a point of pride for my family."

"Is she a good person?"

The butler didn't immediately respond, which meant he opted for an honest answer and not the one he had rehearsed. "She is a fair woman. It has been an honor to address her needs during her reign."

"Thank you," Patches said. "I guess it's time I make a fool of myself."

"If she smiles, she's being cordial. If she grins, she's being sincere. It's a lesson that has served me well."

"They don't pay you enough," Patches said as he followed the butler from the room.

As they wound through the maze-like halls, Patches kept stopping to inspect the paintings. Many of them were older than the United States and held a quality that made them look elegant to the point of being gaudy. The palace held more artifacts than most museums, and each one of them screamed money. He wondered if the monarch dictated what to put on display or if it was inherited as a family tradition. He had a thousand questions that he'd need to meter when meeting the queen.

The butler held up his hand at the door, halting Patches' approach. He opened both doors and stepped to the side with a bow. "I present Patrick Kilgannon." Patches cringed at the sound of his name, both because nobody called him that and they had done research on their guest.

He puffed out his chest, sucked in his gut, and walked into the room. The dining room had at least enough chairs for fifty people, but all remained empty. At the end, nearest the door, the queen sat alone with a modest spread of food in front of her. Had one of the most powerful women in the world not occupied it, he'd have laughed at the formality.

The doors closed behind him, preventing a quick retreat. He crossed the room as he debated how to introduce himself. Was he supposed to kneel? Did he offer a handshake? She stood and decided for him as she offered a hand.

"It's a pleasure, Your Majesty."

"The pleasure is all mine." She gestured to the chair to her left. "I owe you a debt of gratitude for saving my son."

"He already paid the debt. I owe Osc— Prince Oscar for rescuing me from a dire situation."

"So he told me. Oscar has a knack for finding trouble. That boy will be the death of me." She gave a slight laugh.

Patches sat down while he studied the woman. She was well over a hundred, but it'd be hard to tell how many years beyond. The technology in this country seemed years beyond the Free Republic, and with it, who knows how many birthdays she'd see. She lifted the spoon from her soup while Patches held his hands neatly folded in his lap.

"Where are my manners? I've asked the staff to leave us be. I hope you don't mind serving yourself."

"Ma'am, this is already nicer than the paper napkins

at my house. It smells absolutely delicious." It had been days since he ate and he had to slow himself. Otherwise, she'd believe him boorish.

"I hope you don't mind if we talk business while we dine."

Patches ladled what appeared to be chicken soup into his bowl. "Where I come from, we'd normally gather around the television while we ate."

"I've done that as well. But don't tell anybody."

"Like anybody would believe I had dinner with the queen."

Patches froze as he inspected the two spoons to the right of his plate. If he knew anything of the woman, he'd risk it. But with tension and uncertainty mounting, he feared even the most innocent mistake could cause an international disaster. He'd have eaten with a fork if there weren't four to choose from. How did royalty view slurping?

"Work from the outside in. I had that beaten into me as a child. I claimed one spoon could be used for an entire meal. Let me tell you…" She raised her spoon to her lips and sipped her soup. "Father was not happy."

"It sounds tedious."

"The responsibilities of the crown seem to require me to know the difference between a salad and dinner fork. To the best of my knowledge, it has yet to start a war."

Patches bit his tongue. A joke about war while her country persecuted two countries? Either she was oblivious or sadistic, and after his week, he found it telling about her personality. He sipped soup from the correct spoon, savoring the taste of the broth as it flooded his mouth.

Noting the plate across the table from him, he

wondered if Oscar intended to join them. "Is the prince coming?"

"He sends his regrets. My son is attending to his military duties this evening. I thought it only appropriate that a Child of Nostradamus meets his British equivalent."

The queen tapped the table, and for a moment, Patches thought she might have a tremble. But as the screens expanded, he discovered the massive table was nothing more than a computer monitor. He had been enamored with the age of the items; he hadn't thought they'd be new. The deceit had him wondering if the theme translated to the people as well.

The doors opened, but there was no butler to introduce the man. He shut his own door as he walked toward the table. Unlike the queen, there was no handshake as he stood next to the empty chair. With a nod from the queen, he took his seat without a word.

"Patrick Kilgannon, this is the leader of the Knights of Winchester, Magus."

"Champion of the queen," he added.

"That's a mouthful," Patches said, but neither the queen nor Magus found it humorous. He returned to his soup before he wedged his foot further into his mouth. The prince spoke ill of the man. Patches thought this was the perfect opportunity to discover the truth behind the man's hatred. Not just that, but he wanted to find out why the man supported the Long Watch.

"They informed me that you saved the prince."

Patches caught the man staring. He must have been approaching fifty, but the silver hair made it hard to pinpoint his age. He allowed the stubble to cover his face, revealing a mix of salt and pepper. But it wasn't the man's weathered face that struck him as interesting, it was the suit he wore. In a safe house in London, Patches had a nearly identical one stored away. The borderline superhero costume offered another bit of proof that Registry had been here before being freed by Skits.

"Mmhmm," Patches said, trying not to open his mouth while he ate.

"The crown—"

"Owes me a debt." Thanks to the man across the table, Patches had experienced the worst week of his life. He delighted in stealing his thunder. "Her Majesty already mentioned it."

"I thought a Child and Knight would have plenty to discuss," the queen said.

Magus leaned forward, resting his elbows on the table.

"Elbows," Patches said, surprised that the queen grinned. "I have plenty of questions."

"As do I," Magus said.

"Inhibitors. Smart move." Despite the man's warning, she stood. She should have erred on the side of caution. But she wanted to provoke him, to do anything that would give her reason to collapse his ribcage and drive his sternum into his heart.

His sleeveless hoodie made him look homeless, but it showed off his arms. He was a large man, with enough muscle to show that he worked out, but not so much that he lived at the gym. Even the shaved head and stubble of his beard said that he took care of himself, but not that he tried hard. Everything about him appeared calculated.

"Don't say I didn't warn you."

She ducked as a fist swung overhead. Kicking her foot back, the man caught her heel and attempted to spin her leg so it'd pop out of joint. With a push, she spun about, slamming her heel— He blocked with a forearm. Eve landed on her butt, already rolling backward into a crouch.

"Points for improvisation." His tone didn't mock her as much as it stated the obvious.

Eve wrapped the anger around her like armor. Jasper had taken part in the execution of those Caledonians in the name of the greater good. Whoever she answered to had given her permission. Not only did it not sit well with Eve, but it also left her skin itching as she vibrated with rage. They might need allies, but somebody had to pay for these crimes.

Eve tried to summon her abilities, to hurl them against the man, to scramble his internal battery. She flung her hands forward, relying on them to focus on her powers. There was nothing, no tinge of what made her a Child of Nostradamus. She'd curse Genesis Division for ever making power inhibitors. Thankfully, she spent years training her body in spite of her gifts.

He held his position, his toes changing direction as he attempted to predict her next move. Eve didn't want to disappoint with a lack of improvisation.

"I'm having a bad day." She reached her fingers through the grate and spun on her knee. Releasing the metal, it whipped through the air.

He moved quicker than she expected. If she had her abilities, she'd be able to pinpoint his enhancements. For now, she'd have to assume he had gotten upgrades and paid a premium to avoid scarring.

Punching remained an option.

She sprung forward, attempting to drive her knuckles into his throat. One moment he was there, and the next, he spun out of the way and slapped her on the back of the head. Dropping low, she attempted to sweep his legs out from under him. Hopping over her foot, he brought up his knee, prepared to drive it under her chin. She caught it, and instead of stopping his momentum, she used it to stand upright, smashing her elbow across his jaw.

She spun, bringing her right hook to clobbering his ragged face. Blocked. She shot a left jab forward. Blocked. Despite the change of tactics, switching feet, and moving between punches and kicks, it appeared the man predicted the future with each counter to her attacks.

He slowed with every block. Keeping at it, she wanted to wear down his servos and ride him until his battery drained. Even if she wasn't landing a solid fight-ending strike, she could keep going until his she broke his forearms. Then she'd have no problem beating the shit out of him.

"Enough," he yelled. But she wasn't done, nowhere near close to it. Every punch was for the bodies she covered with fresh earth.

Cupping her hands together, she stepped into the swing, twisting her body to add extra oomph. When he attempted to block her, he misjudged her strength. The enhancements didn't stop her anger. Her attacker stumbled backward and fell to the ground.

He tried to scramble to his feet, but she was on him.

She slammed her palm in the space between his shoulder blades, putting him onto his belly. Raising her heel, she prepared to slam it on his neck. Regard for his life vanished. Eve wanted to hear the bone break. There'd be justice as she left the body on display for the entirety of Gallowglass to see.

He rolled out of the way as her heel broke the stone. Swinging about, he snaked his legs between hers and used her weight to knock her off-balance. Unable to adjust her feet, she landed on her ass with a thud.

The man moved with speed, impressive even for the enhanced. He straddled her waist, arms trapped beneath his legs. She attempted to buck her hips, to throw him, but he rode her like a bronco. When she attempted to snag his head with her legs, he leaned forward, making it impossible. He could easily strike and break her jaw or collapse her windpipe. But he made no move to kill her.

Eve cursed herself for falling victim to a man with a rudimentary knowledge of fighting. But when Alyssa came into view with Jasper in tow, she prepared for her mentor to tackle the man. Between the two of them, he wouldn't be able to outrun or outfight them. Her muscles tensed as she prepared for another round beside Alyssa.

"Long time no see, Alyssa."

"Preacher." Her mentor nodded. "I wish we came under better circumstances."

He clamored to his feet, no longer concerned with Eve. What had happened? The man's muscles eased, and Eve suppressed a growl. This wasn't how she intended the fight to end.

"Have our kind ever known better circumstances?"

Alyssa offered a hand to Eve, pulling her off the

floor. Eve had listened to a thousand tales from every Child of Nostradamus about the Warden's uprising. But none of them had mentioned the name Preacher. Was he another of the Knights with their need for superhero monickers?

"I should have guessed you'd be at the center of this resistance."

When he stepped closer to Alyssa, Eve expected the woman to take a step back. The thing she valued most was her personal space. But she held firm. Just like that, the exchange turned intimate. Eve's eyes widened as she realized the implications.

Eve brushed off her ego like the dust covering her pants. Knowing that he and Alyssa had a past somehow made the lack of victory sting less. Eve wanted to believe her mentor had trained him and that was how he'd bested her. The lie would work for now, but eventually, she'd start beating herself up for letting him get the best of her.

"Who is this?" asked Eve.

"Eve, meet Preacher," Alyssa said. He unfolded his arms from his chest, reaching out to shake her hand. Eve snubbed him by not returning the gesture. Childish, she knew, but her pride got the best of her.

"Should that ring a bell?" she asked.

"You'd better know him as the Warden's son."

"What is a Child of Nostradamus doing in London?"

"Tourism," Patches said. The niceties had ended, and it was time for them to get to the heart of the matter. However, Patches refused to partake in the roundabout manner Magus used to interrogate. "Let's stop the smoke and mirrors. Ask and you might—"

"Is this an assassination attempt?"

Patches nearly choked on his quail. "No. This has nothing—"

"You murdered officers."

"As I was saying…" Patches had nearly died, or maybe he did die, and he hadn't dwelt on his reality. But as he tapped his foot, the energy rippled along his muscles. With his abilities at his call, he didn't fear the Knight. Dying had made Patches calm, and he wielded the composure like a weapon. "I never expected to see the queen, though it has been lovely."

The grin returned. She might respect Magus, but she also took joy in how much Patches frustrated the man. He needed to keep a tally.

"As for our officers?"

"Our countries aren't so different. Law enforcement here also likes to bully innocent people."

"And so, you killed them?"

"I defended myself."

"Murder is still murder."

"You want to discuss murder?" Patches dropped the fork onto his plate and pushed it to the side. The man across the table had supplied his kidnappers with the technology that kept him imprisoned. "Let's discuss the militia that kidnapped me off the street for my accent. They kept me locked up until they were ready to hang me."

Patches pulled down the collar of his shirt, revealing the burn marks. The queen didn't seem thrilled with the accusation, but Magus hardly made a face.

"Surely a Child of Nostradamus could free himself."

Unlike Magus, the queen's voice held concern. If she faked it, she was a master of politicking.

"I could have, ma'am, if it weren't for technology used by the Knights of Winchester that turned off my abilities."

"Magus?" The genuine surprise in her voice was comforting.

Even Magus had been surprised. "How do you know—"

"I recognize Registry's technology." Patches watched as the man's lip quivered. He had no love for the liberated Knight, so much that it nearly broke his steely facade. Patches pressed on.

"Eleven Caledonians—"

"Scots," Magus corrected.

"Caledonians," Patches repeated. "They hung them from the balcony, celebrating as their necks snapped. Your people, Your Majesty. Brits. They're murdering in cold blood like domestic terrorists."

"Is this true, Magus?"

"Technology has gone missing from the Knights. We're aware of it and dealing with the situation accordingly."

Patches grew tired of the man's deflections, so much that he fought off a yawn. It had been days since he had a night of restful sleep. At this rate, he might collapse at any moment. He longed for a bed where he could bury his face in the pillows.

"It's not simply missing. It's being given to them. They're bold tech junkies scouring the streets for anybody not like them. Bigots run the streets of London."

"How dare you?" Magus' fist slammed on the table. "You speak ill of the queen with—"

"Pardon my next words," Patches said with a nod to the queen. "I highly doubt she oversees her streets. Our president doesn't see to the public's safety. This reeks of somebody abusing their position. Suspicious that they have ties to the Knights."

"The audacity!" Magus stood, the force knocking over his chair. "I could have your—"

"Head?" Patches pulled the collar down again, standing and leaning over the table so Magus could clearly see the bruises. "They already tried. It didn't take." The anger in the pit of his stomach tempted him to jump over the table. "Did I get too close to the truth? Angry you've been—"

"The Knights of Winchester are honorable and uphold the values of the crown. Can your Children say the same?"

"Honorable? Was Nexus honorable when he attacked Troy?" Patches didn't want to talk anymore. It was useless when Magus believed the rhetoric he spewed. He had dealt with bullies his whole life, and Magus was no different. "If I hadn't killed him, we could ask." He barely recognized the words coming out of his mouth.

"Nexus and Lux dissented."

"Sounds like a common..." Patches fought off a yawn. The last several days were catching up with him, and he struggled to maintain the adrenaline rush. "... problem."

"It appears we have lengthy conversations ahead of us," said the queen. Patches wanted to believe she was innocent. She had been nothing but respectable. But how could a ruler be so blind? Patches found his lids drooping despite the anger.

"Your Majesty," he paused, searching for the right words. "Your house needs cleaning."

Patches dropped to his chair.

"He comes to sow seeds of doubt," Magus said.

"I have no doubt there is truth behind his words. But until we have this sorted, he's best secured with the other American."

"Skits," Patches whispered. His muscles had transformed into dead weight. He couldn't suppress the yawn. This wasn't fatigue. They had— "What did you do to me?"

"The soup took longer to take effect than I thought. But I am impressed you withstood the sedatives for this long," she said.

"But you drank…"

"Technology is a wonderful thing. Poison used to be a constant fear."

Patches tried to slam his foot on the floor, to call on his powers, but his body refused to obey. He could see, but it appeared as if he were watching through a camera lens. Fighting with his eyelids, he found himself losing the battle. Neither the queen nor Magus reacted as the world turned black. Once again, he'd allowed himself to be the victim.

"This is becoming familiar," Alyssa said.

Sitting at a makeshift table beneath the abbey touched upon her nostalgia. Not long ago, they had sat at a similar table beneath the streets of New York City.

Just like then, Preacher had been at the heart of a rebellion attempting to fight oppression. It seemed the themes were the same, only the accent had changed.

As she stared at the man across the table, she could see the crypts behind him, plaques describing who lay within. To their side, a tomb sat as high as the table and she tried not to focus on disturbing their rest. It smelled of cool earth, but behind that laid the scent of decay. Nobody should be able to detect the smell of decomposition, let alone have the vocabulary to describe the sweet, acrid taste it left on the back of the tongue.

"How is Ned?"

At the mention of his name, her mind focused on the smell of his cologne. Ned claimed to be the leader of the rebellion. But she knew that Preacher and he shared the title. As Needles, Ned caused problems for the Warden, breaking into his computers and agitating the people to action. But it was Preacher who trained the troops, arming average citizens with the knowledge necessary for an uprising.

"He is well," she said, fighting to stop the heat rising in her cheeks.

Preacher stopped rubbing the stubble on his head, and an eyebrow raised to almost comical proportions. He smiled. "This brings me joy. I am happy for you."

"How the hell are you the Warden's son?" Leave it to Eve to break a sentimental reconnection with her inability to read the room. Thankfully, Preacher never shied away from answering for the sins of his father.

"The Warden was both a telepath and a Child of Nostradamus. We'll never understand it, but his gifts allowed him to disconnect his consciousness from his body. For a time, Ivan Volkov inhabited my father's body. He became known as the Warden."

"This is like a comic book," Eve said.

"Unfortunately, it is. A woman named Ariel rescued me. She was one of my father's mentalist research subjects. We escaped to the Outlands, where I was raised. Later, Ned and I…" His words trailed off.

"The rest is written in history," Alyssa said. She avoided explaining his involvement and how he had been present during Ivan's final moments. Eve had heard how Conthan killed Ivan's host, Preacher's father. She did not feel the need to put his pain on display. But as she stared into his eyes… he had yet to make peace with his past.

"Is that when you became Preacher?" asked Eve.

He let the tension out as he chuckled. "It's a nickname given to me by Ned. He said the digital revolution required codenames. Apparently, I have a knack for delivering advice. It's thanks to Azacca and his followers that it grew into something more."

"Adelaide?"

"Sister Adelaide," he smiled. "Is she well?"

"She thrives," Alyssa said. "She serves as our welcome committee at the Tower."

"Good. She deserves nothing but the best of life. But yes, she is one of the devoted."

"So you're a God?" Alyssa cringed at Eve's bluntness.

"No. In a time when faith in mankind reached a low, they needed something to believe in. Someone. They turned to the preachings of Nostradamus. You can thank Eleanor Valentine for bringing about this devotion to Children."

Alyssa often cursed the psychic. Had she known as she wrote those letters how she'd reshape the world? Did she see the rise of a religion based on her post-mortem involvement? But in the face of evil, people had needed something to lift them and drive them to action. For this, she'd be eternally grateful to the woman.

"With the Knights at the queen's disposal, we needed Children of our own." Jasper had sat at the table, keeping quiet, listening intently to their conversation. As she fiddled with her nails, it seemed as if nothing they said came as news. It meant that Preacher had become more comfortable telling his tale. Something about this warmed Alyssa's heart.

"Have you not seen enough war, Raymond?" The mention of his birth name made Jasper drop her jaw. He might have grown more comfortable, but he had only taken the first step on a lifelong journey. She didn't want to see the man continue to break himself, not after all he had endured. Reaching across the table, she rested a hand on his.

"I…"

"You have offered more than any man should. You've paid for the sins of your father. It's about time—"

"You haven't paid for the sins against the dead Caledonians." Eve's words were quiet, barely more than a whisper. "Who pays for *them*?" They might have been hushed, but they cut like a finely-honed blade.

"Evelyn Cowan," Alyssa barked. Never had she needed to use the woman's full name. The girl's words came from a place of anger. She still believed in a sense of right and wrong in the world, black and white. But in war, the two ran together and turned from gray to crimson.

"I'm going to get Blue." She stood, knocking her chair over. Shoving her hands into her pockets, she stormed from the crypt into the tunnels, leaving them in an awkward silence.

"Jasper," Preacher said.

"I'm not her favorite person."

"Please," Preacher said. Jasper nodded and walked out in pursuit of Eve.

He had indeed softened. Alyssa noticed it in the way he fought, controlled and calculated. Once upon a time, he had been an angry young man, and as time wore on, the anger consumed him. Then he became the Preacher, and Alyssa saw a man controlling his emotions, but not soothing them. He had an indomitable will, but he hadn't allowed himself the opportunity to heal.

"You've changed," she said, her fingers gripping his hand. "I can't quite explain it, but this isn't the same man who rallied the troops."

"I avenged my father, and for a time, that brought me peace. I expected Ivan's death to wash away years of guilt. But then I thought of the men and women who suffered because of him." Preacher stood, pulling his shirt over his head. He had covered his body in small black lettering. "These are their names, at least those I can recall."

"These are not your burdens to bear alone, Raymond." She reached out, as if she might read his body like braille. "Does this bring you peace?"

"For some of us..." He pulled his shirt over his head. "There is no peace. All we can do is seek an unobtainable redemption."

And like that, he cut through their pleasantries and spoke to her soul. If she didn't know better, she'd believe him to be a telepath. But as he returned to his seat, he held her hands, squeezing them between his palms.

"If we cannot obtain it, then why keep pushing forward?"

"We pay penance by assuming a burden greater than we should be capable of bearing. We do it because there are two young women upstairs who still have a chance at a future that isn't riddled with regret."

"I know you don't practice confession, but should you ever need it, I am here. From one soldier… no, from one survivor to another, I *am* here."

"Assalamu Alaikum."

"I see you," he said. "But while we have the room, tell me about the blush in your cheeks every time I say Ned's name."

Chapter Twenty-Six

2039

The lights flickered on, and Patches only wanted to roll over and go to sleep. It had been too long since his head touched a pillow. Nobody would deny him another hour under the blankets. Pillow… blankets…

Patches shot up, fists clenched. Yet again, he found himself a prisoner in a cell. Slamming his fist against a glass wall, he hissed at the pain. They'd nullified his powers yet again. It was official, he no longer liked Londoners. They could burn in Hell for all he cared. At least this time, they hadn't subdued him with a concussion.

"Careful, hotshot."

In the cell next to his, a woman sat on the edge of her bed. She wore casual street clothes, and even with her back to him, he could see she was small. But it was the matted neon-blue hair that gave her away. He had seen enough photos from Eve to know he had finally found her aunt.

"Skits?"

She turned, eyebrow raised. "Do I know you?"

Her eyes narrowed. There was no hiding her suspicions. If Patches hadn't studied the photographs, he'd fear she was a plant by the Knights to garner information. But it seemed she held the same worry.

"We've played this game before, Magus. If you think I'm going to talk—"

"Eve and Alyssa, they—"

"Dammit." She rolled her eyes and let out a long sigh. "Did they really come here to save me?"

Patches threw back the blankets and sat up. The world spun, and he feared he'd hurl. Unlike the Long Watch, this cell had a toilet, sink, and even a desk. He shouldn't have intimate knowledge about prison cell layouts and be able to rate them. His life had taken a plunge.

"You're welcome."

"I didn't ask for a rescue."

"Aren't you a delight?"

"I'm not leaving until I complete my mission."

"About that mission. That one where you tried to kill the queen and saved Registry? Fuck you."

"Who the hell—"

"Because of you, there are bodies in the ground. My first day at the Tower and people died. All. Because. Of. You." The rage from earlier carried over and there was no holding back. He fought through the dizziness, determined to make her understand the consequences of her actions. It'd take the rest of his life to unpack these events. But right now, he found the person who knocked over the first in a long line of dominos.

"Wait. You haven't heard, have you?" Patches pushed off the bed, staggering until he leaned against the wall separating them. "You're the reason people died. Innocent people."

"That's—"

"Shut up," he shouted. "Four people are dead because of you."

"I followed orders," she snapped.

"That didn't seem to stop Alyssa from leaving? She wised up. She's not to blame for dead Children. In fact, she was at the Tower protecting us. And you? Sitting here whining that you didn't kill somebody? Well, good news, you did."

Silence filled the cells. Skits didn't have a snappy retort to his words. He prepared a list of insults to hurl should she open her mouth. He'd rescue her because of his friendship with Eve. But he didn't have to like the woman and the choices she'd made. Unlike her, the line between right and wrong was well marked.

"I didn't ask to be rescued."

Her words lacked the animosity from before. Hearing her quiet, siphoned away an ounce of rage. He still wanted to yell and berate the woman, but it wouldn't make him feel any better.

"And I didn't ask to be hanged and drugged, but here we are. Be happy your family thinks more highly of you than I do." He might not be shouting, but he wanted to make sure his words cut.

"Hanged?"

"I don't recommend it. So, what's the plan?"

"Power dampeners. No locks to pick. The Knights of Winchester have had decades to perfect containment. Since I've been here, they have filled most of the cells with their cadet rejects."

"They put their own in jail?"

She let out a laugh. "Jail? This is a holding cell until we're sacrificed. They make the cadets fight their rejects to earn a position within the Knights."

The Tower seemed utopian by comparison. He wondered if there were cells there for Children who didn't align themselves with their values. Had Conthan ever had to fill them?

"Not much of a rescue," he admitted.

"Have you met Eve? If she's decided to rescue me, it's only a matter of time."

Dammit, the rage drained away with a single statement. Patches had to laugh at the description. He appreciated that somebody else acknowledged the woman's tenacity. "She's relentless. Has she always been like that?"

"That girl…" Skits pounded on the glass three times before giving up, "she learned it from her aunt."

"In that case." Patches tapped on the glass door. He eyed the lock, trying to figure out how it opened. "I say we get out of here."

"We're powerless."

"How far before the dampeners wear off?"

She shrugged. "I've been locked in here for months. I couldn't tell you."

He flicked his wrist and the metal of his watch flowed over his hand until it formed a gauntlet. Skits stood, suddenly onboard with his escape plan. He had never used the glove without a bounty of stored energy. Anything would be better than remaining trapped in another cell.

He hesitated, fearful that it'd turn into another trial, testing to see what horrors they could inflict. They had all but robbed him of the will to survive. Now the queen and Magus conspired to do the same. With every blink, the burlap sacks haunted him. Faceless Caledonians sacrificed because of Magus and his need for genocide. Skits targeted the wrong person. The queen might be a tyrannical ruler hiding behind the sweet grandmother act, but Magus was a butcher.

Revenge wasn't the healthiest motivator, but it'd have to do. They might have robbed him of his abilities, but they had been careless, thinking their prison unbreakable. Without the cuffs, he had access to technology.

"Arrogant pricks."

"What are you doing?"

"I came with more than powers." He closed his eyes as he pressed his palm against the lock. The blast knocked him backward, smashing against the desk and burning the skin along his fingers. He'd be dealing with burns, but it was nothing compared to the sensation of having his insides siphoned through a straw.

"What are you waiting for?"

"Oi," he barked. "She *does* take after you. Registry didn't design this to be used by humans."

Skits pressed herself against the front of her cell, looking down the hallway. In all the time with Eve, Patches never thought to ask about the woman's powers. If they cleared the cell, could she teleport them away? Or did she have some sort of scream that'd render the Knight's brain dead? With his luck, she'd be a Child with the uncanny ability to change colors.

Patches shouldered the busted glass, staggering through. His limbs turned sluggish, and he had to will them to move. As he held up the gauntlet, Skits rolled away from the wall, curling into a ball on the bed. The blast smashed through the glass and he fell against the wall. The first time might have been unpleasant, but the second, he swore his stomach was being crushed into a tiny ball. His skin grew cold and tiny pinpricks stabbed at his arms.

Skits kicked the glass until it came down in a sheet. "We need to run. Now."

"Go," he gasped.

He half expected her to give him a salute and then return to her mission. Instead, she threw his arm over her shoulder and hoisted him from the wall. His legs threatened to give out, and she grunted, supporting his weight.

"I see you're new to the Nighthawks. Nobody gets left behind."

The resemblance between Eve and Skits' determination had reached uncanny levels. She started down the hall, half-dragging Patches.

"Sentinels," he muttered. "We're called Sentinels."

"That's a stupid name. Let's go."

It was as if Eve spoke. He couldn't wait to see them in a room together. He just had to escape… again.

"Looks like he's not going to wait for your men," Oscar chuckled.

Oscar eyed Magus as they watched the projection of their prisoners escaping. This barbaric method of testing cadets before allowing them into Knighthood had become the norm. It surprised him when Magus took charge of the Knights that he didn't disband the tradition. Even though he remained an obstacle on the battle-field, he hadn't turned soft.

They had been an hour from sending Knights to release them from their cages when Patches proved himself resourceful. It helped that Oscar hadn't told him about the weapons the man carried or that they appeared similar to other devices used by the Knights. He enjoyed the surprise on Magus' face.

The situation had played out exactly as he expected. Alerting Magus to the man's presence in the palace proved an irresistible target. Oscar removed himself long enough for the Knight to conspire with his mother. Magus only gave credit to the conspiracy he had woven. Magus had become predictable, and convincing him to put the Children on display didn't require manipulating his thoughts.

"Do we know his abilities?"

Oscar shrugged. "Strength. Speed. He didn't flinch when shot. What about her?"

"Plasma generation. Her powers are well documented after the Battle for Chicago."

Oscar found it infuriating that he couldn't read the minds of Children. He wanted to hear if Magus found the man's resourcefulness impressive. Patches needed to survive the encounter with the cadets. If he managed that, then Oscar would have the ally he needed. But it wouldn't be just Patches. The girl had an axe to grind and who better to take out her aggression than on the man who imprisoned her?

"Deploy the cadets," he said. Somewhere, technicians released his hounds into the training facility.

Since Londoners protested a walled-off Croydon,

Nexus had moved their training facility to their headquarters. Oscar doubted the man's altruistic intentions. While he claimed it was to provide more housing opportunities for Brits, Nexus never cared about commoners. Oscar's network of spies suggested it was more so the order could slaughter cadets without the public's watchful eye.

Magus eyed Oscar. "By now, you're normally rolling your eyes. Why are you invested in this man?"

There was no point in lying. "I let my ego get in the way. I should have seen to the militia with a squadron."

"Foolish move, Prince."

"They were of no concern. It's the closest to battle I'll see during this war. I didn't think they'd regroup as quickly as they did. If it wasn't for him, I'm not sure I'd be alive. That Child saved my life."

"A debt?"

Oscar shrugged. "Debts are beneath us. But you can say I'm intrigued by a man who threw himself into danger. I'll try not to cheer for him too loudly."

Magus gave a slight laugh. "I thought you might sympathize with the man. That's why I sent my best cadets. Their powers should be enough to end the threat to your future throne."

The mention of the throne served as a warning. Magus had no intention of supporting his ascension to king. He pretended that the strength of the Knights would stand behind him. A fallacy that he attempted to lord over Oscar. He assumed his powered subordinates were necessary to protect the crown. Oscar refrained from laughing at the man's audacity.

Magus would discover the threat soon enough.

"Some rebellion," Eve said. "No guys with guns? Are you even trying?"

When Alyssa talked about the rebellion in New York, there had been hackers, Children, and a small army ready to stage a coup. Before they left the abbey, Eve counted four people. They claimed there were two dozen positioned within the city, occupying positions within the government. But when she demanded he call them for reinforcements, he simply said, "Force is not how you win a war." Eve had little faith in their subvert path to success.

"My family is fighting for their survival," Jasper said. "There aren't enough Caledonians to wage war. We have to be precise in our strikes. Sorry, we don't measure up to your American sensibilities."

They sat in the back of the truck. For the last hour, they waited for the guards to change shifts. Jasper continued checking her watch every few minutes. She seemed just as irritated to be here as Eve was to have her with them.

"That bad?"

Eve saved her rage for the men in charge. She didn't agree with Jasper or Gallowglass's approach, but after dwelling on it, she couldn't be mad at what she didn't understand. It didn't mean she forgave the woman, but perhaps it wasn't as black and white as she believed.

"They're starving my people. The power is sporadic, and there is a constant threat they'll taint the drinking water. The prince is vicious, and he doesn't care who suffers as long as he claims victory."

"Is what Preacher said true about the clans?"

"We take pride in our ancestry. It's kind of foolish if you think of it. But if it gives them hope, then so be it."

"Kilts and all?"

"You haven't met a man as ferocious as one who freeballs."

Eve's jaw dropped. Had Jasper made a joke? Or was she serious? It was hard to tell, and the idea of a small army of Caledonians wearing kilts as their junk swung in the wind made for a funny sight. She knew the northerners were bold, but even that caused her to nod, impressed.

Jasper doubled down. "No, I'm not kidding."

Alyssa remained silent in the front of the box truck, lying down on the seat to avoid prying eyes. She found it impossible to read the woman. After talking with Preacher, she had a renewed sense of calm, similar to her demeanor when instructing the cadets. While Eve thought about their talks, the resentment she felt for the woman washed away, stored for the people who made these terrible decisions necessary.

While Preacher assumed a nickname from the church, she hadn't believed him too big on faith, certainly not the way he appeared. But with one conversation, Alyssa exited with vigor and determination. Eve wanted to ask if this was a benefit of being around other veterans of Chicago. Did doing more than surviving after a war help pull each of them away from the dark place?

Eve stewed in her lack of understanding. When there weren't people to save, she'd need to reflect and digest her anger.

"You're sure they're in there?"

Jasper nodded. "Last report said both the prince and the head of the Knights were inside."

"That's not exactly a resounding yes." Eve prayed the information was accurate.

"It's time," Jasper said.

"Blue, you remember the plan?" Eve asked.

The synthetic's head turned toward her and didn't give any indication he understood. That was as good as a yes. "Alyssa, are you ready?"

"Yes." Simple and to the point.

Eve closed her eyes and imagined walking across the street. Inside the building, there was an abundance of electrical systems and people; each causing the magnetic fields to bend. Once inside, her abilities would be useless, but at least for now, she served a purpose. Blocking out the white noise, she could see the delivery door granting them access to the Knight's not-so-secret base. There were cameras, scanners, locks, and hydraulics protecting the door. She wanted to ask if the hardware was to keep out intruders or to keep their cadets locked inside. She feared the answer.

It became easier every time she did it. Reaching in, she pretended she tore at the waves like they were wires. After enough roughing about with the electronics, the power stopped flowing. The sudden vanishing of electronics most likely sounded alarms, but at least they'd have the element of anonymity. For all anybody would know, they came with a small army. Too bad their army consisted of four. Still, Eve didn't hate the odds.

"We're covered, and the door is blacked out."

Alyssa didn't reply as she tossed open the door and jumped out. Jasper and Eve followed, checking the street for any sentries guarding the building. The lack of human security meant they were reliant on computers and tech, or they were full of themselves. Eve would put money down that they thought nobody would dare violate their sanctum.

The building spanned several blocks and lacked the gothic architecture of other nearby buildings. She expected something grand like the Tower, but if Jasper hadn't identified it, they'd have driven by without another thought. The only thing that looked awkward was the absence of windows. She'd seen government buildings like it in the Free Republic. The people inside were nothing more than prisoners, isolated from simple joys like sunlight.

They crossed the street where the road veered downward to a loading back. Without power, they'd be relying on brute strength. It'd serve as a warm-up for what awaited them on the other side.

"Ready?" asked Eve. The three women jumped up onto the dock and squared off against the door.

Alyssa nodded, reaching to the bottom of the door. Wedging their fingers in, Alyssa and Eve grunted as they raised the back door. They made it a few inches before it jammed in place. She was about to call for Blue to help when Jasper joined them. It was cute that a human thought—the door lifted another foot.

"What the hell?"

"Never skip leg day," Jasper said, dropping to her stomach. She and Alyssa crawled under. Eve followed suit.

Inside it looked like a warehouse with shelving filled with boxes and large palettes lying yet to be unpacked. She expected there to be high-tech equipment or at least a mad scientist lab. But it was no different from the delivery room at a grocery store. Unlike the local market, this made her skin crawl with the number of electronics at work in the space.

"I'm blind," Eve said.

"Electronics are still working," Alyssa confirmed. Eve should have asked for a pair of the contact lenses Alyssa used. Seeing the screens might distract her at first, but the more she could see without her abilities, the better she'd be in a firefight.

Jasper pulled off her backpack. Seconds later, she produced a small puck no bigger than her palm. Attaching it to the side of the garage door, she gave Eve a wink.

"It's our distraction."

"How many do you have?" Asked Alyssa.

"Enough," Jasper said. "It'll keep them scattered."

Eve double-tapped the collar of her suit and let the current flow about the surface. She zipped Eleanor's jacket, ready for battle. No amount of cockiness could offset the creeping sense that they were about to walk into the lion's den. But at least here, they'd be able to deal with the prince and hopefully find Skits. With one more on their team, saving Patches would be easy. They just needed to survive.

"Sentinels?" Alyssa held her fist out. Eve rolled her shoulders before bumping her knuckles.

"Sentinels." She gave her mentor a wink. "Let's go."

Chapter Twenty-Seven

2039

Skits continued looking over her shoulder though the hall remained empty. The woman didn't trust her eyes and froze every few steps, cocking her head to the side before continuing. It had only been minutes, but Patches was doing more walking than dragging at this point. In another five, he'd be able to walk without her support, even if it was at a snail's pace.

"Dead end," she growled.

The maze had metal walls, as if they were recent additions. For all Patches knew, they were as old as the palace itself. They had yet to see a door, and at every intersection, Skits moved as if she knew the way out. But at the end of another long corridor—

"It's a door," Patches squinted, certain he could see a thin dark line down the center of the wall. "Like an elevator door."

She helped him along until they reached the end. He tried to wedge his fingers into the split in the wall, but without his powers, it'd never happen. Skits, however, had already dropped to a knee at the side of the wall, peeling a metal panel away and throwing it to the floor.

"Cover my six. This will take me a minute."

Patches braced his back against the elevator doors. He held up his gauntlet, palm out, ready to fire should somebody round the corner. The muscles in his arm quivered, and he had to use his other hand to steady himself. Despite the strength returning to his legs, it appeared it'd be a slow road back to normal. He wasn't sure he'd survive another use of the gauntlet, not until his powers returned.

"Conthan is your brother?"

"Yup."

"You guys don't seem—"

"Dammit. I'll kill your face." The smell of burning filled the corridor. It took him a second to realize she was speaking to the circuit board.

"You're different."

"He had foster care. I had the psych ward. You can say we had different upbringings."

"Psych ward?"

"It's the place where they put crazies. Though my cell wasn't as nice as the ones we had just escaped from. What I would have given for my own bathroom. Agnes hogged it all hours of the night talking to ghosts."

"She could talk to ghosts?"

"No, idiot. We were crazy."

"Were?"

"Some of us got better."

"Debatable," he replied.

"*That* you balk at? But not a note from a dead psychic who instructed my brother to rescue me from evil orderlies?"

She had a point. The more he listened to stories from Children, the more he believed they each came from traumatic backgrounds. But like the other Nighthawks, she referenced Eleanor with a mixture of appreciation and disdain. They at least had that in common.

"Almost have it," she said. She had pulled wires from the wall, hanging in a knot. Three circuit boards dangled out of the panel. With a piece of wire, she continued touching spots on one board before turning to the other.

"You know Eve idolizes you."

"I thought I taught her better. Conthan will have my head if something happens to her."

"She has the same stoic demeanor. Have I mentioned how annoying it is?" He dropped his arm, unable to keep it up any longer.

The doors hissed as they opened. Patches fell into the elevator before she caught him by the wrist. "I'm a fucking delight. I'll stab anybody who says otherwise."

Aye, definitely related, he thought.

Once inside, he looked for the buttons but found the interior smooth. Skits banged on the walls in search of a panel to break open. The doors hissed again, shutting. Seconds later, the elevator jerked upward, moving fast enough Patches had to brace himself against the wall.

"This can't be good," she said.

As if they passed through an invisible barrier, a knot in Patches' stomach unfurled. Tapping his foot, he found the energy returning to his muscles. The dampeners no longer inhibited his abilities. After being locked up twice, he wanted to be ready for whatever awaited them on the other side of the doors.

"Hit me," he said.

"You're annoying, but—"

"Hit me!" he yelled.

Skits drilled her knuckles into Patches' jaw. Seconds earlier, he'd be fearful of losing teeth. There was no pain. No spin of the head. The energy rippled across his body, a warmth he never wanted to end.

"Do it—"

She repeated, once, twice. Even with her enhanced strength, he only had to catch himself with the last blow. Skits didn't pull her punches, and for some reason, that assured him of what was coming. But until then, he was ready for whatever waited for them on the other side.

"Can I keep going?"

"I see where Eve gets it," he said.

He pushed her to the back of the elevator and stood between her and the door. It had nothing to do with the small woman. Drugged, hung, drugged again, and shot at, he wanted somebody to pay. Whoever waited for them on the other side of the doors was about to receive a world of hurt.

"Hey, I can handle myself."

"How'd that work for you?"

"Touche," she replied. "Ready to fight for our freedom?"

"Fuck freedom," he growled. "I want to crack skulls."

"I see why my niece likes you."

The elevator slowed until it stopped. There was no ding. Patches held his breath as he braced himself for a barrage of bullets. He imagined the power flooding over his body, and he'd use it to crush every one of the Knight's flunkies. Before he left, he'd have Magus by the neck and force him to submit.

First, he needed to find him.

Oscar's attention divided as he watched the screen. Magus remained tense, and while he enjoyed the man's discomfort, there were pawns that needed attending to for the next stage of his plan. If Patches survived the cadets, they'd flood the facility with gas, rendering him inert. If the Children of Nostradamus survived, they'd need his help if they were to reach Magus.

While his body remained fixated, he let his mind drift. Voices from throughout the facility bombarded his senses, a fury of white noise. He couldn't make out their words, but with a slight nudge, he could focus on one or two. Imagining the floor plan, he took two steps, crossing an uncanny distance through walls, so he stood in another control room. There were a dozen humans overseeing the facility, each one focused on their screens.

Oscar's jaw tightened as he strained to hear their individual thoughts. If he didn't move quickly, he'd begin sweating and find himself on the floor blacking out. He hated that despite experimenting for years with his abilities, they remained nothing more than parlor tricks.

Seconds later, he occupied the same space as a technician. Resting his hand on the man's, he could almost feel the warmth of his skin under his palm. He forced the man to raise his hand, poking a finger at the screen. Several menus later, he found the security systems within the training facility. With a flick of his wrist, he disabled the safety measures meant to ensure their victims didn't escape.

"Sir, there's a—"

Oscar moved quickly, touching the man's forehead with his finger. *Ignore the warning. There is nothing to report here.* Whispering was easiest when he could see them, but late at night, he practiced on the staff in the palace. The man coughed before ending with, "Nevermind."

While he whispered to the training session's safety coordinator, he looked at a series of warnings on the screen. These alerts, however, had nothing to do with Patches and Skits. Somewhere, there were trespassers and it had triggered the alarms. But with another whisper, the man disabled the alert.

If they could trace his actions, he'd be killed for treason. No matter how much he explained his goal of removing the Knights from opposing his rule, the public wouldn't agree. Even his mother might question his actions. But he was determined to unify the empire and bring down the insurgents in the North.

"We're about to see why my cadets are superior," Magus said.

The man's words were a distant echo as if he had said them from the end of a long hallway. Oscar forced his body to nod before he turned his attention to the rest of the facility. Somewhere he heard screaming, the sound of—

Interesting, he thought. Voices were being snuffed out before he could track them down. It could only mean that whoever intruded dispatched the guards. Normally, he'd want to show off the military's force and execute anybody who challenged him, but Oscar shied away from an opportunity. This could be the distraction he needed. The universe smiled upon him, further proof that he was meant to sit on the throne.

He returned to his body, smiling. Magus did not know what had transpired under his nose. The man's ego would be his downfall. But for now, he wanted to watch his trainees suffer.

"Let's hope they're more capable than Nexus."

Oscar couldn't help himself. Taking jabs at the Knight while he did not know of the disaster coming his way seemed sadistic, but he'd make his apologies as he stood over the man's corpse. He was betting on Patches and Skits emerging victorious.

Alyssa pulled the hood over her face and watched as her hand faded from view. The illusion wasn't as perfect as Gretchen's ability to bend light, but it kept her from standing out against the scenery. With Registry at the Tower, she could only imagine the technology he'd be able to create. Perhaps this is why Canada had been eager to offer sanctuary for Children seeking refuge. If only the Free Republic had done it from the beginning…

Despite Eve's protests, she demanded they rely on stealth until they couldn't. The girl had taken to the leadership role, even if it hadn't provided the results she wanted. But her ability to persist and not wallow was the definition of being a leader. If she continued, she might one day replace Alyssa as the head of security at the Tower.

"…care if it's treason, they're monsters." The voice cared enough that he quieted at the mention of monsters. Two men guarded the entry into the storage area, both of them wore tactical vests with hands resting on guns hanging from their necks. If they spoke about *them*, it meant they weren't Knights.

"Keep saying it and they'll be coming for *you*." The man on the right was taller than his companion by almost a foot. Both were thick enough to show they cared about their physique. Had they been run-of-the-mill humans, she'd easily dispatch them without breaking a sweat. But in London, she had learned that the Body Shop had become a way of life. Either of them could be more machine than man.

"I could arm wrestle them," Leftie said.

"Get powers installed this time around?"

The videos flashed in her eye. Unlike previously, she slowed down the speed so she could process the demonstrator. There were a mix of martial arts, acrobatics, and weapons tutorials. Her muscles twitched, and she couldn't help but let her fingers move as her body absorbed the visual stimuli.

The last video played, and she smiled at the sight of a ballet dancer. He might come across as gruff and arrogant, but only Ned would end her battle scenarios with a touch of elegance. When she returned, *if* she returned, there would need to be an honest conversation between them. The word love, an emotion she feared she didn't understand, came to mind. She locked it away, saving it for after she bared her sins for him to see.

Alyssa stepped between the two men, who continued talking about picking up women at a nearby pub. There were lewd comments about the type of sluts they preferred. She almost pitied them for working for the Knights. After their lewd words, however, there was no regret in what she was about to do.

Knowing nothing about the tall man's enhancements, she decided he deserved her fury first. Her fist shot out, leading with two knuckles. They smashed into his windpipe. His companion was already lifting his weapon, ready to fire into the emptiness and risk his buddy's life.

Spinning on the ball of her foot, she ducked under the weapon. In a fluid motion, she hit the magazine's release. The trigger clicked, but nothing fired. When nothing happened, he swung the gun wide. Alyssa stood, clapping his ears, forcing him to shout. Before he could reach for his earpiece, she repeated the jab to the throat, silencing him.

The other man leaned against the wall, raising his gun. Leaning forward, holding the short man, she kicked, knocking his tall friend's hand away from the gun. She repeated the maneuver, this time thrusting her heel into his knee. The bone snapped, and he dropped to his good knee.

Alyssa arched backward, planting her hands on the ground. Kicking off, her world spun until she was sitting on his shoulders, his head between her legs. There were a dozen graceful ways to end the encounter, but with a spin of his head, his neck cracked and he died before crumbling in a heap.

The shorter man tried to grab her, but she somersaulted between his legs. She slammed a fist into the back of his leg, taking him down to a knee. With a quick spin, she had the gun strap. Bracing her feet on his back, she pulled. He attempted to bat her away, to drive an elbow into her side, but with the leverage, he couldn't reach.

It started with silence, and as his body grew limp, it ended without a word. She held on for a few more seconds before letting go. The man slumped half over his partner, both of them additions to an unnecessary body count. If the men in power didn't abuse their status, commoners wouldn't suffer the consequences.

"Good riddance," Jasper said, jamming her boot into the ribs of a man.

Over her shoulder, Alyssa watched the mix of emotions run across Eve's face. The fact she didn't share Jasper's sentiment gave her hope. In moments of rage, she feared Eve walked a path toward destruction. Alyssa wanted nothing more than to shoulder that burden, to keep her safe from a cruel world. But she couldn't rob the young woman of her choice.

Eve didn't need her eyes to see, not as Alyssa's uniform bent the light. Her hand rested on Alyssa's shoulders. She leaned close, speaking in a whisper. "Despair not of the Mercy of Allah: for Allah forgives all sins."

In all her recklessness, Eve demonstrated maturity that betrayed her years. Before other Muslims arrived in Troy, she had shared stories with the young woman. Of her own accord, she studied like a young scholar. Eve would say Alyssa took the teenager under her wing to study the art of combat to make her strong. In all those years, she never confessed it had been to repay her for a kindness so few had shown her people.

It hadn't been so long ago that Vanessa, her own mentor, had taken her and set her on this path. She, too, had tried to shoulder the burden of those around her, and only when she relied on the community she built did she discover her potential. Alyssa wanted to pass on that legacy.

"Thank you, child." With every act of violence, she

feared her soul slipping away. But with a single state-
ment, Eve reminded her of the joy she found in her faith.
If she dared to question his will, she'd ask if he had sent
Eve as his emissary.

Eve wouldn't let her dwell. "How much further to
the control room?"

"We're not close. It's—"

"Then we better get moving." Pointing forward, she
embraced her role. "Alyssa, scout. We'll pull up the
rear."

She couldn't shoulder Eve's burdens. But with
actions, she let the young woman know she believed
in her.

"I've got the lead." Further, into the beast, they
climbed.

Chapter Twenty-Eight

2039

He had walked outside his body nightly. It offered freedom. In the other place, he wasn't the queen's abomination or the prince. It wasn't long before he learned to listen to conversations on the far side of the palace. At first, it had been glorious, a way to eavesdrop and gather intel on the world around him. But quickly, he'd learned that whispers behind closed doors cut the deepest.

Even now, as he shifted between watching the screen with Magus and stepping between worlds, he could hear their opinions of him. Some feared him, but most viewed him as an unworthy heir. It was an improvement, but nowhere near the level of respect they gave the queen's deceased son.

"He would have been a *real* king," a woman whispered to her fellow guard. The man nodded. With a thought, he could have them turn on one another, racked with suspicion and fear. Killing them would bring a moment of satisfaction. He refrained. Knowing their lives were forfeit to his whims was enough to remind him of his power.

"The show is about to begin." Though he stood only a few feet away, Magus' voice was barely audible.

Oscar continued roaming the halls, each connection to a guard taking him to a different part of the building. Without his body, his mind moved over great distances with little effort. Somewhere, there were Children daring a rescue, and he wanted to see how they progressed. If their intrusion offered him more leverage against Magus, he'd accept their meddling.

Who are you?

Oscar froze, the muscles in his body tensing. For all the listening he did, never had a human spoken directly to him. Had the Children come with a mentalist? By all reports, they had a turbulent relationship thanks to the events leading up to Chicago. Should that be the case—

It is not the case.

There had only been a single time he encountered another telepath. Grinding his jaw, he attempted to take steps toward the hospital. Outside the building, the world turned a brilliant white, and he almost shielded his body's eyes. While he could move unencumbered, his abilities had limitations.

The world had all but vanished, and he reached the boundaries of his gifts. He prepared to relax and let his mind rocket backward until he saw only through his physical eyes.

A hand.

We have been waiting.

His sense of safety vanished as he clutched the limb's wrist. The entire world flashed white, and he thought he had gone blind. There was no sense of up and down, and no concept of depth. All about him stretched a boundless emptiness. This was unlike eavesdropping.

Here, there were no people for him to observe as a ghost.

Where am I? he asked.

You are in the other place.

Great, cryptic, he thought.

Not cryptic. They could hear his thoughts as if they were being said aloud. It wasn't much different from when he walked from his body to spy. Were there more like him? Years had passed since the last report of a mentalist in the empire. Had they grown careless with their screenings? Or was this another—

There are no words to explain where we are.

It defies definition.

Two voices? Similar, but different. But who—

He appeared in-between blinks. Other than being naked, Oscar could be staring into a mirror. Every detail reflected him. On the collarbone rested a single difference, a missing scar from when he broke his collarbone. For all intents and purposes, the man studying him could be a—

"It can't be. You're not—" It hadn't been his imagination in the hospital. The versions of their progenitor living in the tubes were like him?

"How many years has it been since you woke?"

"A lifetime," Oscar said. "Are you like me?"

A second man appeared, standing behind the first. It was awkward to think they were carbon copies of him, duplicates of the original Oscar. But for years, he hid this secret, never sharing his gifts with another, and now, there were two people who could understand him in a way that even the most trusted confidant couldn't.

"Are we not the same?" asked the first.

"Born with identical genes," said the second.

"What of the third?" Oscar waited for another man wearing his face to appear. He had made peace with the idea that his younger years were genetically manipulated memories. But to think there were untainted versions gave him pause. All the years he spent alone, a spectacle for the court. If they had been awake, at least he'd have had somebody to relate to. He went from isolated to hopeful in seconds.

"What makes us unique is different for each." The second carbon copy took steps forward until he stood next to his brother... to our brother.

"But he'll wake too?" asked Oscar.

"Perhaps," answered the first.

"We do not know," added the second.

"How did you learn about..." Oscar gestured to the vast space. "This?" When Oscar first opened his eyes on the lab table, he had been terrified. Despite being in an adolescent's body, he barely had the verbal capabilities of a toddler. "How did you learn to speak?"

"We've been listening for some time." The first clone turned his head, studying the nothingness. "We've been hiding within our flesh."

"Studying the world and its people."

Oscar imagined if they had been there as he learned about his abilities. Would he be stronger? Did it vary, or were those identical as well? If they had stood by him, there'd be no stopping his ascent to the throne. *His* ascent. Did they share his ambitions for grandeur? If they were truly identical, would they support him, or would they serve as rivals? Suddenly, his curiosities turned cautious.

The first reached for Oscar, a single finger aiming for the space between his eyes. Oscar wanted to swat away his hand, but he also wanted to see what talents he discovered while suspended in a tube. He closed his eyes, ready to wince his way through the pain. The finger pushed against his forehead, and for a split second, he saw nothing but a searing white light.

His eyes shot open as a hand smacked him in the chest. The wind knocked from his lungs. He stood in the observation room. Magus gave him a sly side-eye. Oscar could have threatened the man, but instead, he turned his attention to the monitors.

"Are you well, Prince?"

"Your newest gladiator is about to clobber your cadets."

Even as he plotted the demise of the man standing next to him, his mind continued to drift back to the lab. Suspended in liquid were three bodies, two of them wielding gifts much like his own. While he couldn't violate the Knight's mind, he wondered if one of his siblings had figured out how. If they relied on nothing but telepathy to communicate with the outside world, then maybe they'd be able to teach him new tricks to eliminate Magus. He tucked away the idea as a backup plan. For now, he needed to focus on Children fighting Knights.

"Do we make a gentleman's wager?"

Magus snarled, unamused. That only made Oscar happier as he plotted his victory. One he'd gladly celebrate with his newest allies.

Patches tore the doors to the elevator open. If they wanted a demonstration of his abilities, they'd get it. As he stormed into the open, he braced himself for a fire-fight in the Knight's headquarters. Suddenly, he felt embarrassed holding the chunk of shorn metal in his hand.

"Points for an impressive entrance," Skits said.

"We're being toyed with." Patches dropped the metal. They stood in another ridiculously long hallway. "Brits certainly love their mazes."

"Lead on, Hercules."

If they were smart, they'd have attacked here, in a place where they couldn't maneuver or find cover. The fact there were tech jockeys armed to the teeth trying to kill them could only mean one thing. Whatever waited for them at the end of the hall was even worse.

"You know it's a trap, right?"

He conjured a thousand insults that would make even his grandfather blush. Instead, he gave her the finger. "I'm not a complete idiot."

They were almost out of hallway when a hiss echoed. The end of the hallway opened, and he expected another elevator. How far underground could they be at this point? But instead of a small room, he could see daylight on the other side. Even though he knew it was a trap, part of him hoped it led to the streets of London and he'd be able to flee. He'd be able to get Skits to safety before he came back for Magus.

Yes, he decided that his personal safety didn't matter. Not as long as that tyrant continued mutilating innocent bystanders and threatening Caledonia. With one fell swoop, he'd be able to give the Gallowglass a fighting chance. The thought surprised even him. For once, heroism overrode his desire for the safety of a library.

They reached the opening, and to his surprise, it led

into a rubble-filled London. It appeared as if a bomb had gone off. Buildings struggled to stay upright, and the streets were filled with rubble. How long had he been unconscious? This looked like the work of years of destruction.

He sniffed the air and the stale smell of earth ruined the illusion. Even though there were buildings lining the intersection, they hadn't recreated the dampness of London weather. He looked up as clouds moved along the sky. Every few seconds, a shimmer revealed the digital recreation.

"It's the training facility," Skits said. "The sky is fake. It's several stories high. This is where they send their rejects to play a game of cat and mouse."

"Dammit," Patches said. "Means we're the mice."

He turned to see bright red beams blocking their retreat. He might survive, but they'd sear his flesh. Turning back wasn't an option, and not from fear of being burned alive.

"How many are coming?"

"Always three. To make the cut, they need to take us out and survive."

"Active abilities?"

She shrugged. "I've only met a few Knights. Their powers were impressive."

Patches' eyes widened as a burst of heat brushed against his skin. A bright blue liquid fire covered her hands, creeping its way up her arms. It burned at the material of her shirt, and suddenly his abilities didn't seem as impressive. He understood why Eve cursed her gifts. When your dad can shoot lightning, and your aunt can make fire, seeing electromagnetic fields didn't stack up.

"Can you fight?"

"A little. New to this superhero thing."

"Nothing we're about to do is heroic." She meant the brutal killing about to happen. It was them or the Knights, and he was tired of failing. For once, he wanted to do a victory lap. But to do that, it meant putting their opponents down, and he doubted they'd listen to civility.

"I'm in." There had always been a line in the sand. After the last few days, not only had the line become blurry, he'd readily walk over it. If he faltered, all he had to do was recall the eleven bodies strung from the balcony.

"Follow me," she said.

They ran down the street until they reached a building with boarded-up windows. Ducking behind an overturned car, she poked her head up. He followed suit, looking for signs of movement, but everything about the fake city looked as if it had been abandoned.

"We need something at our back. Don't let them surround us. Assess their powers before making a move." Patches attempted to digest the wisdom as she dished it out. As one of the original Nighthawks, he expected her to be seasoned, but as she rattled on about selecting a battlefield, he found himself drifting off. He didn't want tactical warfare. He wanted to smash the bad guys.

"Kid." Her hand came close enough to his face, making him recoil from the heat. "They're trained killers. Don't dick around on me."

Patches wanted to gloat about going toe-to-toe with Nexus, but that ended in him nearly dying. Instead of speaking, he dug his fingers into the metal of the car's door. Jerking back, he tore it from the frame. He'd missed the limitless strength that came with his abilities. His opinion of his gifts had changed drastically in the last month. Before, he feared their potential. Now, he found them intoxicating.

"I get it. You're strong."

With a grunt, he whipped the door through the air, clipping the corner of a nearby building. The door smashed through the glass, spraying it across the street. She growled before he pointed at the building. A man in a black suit rolled out of the way, exposing himself as he dodged the projectile. They froze in the street, waiting for Patches' next move.

"Not just a pretty face," she said.

Patches couldn't put his finger on it, but something in the woman changed. Eve had talked about the wild streak and how Skits was dangerous in battle. There had been hints at the tenacity, but also how her lack of inhibition bordered on psychotic. Even Alyssa confirmed her former partner's reckless approach to life. The shimmer in her eyes summarized every story they told. Skits stepped away from her inhibitions as the flames around her hands faded from blue to white. It should terrify him, but he embraced her chaos.

The fire flowed through his body, controlling it like Alyssa had taught him. He drew it into his chest until it felt as if his ribcage might rupture. Tensing his muscles, he forced the burning into his legs.

"Keep up, grandma."

"Who the hell—"

Patches pushed off, leaving Skits behind as he launched into the air.

"This place is a maze," Eve whispered.

"Would you build a lair with direct access to your bedroom?"

Eve had never thought about the dangers of being accessible. It made sense. Flat land surrounded the Tower, and then the walls went up. Breach the wall, and there was still time for its residents to get away from the ground floors. It had done little good when the synthetics attacked. She shivered at the thought of not having those precious minutes to get the families to safety.

Eve pressed her back to the wall, stealing a glance around the corner. It was another long gray corridor, except doors lined the right side of the hall. Somewhere ahead of them, Alyssa scoured the facility, looking for targets. But at this point, they had only found a dozen humans. Even the Tower housed more people casually strolling from the lobby to the gardens. Something felt incredibly off. She waited for the other shoe to drop.

"Why aren't there more guards?" asked Eve.

"They never have many. Who would attack a building filled with Knights, but... this is surprising even for them. Maybe it's a trap?"

Eve eyed Jasper. Up to this point, her intel had been accurate, but that didn't mean she wasn't playing for the other team. Perhaps in time, she'd be able to read the magnetic waves put out by the freedom fighter, but she had never thought to use her abilities like that before. She cursed herself for not spending more time exploring the potential of her gifts. When this was over, she'd stop fussing about being a soldier and start turning her efforts inward.

"I never asked. How did you get the plans for the building?"

"Seduced a Knight. Stole his Data pad."

"Oh." Sleeping with the enemy? Jasper held a level of commitment that surprised Eve. She'd crossed the ocean and stepped into hostile territory to save Skits, but would she have sex with the enemy to get what she needed? She pushed the thought out of her head.

"What are those rooms?"

Jasper shrugged. "Broom closets, for all I know. I memorized the layout, but not everything had details."

Eve swung into the next hallway, keeping her back to the wall. Resting her hand on the door, she let her powers drift outward, but the white noise made it impossible to detect if soldiers awaited them on the other side. She flung the door open, sliding inside. Fist drawn, she prepared to wail on the first person she reached.

"What the hell?"

She had stepped inside a break room. On one side was a typical kitchen set, while the rest of the room held circular tables. Three soldiers sat, each of them slumped over. Anticlimactic. She loosened her fingers, annoyed that she had yet to break somebody's jaw.

"Alyssa's doing?"

"Perhaps? But why didn't they move when the door opened and nobody entered?"

"Lazy guards," Jasper said.

Nothing about this gave Eve confidence. With no fanfare, she shoved past Jasper and went to the next room. It was nearly identical, a break room for the guards to unwind or have lunch. Two women sat at a table, and another by the stovetop had collapsed. She'd seen Alyssa's handiwork, and even Eve couldn't believe her mentor took them out where they stood with no fighting.

"This isn't Alyssa's doing."

"No, it is not." The voice came out of nowhere. Alyssa pulled off the hood, and her body shimmered into view. "It's like this everywhere. Every guard is unconscious."

"They're sleeping?"

Alyssa shook her head as she pushed a woman from her chair. The guard fell to the tile, not making a sound. If her chest didn't rise and fall, Eve would believe she stood in a room of corpses. They expected to fight, to claw their way toward the prince, to Skits. But it was like all opposition had been removed.

"Gas? Drugs, maybe?" Eve couldn't imagine a weapon capable of this.

Alyssa shook her head. "I've seen this before. The Warden single-handedly turned all of New York into rage-induced monsters. This has the fingerprints of a telepath."

"Why didn't he do it to us?"

"Not us," Alyssa walked over to Jasper. "Children have a natural immunity to the intrusions of a telepath. We're shielded from most of his tricks."

"But, you…" Eve turned to Jasper, poking the woman in the chest. "Why are you still standing?"

Jasper swiped at Eve's finger. "What are you implying?"

"Are you a Child?"

"If I had powers, I wouldn't have wasted time pretending to be part of the Long Watch."

"Preacher would have known if she were a Child," Alyssa assured Eve.

"Then why aren't you asleep?"

Jasper leaned in, bearing teeth as if she were about to snarl. The accusation touched a nerve, and it was the first time she had seen the woman get angry. Eve thought about how convenient the plan had been. Everything hinged on her knowledge of the Knight's facility. Had she been luring them into a trap this entire time?

"This is the hallmark of a telepath," Alyssa said. "They play games. The prince could very well be in this room watching. They meddle because they can."

"I'm here for my people," Jasper growled. "Question that again. I dare you."

"I trust her," Alyssa said.

"But…"

Alyssa rested a hand on Eve's shoulder. "I trust Preacher with my life. More importantly, I trust him with yours."

With a tug, Alyssa pulled Eve away, giving Jasper breathing room. Eve considered apologizing, but her anger about the Long Watch still hadn't been resolved. Jasper might not be the enemy, but Eve wasn't willing to forgive her for partaking in those deaths. She'd reconsider when the vivid memory faded, which meant no time soon.

"It begs the question, why incapacitate the guards?"

"He's rolling out the red carpet," Jasper said. "That arrogant twat has given us an invitation."

Alyssa nodded. "It sounds like something the

Warden would have done. He believed being a mentalist meant he was unstoppable."

"Then I guess we take him up on his offer," Eve said. She turned, smashing her fist on the table. The wood splintered. Neither Alyssa nor Jasper commented on her outburst. There was no point in attempting to preserve a straight face like Alyssa. There were many traits she inherited from the woman, but remaining calm had never been one of them.

"Jasper, lead the way."

"There could still be Knights," Alyssa warned.

Eve pulled her hand from the broken table. "That's what I'm hoping."

Chapter Twenty-Nine

2039

Patches prepared to crush the Knight with his knee. He forced his eyes to stay open as he soared through the air. His knee impaled the man. The asphalt exploded as he slammed into the street. He closed his eyes and turned his head, digging his fingers into the pavement. It hadn't been a graceful landing, but he safely pinned the Knight beneath—

He realized his knee had passed harmlessly through the man. He spun about in time for the Knight to ensnare his leg around Patches' neck, throwing him. Patches went limp, welcoming the sensation of his body smacking against the pavement. Each bump sparked another fire in his chest, strengthening him. The invulnerability was a welcome change from feeling helpless in a prison cell.

Skits ran toward him, but he wanted the man put down before she joined. He wanted vengeance without interference. Jumping to his feet, he drew back his fist. One strike and he'd punch a hole through the man's chest. As he lunged, knuckles ready to break the

Knight's sternum, his hand passed through his chest. From behind, the man kicked the back of his knee, dropping him to the ground.

Patches spun on his knee, throwing an arm out, expecting to catch him in the torso. But again, his arm slid through the man. A knee came up, catching him under the chin with enough force his teeth rattled. When his hand passed through the Knight's leg, he switched tactics. He slammed his fist on the ground and the street imploded. The Knight staggered backward.

Assess, Patches thought.

When the man launched a jab at Patches' face, he caught the man's fist, or so he thought. The fist phased through his hand and his knuckles smashed against Patches' face. All the strength in the world wouldn't help him if he couldn't touch his target. He couldn't sort out how he did it, but he switched between tangible and intangible with ease. But how could he—

"Duck," Skits screamed.

He dropped to his knees, covering his head. She stepped on his shoulder, launching herself into the air. She shoved a fist through the man's body. He shrieked, and as he attempted to pull away, Skits' body flared to life, the blue fire burning away her shirt until all that remained was a naked woman on fire.

The Knight tried to flee, to back away, but she followed. Waving her hands through his body, she caressed as much of his body as she could. The Knight's suit didn't burn away. The material bubbles, mixing with the color of his skin until the two fused together. Patches had wanted to kill the Knight seconds earlier, but this teetered on torture. *Good*, he thought.

The shrieking continued until Skits was lifted off her

feet, hovering two feet above the street. An invisible force knocked her to the side. The air scrambled, and for a second, a slender, bald woman blinked into existence. Before he could sort out where she came from, the air swallowed her again.

The man's shrill screaming continued. Patches savored the man's torment as the Knight pulled at the suit's burning fabric. The smell of burning hair and flesh filled his nostrils. He wanted revenge, but burning a man alive, even that might have crossed his—

Something hit Patches in the back hard enough that it sent him flying along the street, bouncing like a skipping stone on a still pond. His powers dispersed the impact, but the blow had been hard enough to make him grunt. Fire filled his body as his abilities stored the energy. His chest burned. He thought the loud thumping came from him, but as he stopped, he saw it was from a giant stomping toward him.

"Four arms?"

Two hands clasped together overhead while the two arms protruding from his upper torso drew back, ready to punch. The club-like fists came down, hitting him in the back between his shoulder blades. Patches flattened out, his cheek pressed against the cold pavement. The Knight followed the move by slamming his foot on the side of his head. He approached his threshold, where his body would burn from the inside out.

"One down," the Knight shouted.

"Not even close," Patches growled. Pushing his way to his knees, the Knight shifted his weight, thinking it enough to keep him down. He hardly noticed. The man's hulking frame didn't slow him as he lunged, grabbing the four-armed bastard by the waist.

Leaning back, two hands planted on the ground while the other two held Patches by the shoulders. The Knight attempted to throw him, but Patches' fingers dug in, breaking the skin and sinking into flesh. Patches flinched at the high-pitched screech. They crashed onto the street, each racing to get to their feet first.

Patches held up the gauntlet and fired. He didn't expect to hit the Knight, but he had surpassed his limit and needed to burn off stored energy before it rendered him unconscious. The four-arms came together, making a shield. The blast smashed into the Knight, leaving metal arms covered in bits of flesh. It shouldn't surprise him that the Knights augmented their abilities with tech like every other human in London. It just meant it'd be more fun tearing him apart.

Skits flailed, her feet barely touching the ground. She wrapped her fingers around something about her neck as she fought to breathe. Whatever the invisible woman used, Skits would sport a bruise along her neck similar to his. Patches held up his hand, powering the gauntlet as Skits tossed a thumbs up. Swinging her legs to the side, she spun her attacker into the path of the white and orange ball of energy. The Knight shimmered into existence, staggering while she fought to keep the wire secured about Skits' throat. She wasn't fast enough. The fire surrounded Skits' hand, and she cut the garrote, staggering away from her attacker.

We might survive, he thought.

He wanted to pat himself on the back, but four-arms charged, all fists drawn ready to strike. Alyssa would be proud as he noticed the man's toes, giving away his next strike. The top left came at his face, but he blocked it with ease. The lower right aimed for his kidney and he caught the man's knuckles, squeezing until the metal crushed in his hand. He leaned out of the way of the next punch, but the Knight landed a blow with the last hand, striking his sternum enough to force him back.

"Die, Child."

When the Knight thrust another fist, Patches caught him by the wrist. Shoving the gauntlet against the bicep, he fired the laser and pulled at the man's arm. It was worse than scorched flesh bonding to the Knight's suit. At this proximity, he feared he'd never be rid of the smell. Patches severed the arm. He debated on using it as a club, but the Knight grabbed him by the throat, thumbs pressing on his Adam's apple.

Had they conditioned them to ignore the pain? Or was that part of the tech flowing through his body? Patches didn't care. He curled his fingers into fists as tiny colorful orbs filled his peripheral vision. The world turned bright red as he fired again. The laser cut through the man's arm, and now his right side lacked limbs.

"Not," he hissed, "today." Pressing the gauntlet into the man's face, and let loose an explosive blast of energy. He forced his abilities to direct the fire into his hand, feeding the gauntlet. Unlike in the hallway, he had plenty to spare. The Knight's fingers loosened and Patches dropped to a crouch. Lasers, he needed lasers. With an upturned stroke, the man's lower arm blocked part of the beam, but not enough to prevent it from cutting through half his torso.

He wanted to say something pithy, even spiteful as the man came to terms with his mortality. The laser had cauterized the wound, preventing blood from pouring out. But it wasn't enough. A slow death wouldn't give

Patches the satisfaction of victory. It didn't satiate the ghosts of eleven Caledonians killed for their nationality.

"Fuck you," Patches said. Tightening his fist, he pointed the gauntlet at the man's face. One burst of bright red light.

A black hole replaced his right eye, but it wasn't enough. The man was all but dead. His brain just hadn't come to terms with it. Screaming into the Knight's face, Patches repeated the gesture with the other eye. Before the body collapsed, Patches clenched his hand tight, letting a laser sever the brute's head.

The body fell as the head rolled away.

Despite the bile building in his stomach at the image of a decapitated corpse, the ghosts quieted. The gauntlet had siphoned his abilities, draining him until his muscles relaxed. Revenge and technology made for a cathartic combo. This made up for one body hanging from the balcony. He only had ten more to avenge, and that would come when he held Magus' head in his hand.

Turning his attention to Skits, he found the woman didn't need his help. The liquid fire she created hung in the air, blocking a two-foot blade wielded by a woman no older than Patches. Skits' entire upper body flared a brilliant white as the fire wrapped around her. It'd be beautiful if not attached to a ruthless woman.

The Knight thrust her blade forward, an easy strike to Skits' chest. As it plunged into the fire, it appeared to melt away, leaving the Knight with a handle and stump of a knife.

He swore Skits laughed.

Mirroring the Knight's movement, she plunged her hand into the woman. The Knight didn't flail or retreat. As the hand burned out her back, creating a crater in the

Knight's body, Skits kicked her, pulling her arm free as the woman fell. Dead.

She stood over the body, snarling before she spat on the corpse. If they had been alone, the fight would have gone differently. For now, they needed one another. These were cadets, the uninitiated. Would the Knights prove more of a challenge?

Patches spun about, looking for reinforcements. This had been a test, a trial for them to pass. But where were their judges? He searched the sky, looking for drones or cameras.

"It's a mirage," she said. "The sky isn't real. But they're up there somewhere watching."

Patches pushed the fire into his hand until the lights on the gauntlet glowed. Pointing skyward, he fired. He wasn't sure what to expect, but as it struck a cloud resembling a dragon, the entire ceiling shimmered and blinked. Panels fell and he could see the honeycomb pattern that made up the tallest of buildings in the distance.

It wasn't the blue skies that interested him. The black window in the corner of the football-sized room piqued his interest. That's where their jailers safely watched. A tightness in his gut said that it was Magus standing in that room watching. Knowing the man sent his cadets to the slaughter while he stood by made Patches hate him more. Revenge fueled him.

Slowly, he pointed at the window.

"I want Magus," he said.

"Okay," Skits said as if it were a simple request. "I was going to head back to my cell and pout, but killing the Knight's leader sounds fun too."

The word killing should have made him flinch or

caused his inner voice to say, "No, don't do it." But he wanted nothing more than to make the man suffer a painful and agonizing death.

"For the Caledonians," he whispered.

"Ruthless," Oscar said. "Better luck next time, mate."

Oscar studied the three bodies. Patches and his companion had proven themselves capable. But were they powerful enough to eliminate the man leading the Knights of Winchester? He'd gladly watch and find out.

Magus didn't budge as the two Children vanished from the screen. He expected a threat, or at least a sly comment. The Knight's chest continued rising and falling, but there were no other signs of life. He wondered if his doppelgängers infiltrated the Knight's mind. Just as he was about to attempt to force his will on him, the Knight thrashed about.

His fists passed through the projection screen and into the computer. The table that served as a desk for techs exploded. He let out a growl before turning to the wall, and slamming his fist into the cement. Debris filled the room as he pulverized a chunk of the wall, obliterating blocks of concrete as if they were made of paper.

Oscar spat a bit of cement from his mouth, waving his hand to push away the cloud of dust. "It seems our guests struck a nerve."

Magus faced the man, growling as if he'd unleash his anger on the prince. Oscar didn't fear the Knight, not in a physical sense. They had conditioned the Knights to serve the crown, and despite his and Magus' constant vie for power, he wouldn't dare strike the queen's heir. Their unwavering loyalty was almost endearing.

"I will avenge my cadets." The words came between breaths, his chest heaving. Oscar wondered how much of the damage resulted from the man's gifts or if it was innate abilities his kind gained with the onset of their powers.

"They're seasoned fighters. You should alert the Knights."

Oscar laid the trap, subtly putting the man's ego in jeopardy. Magus might best him in a show of strength, but he hadn't been raised in the court. Compared to the *allies* of the crown, he was but a simple man driven by basic urges.

"I'll dispose of them myself."

Baited and hooked. Oscar fought to keep the edge of his lip from turning upward.

Magus turned to leave the viewing room. He touched his earlobe, turning on his comms. "Where are the Children?" He waited for a moment before touching his lobe again. "Is anybody there?" He waited a few seconds before cursing. "Communications are down. This can't be a coincidence."

Oscar wanted to pat himself on the shoulder for ensuring that Patches and his companion had the advantage. Not only were there two Children on a search-and-destroy mission, but there were also others roaming the building. The cards were slowly being stacked in his favor. Once they eliminated Magus, then there'd be nobody stopping him from ensuring his rightful place on the throne.

"Is the hub compromised?" asked Oscar. He knew

the answer, but it wasn't the Children who had infiltrated the Knight's Central Command.

"There's no way they reached the hub."

Magus stormed from the room. Oscar debated fleeing for safety, leaving the compound so his unwilling allies could focus on a single target. It might have been hubris sadism, but he wanted to see Magus fall. For all the years the man taunted him, it was his turn to lord over the fallen Knight. Unless he saw the corpse, he couldn't claim victory.

They reached an intersection and Magus paused. Oscar took pleasure in the man's conundrum. To go left, he'd have a straight shot to the stairwell leading to the training area. But to the right, the hub, the operational brain of the entire building. Would the man let anger consume him, or would his logic override his bravado?

Oscar couldn't be bothered waiting for the man to act. It was the entire reason for this charade. He pushed past Magus, hoping to elicit the man's ego. "They'll be down here. We can cut them off."

"We need to alert the Knights." The man's fist slammed into the wall as he turned right. Even with the reinforced steel, he managed to pound a hole into the metal as if it were nothing. Oscar understood the man was strong, but perhaps even he didn't understand the extent of his abilities.

Wise play, Magus, he thought. But his appreciation meant that perhaps Patches and his friend wouldn't be enough force to kill the man. *No loss for me.*

Magus started in a jog and despite Oscar running at top speed, he couldn't keep up with the Knight. As Oscar rounded a corner, Magus had already shouldered his way through the security gate. Steel and concrete fell as he tossed the gate to the side. Even making the cautious choice, his emotions were getting the best of him. The station might not stop the Children, but anything to slow their approach would have been helpful. Oscar wondered if he was leaving a trail for them to follow.

But even Magus had to slow for the door protecting the hub. It appeared less like the average door and more like a bank vault. The defenses in this wing of the building were carefully hidden, but Oscar knew they were in place as much for the safety of the humans inside.

The floor rumbled as the hydraulics withdrew. Oscar prepared to step outside himself as he approached. If necessary, he'd let the room of technicians attack the man, citing the Knight's barbaric ways. They'd all die at the hands of Magus. Oscar cursed himself for not ensuring there was footage should the Knight survive. It wouldn't change his position beside the crown, but any damage inflicted on the man's image with the public would be to his benefit.

"Something's wrong," Oscar mumbled. At this distance, there should be whispers from stray thoughts. On the other side of the door, there wasn't a single thought. Had the Children broken through the security undetected? For the first time, he feared he might have gotten in over his head.

Before the door could open, Magus squeezed through. "Bloody hell."

As the room came into view, Oscar raised an eyebrow. The walls of the room were coated in ribbons of blood. Bodies littered the floor, skulls bludgeoned. Magus waded through the gore, his shoes squeaking as he walked into the room. Oscar was about to ask what could have done it when he spotted a young man with his hands still wrapped around the neck of a colleague.

"They killed each other." Oscar's words were as much a question as a statement. "What could do this?" Oscar neglected to add that he could have unleashed this level of hysteria.

"Pheromones. Voice modulation. No Knights with those abilities."

"Pheromones?"

"It's a trap," Magus said. "They're not alone."

Impressed by the man's skills of deduction, he played stupid. "What? I'm not following."

Magus led the Knights with a chip on his shoulder, but he was far from incompetent. Oscar might not like his philosophies, but the man knew his people's powers.

"Neither Ayer nor Kilgannon could do this. There are other Children in the building. This was a setup."

Oscar struggled to hide his smile. Under other circumstances, Magus might have been right. But still, the man didn't see the betrayal unfolding about him. Oscar wanted to confess as the man lay dying. Had their newest arrivals used their abilities to slaughter a room full of humans? If so, they were more ferocious than he gave them credit. He understood his mother's fear of the Free Republic and its growing powered population.

"Something on the screen is moving." Oscar stepped into the room, careful to avoid the growing puddle of crimson. "There," he said, pointing at a nearby station. It took a moment before he realized the numbers were counting down. "Is that a bomb?"

Magus shook his head as he kicked a tech out of the

way. He tapped the projection, but nothing happened. "It's in the electrical systems."

Oscar leaned against the doorway, bracing himself should something explode. His gaze narrowed as the countdown reached five seconds. Four. Three. Two. His teeth ground together. One. There was no boom, no sound at all. He opened his eyes, surprised at the lack of light. The squeaking in the control room continued, and he feared Magus would strike him in the blackness.

Red safety lights flooded the room. The blood along the floor and walls turned black. The carnage had been bad enough under the white lights. Now it resembled a horror movie. But in the room, only one monster stood, both his hands high over his head as he slammed a computer.

"I want their heads!" Magus howled.

Chapter Thirty

2039

"Should that happen?" asked Eve.

Alyssa blinked three times in rapid succession. When she opened her eyes, the room transformed into a green wonderland. She never wanted permanent enhancements in place of her organs, but she swore to never leave her apartment without a set of contacts again. As her eyes acclimated to the infrared spectrum, she inspected the room for any hostiles.

"It shouldn't have," Jasper said. "I mean, it wasn't my doing."

After roaming narrow hallways and descending stairs until they were deep beneath the streets of London, she was thankful to be in a wide-open space. Metal beams ran the length of the room, while girders stretched several stories high. This far underground, they most likely held up London's infrastructure. Seconds passed, and the room flooded with a soft red light.

"Power's cut," Eve said. "Think it's Skits?"

"Or Patches," Alyssa said.

A door creaked open on the far side of the room. Even with the contacts, she couldn't make out any semblance of a person. But with Children, it wouldn't surprise her if their abilities rendered the tech inert. She backed up until she bumped into Eve.

"We're not alone."

She pulled the hood over her face. If the prince rendered the human guards unconscious, it meant the next people they faced would be Knights. It pained her to think of Children as targets, but with only her and Eve, it meant no holding back.

"Four," Eve whispered. "Trying very hard to be stealthy. Tech. Maybe suits, maybe enhancements."

They had room to maneuver, but no tactical advantage. With the lights out, Eve's abilities would be useful, but it'd be better if she could shut down their tech. Perhaps if they were lucky, they'd be more machine than man and she'd be able to render them like statues.

"Can you shut them down?"

"Trying. I can't find them. They're more like empty pockets."

A long hiss filled the room. Alyssa reached to her legs, pulling the batons free. Before she ran into the darkness, Jasper spoke. "I found them."

Alyssa spun about to see four figures stepping out of the shadows. Her contacts didn't register their heat signatures. When this was done, she'd demand Registry explain every piece of tech he had ever made for the Knights. He'd be an asset to the Tower if she didn't kill him first.

"What do we have here?" Bold. Cocky. They didn't fear them.

"Intruders? That's a first." The woman's voice stressed the s.

"Rebels?" asked another. Two men and two women, based on their statures. The man on the end didn't wear a shirt or vest, leaving his skin exposed. Heat? Something based on his epidermis. One of the women had her arms exposed. From her forehead, horns protruded like a mountain goat. The other two looked no different from the Knight in the garden.

Learn. Adapt. Alyssa trained a generation of Sentinels. Where she taught control, the Knights learned obedience. In place of compassion came an undercurrent of dominance. They might share supernatural gifts, but that's where the similarities ended. She couldn't speak for Jasper, but Eve had spent years preparing for this moment. Alyssa only hoped she was as good a teacher as she was a fighter.

"We don't want to fight." Even Alyssa could hear the lie in her words.

"You're trespassing in our sanctuary."

"You incapacitate our guards. And then claim you don't want a fight?"

Interesting, Alyssa thought. They didn't know the guards had been toyed with by a telepath. It meant the Knights, at least their foot soldiers, weren't aware that the monarch-to-be manipulated them. Perhaps they should know?

"Your guards are under the influence of a telepath."

"Too bad your mind tricks won't—"

"Not us," said Alyssa. "Prince Oscar."

All four of them laughed at the statement.

"The heir to the throne? A telepath? Tastes of desperation."

It had been a long shot, but she had hoped their hatred for mentalists rivaled their sense of honor. Her allegations didn't stop them from advancing. Jasper held a hand to her thigh and the material along her pants crawled like ants. It explained the strength earlier. Her entire outfit was composed of tiny machines. The Caledonians were more resourceful than they let on. She wondered how much of their technology could be traced back to Registry or Genesis Division. The nanites pulled away, filling her hand until it solidified into a gun. Jasper was the first to react. Two shots. The hissing Knight gracefully bent out of the way where another plucked the bullet out of the air.

"Cute," the man said.

"I thought so. Now go boom."

The explosion wasn't large, but it split the four. The hisser jumped out of the way, bounding like an animal, and the horned lady shielded her face as the blast knocked her backward. Only the man who caught it was unmoved. In one action, Jasper had given Alyssa enough information to choose her targets.

There was no more need to wait.

"Kill them." Two Knights ran toward Eve and Jasper.

Eve tried to gawk as the third levitated off the ground and rocketed forward like a human bullet. Despite all the abilities at the Tower, nobody defied the laws of gravity. She had thought Nexus... *Tech*, she thought. There wasn't time to be graceful. She anchored her feet and screamed while thrusting her hands forward.

To onlookers, she had lost her mind. Unlike Dwayne hurling lightning, she disrupted invisible forces. The only person who grasped her intentions was the human rocket. He closed in. But as she reached through the electromagnetic fields, she created chaos in his electronics. He skidded along the flood, rolling like a rag doll. She dodged, jumping behind Jasper, who continued pulling the trigger of her gun.

She jumped to her feet as a woman swiped at her face. Even in the dim light, Eve noted her fingers were like claws, longer and more rigid than normal. At first, she thought the Knight wore a distinct set of armor from her skin, but realized it wasn't armor. Bones protruded from her body like spikes, her entire chest hidden behind bone. If she didn't know better, she'd have thought it was Conthan's childhood friend. It was rare to see Children with identical gifts. It meant she understood the extent of her abilities.

Eve slammed a fist into the woman's chest, hoping she had the brute strength to snap the bone. Crying out, she regretted the decision. The electricity from her suit left burn marks, but it didn't stop her from breaking something in her hand. The woman smacked Eve across the face, dragging her talons across her cheek. Eve tried to roll with the blow, but the stinging meant blood.

Years. *Years* she spent training with Alyssa. She couldn't win with brute strength. But Alyssa's teachings rarely relied on muscle. When the second swipe tried for her neck, she caught the woman by the elbow. Spinning, she pulled, hurling the Knight over her shoulder. She growled as shards of bone protruding from the Knight pressed into her back, threatening to pierce her suit.

The woman landed next to Jasper with a crack. Eve

spun about to see Jasper backing away from the man. "Switch," she said. Jasper hadn't trained with them and hesitated. Eve shoved her out of the way as the man tried to wrap her in a bear hug. Unlike the other Knight, it wasn't obvious what powers the man had. His naked torso should have given a hint, but she didn't have time to speculate.

She erred on the side of caution as she slammed her foot against his chest. He caught her ankle before she could retreat. Hissing filled the air, and her leg burned as something tried to eat through the fabric. Corrosive skin. *Mundane,* she thought. He slid his hand along her calf, melting away her suit. She slammed her foot against his chest, trying to pull away.

"Let. Me. Go." If the screaming didn't convince him, the toe of her other boot did as she spun in the air did the trick. It wasn't as graceful as Alyssa, and nowhere near as effective, but he loosened his grip as blood ran down his face. Eve fell to the floor and scrambled to get away from the Knight.

"Switch," yelled Jasper.

She placed her arm on Eve's shoulder, using it to steady her arm. The shot struck the man in the face. Jasper screamed as the bony Knight rammed into her from behind. The Knight she shot didn't seem bothered by the bullet. As the flying man tackled Eve, the bullet exploded. She barely had time to see the side of his face tear away.

"You're going to pay," said the man.

"Put it on my tab." Patches would be proud of the witty banter.

She rolled with the man on the ground. Before he could gather himself, she crawled on top of him. She pinned his arms with her knees. "Not used to a lady on top?" Maybe Patches had rubbed off *too* much. The high ground did nothing other than make the Knight laugh.

Without moving, an invisible force pushed her back. In the security lights, something surrounding his body shimmered.

"Shit."

"Kill them." Two of them ran toward Eve and Jasper.

Alyssa charged, angling her approach to come at the Knights from the side. Three of them didn't take notice, but the hisser found her a suitable target. Whatever the woman's abilities, she saw through the technology rendering Alyssa invisible. If she could take out the Knight, she'd be able to rely on stealth to dispatch the others.

The man who caught the bullet leapt forward and rocketed toward Eve and Jasper. Of all the Children at the Tower, she had never seen one fly before Nexus. Even powered by technology, the idea of being weightless impressed her.

The Knight crouched low to the ground, her hind legs shifting as she tested the traction. Alyssa tightened her grip, holding the batons flushed with her forearms. The woman was going to jump, and if her powers were as uncanny as the others, she wanted the woman off-balance when she slammed the weapon against her chest.

As she predicted, the Knight leapt. Alyssa tucked into a ball and leaned into a roll. Sailing under the— The Knight grasped her ankle. The change in direction nearly wrenched her leg from its socket. The woman spun her body about, landing with the pristine grace of a gymnast. Alyssa flipped a baton around, charging the tip before thrusting it forward.

The Knight released her leg, easily retreating out of reach. At this distance, Alyssa could see the woman's face, morphed with a flat nose and wide eyes. The Knight didn't waste time. Instead, she spun, intending to clock Alyssa across the face. Forearm up, she blocked the blow, stopping the momentum. But she maintained her balance, retracting her foot quickly before slamming the heel into Alyssa's cheek.

Fine muscle control. Speed. Grace.

Alyssa got her feet under her, crouching low for the next strike. She raised the batons. To anybody watching, it appeared as if they hovered in the air. The weapons ruined the element of surprise, but if this Knight had gifts that enhanced her other senses, invisibility didn't offer any protection.

The Knight's body stayed limber, constantly shifting her weight. But with her fists up, protecting her face, claws extended from between her knuckles. It wasn't the first Child to have abilities similar to an animal. Eve's father compared his gifts to an electric eel. If Alyssa was right, that her gifts were based on animal physiology, it meant she had gained an advantage.

No comments. No pithy sayings. The woman leapt again. She ducked under a swipe of the baton. Swiping with her right hand, she paused short of Alyssa's upturned forearm. Instead, pulling her hand back, slipped inside Alyssa's defense and dragged her claws across her arm. If it hadn't been for the suit, she'd have torn through the skin. Dropping low, she spun, attempting to sweep Alyssa's— No. She stopped short, angling her heel up, catching Alyssa in the chest.

Direction. Stop. Redirect. The woman thought herself the superior fighter, but Alyssa had let the woman land her strikes. Her abilities flared. As her eyes processed the Knight's technique, her muscles adapted, synching as if she had trained for this very moment. It would have taken Alyssa months, if not years, to learn the woman's habits and how to counter them. Thanks to the Nostradamus Effect, it took three seconds.

The Knight led with a left hook. Alyssa dropped the baton, the weapon shrinking no bigger than her fist before it secured to the magnets on her thigh. She feigned a block. The woman stopped short again, but before she could retract her fist, Alyssa caught her wrist. The Knight tried the same technique with her knee. Stop. Retract. Strike. She tried to dig the toe of her boot into Alyssa's kidney, but Alyssa knocked her leg out wide. Alyssa jerked her arm, pulling her in tight. Before her next kick landed, Alyssa ducked, catching the woman behind the knee.

Alyssa strained as she lifted the Knight. The Knight cursed, using her free hand to jam claws into her shoulder. Bone struck her clavicle, and she screamed. The woman tried again, ignoring her as Alyssa plunged the woman downward. Her body folded around Alyssa's knee, but there wasn't a snap of the vertebrae. Like a cat, the woman proved to have a spine capable of bending.

Alyssa cursed.

The knee slammed into the side of her head as the woman prepared a backward handspring. Alyssa reached into her boot, opting for the blade over the baton. She caught the woman's leg, a messy attempt to latch onto her. Claws scraped at her side, shedding through the fabric. Alyssa cried out, the wounds deep enough she'd need stitches.

It wasn't elegant as she shoved the blade into the woman's leg. Wrenching it backward, she tore at the muscle. The Knight's high pitch scream hid the sound of the blood splashing against the floor. Alyssa didn't want to handicap the woman and leave her immobile on the battlefield. She twisted the blade until she struck the bone. With another spin, she found the artery. Blood poured out, spraying enough that it doused Alyssa.

The woman stopped attacking and clutched the wound, desperately attempting to halt the flow of blood. It was too late. Shock would set in within seconds. Alyssa shoved the woman's body away. Tucking the knife into her boot, she rotated her shoulder, taking inventory of her wounds. Painful, but nothing lethal.

Alyssa didn't wait for the body to convulse as she darted away. Jasper and Eve needed her. Skits needed her. Patches needed her. But what she needed right now was reinforcements.

"Jasper," she yelled. "Distraction, now!"

Eve's fist stopped short as she hammered away at a Knight's face. It wasn't a physical barrier stopping her, more like an invisible force stealing the inertia of her strikes. Try as she might, she couldn't break through and pummel the jerk.

"You braggart," he laughed. While she couldn't penetrate the field, he could still move unhindered. He freed his hand, reaching for her throat. Before she could lean back, invisible extensions of his fingers wrapped around her throat. The fight wasn't going according to plan.

"Help," she choked. Jasper wasn't fairing much better as the bone-covered Knight raked her nails across the woman's torso. One of her bullets exploded and Eve prayed it pierced the woman's bony armor. But no, other than making her hesitate, the woman's exoskeleton remained intact.

"You're all going to die."

Eve tried to spit back another witty retort. His phantom fingers forced her to swallow her words and focus on gasping for air. She grabbed his wrist, trying to dig her nails into his arm. Her gifts flared, and she tried to pull at the electromagnetic field the way she did security cameras. With enough time, she might give him a headache, but unlike Patches, she couldn't siphon the energy from his body.

Her vision blurred, peppered with dark spots. Eve only had seconds before he choked her unconscious. Her grip along his wrist relaxed and, for a second, she could feel her fingers touching the skin along his wrist. She didn't have time to question how she had penetrated his shields. Her nails bit into his wrist, tearing into the skin until she scratched bone. She could barely hear his screams over the deafening white noise as her blood boiled.

In a match of strength, Eve had few rivals. She pulled at the flesh, freeing herself. She rolled over, gasping for air as she scurried away. He reached for her leg, but she spun away. If she couldn't punch the guy, couldn't knock the wind out of him, how was she supposed to fight him? What would Alyssa do?

"Jasper." Her voice came out in a raspy whisper.

Her breathing came in short ragged gulps, but not enough to quench her lungs. Spinning about on her knees, she barely had time to cross her arms and block the Knight's knee. He hopped to his other foot, trying with his other knee. Eve leaned back, his shielding brushing against her chin.

Alyssa didn't win fights with her fists. Most often, she grappled with her opponent until they submitted. Eve had been on the receiving end more times than she could count. She cursed each time she had to tap out.

Before he could bring his foot down, Eve caught his boot. She didn't need to touch him to push him around. She leaned in, the back of his knee resting on her shoulder. Jumping to her feet, she lifted him, holding his waist as she drove him shoulders first onto the cement. Lifting his ass up, she slid under him, folding his body in half. Her leg hooked over his neck as she held him in place.

"Submit." Her voice grew louder, but it felt as if sand filled her throat.

"Going to kill you."

Eve had him secured, and despite his thrashing, he couldn't get away. But it'd only be a matter of time before her arms tired, or he found leverage to push her off. How many times had he waited for a victim to grow tired before he pulverized them with his force field? Not only could he throw a punch, but like Patches, he wouldn't feel a thing.

Eve's eyes lit up. Patches was the answer. He could hardly feel it when she slapped him. But if she squeezed his cheeks to make him look her in the eye, he complained about her rough grip. If the two men were anything alike, it came down to exerted force. Even though their powers manifested differently, maybe they charged their batteries similarly.

Resting her hand against his thigh, she slowly pushed. The Knight kicked with his other leg and tried pulling at her ankle, but she remained focused. Where her limbs held him in place, she couldn't penetrate his shields. But with the soft touch of her hand, her fingers pushed through the shimmer. It was everything she could do not to cheer. Paying attention to the powers of other Children paid off.

"This is going to hurt," she growled. Her hand wrapped around his thigh, fingertips digging into his suit. Even if she couldn't tear through, crushing his muscles remained an option.

"Jasper," Alyssa yelled. "Distraction, now!"

It only took seconds before the rumble of explosions filled the building. Jasper had been placing the charges as they wound their way into the middle of the complex. It might distract others, but the man she held to the ground renewed his flailing, threatening to buck her. She tensed her muscles, struggling to hold him in place. Squeezing with her hand, the meat of his thigh compressed until he screamed. She wanted to break his femur, leaving him useless in a fight.

A groan filled the room as if the building itself spoke. The floor vibrated, softly at first, and then turned violent. Whatever the explosions did, they hadn't finished their job. When the first chunk of the ceiling collapsed on the far end of the room, Eve realized the entire building was about to come tumbling down.

Jasper had fallen to the ground, and Alyssa charged to save her. But even in the dim light, Eve watched cracks split along the ceiling. Their opponent stopped being the Knights and now was the building itself. They could trade blows and show off their skills in battle, but none of them had abilities that'd survive being buried alive.

Her tactics changed. She let go, rolling away from the man. Instead of clutching his wounded leg, he tried to snatch her jacket. Eve evaded. Climbing to her feet, she spotted Alyssa on top of the boned woman. The fight had ended. Their priority turned to survival.

Eve ran.

Alyssa ran toward Jasper. The woman with horns stood over the Gallowglass. She held a sword nearly as long as she was tall, ready to bring it swinging down to cleave Jasper's skull. The rebel might be laced with technology, but she hadn't trained to fight Children. The Knight's tenacity would prove her undoing.

"Now!" Alyssa screamed louder.

This time, the rebel listened. The roar was distant, but the tremors caused the floor to shake. It started as a gentle hum. The pucks exploded. Alyssa thought they'd be nothing more than grenades chipping away at the structure to distract wayward Knights. But as the rumble grew louder, the entire structure shook. Beneath the streets of London, she wondered if it had been a wise decision.

The fighting stopped as silence replaced the explosions.

A second wave of rumbling tore through the structure. Alyssa tried to recall every time Jasper had placed the charges. Alyssa had assumed it had been haphazard.

The entire building quaked. The underground portion of the Knight's headquarter spanned several blocks, and Jasper had destroyed it all. While she and Eve had been on a mission to save their friends, Jasper had treated it like a suicide mission. Above them, the streets of London fell into the subterranean base.

Alyssa screamed. "Run."

Cracks split along the ceiling. Slabs of cement exploded, raining down debris. Alyssa ran toward Jasper. The horned woman didn't seem concerned with dying as her upper body tensed. Grabbing the baton on her thigh, she flipped the switch, charging the end. Hurling it, she needed speed over accuracy. Spinning through the air, it smacked against the woman. The electricity jolted her enough to force her back a step.

Alyssa used the extra second to pile drive into the woman. The sword fell to the side with a clunk. Something bit into her shoulder and she glimpsed the woman's arm. Her exterior had become calcified, layered in bones until it turned into body armor. It reminded Alyssa of Conthan's childhood friend. Nostalgia would have to wait until she dispatched the Knight.

"Traitor," the woman yelled. The landslide swallowed her cries at the far end of the room. They didn't have time to fight, not if Jasper's handiwork was going to bring down the entire building.

They tumbled to the ground, but Alyssa's grip tightened. A bone-covered elbow slammed between her shoulder blades and she fought to hold on. She tried reaching for her boot, but their entangled legs made it impossible to snatch the knife. The woman slammed her forehead into Alyssa's face. When she pulled her head back, the plate above her brow dripped with Alyssa's blood. She had broken Alyssa's nose, but she couldn't focus on that now.

The Knight crawled onto Alyssa, using her weight to hold her in place. Sarah's growths had been similar, a result of her body creating too much calcium. Neither had had bone covering their joints, making them vulnerable to a well-placed strike. If only she could reach her boot...

Grabbing the Knight's horn, Alyssa pulled until the woman screamed. The tip broke free. With another fist to the jaw, Alyssa spat, blood from a split lip spraying across the woman. She drew back again, knuckles posed to dislodge Alyssa's jaw. With the tip of the horn, Alyssa swiped across the Knight's throat. The tip sank into the soft flesh under her bony jawline an inch to the left of her jugular. She used her weight to pull, the bone tearing through flesh.

She didn't have time to ensure the Knight died. Jasper was at her side, reaching under her armpits, pulling her to her feet. Eve had already taken to running as the remaining Knight hobbled after her. It was no longer about killing the queen's elite guard. They needed to survive the avalanche.

Following Jasper, they chased after Eve.

Eve easily outran the limping Knight. Searching for an exit, she found a pair of double doors. The smashing of concrete made it impossible to understand Jasper and Alyssa's shouting. As long as they continued barking at one another, it meant they were alive.

Slamming into the doors, she stumbled and skidded along the floor of the long hallway. The wall stopped her slide. Jumping to her feet, she spun around as the doors continued swinging back and forth.

Open.

Alyssa had nearly reached the Knight she had wounded.

Close.

Unlike the warehouse, the hallway didn't have cracks tearing through the ceiling.

Open.

Alyssa paced herself with the man, and with an out-turned foot, tripped him.

Close.

Had Jasper known her explosions would bring down the building?

She pushed the door open, but it wasn't her friend dashing into the room that caused her jaw to drop. The ceiling tore open, concrete and earth filling the cavernous warehouse. Even as Alyssa and Jasper dashed into the room, she couldn't help but watch the carnage. The Knight she crippled struggled to get to his feet. A concrete slab fell on him, and she wondered if his powers saved him or did they have limitations. If they held fast, would he endure a slow death? Eve found she didn't care how he died, just that he got what he deserved.

As quickly as it started, the rumbling vanished, replaced by creaking from further into the building.

Alyssa and Eve braced themselves against the wall, panting.

Dust filled the hallway. With the faint red lights, she struggled to make out any movement amidst the rubble.

"Better than expected," Jasper said.

Eve raised an eyebrow. "What do you mean?"

"She wasn't leading us anywhere. She placed the charges to topple the city."

"Aye. And they deserved it."

"Did Preacher know?"

"He's not a Caledonian. His methods—"

Eve punched Jasper in the gut, lifting the woman off her feet. If she hadn't been an ally, Eve would have risked breaking her jaw. She shoved her against the wall. "This isn't over. Not by a long shot. Before we leave, you and I are going to have a talk. Get what I'm saying?"

Jasper slid down the wall, coughing as she wrapped her arms around her torso. Eve's eyes were nothing but anger, fury waiting to be unleashed. She stopped caring that she did it to protect her people. They had just killed four people to save their friends. She wouldn't fault Jasper for being an extremist in dire times, but her 'at all costs' approach infuriated Eve. Unlike Jasper, Eve wouldn't sacrifice one ally for another. It was the only thing keeping her alive.

"Do you understand?" Eve leaned closer to the woman's face. It wasn't a rhetorical question.

"I..." Jasper's breath came out ragged. "I understand."

"Good." Eve turned to the destruction the rebel had caused. It was impossible to discern what was part of the Knight's headquarters and what came from the streets of London. The dust had grown thick enough she had to cover her mouth for fear of choking. The dark red haze whirled about as groans continued filling the space. She couldn't tell if it had finished or if more of London would topple down on them.

"How many died to prove a point?" Eve muttered.

"This is the price of war," Alyssa said. Blood coated the woman's face, even as she tried wiping it away with her sleeve, streaks of crimson smeared across her cheek. "Every loss, every victory, they come with casualties."

"Pointless," Eve said.

"Not for them," Alyssa eyed Jasper. "This happens when people are left with no options. She, too, saw the hanging bodies. I don't condone it, but I sympathize."

The vacant softness in Alyssa's eyes was the same as when her fathers talked about the horrors of battle. It was as if the brain refused to process, instead replaying a reel they couldn't stop watching. Eve had fixated on becoming a Sentinel. She hadn't thought about what would happen when she assumed the mantle. It wasn't long ago, with her first chance to prove herself, she froze while synthetics stormed the Tower. The anxiety had vanished, replaced with anger. Did her eyes hold the same sadness as she imagined the grave of the Caledonians?

She no longer blamed Alyssa for her involvement in the Wetworks. If their actions prevented *this*, then it was worth the burden.

"Are you okay?" asked Alyssa.

"No."

"If you need—"

"We need to go."

Rescue first. Cry later.

Chapter Thirty-One

2039

Every human massacred. At first, he applauded the efforts of his siblings, but it appeared they lacked his fineness. They'd have much to teach one another when this scuffle concluded. He wanted to learn more about the white room, and he'd teach them about surgical precision in their attacks. Together, they'd be an unstoppable force. But first, he needed to ensure he collared the only people resistant to his manipulations.

He continued following Magus as they doubled back and headed toward the staging ground. Unless Magus had an uncanny ability to track his prey, they could roam the halls for hours before they found Patches and Skits. If their efforts dragged out, he feared they'd bump into more Knights, and with soldiers at his back, Magus would have the advantage.

"Do you hear that?" Something echoed through the halls of the building.

"Are you daft?"

"It's a—"

Oscar braced himself against the wall as the floor

trembled. The emergency lights flickered, leaving them in pitch black. While the floor rocked like an ocean wave, the walls buckled, plaster pelting him in the face. What started as a minor quake threatened to level the building. Of all the ways he could die, he never suspected a natural disaster.

"We're under siege." Magus' shouting reinforced what the prince already knew.

Somewhere nearby, he heard screaming through the roar. The high pitch bellowing belonged to a woman. Could they be lucky enough to have found Patches and Skits?

The shaking lasted only a minute. As the world stabilized, Oscar wondered who might be responsible. Was it the intruders he allowed into the building? Or had Patches and Skits brought down the structure? While he wanted Magus dead, he feared the cost of victory came with too steep a price.

"Who dare—"

"I heard voices," Oscar said.

Amongst the rubble, the Knight stood silent. Oscar squinted, trying to make Magus in the darkness. The building continued to moan, hiding his breathing. If he didn't give Magus a direction, all of his efforts were for nothing. He refused to let the man get away unscathed.

The lack of lights provided him cover to step outside his body. The moment his mind propelled forward, time moved at a glacial pace. He'd be able to scour the complex looking for the empty voids created by Children. The man might grow suspicious about how he located the prisoners, but there was no point in worrying this close to his goal.

Unable to steal sight from humans, the world

remained as dark as the one he saw with his physical eyes. But unlike reality, thoughts and emotions governed this world. Even minds he couldn't read shone like a beacon. Magus had lowered his guard, the rage almost tangible enough to taste. The Knight maintained his composure, but here, there were no lies. Magus had reached his breaking point and began slipping.

Good, he thought.

It wasn't only his emotions Oscar detected. Fear. He stepped through walls, following a delicate thread. Pulling at it, he discovered the source. Like fingerprints, every person has a unique presence. He might not have been able to pinpoint Patches, but after touching his mind at the hospital, it had a familiarity. Oscar pulled harder and found the man was far closer than he could have hoped.

Patches stood over a void. It made sense that somebody who fought a telepath had learned to shield themselves from casual intrusions. If he had time, he'd have tried pressing to see if he could break him before the pain made his eyes water. There would be time for that. But first, he needed to finish executing his trap.

"I swear I heard a woman screaming."

"Where?" Magus moved closer, his boots scuffing along bits of broken drywall.

"I don't know," he lied. "Through a wall. Here, maybe?"

He pressed his hand to the wall. In the darkness, Magus' eyes looked like two floating orbs. The man had turned on his enhancements. The Knight had always scoffed at the need for technology.

Hypocrite.

Pressing a hand against the wall, Magus gave it a slight push, as if it'd crumble from his efforts.

"Stand back, Prince."

Magus used a title he didn't respect. The Knight took several steps back, his boots scuffed against the floor as he found his footing. Dashing toward the wall, he crashed into the concrete. The wall crumbled inward. The security light in the next room was almost blinding. It illuminated Magus' white suit, making him appear as if he glowed a bright red. The man picked up speed, leaning his shoulder forward as he smashed into the next wall.

Oscar smiled as he spotted Patches.

The Knight grabbed the man and didn't slow. Another thunderous boom sounded as the next wall collapsed. The darkness swallowed them. Patches relied on his tech, creating bursts of light illuminating Magus' upper body. He didn't need to see to know that the two men were about to square off. There'd only be one who emerged from the room. His plan had come to fruition.

"It's over, Magus," he mumbled.

"They're asleep?" asked Patches.

A man and woman in suits had collapsed at their stations. Projection screens lined the far wall, displaying thousands of computer screens. They flashed, switching between the cameras throughout the city. What were these two technicians watching for? His finger brushed the CPU behind the woman's ear. Holding his fingers over the woman's throat, he double-checked that he hadn't imagined her pulse.

With no visible signs of bruising, he could only speculate at the cause.

"Subsonic vocal cords. Condensing the air in the room. There are a thousand powers that could do this. It means there are more Knights in the building." He got off the floor, trying not to stare at Skits' naked torso. She didn't seem to care that she bared her breasts for all to see. Patches would shower with a t-shirt on if he could.

"We need to be careful." He wanted a fight, but not with one of the flock. He'd only be satisfied when he watched the light in Magus' eyes fade.

"Or not." Skits, however, wanted to fight everybody.

Patches froze as the overhead lights shut off, thrusting the room into darkness. Blue light flooded the room. Not only could she vaporize flesh, but she also made for a handy nightlight.

"This place is a maze," Patches said. "We could be here forever and not find Magus."

A deafening boom tore through the room. Patches fell against the wall as the floor shifted. Cracks ripped along the walls. The light from Skits' arms blinked, and once again, they stood in darkness. He pushed off, catching her around the waist. Pinning her to the ground floor, he covered her body as the drywall from the ceiling rained from above.

The world continued shaking.

"Earthquake?"

"Bombs," Skits yelled. "Somebody is bringing down the building."

"Gallowglass," he shouted.

Concrete struck Patches with enough force he nearly squashed Skits. His powers dispersed the impact, but it only meant his entire body hurt. The fire in his limbs intensified, burning hot enough that he feared his skin melting. He needed to drain his battery before the pain left him comatose.

"Get off me," Skits yelled. When he hesitated, she barked the command louder.

He rolled off as she spun about. Her body flared blue, hot enough that it tempered the burning from inside his body. She tucked into a ball, shrinking herself as she waved her hands in the air. The blue light hung in the air as if she had painted with heat. It only took a second before she created a vibrant barrier, vaporizing rock as it fell. He pulled in tight to her side, half tucking his legs, half covering her body.

Skits screamed as the blue faded, replaced by a searing white light. As the concrete grew larger, her volume increased. The wailing didn't stop as the ground settled. Dust filled the air, and she held her position.

"Skits," he said. "Skits, you can stop."

The light vanished and she collapsed, hands dropping to her side. She turned her head as her eyes rolled about. Patches worried she'd injured herself until the smile appeared. They nearly died as the building fell apart around them and his companion found it humorous.

"Pro tip." She sucked in air like she had run a marathon. "Teammate says move, you move."

"Received."

Patches got up, inspecting the damage. The walls were mostly in-tack, but the ceiling had seen better days. Whatever destroyed the building did a fine job, and they'd be buried two floors down. It couldn't be a coincidence that they were loose and somebody blew up the Knights' headquarters. If it had been the Gallowglass, he had questions. But what if it was Eve? Blowing up a building didn't strike him as a tactic she'd use.

"We need to keep searching," Skits said.

"Magus could be buried."

"I'll believe it when I see his corpse."

Patches held out a hand when the tremors started again. If the ceiling continued collapsing, he'd have to rely on Skits. His muscles already burned. It reminded him of the fight with Nexus. He wouldn't be of any use if he fell victim to his own powers.

The wall exploded. He shielded his eyes just before something caught him around the chest. Hands? He opened his eyes to see Magus driving him into the hallway and through another wall into an identical surveillance room. Patches' abilities absorbed the impact, preventing his ribs from shattering and his spine from snapping. If he were anybody else, he'd be dead.

Patches pushed a hand against Magus' face. "I owe you." He wasn't anybody else. He didn't need to summon the fire. His entire body raged against him. The glove lit up. The blast from the gauntlet showered about Magus, halting his stampeding through another wall. Patches continued, deciding the man deserved to have his face melted. His palm grew hot as the energy continued pouring out. The Knight deserved no mercy, no chance to fight. Patches wanted the tyrant dead.

"Ya diddy," Patches shouted.

Magus stepped back. As the orbs vanished from Patches' sight, he expected to see a melted mass where the man's head should be. He gasped when the man's toothy grin came into sight. The man's face, even his white suit, none of them had the smallest of scorch marks. Whatever powers the Knight possessed, they made him immune to a blast from the gauntlet.

"I see you know Registry," the man goaded.

With a flick of the wrist, the gauntlets reverted to bracelets. If frying the Knight didn't work, Patches had other skills. Foot braced against the wall, he pushed off, willing the fire into his upper body. Patches intended for the uppercut to tear the man's head clean off his shoulders. Magus staggered backward, but it did little more than shove the man. He repeated, this time drilling his knuckles into the man's gut.

Magus' boots skid across the dust-covered floor, but other than moving a few inches, it appeared brute strength only amused him. Patches didn't care. With each blow, the pain rippled along his skin, stoking the internal flames. Eve taught him to follow through, to use his powers to gain leverage. Each punch struck with a boom. Magus held still, hands on his hips. The Knight laughed, thinking that Patches attempted to wail on the man.

"It's futile, Child. You can't hurt me."

It was Patches' turn to laugh. "I wasn't trying to."

With the stored energy rampaging through his body, he slammed his heel on the floor. The fissures in the concrete spread. It collapsed. Patches tried to spring away, but Magus caught him by his shirt, dragging him into the falling rubble. Unlike the quake before, the falling floor was deafening. He slipped into a cloud of dust, unable to make out the Knight. Patches pulled at the man's wrist, but Magus held tight. With a final tug, Magus released him.

On the floor below, he slammed against something hard enough it knocked the wind from his lungs. He tried to roll out of the way but found rubble blocking his escape. If he was lucky, Magus would be pinned beneath the rock and Skits would get her wish to see a dead body.

Patches' only luck seemed bad.

As the dust settled, Magus stood over him. While the blasts hadn't hurt, at least now the Knight's suit had been tarnished. It was a start.

"You—" Patches coughed. "Got something on your superhero costume. Sorry."

Magus didn't appreciate his wit.

Oscar was ready to climb through the hole the brute had made when something moved. Skits had been lying on the floor as Magus clotheslined her companion. Despite needing her to help finish Magus, he understood the woman had no love for the monarchy. If he revealed himself, he might find himself on the other side of her awesome abilities. Oscar stepped out of sight. This close to victory, he erred on the side of caution.

He will not stand in your way.

Oscar resisted the urge to swat at his ear. It echoed as two voices spoke in unison. He had questions for his siblings. Did they require one another to pull off nullifying the entire base? Or was that a taste of their abilities? So close to his victory over Magus, he focused his thoughts, ignoring the gnawing questions. There would be time as he prepared the army to move north. Then he'd not only have the full weight of the military at his disposal, but hopefully a new set of powered soldiers to aid him in his conquest.

The prince will be king.

The walls and red light vanished, and again he stood in an infinite white. He growled at the inability to resist their beck and call. It was one thing to seek this *other*, but to be at their whim left him gritting his teeth.

"I have no time for this," he yelled.

Here, time has no meaning.

An eternity, hidden in the blink of an eye.

Educational, but their words held an air of arrogance. If they were one of his subjects, he'd have used his rank to demand respect. But did these men see the title as anything other than a hollow word?

"The king who would be." Spoken aloud, it was as if he uttered the words himself. If he didn't know better, he'd have thought his inner voice prodded at him.

"In due time," he said. "With Magus out of the way, we'll be one step closer to unifying the kingdom."

"Did you appreciate our assistance?"

There was no point in lying if they could read his mind. "Impressive, but unnecessary. The humans are—"

"Fodder." A naked man stepped out of the white light. With each step forward, his skin rippled, transforming until he wore a tailored suit. He reached up, adjusting his tie. Oscar found it amusing that they shared the same nervous twitch. His sibling had never worn clothing before, and the first article he chose matched Oscar's favorite suit.

"Citizens of the empire are not fodder." Like a movie set, a simulation of the hospital played out in the background. The Long Watch murdered one another. His actions betrayed his words.

"You are a curious creature." The second brother stepped out of the nothingness. Unlike the first, he remained naked. Oscar assumed they'd be identical in every way. But a simple decision reminded him they were as unique as him. He thought about how the queen viewed him. At first, she treated him as her dead son. Over time, she grew to accept that while they were similar, he had his own identity.

"Curious?"

Neither moved. Their ability to stand perfectly still unnerved him. They might have better control of their telepathy, but neither of them had lived outside of the lab. He reminded himself that he was the prince of the most glorious empire in the world. If he could stand against Magus or the queen, he had nothing to fear from his copies.

He walked toward them. "Why have you brought me here?"

"Do you know how we learned to talk?"

The clothed Oscar led the conversation. The question had come to mind. He assumed scientists somehow ingrained it in their genetics. But he remembered those first weeks in the hospital. Doctor Wentworth visited him hourly, talking through his observations with each assessment. Oscar learned to speak by the second week. His vocabulary limited to the words the doctor used. No, they might learn quickly, but they had gained the skill through other means.

"We learned from probing the minds of scientists. By human standards, they consider their minds brilliant. Simple, yes, but filled with knowledge."

"We learned," added his naked counterpart.

"Their minds are weak, information presented for the taking."

Oscar had listened to conversations from a distance,

but he never thought to pull at their thoughts, to consume them. Had he squandered his gifts? Or did their telepathy grow out of necessity? If he lacked his other senses, perhaps he'd have relied more heavily on his sixth sense.

"Do you know what else we learned?" The naked man turned to their suited sibling. Oscar decided he needed to name them and stop thinking of them as clones. Oliver and Owen. It was foolish, but just as he had fought for his independence from his progenitor, he wanted to honor that with these two.

"They are a cruel species," said Owen.

Oliver repeated the twitch, adjusting the knot of his tie. Oscar recognized the tells of his impatience. He didn't need to be a telepath to know Oliver grew frustrated with Oscar's lack of knowledge. While he agreed that mankind had its cruel moments, he had never thought of them as any worse than any other apex predator.

"In their labs, they create intending to prevent their decaying bodies. But at the same time, they seek to destroy. They are a paradox."

"We are a complicated species."

Them.

Not we.

Owen reached forward, fingers grazing Oscar's cheek. Even though he knew they were miles apart, he could feel the skin against his stubble. It was far more intimate than strangers should be with one another. But were they strangers? The circular logic threatened to drive Oscar mad.

"You sympathize with them?" asked Oliver.

"He believes he is human," added Owen.

Before he could reply, their heads turned right, staring into the nothingness. He followed their line of sight and saw nothing. Did they experience the white room differently? The list of questions grew.

Go.

"Go," they spoke in unison.

He slammed into his body with enough force that he braced a hand on the wall for support. They summoned and dismissed him as if he were a toy. Oscar growled. When he finished here, he'd need to go to the hospital to receive his shot. While there, he'd have a conversation with his brothers by whatever means necessary.

"Patches!"

He pushed his anger toward his siblings aside. For now, he needed to focus on the demise of Magus. Peeking around the corner, he watched the room fill with a blue light. Skits' right arm shone with liquid flames. Patches and Magus might be strong, but her gifts were flashier. As she dashed from the room, he decided it was time to follow… from a distance.

There was no point in hiding the grin. He *would* control the Knights.

Patches' boot should have crushed the man's testicles. The Knight made no move to block, secure that it'd accomplish nothing. Magus didn't flinch. The layer of protection robbed him of his ability to fight. He scoured the room, but in the dim light, he couldn't find anything to use as a weapon. Unlike the computer stations above, this one held old school desks like his teachers used to sit behind. Dozens of humans slept on their desks or on the floor where they had collapsed. Closest to him, he caught sight of an arm sticking from beneath the rubble. More victims, thanks to Magus and his damned Knights.

He sat upright, the gauntlet on his left hand wrapping around his fingers. Five short bursts from the palm of his hand. The attack only made the Knight squint. The energy in his muscles depleted, leaving him nothing more than a strong human. Doubt doused the rage. He feared he had gotten himself into yet another dangerous situation. It was the Long Watch all over again.

"Want to keep trying?"

Magus' arrogance stoked the anger. Thinking of Calum hanging from the balcony, he wanted to sink his fingers into Magus' eyes and tear him apart from the inside. Killing this man could save hundreds, if not thousands, of Caledonians. He needed to pay, and Patches wanted to be the one to make good on that receipt. But it was Alyssa's voice that chided him to stop repeating his failures. If one tactic doesn't work, move on.

He grabbed a handful of rubble and threw it at Magus' face. While his fists couldn't penetrate the shield, all but the tiny pebbles passed through the barrier. Magus swatted at the dust as he slammed his foot on Patches' chest, pinning him to a slab of concrete. If he were anybody else, it'd have given Magus the time to clear his eyes. But the blow rippled along his skin, the power refueling his battery. While Patches studied the man's abilities, the leader of the Knights should have been doing the same.

"Big mistake," he said.

He grabbed the man's ankle and pushed his leg away. The Knight could hide behind his shield all day, but it didn't mean Patches couldn't move the prick. Even as Magus leaned forward, using his weight to pin Patches, it wasn't enough to hold him in place. Grabbing his other ankle, Patches jerked back. Magus slammed his back on the floor before throwing a heel against Patches' chin.

He tasted copper. Stopping a bullet hurt, but it didn't compare to the strength Magus wielded. It made sense why Oscar feared the Child. He prepared to tackle the man when a light blinded him. Skits dropped through the hole in the floor, landing between the two titans. From the shoulder down, her arm vanished in and out of sight in the plasma. He wanted to be the one to beat Magus, but if working with Eve had taught him anything, it was to accept help when necessary.

"Pick on somebody your own size." Skits understood the art of a quip.

Magus threw a fist, too slow to hit the nimble woman. She ducked and spun out of the way as he followed through with his knee. Her arm dragged along Magus' torso and Patches expected to smell burning flesh. But just like his punches, she didn't penetrate the invisible barrier.

Shield. Dirt and dust made it through. His fist couldn't. Size? The pebbles hadn't been able to break through. If Eve had been there, she'd have compared his abilities to a dozen Children at the Tower. Now he kicked himself for ignoring every time she showed off her knowledge of superpowers.

"Die already," Skits barked.

Magus growled as the fabric of his uniform vaporized. The heat penetrated, but again, he held firm, gripping her by the wrist as she attempted to drive her fingers into his sternum. Skits screamed, leaning forward but not gaining ground. Like him, she hadn't figured out how to penetrate his shield. Even if she couldn't break through, perhaps the heat would burn the man alive?

"Shit," Patches mumbled. They had a new problem.

Like Skits, Magus' hand burned a vibrant blue.

Chapter Thirty-Two

2033

Ceann closed his left eye as he focused on the image in the scope. The computer in the rifle presented a steady flow of information. Distance. Humidity. Wind speed and direction. From a mile away, he processed every statistic, letting them aid his years of training.

The White House.

When his superiors enlisted him for a mission on enemy soil, they offered him the only thing that mattered—freedom. He served Her Majesty, but he focused on her offer, and if necessary, he'd fight his way past man and machine to reach his target. There was no point in asking why he needed to kill a civilian in one of the most heavily protected locations within the United States. There were no questions, only a sliver of hope she'd make good on her promise.

Servitude is often mistaken for loyalty.

Ceann rolled over, pulling the pistol free from his chest holster. In a fluid motion, he prepared to terminate the witness. His heart raced as he held his breath, maintaining a half sitting position with his finger resting on the trigger. The roof remained empty. The explosive device attached to the access door remained undisturbed. Just because he couldn't see the enemy didn't mean they weren't present.

With a quick double blink, the contact lenses switched to infrared. When they revealed nothing, he reached left to his ear, pinching his lobe. There were those in the order capable of blending into their surroundings, but their heartbeats gave them away. After years of living in the academy, among Knights determined to claw their way upward, paranoia had become his most useful weapon.

They sent you on a fool's errand, boy.

"I have a name," Ceann growled. Since he stepped out from under Feral's torment and received a moniker from Nexus, he refused to become one of the nameless.

Ceann.

Telepath. Ceann focused on the man's voice, a mixture of gravel and an undercurrent of seduction. There were thousands of reports about mentalists running loose in America, but he hadn't believed them to be true. While the British Empire had seen to their elimination, it seemed the United States hadn't been as thorough.

The Knights trained for every uncertainty.

Ceann imagined he sat in a pool of black. The liquid flowed upward, racing across his body. It had coated his entirety when he felt a hand bash against his chest, hurling him backward. Training took over as he spun in the air, landing on his knees, prepared to put a bullet between the mind-witch's eyes.

Light siphoned away until he remained in an infinite black.

He held up his hand, expecting to stare down his

arm through the sight of the pistol. The telepath had blinded him and stolen his…

"This isn't real," he muttered.

Her Highness employs Children? How efficient.

It might be his first encounter with a trickster, but there were enough files on telepaths to know their limitations. Ceann curled his fingers into a fist, allowing the power to ripple down his arm. In reality, his abilities were invisible, but in this place, his hand glowed a vibrant shade of teal.

"Come out, mate. I know your limitations with Children."

A tall, lanky man emerged from the darkness. For a moment, Ceann thought he wore equally dark clothing, but watched plumes of smoke wrap around his body as if they were alive. The manner in which he moved defied physics, but they spoke to his confidence. The telepath didn't fear him, but he should.

"I am not here to trade blows with you, boy." Ceann's fist tightened at the word. "It is true, I cannot infiltrate your mind, not like a human. But Ceann, you think loudly, it's near deafening."

As the man walked closer, the telepath's skin melted away, revealing a thick, almost portly man. With another step, he transformed into a young man. Ceann froze as the mentalist glided closer. Ceann knew every line on this man's face. He had studied his target, his habits, his associations, but most of all, the arrogant expression in every photo.

The telepath held still other than a single raised eyebrow. "You know this face?"

Ceann let the power in his arms flow through his body, reminding him he was not just a Child of

Nostradamus, but a Knight of Winchester. He had come here to accomplish a mission, and now the enemy of the queen stood only a couple of feet away.

The light around his arms turned a fiery red as he slammed his fist into the man's chest. The energy thrust forward, surrounding the man. It should have killed him, forced his cells to decay at an alarming rate. But instead, the telepath let the energy pool in his chest before the tendrils of black smoke swallowed it.

Your actions speak louder than your thoughts.

While the words were loud and clear, his lips didn't move. Ceann stepped backward, careful to recall where the edge of the building had been. He couldn't tell what was and was not real and didn't want to fail his mission because he fell off a roof.

She sent you to terminate Mr. Griffin. I consider him nothing more than a nuisance, a means to an end, but I can imagine a human fearing him.

"Her Majesty fears no one."

"Come, Ceann, it does not require a telepath to know you question her motives."

"The Knights—"

"Are loyal. I see she has bred and trained you like dogs. Subservient and unable to think for yourselves."

Ceann was about to speak before biting his tongue. A man capable of reading the minds of those around him was dangerous. But a man capable of making his enemy speak without torture, that was a gift worth fearing. He was being held against his will, but he refused to provide the enemy with intelligence.

Each time you speak their names, the anger is palpable. One of the black tendrils snaked closer, wrapping itself around Ceann's leg. He held fast, unwilling to let the telepath see panic. *You hate the very thing you've become. You and I are not so different, boy.*

"We're nothing alike, telepath."

"I beg to differ."

Alike in so many ways.

Ceann stopped arguing. The telepath had no problem speaking for both of them. If the Knight argued, he'd appear defensive. If he agreed, it'd allow him a means of connecting with his victim. Instead, Ceann summoned his abilities again, ready to turn them on himself if needed.

"They stole something from you." The telepath moved close enough that Ceann imagined the sensation of warm moist air blowing against his cheek. "But it's not your name. No, you were a wretch before the Knights pulled you from the safety of your family. They stole," he paused, staring Ceann in the eyes, "someone."

Ceann put his hand to his chest, ready to unleash his powers. He wondered if the veins of his body would blacken as they had for Feral. Would he feel pain as his body withered and his cells died, or would he remain detached in this room without walls? His options had been taken away, but he would not allow the telepath to infiltrate his mind and turn him into a puppet.

"She meant something to you. She was nothing more than a babe when they killed…" Ceann couldn't hide the disgust on his face. The telepath's eyes went wide. "Oh, boy. We are far more alike than I gave us credit. Killers created by a cruel world."

Ceann's hand hovered over his heart before slowly pulling away. "Can you see her?"

The man's expression turned sinister as Ceann lowered his hand. He barely had a memory of her, an echo that long ago stopped being real. If he opened his mouth, he would almost speak her name. Almost. Whatever the programmers had done to him had wiped away any memory of this person, leaving a hole in his brain *and* heart.

The telepath did not try to wrestle with him, even his smoky limbs held in place. Unlike the rest of the Knights, his powers fought against the programming, attempting to restitch the fragments together. But even he couldn't resist their machines. He believed they had won and that his life before serving the queen was nothing more than a dream he couldn't remember.

Erica.

Ceann stiffened at the name. He couldn't be sure, not entirely. Was that her name? The tightening in his chest confirmed what his brain didn't understand. He had never described a word as beautiful, but this—*Erica*—resonated through him. Yes, it *was* her name.

Years of torture in the name of the crown came crashing down. Ceann had served loyally, unwilling or unable to question those above him. With a shake of his head, he remembered his training, the dangers of telepaths and their ability to manipulate a target. Ceann prepared to fight, even if he did not know how to escape the void.

"Trickster, you—"

Ivan. He stepped to the side to reveal a lone girl, a light without a source bathing her in soft white. Ceann lurched forward as the pieces of a broken memory reformed. She had been his only friend at the academy, the one person who saw him as more than a cadet. But his friend had died.

"I killed her," he whispered as the dam broke.

"Your hand, maybe," Ivan said. "But it was *them* who pulled at your strings, puppet."

Ceann replayed the scene in his head. The moment she had died, something in him snapped. He exacted his revenge on Feral, the man who forced his hand. But it wasn't enough. There were more who needed to suffer Ceann's wrath before he satiated his need for revenge. His heart raced, the rage building as the girl remained still in the light.

Between blinks, he returned to the roof, still half sitting holding the gun. Wherever the telepath had taken him, it had been an illusion. He laid back, head resting against the cool concrete, his chest tight and arms burning from holding the position.

"Erica," he whispered.

The gun rested against his chest before he returned it to the holster. Rolling over, he took a moment to inspect his rifle. Undisturbed, it remained pointing toward the White House. How they expected him to penetrate the White House and kill Jacob Griffin hadn't made it into the brief. The how didn't matter, just that he accomplished the mission.

Once he brought his eye to the scope, he could see the White House in disarray. A hole had been blown through the corner of the Oval Office and inside stood Jacob. But it was the men and women in the rose garden that interested him. He could have landed the shot, blown a hole through the chest of his target, but outside the White House stood a more important target.

Ceann turned the rifle slightly, focusing on Jacob. From a mile away, the man's arrogant smile turned toward the rooftop. A smirk spread across his lips before he gave a nod of the chin. For a split second, Ceann swore he had Ivan in his sights. It would take the slightest of pull and Jacob Griffin would be no more, another enemy of the queen eradicated. But…

But…

"Erica," he whispered.

The telepath had restored the humanity stolen by the Knights. He had done unspeakable things in the name of the crown, but they all stemmed from a single act. Ivan restored his memories, breaking down walls built by the programmers, and now he remembered the early days at the academy.

We are not your enemy.

In an act of defiance, he pivoted the rifle. A single human stood next to a man producing bolts of lightning and a teenager with plasma pouring out of her hands. Every Knight knew the tyranny of the United States. Atop this empire of lies and decay stood president Cecilia Joyce.

The rifle hardly kicked against his shoulder as he squeezed the trigger. He pushed to his knees, certain that his aim had been perfect. He didn't need to see the woman slump over to know that he had murdered the second most powerful woman in the world. It wasn't the intended target, but he'd be able to pass the polygraph by saying the telepath made him do it. It *was* the truth, at least partially.

For Erica. Ivan's voice whispered in his ear.

"For Erica," Ceann repeated.

Ceann walked toward the door leading into the building. Ivan wasn't wrong, it had been for Erica. The simplest act of defiance continued, shattering the construct built by his jailers. As a child, he hadn't been able to stand up to the Knights, but they had named him

Ceann. It was he who invented the name, giving him his reputation, King of Monsters.

Stand by our side, Child.

"I am a *free* man. I serve no one."

Burn it to the ground, King of Monsters.

It was the last he heard of the telepath's voice. Was it the plea of a madman, or had he broken through Ceann's armor and read his thoughts? Either way, the image of the palace reduced to ash provided a sense of peace.

Ceann had a new mission.

Chapter Thirty-Three

2039

"Motherfucker!" Skits shouted.

She pulled back, instead punching him in the face. Unlike before, his head cocked to the side, jerking with the force of her fist. The fire from her fist should have melted his face, but the heat only burned away the collar of his shirt.

Magus' arm vanished in the blue light. He swiped at Skits, but she ducked, landing a punch to the gut. Whatever had protected him had vanished, replaced with fire. It was almost as if he and Skits had identical—

Patches figured it out. "He steals powers!" he shouted.

"I figured—" Skits had speed, but not enough to dodge every hit. Magus' punch missed, but he swung his arm back around, his knuckles striking her in the jaw. She spun with the blow, using the momentum to launch a kick to his face. He caught her by the leg and leaned back, taking her off her other foot. She plowed into the wall. She clutched her head as the plaster cracked under her weight before she dropped.

"Impressive." Magus held up his hands as they ignited in a shower of blue light. "I much prefer this." Patches tried to recall every time Skits used her abilities. She created shields, turned her entire upper body into fire, and used the heat to melt away anything in her way. Never did he note a weakness with her gifts.

Unlike Skits, the fire clung to his skin instead of hanging in the air. It meant that while he stole the gifts of others, it didn't come with mastery. Somehow, that didn't ease his nerves.

"Do you burn?"

Patches had watched Skits burn through the uniform of a cadet. The fire scorched the material and then burned through their skin. Bullets might not penetrate his steely hide, but if gas knocked him out, he wasn't confident that a fist full of plasma wouldn't kill him. He needed distance.

He slammed his elbows on the concrete slab, welcoming the burning in his muscles.

"Is that defeat written on your face?"

Magus didn't seem in a rush as he paced. Cocky with his newfound abilities, he taunted Patches. Every few steps, he'd feign a step forward, like it might be the killing blow. Like his cadets, the man oozed arrogance. Nexus had done the same, and that ended with him dead on the lobby floor. Redecorating this office with the corpse of a Knight struck him as appropriate.

"No," Patches said, mustering defiance in his voice.

"You were dead the moment we met. I just hadn't killed you yet."

It was as if the prick stole his dialogue from a comic book. If he bought enough time, Skits could rally and clobber him. At least then nobody would walk away with third-degree burns.

"That's what your cadets thought."

Patches' elbows broke the slab of concrete. On the next attempt, he felt the rebar poking through, but not close enough to hit it with his arm. He raised his foot, ready to smash it against the floor to continue charging his battery.

"As did your fellow Caledonians."

Killing the cadets had been for survival, the only way to walk away with his head on his shoulders. But the Caledonians? Magus had slaughtered them, victims of their lineage. The comparisons were as unalike as the two Children. A growl started in his belly until he howled. The Knight prepared for genocide, and the last person standing between him and countless deaths was Patches.

He stood for Calum. He clenched his fists for the woman he had left behind. He roared for the bodies suspended from the balcony. Magus thought them the same, both killers. His throat burned as the fire coursed through his body. Patches wasn't a cold-blooded murderer.

Patrick Kilgannon would be Caledonia's protector.

"Outmatched pup." Magus' arms flared, the smell of burning ozone filling his nostrils. He took his first step forward and Patches turned, snatching the rebar. He pushed the fire into his upper body. Jerking it free, he used the concrete on the end like a club. Swinging, he wanted to drop Magus, to crush his face. When he fell, he'd use the rebar to castrate the man.

The Knight's upper body blazed. His suit vanished as it coated his body. He held up an arm, preparing for the impact. The blow launched him across the room, skidding along the floor only a few feet from Skits. Without missing a beat, Patches jumped, spinning the bar around, ready to drive it through his eye.

By intent or by accident, he threw his arms up, creating a wave of liquid fire. The rebar drove into the plasma, dripping along the floor as it melted. Patches stopped as his hands nearly passed into the wall of plasma. Holding the last foot of metal, he clutched the concrete and slammed it into the fire, forcing a growl from Magus.

What made it through was only bits of rubble, but it was a start. He turned to find another piece of concrete to drive into the man. Pain shot through his body. He couldn't feel Magus graze his calf. The smell of burning flesh and jolts of pain surging through his leg did that. Patches screamed in agony. It was only the lightest of touches, but the damage had been done. He couldn't force himself to look. He needed a weapon, a large one.

With each step, the fabric pulled at the wound, tearing the skin. He'd need medical attention. As he put his foot down, agony rattled his bones. He pushed it aside, focusing on the burlap sacks on the heads of the Caledonians. Hissing, he thought of the rope groaning as they hung lifeless in a place of healing. If he hurt, it meant he wasn't dead.

He picked up a piece of concrete twice the size of his body. His muscles strained at the weight, but nothing mattered. There was only vengeance. Magus pushed off from the wall, hand forward, ready to burn through his chest. His entire body was already on fire as he hurled the slab of concrete.

He didn't wait to see if it killed the Knight. He

searched for something bigger, heavier. Magus swore as the plasma intensified, barely stopping the slab from crushing him. Patches found the largest chunk of rock in the room. He ignored the lifeless technician protruding from the side. Another death because of the Knights of Winchester. The power rippling through his body turned from aching to searing. He had passed the point where he could control his abilities. Every scuff of the foot, even the touching of the concrete, added to the over-abundance of potential energy stored in his muscles. If he didn't unleash the power, Magus wouldn't need to kill him.

He grabbed the rock, needing to lean back to leverage it off the floor. As he lifted it above his head, the technician's body fell from a crushed office chair. Patches had seen too much death in the last few days. One more, and he'd be able to wipe the slate clean. One. More. Death.

He stumbled, balancing the weight above his head. Magus' body burned bright, vaporizing through the slab that pinned him to the floor. If Patches couldn't break his bones, he'd be content with burying him alive. There was plenty of concrete left to build the Knight his own personal tomb.

Patches took tiny steps as he approached Magus. Even with his abilities, the section of ceiling threatened to drive him to his knees. The Knight had nearly broken through, the white light of his body making a whooshing sound as it incinerated the rock. It hadn't stopped him, but it made him angry. The next would do more than make him growl.

"This," Patches grunted under the weight. "Is... for... Caledonia."

Magus extended his leg, his foot brushing the burned section of Patches' calf. His muscles quivered as the pain renewed, threatening to bring him toppling down. Between blinks, the fire evaporated. It didn't matter. With a final grunt, he pushed the rock, dropping the concrete on the Knight.

It was over.

"You killed him." Oscar hung from the hole in the ceiling, dropping onto a desk. The prince's face, even in the dim light, had a smile stretching from ear to ear. Without getting his hands dirty, he celebrated the victory.

"It's over."

"Not yet." Skits growled. Crawling to her knees, her hand flared blue. "One more needs to die."

"It's over."

As Patches spoke the words, the darkness scurried away. Skits hadn't received the memo that they had won against the Knights. His opposition had literally been crushed, and he couldn't hide his delight.

"Not yet." Skits growled. "One more needs to die."

Barely able to crawl, the Child of Nostradamus refused to stop. While Patches had killed his target, he had been too single-minded to worry about his companion. He reached for the gun at his side, unsure if a bullet could stop her advance. Did he risk it? No, gunpowder and lead were the least powerful thing in the room. It didn't even rank as one of his deadliest weapons.

He stepped back, angling Patches between them. His thumb flipped the safety on the gun, hopeful it wouldn't come to killing the woman. Throwing his thoughts at Skits, he commanded she stop, hopeful he could overcome her barriers. To his dismay, the walls protecting her mind remained impenetrable. Could his siblings intervene? If they could neutralize the entire building, then perhaps they'd —

"No," Patches said. He hissed as he turned, squaring off between them. She climbed to her knees, but Patches held his ground. Perhaps he wouldn't need additional reinforcements.

"Out of my way," she barked.

Patches ignored the order. "Nobody else dies today."

"Move, or I'll make you." Her breaths were ragged as she struggled to stand. "Last warning."

Impressive, Oscar thought. She could hardly hold herself upright, and yet her bravado remained unwavering. Either she was incredibly stupid, or incredibly confident. Neither mattered. If Patches could dispatch Magus, then he'd be more than capable of stopping a wounded Child.

"Oscar." Patches glanced over his shoulder. "Get out of here."

"I'm not leaving you here." A lie, but he wanted to remain in Patches' good graces.

"I'm not asking," he said.

"Kid, I don't want to hurt you." Would she kill Patches to reach him? It was the ruthless behavior he expected of the Knights. Under different circumstances, he'd admire her tenacity.

Oscar backed away, bumping into a desk.

"Oscar, you need to get out of here."

"Thank you," he said. He turned and headed toward the door. Patches moved, limping so that Skits would need to bowl him over. He almost pitied the man. Tortured, beaten, and now facing down the very person he came to save. Oscar pitied the Child.

He reached the doorway, turning back to admire the death of Magus. The Knight deserved— "No."

He had been wrong.

The pale lights were enough to see the slab shift. Patches had drilled the man before dropping a ton of rock on the man, and yet he refused to die. The walls shielding his mind had fallen away. He couldn't make out the individual thoughts, but the man's anger focused on the image of Patches' face.

He's not dead.

Oscar bolted from the room. He prayed for Patches as he fled.

It was time to let fate run its course.

Patches' legs wobbled and the slightest weight on his right foot threatened to make him vomit. He avenged the Caledonians by killing Magus. They should be hobbling their way to the exit. If they were lucky, they wouldn't find any Knights before they escaped. But Skits had other plans.

"Move," she screamed.

"He's not your enemy." He tried to reason with her.

"Who the fuck do you think sent me to kill him?"

Patches' jaw hung open. "But the queen…"

He had assumed they had sent her to kill the leader of the country. Or at least the head of the Knights of Winchester. Never had he considered she'd target somebody in the middle. He found it odd that the Free Republic feared him enough to send an assassin.

Skits tried to laugh, but it came out as a groan. He recognized the wild gleam in her eye. Eve had a similar look when she was about to do something stupid.

"Who do you think sent me?"

The reality sank in. He assumed she worked for the government of the Free Republic. Never had he considered she'd take a contract for a foreign power. But that meant that the queen…

"Her own son?"

She stepped forward before pivoting to spin around him. If he could move without screaming, he might have taken the bait. But his lack of speed gave him a chance to see her misdirection in action. He didn't want to fight her. Instead of closing his fist and clocking her, he tried to shove her back.

The fire in his muscles found its outlet. He threw his palms against her shoulder. The bone snapped as she launched into the wall. She broke through the drywall, bending metal studs. When she fell, he froze. He expected a snotty quip, cursing, even threats to kill him. But as the fire along her skin vanished, Skits remained still.

"Skits?"

The horror set in. He didn't have time to check if Eve's aunt lived. Magus shoved the slab away as if it were a blanket and he grew tired of lying in bed. The man refused to die. But unlike before, it wasn't the plasma burning through the rock. Had the man found another…

"I underestimated your gifts."

The brush against his skin. As Magus touched him,

he stole another set of powers. If Eve were there, she'd assess before striking. He ran through everything he had observed about the Knight. Touch, he stole powers by contact. He didn't wield Skits' plasma. Did that mean he could only mimic the powers of one Child at a time? He'd be strong, and after the rock dropped on him, he'd be unstoppable.

Unlike before, Patches found victory inevitable.

"For a git, you think you're the shit."

Magus clamored to his feet, flexing his muscles as he stared at his hands. Patches understood the power flowing through his muscles. The burn made him feel alive, as if he experienced the world at a heightened level. If it didn't hurt, it'd be intoxicating. The smirk on Magus' face wouldn't last for long.

Magus drew back a fist and rushed Patches. Throwing up his arms, Patches absorbed the blow before soaring through the office. He welcomed the crash into the desks. His neck, spine, arms, butt—every impact rippled across his skin, fueling his abilities. The reverberation of Magus' punch left his bones vibrating.

"Big man," he yelled. "Such an idgit." He added a laugh just to make the man's blood boil.

He welcomed the power in his body. Sitting up, he pointed the gauntlets at Magus. Registry's toys pulled at the power, draining his muscles as they charged.

"We both know that won't work."

Patches continued laughing. He did know. Magus might be one of the most capable Children he'd ever met. With the ability to adapt to any confrontation, he could probably best Eve, or even Alyssa. Patches would not win against a soldier, not with fists. Patches survived life using more than his brawn.

He pointed his palms at the ceiling. Bursts of orange and white energy fired, cracking in the ceiling. Firing again, he let the energy drain away from his body. As quickly as his powers turned him into a hulk of a man, he reverted into a mundane Child of Nostradamus.

The ceiling collapsed, and Magus put on a display of strength. Fists smashed into the rocks, throwing them to the side as if they were nothing more than an inconvenience. The gauntlets vanished and Patches slapped his palms against the floor. Drained, then recharged. It wasn't nearly as much as he received from Magus' blow, but it allowed him to shoot to his feet.

"I'm scared. Watch me quiver in fear. Quiver. Quiver."

"Die, Child."

Magus shot across the room, drilling a shoulder into Patches' torso. With the wind knocked from his lungs, he struggled to drive his elbow into the Knight's shoulder. Magus stopped short of crushing the wall. His hand wrapped around Patches' neck and lifted him from his feet. Unable to breathe, Patches could only smile in defiance. He fired from the gauntlets, the shots harmlessly soaring into the room.

"Not so..." Magus shook his head as he tried to focus. "Where's the bravado now?"

Patches kicked the man with his good foot. With his fists, he continued hammering away at the man's face. Neither did anything to deter Magus.

"Weak," the Knight growled. His jaw had tightened, and Patches watched as the consequences of his abilities clawed at Magus' resolve.

"No." Patches feared he'd go unconscious. "Smart."

He continues punching, each impact growing

stronger. It'd require a tank landing on him to reach Magus' stored potential, but that's exactly what he hoped for.

Magus' growl turned to scream.

Patches understood the pain tearing at Magus. His fingers loosened until he finally stepped back. He shook his arms, trying to shake off the excess energy. But without Registry's gauntlets, every touch stoked a new inferno. Magus had become a prisoner in his own body.

Patches tried sucking in air as he crumpled to the floor. Magus went from shaking uncontrollably to pounding his fists against his head. Patches could almost feel the surge of power from every hit. No matter what the man did, his gifts trapped him.

"I've won," Patches shouted.

Magus turned his anger on the Child. Reaching for Patches. He stumbled, falling to his knees. With every touch, he screamed. It wasn't drilling the man into submission, but Patches found a sick sense of satisfaction watching his powers destroy the man from the inside. Arrogance killed Magus. Patches only supplied the tools.

The man's eyes rolled back in his head before collapsing on the floor. Even as he went unconscious, pain-riddled yelps escaped his lips. It wasn't enough for him to be trapped in a loop of agony. Patches crawled to the man, rolling him onto his back.

The pain might eventually kill him, but that wouldn't silence the ghosts of murdered Caledonians. Wrapping his hands around Magus' throat, he squeezed until the whimpering stopped. The skin under his hands resisted, but he didn't need to cut him. Patches leaned in as the Knight's breath faded, the puffs of warmth against his cheek spaced further apart.

"This is for Calum," Patches whispered. Tears formed in the corner of his eyes, cascading until they dripped on Magus' face. "For Caledonian." The words came out in a sob, but his grip didn't relent.

Minutes passed before he realized Magus' body lay lifeless. He had done this. He won. Without the help of Alyssa or Eve, he avenged dead Caledonians. As he sat upright, straddling Magus, reality set in. The anger faded, replaced with a crushing sense of dread. The librarian from Chicago died with Magus. Now all that remained…

Patrick Kilgannon, the killer.

The sobbing almost drowned out the shuffle of feet. He turned, expecting to see Skits standing over him, ready to exact her revenge. But it was Eve, her eyes wide in disbelief.

"Patches, what have you done?"

As he turned to the lifeless corpse, he asked himself a similar question.

What have I become?

Epilogue

2039

"Do you want to talk about it?"

Patches sat at the kitchen table, banging his forehead against the fake wood finish. With each tap, his abilities dispersed the impact. As his forehead smacked against it for the hundredth time, he froze. Since London imploded, everybody had given him space. With Skits in a makeshift hospital, and the prince running free, he failed. Sure, they'd completed their mission, but his actions had led to an all-out war.

"I fucked up."

Eve sat next to him. He expected a speech, some sort of heroic monologue to bring him around. She gave him a pat on the side of the face. With each touch, he found his internal battery depleting. Even offering a sympathetic touch, Eve trained her abilities.

"Yup, you did."

"Have you thought about giving motivational speeches?"

She ignored the jab. "What happened at the hospital?"

"Oh, that." He had been too focused on being the catalyst for a civil war to dwell on the hospital. His life had been dull in Chicago. If he had friends, he wouldn't have anything to talk about with them. Who would want to listen to him get excited about new acquisitions? But since he set foot on that aircraft, it had been one emergency after the next. It took him time to process his thoughts, and it seemed as if life didn't want to wait.

"Patches..." Her hand touched the side of his face. Something in her body language changed. She caressed his hair like one might a dog. "I saw the hanging bodies."

"Caledonians," he corrected.

"I saw the Caledonians." Her next words came out as a whisper. "They weren't the first."

"What?"

"Alyssa and I buried a dozen Caledonians at a school. It..." She shook her head as she gathered her thoughts. "Horrific doesn't do it justice."

"I went with the Long Watch because I thought they might have information about the Knights. My first mistake was thinking I could handle myself."

Eve leaned back in her chair, resting her hands in her lap. He took the silence as his cue to continue.

"They put me on trial. In hindsight, I think they wanted to show off their trophies. But they let me escape. I thought I could get away and get help to free the woman in the cell. They were toying with me. On the roof they said I could jump, that it'd be a swift death. They wanted me to kill myself. But I couldn't do it. I was terrified. I..."

He might stare at the floor while he spoke, but all he could see were the dead Caledonians who failed to escape. They had been brave, seizing their fate. All he could do was let a bunch of bigots control his future. He had been reluctant to go to the Tower, more so to follow Eve to London. The doubt nipped at his heels every step. But now, he had confirmation.

Tears rolled down his cheeks. "I'm a coward."

"When the synthetics attacked the Tower, I froze."

"Funny."

"I trained for years. First opportunity to save the day. I had a panic attack."

"Great," Patches said. He sat upright, wiping his eyes. "We're both cowards."

"Would you rather be like Conthan? Alyssa? I love them, really, I do. But they're broken. That bravery thing that they do? They've gotten good at hiding their fears. I'd be more concerned if you weren't scared."

Eve did her best to provide a pep-talk, but it didn't cover up the facts. She mentioned the Nighthawks were broken people. Maybe he belonged. That word, *broken*, described how he felt right now. The fire in the pit of his stomach while he fought the Long Watch had vanished. He got his revenge for the hanging Caledonians, and where did that leave him? His ancestors would be ashamed.

"You're not the only one who is scared."

The confession caught his attention. Alyssa hid her emotions. Eve, on the other hand, served as the driving force in this band of heroes. He never expected her to confess anything but determination.

"Now you sound patronizing."

"Whatever." She rolled her eyes, dismissing him. "What are we going to do about it?"

Action. While he wallowed, Eve had already moved

on to figuring out their next move. Patches thought of Calum and the woman in the cell. They had been willing to die to save their home. Eve wasn't any different. When the synthetics attacked the Tower, she put her life on the line. He had gone along because of the circumstances, but given a choice, he'd have stayed at the Tower hiding amongst his books. He tried to stand up for Caledonia, but…

"What if our actions make the situation worse?"

"It always gets worse before it gets better. You were in Chicago. It wasn't a picnic. But they didn't give up. Odds were against them, and—"

"They kept fighting," he finished. He studied Eve, the fire in her eyes as she spoke with conviction. At first, it felt as if they were kids playing a game. Once he saw the bodies hanging from the balcony, reality had set in. It wasn't a game. As they dragged Calum to his death, Patches had felt helpless. He never wanted to feel like that again, not when he housed the potential to move mountains. What would Calum say if they heard his self-loathing?

They never stopped fighting.

"You can't shoulder the—"

"I want to go to Caledonia." He blurted out the words before his fears strangled his voice. While the Caledonians fought for their freedom, he had inadvertently put it in jeopardy. No matter how much he wanted to run and hide, he couldn't desert them. He owed the ghost of Calum. Hell, even Jasper fought to save her people.

His people.

"Oh, good. Otherwise, it'd be awkward when I told you we were going."

He raised his eyebrow. "You already decided, didn't you?"

She smiled. "You're the one that keeps me from making stupid decisions." He could see that it was one of those signature smiles that didn't matter what he said. He might be the cautious one, but she declared veto power whenever she didn't agree with him. "So, what do you say?"

"Do I have a choice?"

"Not really. No. Not at all."

Every instinct told him to pack his bags and leave. What good was a librarian in a war? Having brute strength didn't make him anything more than a foot soldier. No, he'd be best served—

Eve slapped a sheet of paper on the table. He grimaced as he spotted the cursive handwriting. Eleanor P. Valentine. Like every other Child of Nostradamus impacted by her predictions, he questioned her predictions.

"Like you, he once hesitated," Eve quoted. "Was she talking about the Tower? Or now?"

"I hate you," he mumbled.

"I'll make you a deal." She pushed the paper across the table. "When you doubt yourself, tell me. I'll remind you that you helped save the Tower."

"You're the one who—"

"Patches, it's not all or nothing. It's why we're doing this together."

He had friends in Chicago. No, more like work acquaintances. He always preferred books over people. He wasn't sure how to accept help. Eve didn't care, she'd force it on him. She continued to be his opposite in every way imaginable.

"Sentinels for life," she said, holding up her fist.

"You're really trying to make that name stick, huh?"

"Says the guy practicing catchphrases."

He bumped knuckles with her. "I hate you."

"I'm too lovable to hate. Now, let's find some beer."

And just like that, she dragged him into the fold. Is this how the Nighthawks had felt when they fought the Warden? He had always been proud to be a Scot, and even more proud when they declared their independence. His parents would tell him to let go of his fears and follow his heart. But his gram, she'd tell him to make the Brits regret their decision.

He chuckled at the thought of the woman getting fired up. She'd love Eve pushing him out of his comfort zone. Wallowing would not help, and if he left, he'd live the rest of his life with regret. He hadn't stood up to his boss, or his landlord, and he hated himself for cowering. Perhaps this was a chance to make things right?

"I'm in."

Eve stood, patting him on the head. "Like you had a choice."

The cafe boasted a spectacular view of the Eiffel Tower. With the sun rising behind the monument, the scene reminded Alyssa of a painting. She hadn't been to Paris in years, and even then, she had been hunting down a man financing a war in the Middle East. For now, she admired the old buildings of Paris without work clouding her admiration. Normally she'd sit and watch the locals as she eavesdropped on their conversations to see if her understanding of French had improved. But the streets remained vacant.

She sat at a small table with intricate metalwork that resembled leaves. A coffee rested in front of her, the steam rising, catching in the breeze. The attention to detail was tres magnifique. But as she rested her hand above the coffee, seeking the moist warmth, her hand remained untouched. The programmers had done a wonderful job, but they had a long way to go before they achieved an immersive simulation.

The longer she spent at the cafe, the more her abilities struggled with the false reality. As she observed the lack of sensation, her body adapted, ignoring the chair she sat in. Fifteen minutes and she already felt as if she were floating. The pressure against her butt and back had all but vanished. It had never dawned on her that if her eyes experienced a reality different from her body it could wreak havoc. When she had free time, she'd have to explore this new dynamic.

"Is this seat taken?"

But the world around her didn't matter. In the vastness of Paris, her attention turned to him and him alone. Ned stepped from behind her seat, taking an awkward bow. Moving next to the chair on the other side of the table, he waved his hand along the back. He moved as if he had never sat before, struggling to get his butt in the chair.

Alyssa laughed at the absurdity.

"Clunky user interface. The programmers should be fired."

He might be virtual, but the sight of Ned's face warmed her heart. While on the run in London, she hadn't communicated with the man, and now that their identities were known, she threw caution to the wind. Any fear of being discovered evaporated. He had dressed for the occasion, a sweater and pants that didn't have tears in them. Had he taken time to change his avatar to impress her?

"Do I have something on my face?"

Her face warmed as he caught her staring. "I'm admiring the gentleman sitting across from me."

"So I shouldn't admit I'm in my apartment in my underwear?"

She'd expect nothing less. Where Needles ended and Ned began continued to be a shifting line in the sand. Alyssa would admit it to no one, but the image of him on his couch with his chest exposed didn't hurt. She rested her elbows on the table and covered her cheeks with the palms of her hands.

"I've read the reports. So, you're a terrorist?"

"It seems so."

"I watched when I could."

"I suspected. I could feel it."

"The Brits have turned the country into a digital safe room. I wanted to help, but when they caught me, they assaulted the Tower's computers. I swear I—"

"Ned, I know. This wasn't your fight. I came here to watch over Eve and Patches. We rescued Skits. We accomplished the mission."

He paused before leaning forward, his hand reaching across the table, palm up. "You're not coming home, are you?"

Alyssa placed her hand on his. The lack of heat and the coarse sensation of his fingers made her heart ache. She had played out the conversation a thousand times.

Ned deserved to hear the truth, even if it jeopardized their relationship.

"Not yet."

"Alyssa, is this still *your* fight? Or is—"

"I've done horrible things."

"We've all—"

She held her hand to his face, wishing she could feel his lips against the tips of her fingers. Despite the breakthrough in technology, it couldn't satiate her need for human contact. If he had been in the room with her, she didn't think she'd be able to say what she needed. Right now, she'd rather succumb to temptation than speak the next words.

"Please, Ned, listen. I joined the Wetworks to stop bad people from doing bad things. In my heart, I didn't want to see another Ivan Volkov rise to power. My actions were well-intentioned… at first. It stopped being about preventing tyrants and shifted to securing the interests of the Free Republic. I lied to myself, saying it was an order. I blamed Twenty-Seven for enlisting me."

A thousand times she rehearsed the speech, mulling over the thoughts she locked away from everybody, including herself. But it didn't prepare her for the tightness in her chest. Alyssa wanted to blink until the scene ended and she sat alone in her room. It'd be easier to wallow in her self-pity than to confess her sins to Ned. The disguise of a stoic woman fell away, and she feared he wouldn't like what remained.

"I killed because I'm good at it. I let them use me as a tool. In my adult life, fighting is all I've known. They didn't make me a killer. I had become that long before the Wetworks."

Once upon a time, she'd wanted to join the ballet. A night of watching *The Nutcracker* with her parents changed her life. Her mother convinced her father to let her take classes. On stage, she performed with grace and poise. When her powers manifested, the long days of practicing shrank until she only needed an hour to perfect her routine. But she stayed, determined to harness the elegance. Her dream died with her parents. An orphaned girl, she wanted revenge. She gave up the hope of bringing beauty into the world. But combat, that she *could* give.

"The woman you see…" Alyssa's breath grew ragged as she held back tears. She hoped her avatar didn't betray her. "She never existed."

"I can hear the pain in your voice. Really, I do." He leaned forward, placing his other hand on her arm. "But that, pardon my language, is fucking bullshit."

"Ned—"

"I killed a man when I was seventeen."

He bit his tongue while she spoke. It was the least she could do in return.

"Seventeen. I wanted to be glued to a computer breaking into school records or looking at porn. I wasn't doing it for altruistic reasons. I always felt small, and little ol' me could cause some damage. But Dav5d, he was in it for the challenge. If it wasn't for him, I'd have stayed home that night. I didn't want to go. To be honest, I thought about letting him go on his own. But it was Dav5d. He was never like us. He didn't know how to feel small."

Ned's eyes turned down, staring at the simulated cup of coffee. It was hard enough to talk about a life that changed drastically. But he held a soft spot for Dav5d. An unlikely pair of friends. She couldn't imagine

Needles tolerating his idiosyncrasies, but Ned, she often imagined that it was Dav5d who kept that part from being swallowed.

"I let everybody think I pulled the trigger to save Dav5d. But I've always known it wasn't the case."

"Fear," Alyssa said.

"Fear," he confirmed. "I killed a man because I was terrified that I was next."

"Ned…" If only she could hug him.

"The difference between us? I made peace with the truth. There's guilt, plenty of it. I can't change the past. But I can try to be better tomorrow."

Alyssa wanted to ask how.

"Accept who you are, not who you think you *should* be."

She raised an eyebrow. The tender moment had passed, and now he leaned back in his chair, folding his arms awkwardly. The virtual version didn't catch the subtle nuance of his facial expression. But she knew, somewhere in the Tower, the edge of his lip turned up. He was like a child dying to share a secret.

"You knew?"

"I know everything that goes on in the Tower."

"Why didn't you say anything?"

"You're Alyssa Rahim," he laughed. "I've learned that you come about in your own time. This was your secret to share, not mine."

To the rest of the world, he'd always be Needles. Cocky and fiery, he'd continue to be the loudmouthed hacker that everybody avoided. He wore the guise like a suit of armor, letting nobody get close. But somehow, he let the walls come crashing down for her. The boy who accompanied Dav5d to keep him safe was the same as the one who accepted her, even when her faith in herself wavered.

He leaned forward. "I—"

"I love you."

Her control evaporated. The emotions building in her chest came out in a stutter. Leaning back in her seat, she bit her lip. What had she done? She never imagined she'd care for somebody like him. And even as she questioned the meaning behind a four-letter word, she understood she attempted to comprehend its depth *for* him. He had gone from a brother-in-arms to a mild nuisance. But at some point, Ned made her want more than a life of solitude. His patience with her seemed limitless, a trait he seldom showed to the rest of the world.

"But you already knew that, too."

"I suspected as much. Like I said, you come about in your own time."

"Before I can come home, I need to help Eve and Patches."

"I fear for the person who steps in your way."

Outside of her parents, she had never uttered the word love to another person. She didn't know if she should stay and let the feeling linger or leave. Whatever the future held, she walked toward it with a full heart. And he was right. She'd take on an entire army if it meant going home. Except now, it wasn't because of a sense of duty.

"I should go," she whispered.

"Me too. I think the laundry is done." Heathen. The image of him in his underwear tightened the knot in her stomach.

"And for the record..." His avatar managed a grin.

Even if it paled in comparison, it made her smile. "I loved you first."

She laughed, a belly-deep roar that eased the tension in her body. "Ned, this isn't a competition."

"That's where you're wrong, Ms. Rahim."

His avatar faded from sight. For a moment, she believed the man had gone soft. But only Needles could turn her affection for him into a sport. It's one she'd play happily with him. Who would love the hardest?

Alyssa left excited to win this match.

From the balcony, Oscar watched as the people of the British Empire gathered. Thousands of candles filled the area outside the palace gates as they mourned the seven-hundred and thirty-two people killed by Scottish terrorists. Despite the soft mists, they arrived in droves. He expected protestors, or even riots, but for the common folk, it remained a solemn event. Lining the gates, he noted the Knights of Winchester, their white suits standing out as the sun set.

He thought he'd celebrate the victory over Magus. The man had vexed him since long before he assumed command of the Knights. But even that victory was muffled beneath the cost of British lives. The people of London would have stormed the gates if they discovered his involvement. The guilt came as a surprise. He reminded himself that he assumed the burden for Britain. Now he'd be able to control the might of the military, aided by the Knights. Scotland would no longer be a pain in their side. But the thought of re-uniting their empire did little to ease his conscience.

"The burdens we bear," he whispered.

Earlier, the queen addressed the nation, assuring them that action would be swift and merciless. She surprised him with the severity of her words. She hadn't needed his voice in her ear or his thoughts nudging her forward. Since Scotland declared their independence, she had played nice with the nation. But as she threatened their rebels and their loved ones, he wondered if it was Magus who kept the queen in line.

"I am an expert at war. One doesn't simply assume the throne. They fight for it and once they are seated, they continue to fight." Her statements echoed in the back of his head. He should have never existed. Since he woke, he had fought every day of his life. Part of him hoped that as the crown rested on his head, he'd be able to stop. But she assured him that the rest of his days would be a battle of one kind or another.

Tiny flames lit the faces of the attendees. As the sun dipped behind the city, the thousands of candles grew brighter. Days ago, they'd have called him the queen's abomination, or worse. But even from a distance, he could hear their thoughts. Attitudes had changed, and they saw him as a savior, somebody who would keep them safe. Their collective ache washed over him, waves beating against a rocky shore. The sincerity in their thoughts… Oscar couldn't help but let the tears roll down his cheeks. It wasn't a victory over Magus that moved him. It was listening to their acceptance. Not as their prince, whom they'd have had to accept no matter their reluctance, but as a Brit.

"Prince, the queen awaits you."

"Of course, Halo."

The young man in the white suit looked like his

brethren. He needed to speak with the queen about Magus' replacement. He had spent the better part of the day interviewing his subordinates. They referred to themselves as the inner circle, the strongest of the strong. While they treated leadership like an arm-wrestling competition, he wanted somebody in place who supported his efforts to the North. Once squashing the rebellion and securing Scotland, he wanted to ensure the candidate would back his ascension to the throne.

Halo was the newest of the queen's guards. The Knights had assigned him to shadow Oscar, not out of fear for his safety, but to demonstrate the role of the Knights within the empire. He obeyed without question. But like with all of his ilk, Oscar questioned if the man did it out of obligation or desire. He wished he could have a candid conversation without the prying ears of Knights seeking information to use against him. Perhaps, one day, they'd truly be allies that progressed past a sense of duty.

Walking from his apartment, he encountered a dozen pairs of human guards. Each stepped out of his path, saluting as he passed. While their spines went rigid and their eyes remained forward, their thoughts wandered. Like the people outside, they were confused and angry. One of them hoped he'd be pulled from palace detail and assigned on the northern border. But the other, his thoughts were cloudy, as if he walked in a fog. Oscar wanted to ask if he knew anybody who died in the collapse. Usually, thoughts like that were the product of the brain preserving itself by keeping painful thoughts at bay.

As he approached another pair of guards, he slowed his walk. Reaching into their minds, he encountered the same white noise as the last. He dove deeper, looking for proof that they were more than confused shells roaming the halls. They maintained their schedule on autopilot, but he couldn't find an original thought. For those drowning in trauma, he could peel back their mundane thoughts and find the source of their pain. No, something unusual was wrong with these guards.

"It's them," Oscar muttered. "Halo, stay close to me."

"What's wrong? I'll alert the—"

"No," Oscar said. "This is a family matter." Code for discreet. It was one thing for the public to know he was a clone. Without his progenitor to remind them, they'd eventually forget. But if two copies of him roamed free, the population would riot. The Long Watch would be useless. The guards, well, they were already useless. Only the Knights and their immunity to telepathy would serve as allies.

"Understood."

He bound down the hall toward his mother's apartment. The Knight that should have been stationed at her door had vanished. He reached for the gun on his hip. Light filled the hallway as Halo summoned his powers. It'd pour from his eyes and mouth, turning him into a radiant nightlight. Gears whined as the Knight's forearm separated. A dozen barrels sprung out as if he were a human Gatling gun. Oscar didn't have time to ask how his powers and the tech interacted.

Oscar's heel slammed against the door. Wood splintered, the lock giving way under his weight. He froze, half expecting his brothers to be waiting for him on the other side. When he cleared the parlor, he eased his way toward the living room. Peeking around the corner, he spotted her foot first, the angle giving away that she sat in her favorite chair.

He found the queen, his mother, leaning back in her favorite high-back chair. She wore her suit from the interview. The white fabric along her chest had turned a dark red. His mother bleeding out almost caused him to ignore the two men standing with their backs to him. He didn't need to see their faces. Their thoughts gave away their identity. Unlike the whisper of humans, their minds were like the crash of thunder.

King.

Their words echoed in his head, whispered with a mix of glee and ambition. His relationship with his mother had always been difficult. She navigated elation and guilt seeing another wear her son's face. But he still considered the woman who demanded his creation to be his mother. Over time, she treated him like an individual, and in this room they'd have their tea. He had patiently waited for her to pass to assume his place on the throne. His ambition didn't supersede his respect for a woman who made the empire a force to be reckoned with. His brothers opted for action.

"What's going on?" asked Halo.

Oscar remained in the doorway, holding a hand for him to remain still. He could easily step aside and with a gesture, he'd eradicate the assassins. Unable to influence the Knight, they'd find themselves hard-pressed to overcome his strength or his gifts. Did his feelings for a woman who provided half his genetic material outweigh the realization his brothers were free? His loyalty remained to the people of the British Empire and the crown.

He stepped out of the Knight's way.

"Your Majesty." Halo's gasps turned to a gurgling. Where Oscar expected the Knight to wield his light like a finely-honed rifle, he staggered forward, a blade buried in his throat. Behind him, somebody held his body upright as the Knight flailed, desperate to keep his fluids from escaping his body.

Throwing Halo to the ground, Oscar found his missing sibling. The third clone had awakened, and by the blood covering his body, he had been busy. Oscar pressed his back to a bookcase as the third man wearing his face stood amongst his siblings. The trio wore lab coats from the hospital, each of them streaked in red. But it was the name tag on the third that stood own.

Dr. Wentworth.

They smiled in unison. *We are king.*

— THE END —

Read Next

The Dawning of Superheroes

Awaken the Daughter

Anoint the Daughter

Ascend the Daughter

The Night Quartet

Nighthawks

Night Shadows

Night Legions

Night Covenants

Morning Sun (Prequel)

Wayward Orphans

Sentinel Rising

Seraph Falling

Explore the Universe

The Children of Nostradamus Universe Codex
Lore. Technology. History. Characters.
www.remyflagg.com

About the Author

Jeremy Flagg is the creator of the dystopian superhero universe, CHILDREN OF NOSTRADAMUS. Taking his love of pop culture and comic books, he focuses on fast paced, action packed novels with complex characters and contemporary themes. He continues developing the universe with the Journal of Madison Walker, an ongoing serial set two hundred years in the future.

Jeremy spends most of his time at his desk writing snarky books. When he gets a moment away from writing, he binges too much Netflix and Hulu and reads too many comic books. Jeremy, a Maine native, resides in Charlotte, North Carolina and can be found in local coffee shops pounding away at the keyboard.